STAR-BORN ANOMALY

BLUESHIFT ✦ BOOK TWO

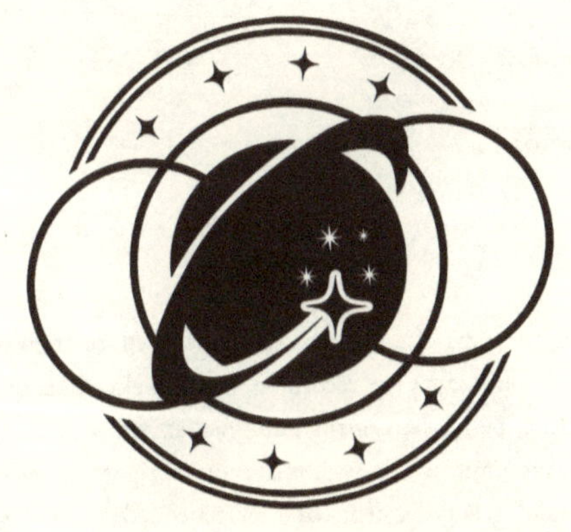

J.E. McDonald

Praise for J.E. McDonald

"J.E. McDonald is an exciting new voice in Sci-Fi
Romance."
-Cynthia Sax, USA Today Bestselling Author

"The intense suspense that kept building was
captivating."
-Stephanie Chapman for Readers' Favorite

"Author J. E. McDonald's debut novel delivers a story
chock full of haunting suspense, humorous dialogue,
scintillating love scenes, and intriguing characters."
-InD'tale Magazine

"This series starts out strong and just keeps getting better
and better. These books are exactly the kind of reading
I need: magic, romance, adventure, demons, prophecies,
ghosts, and dating apps. Perfection!"
-Lisa Edmonds, bestselling author

"J.E. McDonald weaves the two together so seamlessly
that it's difficult to imagine anyone that wouldn't love this
steamy and suspenseful story."
-Indies Today

"McDonald's cast of supernatural characters are always impeccably crafted and leave you eager for the next installment of this delightful series."

-Ashley R. King, author

"A devilishly fun romance."

-Luna Joya, author

"This wickedly compelling story is full of action and romantic tension..."

-J.E. Hunter, author

"...the sexual tension between them is scorching hot, making Ghost of an Enchantment a fast-paced, compelling read."

-K. Caine, author

"This book was filled with suspense, suspense that kept me at the edge of my seat and at times breathless."

-Paranormal Romance Guild

More Works by J.E. McDonald

https://books2read.com/jemcdonald

BLUESHIFT
Star-Crossed Captive
Star-Born Anomaly
Star-Cursed Odyssey

WICKWOOD CHRONICLES
Ghost of a Beginning
Ghost of a Gamble
Ghost of an Enchantment
Ghost of a Summoning

GOLDENLACH RIDGE SHIFTERS
Captive Wilderness
Caged Fury
Conquered Betrayal

CONTENT NOTES

This novel includes content that may be triggering or disturbing to some readers, and is not meant for those under the age of eighteen. Some of these situations include, but are not limited to:

sexually explicit scenes, coarse language, violence, guns and other weapons, thoughts of suicide, thoughts/memories of self-harm, blood, and gore.

A complete list of content notes can be found at www.jemcdonald.net:

Author's Note

Hello! Thank you for picking up my book.

If you've read *Star-Crossed Captive*, you might be wondering where the heck Nia and Mace are. Don't worry! Their story is far from over.

I've always thought of the Blueshift Series as a multi-sided chessboard. Mace and Nia's story, though it was where I started, remains only one pawn in a larger game of inter-system intrigue, danger, and passion. I still need to set up the remainder of the board.

So, rest assured, you will see Mace and Nia again. They're just waiting for their turn in this complex game.

And if you're eager for more of Lexi's story, you'll be seeing her again soon, too.

Happy reading!

-J.E.

For those who have never felt like they fit in.
For those who've always felt alone.
I see you.

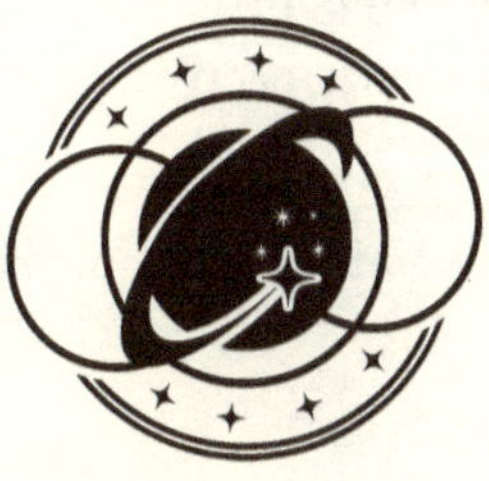

PROLOGUE

File# B11482CX72
Secure communication
100 days after the Calypso's return

General Inger: *Omega Station* is lost, and any ambassador we send turns into one of these automatons, insisting we stop sending negotiators, but they will not return home themselves.

General Dorse: I wouldn't want them too.

Inger: These are CORE officials, some related to the Chancellor. We can't abandon them.

Dorse: They've started calling themselves Calypson like the others. There is no doubt that these... people are no longer human.

Inger: Do we understand what has happened to them yet? Or if it's reversible?

Dorse: Top scientists have been on the task since the very beginning, and none of them will make a solid hypothesis. They're demanding test subjects and access to the *Calypso's* logs. But all ships entering Sector Ten are absorbed without fail, just like *Omega Station*.

Inger: Do we declare war? Send a warship to obliterate the entire colony?

Dorse: The crew of the *Calypso* are obeying our directive and not advancing into our space. But they're creating some sort of gaseous barrier. Our scientists don't know what to make of it. Plus, there are children on board.

Inger: Children die every day from a wide range of hazards, including war.

Dorse: As long as they don't advance toward Jupiter, we have no recourse in launching an attack.

Inger: No one of influence agrees with one another. There are those with their fingers on the trigger just waiting for an excuse, and those not willing to destroy one hundred years of history because of fear.

Dorse: We also have the benefit of distance. They would need to pass through Tellusian space to get to CORE territory.

Inger: My spies tell me the Tellusians are just as nervous and threatened by their presence as we are. There may come a time when doing nothing is no longer an option.

Dorse: Public sentiment—

Inger: Can only last so long. If they become a threat, we will do what we must to exterminate them.

Chapter One

The unforgiving sun beat upon her back, relentless, lethal on this dead world. Wynn sank her glove into the tilled earth and pulled, creating a hand-shaped valley for her seeds. She reached into the bag at her hip, grabbed a fistful, and plopped them into the groove a centimeter apart. Gently, she covered them with soil.

These suckers are going to live.

She wouldn't fail. Not this time. Couldn't afford to. Her days at this outpost were numbered. Either they would replace her with two other scientists, or they would give her a new partner and she'd be forced to quit.

She wouldn't be able to handle working with someone else after everything.

The sound of her exhales echoed loudly within the helmet of her UV-suit. Sweat trickled down her spine to settle in the groove of her ass. Taking the pulse rifle at her hip with her, she shuffled back a pace, and scored another valley into the fertilized soil with her hand. Her seeds fell silently into place before she covered them. Again and again she repeated the process, moving centimeters backward at a time, making room for more seeds. More potential.

A crick in her neck throbbed, and Wynn straightened, rolling her shoulders to get rid of the ache. The landscape spread endlessly before her. Beyond her cultivated fields, dry cracks in the earth reached elongated fingers westward. The wind turbine atop her outpost, the size of her fingernail at this distance, remained motionless, no breeze for relief as she toiled through the dirt. Farther out, the thin line of the supply tether shot through the stratosphere, equipping Research Station 214 twenty kilometers away. And to the south of that, moody clouds formed in shades of purple and black.

She squinted. The bulbous shapes looked bloated with rain. How much acid would they contain this time?

Sun glinted off the solar panels atop the greenhouse connected to her outpost—her favorite place on the planet. Inside, rows of seeds, sprouts, and saplings lived protected from Earth's toxic conditions. With every crop, they'd been making them stronger, more resilient to withstand radiation and acid rain. And one day they would see results.

They.

Her breath hitched, and she swallowed down the lump in her throat.

It wasn't "they" anymore. Just her.

She'd promised herself she wouldn't shed another tear, that she needed to remember the good times with Foster instead of what happened. The memories of death and gore had taken over her nightmares. She didn't need them to take over her waking hours too.

Exhaling a slow breath, Wynn froze when a slice of movement caught her eye. She lifted her hand to block out the sun's glare.

Far above, an object hurtled its way across the sky toward the surface, a white vapor trail blooming in its wake. Space junk or a meteor, probably. Down and down it fell, closer to the horizon. Wynn followed it until it disappeared from sight. The streak of white contrasted against the storm brewing so far away, an inescapable scar, straight and thick—so similar to the ones on her arm.

Bang. The thunderous sound reverberated across the barren terrain when it landed kilometers away. The vibration hit Wynn low in the stomach. She grabbed the pulse rifle beside her, heart racing. The butt of the long-distance weapon in her hand calmed her as she inhaled a deep breath.

It's nothing. Just space garbage.

Then how come she hadn't received an alert? If she could see the vapor trail, then it was close enough for a warning.

Glancing down at the control panel on the arm of her UV-suit, she expelled a defeated sigh. She'd forgotten she deactivated her PALM, her Personal Automated Link to Media, this morning, turning off all communications. Not even the live spaceball game had kept her attention. It had been a relief to disconnect her ocular implant from the grid. An ache always formed behind her eyes after a while.

And listening to the newsreels was definitely out of the question. They were nothing but doomsday predictions of Tellusian strikes, waxing poetic about the proposed genocide of the entire Calypson nebula, and then *her.*

Her image everywhere, and Foster's too. Reporters spouting facts that weren't quite right, conjecture that didn't ring true, and images of the beasts.

Wynn swallowed against the sudden welling in her throat and set the rifle aside. Turning off her PALM had been about keeping her mind from horrific memories, not a means to stir it all up. She shook her head and got back to work, scoring the earth, then dropping seeds.

Foster had wanted it that way, everything planted by hand. *Old school,* he'd said.

But her mind wouldn't settle, and the day he'd died took up the forefront of her thoughts. So similar to today, the heat of the sun, the dryness in the air...

And so much blood.

Stomach rolling, she arrived at the end of her row, turned, and started down the last section. Her pulse rifle remained ever-present at her hip—an unnecessary precaution, but one she couldn't seem to leave in the storage shed. It was idiotic to think the beasts would appear out of thin air. Academy scientists had promised her they'd been corralled for study far, far away.

Even so, having the weapon at her hip eased some of her anxiety.

Wynn inched along, plopping seeds in their new home, covering them softly, then shuffling backward.

As she neared the end of her last row, a shadow crossed her path. Heart in her throat, she jerked straight, and reached for the rifle.

But her gaze caught on the barren landscape before she grabbed hold.

"Holy shit," she murmured.

It was the clouds that blocked the sun. The purple-black swirl now stretched across the horizon without an end in sight. They darkened the sky into twilight, though it was the middle of the day, and swallowed the vapor trail from earlier.

Wynn slapped the panel of her UV-suit, and her PALM reconnected with the grid. Notifications spread across her visor's screen, the first one with an alert about the incoming meteor and its projected impact location. Next was a weather report. *Storm imminent.*

It headed straight for her.

Wynn jumped to her feet, swiped the pulse rifle out of the dirt, and jogged between rows of freshly planted seeds toward her hovercart.

More reports filled her visor, weather advisories, prediction models that covered most of the continent, then disappeared a moment later to be replaced by new ones.

This is so bad. She'd just planted a new field of precious seeds, and they were about to be destroyed by acid and wind. Picking up her speed as best she could in her UV-suit, she swallowed the half-sob that wanted to escape. *Not going to happen.*

As soon as she arrived at the hovercart, she tossed the rifle in the back bed and hopped behind the controls. Heart racing, she pressed the start button.

The engine sputtered, then came to life. She removed the brake and pushed on the throttle, accelerating down the middle pathway toward her fields' central control hub. Brown rows of soil sped by. The silver cylinder towered ahead of her, pointed near the top. She slowed, then jerked to a stop as the first fat drops of rain splattered the ground.

No. She jumped out and ran to the control panel to swipe her PALM. It lit up, a cascade of options falling into sight. She turned off the weather reports clogging her visor's interface to concentrate, then accessed the enviro-net controls. Slapping the screen with a little too much force, she activated the net.

The shielding rippled blue and green around her, stretching upward to protect all four fields like a tent. Wynn double checked the settings. Set to maximum, it would keep every drop of rain from damaging the seeds. Hopefully those first few drops hadn't harmed them. She let out a long breath, her limbs trembling after the burst of adrenaline.

The world around her continued to darken under the approaching storm, then lightning flashed, rippling below the clouds like breaking glass. Thunder cracked a moment later. The sound punched her eardrums. She leaned back, the control hub pressing into her spine, and tipped her head to the sky. Mesmerized, she watched as a wall of rain rolled straight toward her.

The shields sizzled blue and green when the moisture hit, then the swirling clouds took over, darkening the day to night. She squinted toward Research Station 214, and couldn't see the tether through the thickness of the clouds and incoming rain.

But something moved on the horizon below, about to be swallowed by the storm, a dark shape against brown terrain—something that shouldn't be there.

Wynn's chest seized with panic. She reached for the pulse rifle and grabbed nothing but air, remembering too late she'd left it in the hovercart meters away. The urge to run nearly overwhelmed her, but her feet remained planted.

Heart in her throat. She swiped her PALM against the UV-suit's control panel, activating her visor's interface.

Category five storm. Take cover.

The message repeated itself across her vision, but nothing told her what marred the horizon.

Had someone from Research Station 214 decided to check on her when her comms were down? She shook off the idea. They would have driven a hover vehicle, not walked.

A spike of lightning lit up everything around her. Wynn refocused on the thing in the distance in the wake of its brightness. It looked about the same size as a person.

Or an animal.

Thunder cracked louder than the last one, making her jump.

Dread roiling in stomach, Wynn turned, snapped the control panel closed with a click, then forced her feet to move. The wind picked up, swirling and twisting around her legs while the blue and green shields rippled above as the rain continued to drizzle.

She reached the hovercart, grabbed the pulse rifle out of the bed, and tucked it against her shoulder, finger on the trigger. Using the scope, she aimed it toward Research Station 214. The magnifier didn't have enough range to tell her exactly what it was, just a dark, undefined mass, but it was heading toward her steadily, maybe even slowing.

Opening both eyes, she stared above the scope. *Only one.* There was only one of it. If it were a beast, wouldn't it have brought its friends? Its *pack*, the media kept calling them.

Lightning exploded above her, reaching its fingers under the clouds. Wynn blinked away the streaks in her eyes and focused on the form in the distance. It looked like a person. But why would they be out there? She rechecked her PALM, and found no messages from Research Station 214. If they were sending someone, then they would have notified her. It didn't make sense.

The rain picked up, the net above her undulating constantly. Wind slapped against her body, making her sway. The environmental warning pulsed red at the bottom of her visor. She couldn't stay out here any longer.

Wynn slid the pulse rifle between the passenger seat and the dashboard, then jogged around the front of the hovercart to jump in the driver's seat. She pressed the start button. The engine sputtered, then died.

Her chest squeezed, echoed by another rolling rumble of distant thunder. She tried the start button again. The engine sputtered once more, then went silent.

"No. No. No." This had happened before—the day Foster died.

She pressed the button again, and her throat closed up when she got the same results. She smacked the control panel with both hands, then gripped the throttle like she could break it apart.

Lifting her head, she focused on that figure in the distance. It didn't look like it had gotten any closer during the past few minutes. The beasts had traveled quickly, giving her and Foster no time to seek shelter.

Lightning flashed, then another, followed by a louder crash of thunder than before. The sound rattled her helmet around her head, making her grit her teeth.

She picked up the pulse rifle again and looked through its scope. Another bolt of lightning lit up the terrain in the space between her and Research Station 214. She blinked away the bright cracks lingering in her retinas and focused.

The thing in the distance looked the same, a dark shape against a brown horizon, but it was getting harder to see with the rain now spreading between them.

What the hell was it? Her binoculars back at the outpost could see farther, and would give her more information. Wynn lowered the rifle, returning it to its place.

Inhaling a deep breath, she pressed the start button again. "Come on. Please."

The engine rumbled to life. The vibration traveled through her body to her jittery hands. She gripped the throttle and put it into gear. Her foot slammed on the accelerator, the cart shooting off like a pulse cannon. She drove straight down the row at full speed. Once clear of the netting, she slowed and took the turn to her outpost.

No longer within the enviro-net's protection, wind slammed into her like a wall. Rain splattered against the hood of the hovercart and her visor, the percussive sound beating into her head and body. She wiped her vision clear, her hand shaking. Water coated the ground, deep channels forming in the cracks. Without her UV-suit, she would be soaked through.

A warning flashed on the hovercart's control panel, telling her to take cover.

"No shit."

She increased her speed, the squat shape of her outpost growing into a rectangular building on stilts and its connected greenhouse, both made of metal composite and transparent aluminum. Rain coated the throttle, and she gripped it tighter, not slowing until in front of the main entrance. The cart lurched to a stop when she slammed her foot on the brake.

Reaching for the pulse rifle, she turned and searched the horizon. She couldn't see the form through the rain. She could barely see anything at all. Wiping her visor didn't help.

The rifle tight in her hand, she jumped out. Puddles splashed beneath her feet, and her boots slipped in the mud. She should take the hovercart back to the shed, but with the rain so thick, and the strange form on the horizon, she didn't want to waste a second getting safely inside.

Stomach clenching with nerves, she passed the spot where Foster had died, grabbed the handrail, and pulled herself up the steps to the landing. The main doors slid open after a swipe of her PALM against the control panel.

Rain cascaded off her suit as she stumbled inside. She slapped the inner controls. As soon as the doors fully closed behind her, she unhooked her bag, empty of seeds now, and placed it in the wall compartment along with the pulse rifle to undergo their own decontamination process.

A fine mist erupted from above, coating her in cleansing fluid. She held still until it stopped. Moisture dripped from her suit to the floor, then through the grating to the filters beneath.

Wynn turned to face the second control panel, the one that would tell her how many toxins remained on her suit. The panel blinked red in warning. *Too many.* Not surprising after being drenched in acid rain.

Another layer of fine mist coated her before the next door opened. She stepped into the second decontamination room and turned to watch the storm grow in intensity. The shielding above her fields flickered in the distance, but at least it was operational. The inner doors closed, distorting her view.

With a flick of her finger, she disengaged her helmet. Her visor snapped backward, and the astringent scent of cleansing fluid filled her nostrils. She twisted the closure around her neck, pulling it over her head. The rest of her UV-suit followed. A second wall compartment slid open, and she dumped her suit, boots, and PALM inside. She felt a familiar moment of relief as it disconnected and peeled away from her skin.

Standing in her CORE-issue shorts and tank top, she waited as another round of mist covered her from head to toe. The transparent aluminum of the inner door reflected a faint image. Straight black hair cut to her chin, eyes too big for her face, and pale skin—she turned away when the lights on the panel turned green.

The last set of transparent doors released with a hiss, and Wynn expelled a long breath. "Finally." The decontamination process felt especially long today.

She stepped into the entryway of her outpost. The familiar fragrance of green plants wiped away the decontamination fluid scent that followed her inside. Slippers waited beside the door, and she slid them on as the doors sealed behind her with a *snick*.

On her left, the hallway opened up into the kitchen, which led to the living area. On her right, two sets of quarters sat side by side. Across from them was the door to the lab, and beyond that, the entrance to her greenhouse. A short corridor connected the lab to the living area, making it a circular design in a rectangular shape.

Wynn hurried down the hallway, past her quarters, and into the lab. Besides the greenhouse, it took up the largest footprint in the building. Windows wrapped around two perpendicular sections of the walls, and glossy black terminals took up the space beneath.

She gaped at the way the sheets of rain bombarded the transparent aluminum, obscuring the endless view beyond. Rushing forward, she searched the central holotable for her binoculars.

"Where are they?" she muttered when she couldn't find them among the diagnostic tools, scanners, and field supplies. She crouched to check the storage cupboards below, then moved to the wall compartments across from the windows.

She pushed samples and other equipment to the side, and finally found them underneath a case of petrified seeds. Snatching them up, she crossed to the window facing Research Station 214. With a touch to the terminal, she accessed storm controls. The awning outside extended to protect the windows from the direct onslaught.

The cold of the eyepieces pressed against her skin, and the thick downpour hindered her ability to see farther than a few meters. Wynn lifted the binoculars away from her face and changed the settings to thermal imaging. When she resettled them against her eyes, she gasped.

It *was* a person.

Chapter Two

Why the hell was a person *walking* through a category five storm?

Thunder boomed, shaking the building around her, and Wynn's fingers flexed on the binoculars. It made no sense. But there they were, heading slowly toward her more than a kilometer away.

She lowered her binoculars, her eyes seeing nothing on her own through the rain. Lifting them, the masculine shape lurched, made red, orange, and yellow by the thermal setting.

He stumbled forward, and her breath hitched. Was he hurt? The rain had almost knocked her out of the hovercart, so it had to be doing worse to someone walking in all that mud.

Lightning flashed, blinding her for a moment. She lowered the binoculars and bit her dry lip. Should she go get him? She turned, looking toward the main entrance and the hovercart parked there. She could put on a clean UV-suit and drive out there to pick him up.

But.

She hesitated. There had been no notification of a visitor. No one had even checked on her from the research station, though that wasn't unusual. They'd always left them alone out here, even before Foster's death.

If the person wasn't from the research station, then who the hell was he?

She reached for her PALM, intending to check for updates, when she remembered she'd taken it off for decontamination. There were some spares somewhere.

Setting down the binoculars, she checked beneath the holotable's cupboards and found a container of unused PALMs. She pinched the top one.

The gossamer filament clung to her left hand, the plugs inserting into the tiny ports at her thumb, pinkie, and middle finger. Connected to her body heat, it turned on. A CORE insignia rotated above her hand while she waited for it to connect to the grid.

But the icon kept spinning and spinning. *Storm must be interfering with the grid.* No updates then. Huffing out a breath, she removed the PALM entirely, and tossed it on the terminal beneath the window.

She picked up the binoculars again. The person was there, closer now, but slowing. He had to be from Research Station 214, right?

The assumption didn't lessen the unease crawling up her spine at having a stranger approach on foot. It was just so... unheard of. Especially in conditions like these. Lightning flashed and thunder boomed, underscoring the thought.

The hovercart probably wouldn't even work in this sort of downpour, too waterlogged after leaving it outside instead of parking it in the shed. She lowered the binoculars and tried to see through the deluge of rain, but saw nothing but gray.

And someone was stuck out there.

She waged a war inside her mind, contemplating suiting up and retrieving him while simultaneously talking herself out of it. Limbs frozen in indecision, she stood there, waiting, watching, not knowing which way to go or what to do.

A familiar itch crawled over her skin, one she knew would tighten into a sensation of spinning, of losing control, and she'd need to find something to grab onto for focus. A need that she had buried for the past few years because she had this outpost, this purpose, and Foster as a friend.

The beasts had taken all of that away from her.

The thought sent her spiraling further. Wynn set the binoculars aside, and grabbed her forearm over the straight, raised scars that marred her skin. She curled her fingernails into her flesh until pinches of pain erupted.

It should have focused her, but it wasn't enough. The world spun faster, obscuring her vision; the sensation of falling filled her chest. Her exhales escaped her lips in short bursts.

Foster had destroyed her kit long ago—laser scalpel, regenerator, regeneration gauze—almost immediately after he found her in the midst of an "episode" as he'd called it. But since his death, she'd made a new one, had *needed* to.

She'd tried to be strong like he'd asked her to be, but his death had changed everything. Now, reality felt disjointed, spinning, fragmented, and the lure of searing pain promised to make it all go away, to make the ground beneath her feet feel solid again.

She dug her fingernails in further, knew she probably drew blood, but didn't look down. She kept her eyes trained on the cascading rain and wind as it whipped around the outpost, and tried to breathe through shortened inhales.

Fuzziness invaded her sight, and a buzzing noise rubbed the insides of her ears, making her want to scratch her brains out. The spinning continued, getting faster and faster. It would only get worse if she didn't do something *now*. She needed her kit.

She stepped backward, away from the blurring landscape, when her feet jerked to a stop. A form emerged from the pounding rain. Clad in black, the man solidified against a gray world. If she hadn't already noted his route through the binoculars, she would have thought it a figment of her imagination.

The fingers digging into her arm relaxed. Was he wearing a helmet? Or...?

Another flash illuminated the terrain, but didn't shed more light on the puzzle. Shaking her head, she grabbed the binoculars, fiddled with the settings so she could see better, then choked on a gasp. There was no helmet.

Drenched from head to toe, his black jacket hung past his knees. Dark glasses covered his eyes.

He's not wearing a UV-suit.

Her mind blanked, then a tumble of thoughts cascaded one on top of another.

No one could survive a walk across Earth's surface without protection. Then add the acid from the rain? He would have been exposed to a staggering amount of radiation during the past hour.

Her ribs squeezed tight as her stomach churned. Wynn tried to make sense of why a person would do this to themselves, but she found no answers.

And still he headed toward her.

She lowered the binoculars, no longer needing them to see. The man stumbled again, and she inhaled sharply. No wonder his pace had slowed the closer he walked. The radiation sickness would have gotten worse the longer he remained in the elements.

She needed to help him.

The binoculars slipped from her fingers to land on the terminal. *Thunk.* Wynn spun, then darted toward the main entrance and the spare UV-suits stored in a wall compartment. She grabbed the first one, shoving her legs through the pants and into the boots with shaking hands. The four crescent-shaped marks she'd just gouged into her skin glared an angry red at her, but she ignored them as she stuffed her hands in the sleeves, then gloves, and shoved her neck through the helmet closure. She zipped and snapped everything into place.

A flick of her thumb, and her helmet engaged. Then came the agonizing task of making sure every section was airtight and secure. She slapped the control panel on her arm, waiting for the suit's systems to blink on her visor, but it never did.

She'd left her replacement PALM in the lab, and now her ocular implant had nothing to sync to. She looked down at the control panel on her arm instead. It blinked green.

Inhaling a deep breath, she pressed the panel beside the doors. It slid open, and she hurried into the second part of the decontamination zone. Once the doors behind her sealed tight, the next ones opened.

Relentless rain, buckets full, splattered against the outer door like it tried to break it down. Lightning attacked her fields, but she could see the faint blue-green glow that meant the shielding was operational. Another crack of thunder drowned out the sound of her deep inhale. Wynn entered her ID to open the outer door.

Wind suctioned inside the small space, almost knocking her over. Rain slapped her legs and pounded through the grated floor. She hadn't even taken a step outside and water coated her visor.

Wynn gripped the door frame and pushed herself onto the landing. Her boots slipped, and she grabbed the railing to keep from falling. Each of her downward steps felt like she walked on something breakable, something uncertain. The outpost's exterior lights illuminated a path around the building about two meters wide.

One step forward took the energy of four. Her boots sank into centimeters of mud. Water pooled around her ankles. A river ran beneath the outpost, taking islands of dirt along with it. Another boom of thunder shook her entire body.

Gritting her teeth, she trudged forward. *Stupid. Stupid. Stupid.* How could she help him when she couldn't even walk properly?

Wynn plunged ahead, concentrating on the next step, the next stumble. Finally, she cleared the edge of the building and paused. She swiped the rain from her visor and scanned the horizon.

He was gone.

Her breath caught in her throat. He couldn't have just disappeared.

Maybe he'd passed on the other side of the building to aim for the next outpost a hundred kilometers away.

An unhinged laugh burst from her lips at the thought. *No way.*

The laugh turned into a scream when a tall figure lurched toward her from beside the building. She jumped away, and almost fell ass-first into the mud as thunder roared. Lightning streaked across the sky, brightening the terrain. His hand pressed against the exterior of the outpost, his body listing awkwardly. His glasses, a thick band, completely blocked his eyes.

The urge to run, to flee this bizarre scenario, abated when she took in his abused state. Any exposed skin, especially on his cheeks and forehead, was red and raw. The pain must be excruciating. She reached for him, tucking herself under his armpit to take his weight.

"Lean on me," she said, though it would be hard to hear her through her helmet. "Come inside." Her voice shook, then broke, her mind trying to understand why he would put himself through this.

A suicide attempt? Her heart squeezed painfully. Why here? Why now?

He stumbled again, and the force almost brought her to her knees. Gritting her teeth, she aimed toward the door.

Thunder cracked. Wynn jumped, then focused ahead. Impossibly, the storm increased in strength. She focused on the next step, on keeping the man leaning on her from falling into the mud. Each breath strained her lungs from the effort.

It seemed a full day passed before they reached the bottom of the steps. He grabbed onto the railing, relieving some of the strain of his weight. But he stopped instead of climbing upward.

"We need to get inside." The faster they could go through the decontamination process, the quicker she could make him comfortable. Because...

There was no happy ending, no miracle solution, for what was about to happen to him, and she didn't have the equipment to put him in stasis.

Straightening, she pushed those thoughts aside, instead focusing on what she *could* do.

"We need to get you inside," she repeated, louder this time. "I have medicine and painkillers."

He turned his head, like he could hear her through the pounding rain and rumbling thunder. His skin was worse now, blistered, and she swallowed against the hard, dry lump in her throat. The rest of his body would be the same.

She placed her boot on the drenched step, almost slipped, then nudged him upward beneath his armpit. A groan trembled through him.

"I'm sorry," she whispered, but didn't stop her momentum as she nudged him upward.

Through the combined effort of her pushing and him pulling himself up along the railing, they reached the slick landing. Without her PALM to swipe, it took two attempts to punch in her code before the outer doors of the decontamination zone opened. They stumbled inside together.

Wynn reached for the inner panel, pressed the controls, and sealed them inside. Mist flooded the room in a great rush of air, coating them in a white sheen. He braced a gloved hand against the wall, head bent. She remained where she was, supporting his weight.

Beep. Contamination levels popped up on the control panel, the numbers the highest she'd ever seen. The rush of wind swirled around them with more vigor, the next wash of cleansing fluid thicker. Moisture dripped from their bodies in thick clumps.

She looked up at him, encountering her reflection in his dark glasses, the shape of her visor warped, her face pale behind it. His ravaged jaw clenched and flexed. The chemicals at this stage were meant for outerwear, not the skin.

"I'm sorry. I'm sorry," she kept murmuring, though he probably couldn't hear her with the noise of the storm and hum of the decontamination process. "We just need to get through this before I can..." Her voice trailed off, because she could count her options on one hand.

The cleansing deluge finally stopped, and the next set of doors opened. Wynn adjusted her footing and shifted her body forward, guiding him over the threshold into the second decontamination room.

As soon as the door closed behind them, his knees buckled, and he was too heavy for her to stop his fall.

Chapter Three

T he pain.

He had never felt anything like it.

Unimaginable.

But he could not decide if the physical pain was worse than the emptiness, the quiet inside him.

For hours now, days, he had lain alone in the silence, a never-ending echo of nothingness, his own thoughts repeating back to him in a loop.

An aching hollowness had filled him.

They had not warned him it would be this way, though they must have known.

Along the journey, the silence had grown.

Now it screamed at him in deafening waves, gripped him by the throat and choked his breaths, while the taint of the dead planet soaked through his skin and bones.

The urge to leave this place, to return home, drove him hard, but he could not until he completed his task.

Nothing was familiar in this place.

The air suffocated.

The rain drowned.

But he was no longer alone.

His mind remained silent, but an outside source guided him, a light in the darkness.

A lure he could not name.

An energy he could not place.

It would have pulled him forward even if he had not been following orders.

He reached out with his senses, but found his mind empty of thoughts except his own.

But there it was.

A warmth.

A draw.

A distraction.

A comfort from the burning of his flesh.

There were no thoughts to taste, but he could feel *something*, the same pulsing sensation that had led him here, one he could not name.

It hit him in waves, a note of familiarity about it.

Something from long ago.

Or not so long?

It was hard to remember through the pain.

A hand touched his shoulder, and he hissed at the contact.

He took a deep breath.

An unwelcome medicinal scent filled his lungs, corrupting him worse than the radiation.

He coughed, then fell, his legs weak from the planet's attack on him.

The metal grating of the floor pressed into his hands and knees, adding to his pain.

But it grounded him too, reminded him of his purpose.
Of why he was here.
And for whom.

Chapter Four

"Shit. No," Wynn muttered, reaching for him as he collapsed. If he passed out completely, there was no way she could move him on her own. He was too tall, too heavy.

She gripped his shoulder, and he groaned.

"I'm sorry," she said for the millionth time.

He pushed back, his hands braced against his knees, his head bent. Like his cheeks, the skin on the back of his neck and scalp was blistered, peeling in places.

The inner panel beeped. Wynn lifted her gaze and noted the authorization to proceed. Her hand lifted to disengage her helmet, but she hesitated.

Removing his garments first made more sense when he'd been so saturated. It would have soaked deep into his jacket, his gloves, his boots, and could affect her in harmful ways. And the interior door wouldn't unlock until the process eradicated all radiation.

"I need to get this off of you," she said loud enough for her voice to carry through her helmet. "We need to decontaminate your clothes."

A tortured sound emerged from his throat, one of denial. Her hand hovered above his shoulder.

"I'm sorry." Her stomach churned with what she had to do.

He twitched, shifted back on his haunches, then reached a shaky hand up to his shoulder. She stepped to the side and grabbed hold of his collar. The slick material contracted beneath her glove, startling her. She'd thought it the same as what a flight-suit would feel like, but it flexed in a softer way.

The man hissed a breath as he shrugged out of his jacket, bringing her back to her task. She guided the garment over his broad shoulders to reveal the black shirt beneath. It hugged his muscular arms.

The weave of it caught her eye as she pulled his jacket all the way off. Almost organic, the fabric was nothing like she'd ever seen before, like webbing but dense. The jacket fell from his body and slapped onto the floor. She opened the wall compartment and shoved it inside.

"Gloves and shirt," she said, her voice tight with concern. "Everything," she added. "We can't go inside with this much radiation."

She stared at his shoes and swallowed around the lump in her throat. What would his feet look like after walking that far in contaminated mud?

"Boots," she croaked. "We'll start there." She didn't know if she could get them off without his help.

He twitched, then shifted his weight to stand. Wynn ducked down, lifting his arm so she could slide beneath. A groan vibrated through his chest and into her shoulder.

"Sorry," she whispered, guiding him to the wall. "That's it. Just lean here."

She knelt in front of him and undid the first clasp. The style of the boots was new too. They weren't CORE-issue, but something like it, the material having that unusual organic quality. The clasp wasn't magnetic, but some sort of self-adhering fastener. She ran her thumb against the tiny barbs on one side. They flexed, sticking to the material of her glove.

A soft gasp from above snapped her out of her preoccupation. She unclasped the rest of the fasteners.

Placing one hand on the front of the boot, the other on the back, she looked up at him. "Can you step out?"

Droplets of moisture from the first rounds of decontamination fluid clung to his short hair. Framed by blistered cheeks, the reflection in his glasses shone down at her. Her crouched form, her visor and helmet, everything warped in the way his glasses bent around his face.

He shifted his weight, and she pulled. A squelching sound echoed in the small space, followed by his low, sharp groan.

"I'm sorry," she murmured, pulling it off as quickly as possible, not wanting to prolong his agony.

Her movements paused as she focused on his bare foot. Dark moisture, blood and other bodily fluids, caked bumpy skin.

She swallowed, tasting acid. "Next one."

Hissing out a long breath, he shifted the other way. She repeated the process with the second boot to reveal a foot in the same condition.

Wynn stood and tossed his boots into the decontamination compartment. Her gloved fingers twitched at her sides. She'd delayed the inevitable as long as she could.

Taking a deep breath, she reached for the hem of his shirt. "Up and over," she murmured, stretching the material away from his body to reveal more skin ravaged by radiation.

He pushed himself away from the wall with a groan, then helped by lifting his arms. Sculpted muscles and defined ridges took up the planes of his chest and abdominals—a person who did physical labor on the daily.

The thought conjured more questions.

With his help, she pulled his shirt up his back and over his head. A rasping noise bounced off the walls as she lifted it the remainder of the way, his skin sticking to sections of the shirt. He groaned.

She swallowed her apology this time, knowing it didn't help, and tossed the shirt in the wall compartment on top of his boots. Taking a deep breath, she reached for the top closure of his pants. The white of her glove contrasted with the stretchy black material.

Her hands shook as she unclasped the same type of closure as his boots. When it was open as far as it would go, revealing a downward trail of hair, she spread the flaps wide, trying not to touch his skin more than necessary. Gently, she tugged the waistband over his hips, bracing against the sound of his pain.

She tried not to look, but it was impossible with how she needed to crouch to guide the material downward. A thick cock hung between muscular thighs lightly dusted with hair. The skin of his legs was as blistered and red as the rest of the body, and she focused on his knees as she tugged down the garment.

"Step," she said when they pooled around his ankles.

He followed her instructions, shifting his weight one way, then the other. She stood, tossed his pants inside the wall compartment, then faced him. He wore nothing but his glasses. She reached for those too.

His hand shot out. She gasped at the quick motion, at how fast he'd moved after everything. Fingers encircled her wrist like a vise through the material of her UV-suit.

Her heart hammered in her chest. She waited a beat, then two, and when he remained still, she swallowed.

"Okay," she said. "They can stay on for the process." Since they were made of a hard material, they could pass. When he didn't move, she added, "You can let me go."

After another beat, he released her. She took a step back and reflexively touched her wrist with her free hand. Her skin throbbed with awareness where he'd grabbed her.

Keeping her gaze fixed on his face, she reached upward and flicked her thumb at the edge of her helmet, disengaging it. The scent of cleansing fluid wafted over her head. Then came the rest of her suit and attached boots, all the while keeping him in sight. As soon as she stood in her tank top and shorts, she shoved her outerwear into the wall compartment for sterilization and closed it tight.

Wynn touched the panel beside the last door and initiated the final stage of decontamination.

Wind swirled, and with it, a thick fluid coated them. The man's entire body shook. He reached a hand to the wall to steady himself. Wynn twitched. The urge to help him clashed with wariness born from the wrist grab and his nudity.

The process went on, cleaning, disinfecting, always scanning to gauge their radiation levels. The man's chest rose and fell in shallow breaths, his teeth clenching against what had to be excruciating pain.

The encompassing wind accelerated—the final stage of the decontamination process. It ruffled her chin-length hair against her cheeks, then died down completely. The panel beeped, the inner door sliding open with a *whoosh*.

Neither of them moved for a moment, but his labored breaths affected her, a lump hardening in her throat. Straightening her spine, she stepped in close, encircled his wrist as gently as possible, and tucked herself beneath his armpit to take some of his weight.

Damp skin met hot flesh. She gasped. It was like he had an inferno living inside him, and maybe he did because of the radiation infecting his body. But more than that, a sense of familiarity shot through her, one she didn't understand.

She looked up at him, her pale face and wrinkled brow reflected back at her. She didn't know this man. Why would touching him bring recognition? Stars, she'd barely been intimate with anyone. Why would it feel familiar? She pushed the foreign sensation aside to concentrate on the next challenge.

"This way," she murmured, urging him forward.

His first step wobbled, his weight pressing into her shoulder as he regained his balance. Another hiss passed his lips. Gently, she braced her free hand against his sternum, trying to ignore the way his ravaged skin felt beneath hers. The lack of their outerwear emphasized their size difference, him more than a head taller than her.

She matched the pace of his shortened steps, leading him into the entryway, the pinching metal floor changing to low-pile carpet. His body shook beneath her hands. They paused together, and the door to the decontamination zone slid closed behind them.

There was only one place to take him. "On the right."

She nudged him by turning her shoulder toward their quarters. Each shuffled step was like they were climbing a hill. His shortened breaths mixed with hisses of pain. She winced with each one.

They reached Foster's door, and she pressed the control panel beside the door. It slid open, and she sucked in a quick breath.

She hadn't been in here since after Foster's death, but his scent lingered, wafting over the both of them. None of his belongings remained, confiscated the day CORE officials had arrived for their investigation.

The lights turned on automatically as they entered. Tears pricked her eyes as she urged the man ahead, stumbling, toward the bed. She stopped him with gentle pressure on his chest and leaned forward to pull back the bedcovers. Then she guided him downward. He released a groan as his naked body settled, his arms falling to his sides.

"I'll be right back," she whispered, then dashed out into the hallway to the supply closet, grabbing two med kits before rushing back to the room.

The man lay exactly where she'd put him. Kneeling beside the bed, she set the med kits on the ground and opened the first. Her eyes passed over the laser scalpel to the dermal syringe. She palmed it and opened the second kit.

It held medicine cylinders of every type. She grabbed two, snapping the first into the syringe, then held it to his throat.

"This is a painkiller and a sedative," she said, depressing the button on the side. When it emptied, she swapped the cylinder for the other. "And some anti-radiation drugs." She injected it into his bloodstream. "They'll make you more comfortable." *She hoped.* It was hard to know when his body was so polluted already.

Next, she grabbed the regeneration gauze, and flicked her eyes over his body.

She didn't have enough for all of him.

Swallowing, she focused on the worst parts: his face, his neck, his hands, his feet. She crunched the gauze in her hand to activate its healing properties, then laid the strips across each section of red and blistered skin on his neck. Her fingers twitched to remove his glasses, but his reaction earlier made her hesitate.

She finished with his head and moved lower. Thunder and lightning punctuated the time at irregular intervals. Her hands shook as she smoothed the gauze over the reddest part of the man's thighs.

Sorrow rose inside her, clogging her throat. Sadness for this man, for Foster, and for her fields that were probably all washed away. What was the point of anything anymore?

Her breath hitched as an itching sensation crawled over her skin. Her eyes strayed to the three self-inflicted scars carved into her forearm. That familiar need rose in her, but she pushed it down to focus on the man.

With his feet completely wrapped, she used the last of the regeneration gauze over his shoulders, then settled the bedcovers over his body.

"Okay," she said, and he flinched at the word.

Had he found relief, and she'd startled him? She hated the thought, and that she couldn't do more for him, just another shot of painkillers in a few hours.

She had no way to call for help, to get a med team here to put him in stasis, with the storm taking out the grid. It had trapped them together as effectively as being sent to a brig.

Swallowing that disturbing thought, she spoke again, but kept her voice soft. "I'll be nearby if you need anything." She backed out of the room until she stood in the hallway. A tap to the control panel, and the door slid closed, blocking her view of the man on Foster's bed.

She stood there for long seconds, frozen, staring at the door.

Who the hell was he, and why was he here? He wasn't a scientist from Research Station 214, didn't have a CORE uniform. His clothing wasn't CORE-issue either. Apprehension rose in her again, her intuition telling her to retreat.

The solitude and safety of her quarters called to her, but along with it, the kit she'd hid under the sink in the washroom. She lifted her hand and touched the three lines on her inner forearm. Better to keep herself busy than cave to the urge of forcefully muting the world through pain.

She sure as hell wouldn't be able to sleep.

Spinning around, Wynn padded down the hallway and through the lab, the sound of her footsteps swallowed by the constant rumblings outside. The door to the greenhouse slid open at her approach, and she stepped her bare feet onto a grated floor similar to the one in the decontamination zone.

Transparent aluminum stretched before her, a rounded tunnel encasing shades of emerald, viridian, and jade below the strips of synth lights. The storm flashed and twisted above while rain bombarded the panes in cascades, running down the walls in thick rivers.

Taking a deep breath of soil and green into her lungs, Wynn strode forward, focusing on where the metal grating bit at her bare feet. It helped to calm her, those pricks of pain that slowed the spiraling around her. She reached and touched the leaves as she passed. They tickled her skin, a counterpoint to the stinging in her feet.

She kept walking, past the larger saplings, and the tiny ones, to the section filled with pots of dirt. With the shelves bare, the view out of the greenhouse was unobstructed storm. Clouds in every shade of gray, black, and purple swallowed the interior like she stood in the belly of a beast. A streak of lightning tore from the sky. It hit near Research Station 214, or maybe right on it, illuminating the tether like a monument. Another bolt followed, then another, in what looked like an orchestrated attack on the scientific community.

Unbelievable. In all her time on Earth, she'd never seen the equivalent. Her heart raced, and her insides clenched. *Beautiful and dangerous.* She turned slightly, noting the glow of the enviro-net in the distance. It might be operational, but that didn't mean runoff hadn't affected her newly planted seeds.

A crack of thunder boomed around her, rattling the interior of the greenhouse. Wynn clenched her jaw and turned her back on the storm to grab the trowel sitting on the edge of the workbench and the container of unmodified seeds beside it. She would focus on tasks, on making this outpost produce results even as the storm ravaged the work she'd accomplished over the past week.

Tapping on the work surface's terminal, she found a downloaded spaceball game, letting the announcers' voices fill the greenhouse like an echoing cave. When she became bored with that, she changed to a soothing playlist, then an uplifting one, before finding another game.

But no matter what she listened to, her thoughts returned to the person in Foster's room. Another person she couldn't save.

There was nothing more she could do. He'd be dead by morning.

Chapter Five

They called him Carver.

Of course, it wasn't his real name, just the one his superiors used when they wanted to make sure they were talking about the same person, but it fit.

Working for the CORE government day in, day out, it was always the same bullshit. Receive new orders. Follow new orders. Complete the assignment. Reward. Rest. Repeat.

Carver knew nothing else, not since his first kill at the age of ten. Sometimes there were months between assignments, sometimes only a day, never predictable. He couldn't actually *rest*. He lived in a perpetual state of waiting, at the whim of the higher-ups who needed wet work.

Whenever and wherever they wanted him, that was where he went. No questions asked.

He'd been doing the same job for the past twenty years, and knew he was old for an agent. The clock was always ticking. On him. On his next target.

But this assignment? This one was different.

His target, former civilian captain Milo Archibald, hung suspended by his wrists in his own living room, shirtless. Blood dripped from parallel cuts all over his body to the plastic sheeting below, mixing with the piss that had already fallen. *Drip. Splat. Drip. Drip.* It counted down the remaining seconds of the old man's life.

Archibald's wheezy breaths interrupted the smooth sound of the laser scalpel humming in Carver's right hand. He gripped a regenerator in his left. The little room was dark except for the one light behind him, illuminating the old man, but casting Carver in shadows. He'd shut off the bulkhead viewer that played a spacescape of *Lunar One*.

Usually, a sense of justice fueled him as he took the life of a corrupt diplomat, or a rogue agent, or the potential head of a terrorist cell. But this? Carver's skin tightened against his muscles in a way it hadn't in a very long time.

As soon as the unsuspecting man had opened his door to him, nothing had gone as expected. Because the old captain had said, "Ah. Finally. I've been expecting you for a while now."

Despite the perplexing statement, Carver had pushed his way in, and ensconced them within these quarters ever since.

And for the first time since becoming an agent, doubt flickered in his stomach.

He paced in front of the man, not wanting to cut him again, but needing to follow orders and retrieve his answer.

"They just want a number," Carver repeated, his fingers flexing around the laser scalpel.

A fucking number. The guy could say any number in the world, and Carver would be able to end it for him. The old man could lie, could say a hundred, a thousand, a *million*, and Carver wouldn't know the difference.

Because those were his orders: Ask him how many. Get the answer by any means necessary.

How many *what*? What had this man, this regular civilian, done? Carver shouldn't be asking these questions, even in his head. He wasn't paid for questions. It didn't matter how nonthreatening, how innocent, his target appeared, he had a job to do.

Restlessness settled into Carver's body, an agitated sensation crawling over his skin as he continued to pace. He needed to move on, but he couldn't leave without finishing this.

The old man wouldn't give him a number, even a fake one. Carver paced back and forth, his ocular implant recording everything to report back when the job was complete.

"I always knew they'd send someone like you," the old man croaked, his head hanging. Only his toes touched the floor. "I'm so glad Miranda passed on already."

He'd said similar things earlier, things that didn't matter.

"I should have shot myself in the head the day after she died."

The old man had said that before too.

Carver's gaze went to his black case lying on the deck a meter away. There were a hundred items in there that could make the old man talk, but the only things Carver had pulled so far were the regenerator and the laser scalpel. He needed to wrap this up if he wanted to get off the station in the next hour, but instead of heading toward his case, he turned and paced again.

"They just need a number, and this will all be over." Carver would slit the old man's throat, painless, or create that suicide scenario he'd spoken of. "The only person who can make this easier on yourself is you."

The old man lifted his head, and Carver paused. He hadn't done that in a while. A weight settled in Carver's chest as he turned to face the former captain.

He rarely received full workups on the people he ended, but he could always tell when they deserved to die. There was a stench to them. Unmistakable evil soaked into their bones as blatantly as an alert for a Tellusian raid. Maybe because like recognized like, and Carver was as decayed inside as they were.

But when Captain Archibald met his gaze, none of Carver's usual senses tweaked that this man was evil, that he deserved what was coming—that he'd deserved what Carver had already done, and healed, and done again.

"Did they tell you what happened to the boy?" the old man asked.

That was different. The scalpel twitched in his hand, and Carver shook his head before he could think better of it.

Defeat entered the man's eyes. "No. Of course not." His head hung again. "Why would they tell a nothing shadow?"

Insults never landed with Carver. A person could call him anything they wanted, and it wouldn't affect him.

But that softly spoken question twisted his insides tight.

"They just want a number," he said again as he resumed his pacing. "How many?"

He turned the scalpel off, then on again. Then off.

Drip. Drip. Drip. The sound of blood hitting plastic slowed. If Carver wanted to end this, he needed that answer before the old man passed out.

"I've always wondered." Archibald continued like Carver hadn't asked the same question. "Hoped. Even though I knew hope was pointless."

Carver stopped directly in front of him and turned the scalpel on. It hummed.

"I just didn't want him to suffer, you know?" The old man's voice was stronger than before. "We had to sacrifice him to save the others.

He understood." Then Archibald's voice shook. "Do you think that's possible?" Carver watched a different kind of light enter his eyes. "That they wouldn't make a little boy suffer?"

Carver swallowed his scoff, feeding that hope nothing. Throughout his childhood, he'd seen little boys suffer day in and day out. He'd been one of them.

After a moment, Archibald's posture slumped, his gaze returning to the deck.

Carver should take that defeat and use it, manipulate it until the man was sobbing his secrets.

But he... didn't.

He couldn't let this go on, and couldn't understand why he was having such a fucking hard time finishing the assignment.

"I deserve to suffer," Archibald said, his voice only above a murmur.

Carver's fingers flexed on the regenerator. It didn't matter what this man had done. Those weren't his orders. He just needed that fucking number.

Gritting his teeth, Carver stepped right up to him. He turned on the regenerator, and a different sort of buzzing filled the space. Looking down, he healed the oldest cut first, the one near his collarbone, while he gripped the laser scalpel in his other hand.

Once they were all healed, he'd start with the laser scalpel again. The old man would wear down. Eventually.

"Would Miranda want you to suffer like this?" he asked, trying another tactic.

The old man's response came so fast, Carver hadn't finished asking the question. "She knew what was at stake. We all did. She'd be doing the same thing right now if she were alive."

The ferocity of the statement crashed through Carver. What the fuck was he talking about?

Not my orders. Don't ask questions.

Carver concentrated on the next cut and watched how the two sides meshed together while listening to the drips slow.

The old man twitched as his wounds healed, and stared at Carver, unrelenting, while the regenerator buzzed between them.

"Maybe you can help him?"

Carver didn't ask. Didn't want to know.

Not my assignment.

"Maybe you're not as bad as what they want you to believe."

And maybe it was all a test. Carver wouldn't put it past the CORE to have some sort of loyalty task he had to pass, or be terminated by another agent the next day.

But something told him this wasn't that.

He healed the last of the cuts on the old man's chest, dropped the regenerator on the deck, then leaned into his space until their faces were only a centimeter apart. With a flick of his thumb, he turned on the laser scalpel, then held it close to the man's eye.

Archibald barely flinched, even though Carver could feel the heat from the tool just as much as the old man would.

"You're strong, I'll give you that," Carver said, hating the hint of desperation leaking through his voice. "You don't have to prove anything, but I can't leave until I have that number."

They stared at each other, the scalpel humming between them, the old man's gaze jumping between Carver's eyes, searching. A look of understanding, of resignation, swept over his features.

"Twelve. But you'll never find them all." Then the old man moved quicker than Carver would have thought possible while being suspended by bleeding wrists.

Archibald lurched forward, right into the path of the laser scalpel, impaling his face against the heat of the tool. Carver dodged, but not fast enough, trying to pull the device away. The old man's scream tore between them, followed by the scent of burnt flesh. The laser sank into his cheekbone, then his eye, before Carver could retreat far enough.

The scalpel had done a lot of damage, but not enough to kill him, and the old man let out garbled shouts of pain. Carver stepped close, grabbed his white hair, and tilted his head for the killing blow—one swipe across his throat.

Silence enveloped the room in the next instant, punctuated by Carver's fast inhales. *What the fuck was that?*

Carver's grip flexed on the scalpel. He took a deep breath as he stared at the hanging body, the bulk swaying gently back and forth.

Fuck. Fuck. Fuck.

This was sloppy. He didn't have the time to make it look like a suicide now. That meant it would look like a murder.

Murders meant questions. And questions made his superiors twitchy.

His chest rose and fell like he'd just done laps around the station. This felt like his first kill, messy and filled with too much emotion.

Emotions get you terminated.

Carver shut everything down inside him and focused on what needed to be done. First, he swapped out the tainted plastic for a clean sheet, taking the bloody one to the reclamation chute and shoving it inside to be incinerated.

Then he cut the body down from the overhead, removing all trace of the ties he'd used. He picked up the regenerator from the deck and used it to heal the cuts on the old man's wrists. That he had to do. Murder was one thing. Torture was another.

Maybe the cleaner could play this off as a crime of passion if the man had a girlfriend or something, but it wasn't likely with the way Archibald had been talking about his late wife.

Using a cloth from his case, he wiped the blood off the body as best he could, but there was a lot on his pants. He removed those too.

Hefting the dead weight over his shoulder, Carver carried the man to his quarters and laid him out on the bed before covering him in blankets.

Lastly came Carver's clothes. He peeled off the flight-suit and swapped it for business garb before tossing the blood-tainted items into reclamation as well. Then he hit the destroy and recycle button before returning to the main living space.

With one last glance over his shoulder toward the bedroom, he picked up his case to leave, then hesitated. Usually, he would reconnect to the grid at this point and send all his recordings and data to his superiors, but that agitated feeling traveled over his skin again.

Carver took a deep breath, then another, before touching his PALM to access his ocular implant's interface. He watched as what had happened over the past few hours sped by in reverse. With a touch of his finger, he paused his feed at the moment Milo Archibald opened his door for him. He went forward again, cutting the sections where his superiors could find fault, where Carver had hesitated, where he looked weak. Then he took out the parts where the man talked about the boy.

I don't have time for this.

And he didn't, but Carver did it anyway, cutting and blending with touches to his PALM, adjusting the readout, adding still moments, so everything matched up.

He would have cut more, but couldn't linger any longer. He paused at the last part where the man spoke of the twelve. Carver needed that part, or he couldn't complete this assignment.

So why did he hesitate even then?

Hesitation means death.

He left the remainder of the recording untouched, knowing he'd get a reprimand for the cause of death. He didn't have time for anything better.

With the recording altered, he meshed the timestamp with the current time, and strode toward the exit, his black case slung over his shoulder.

He stepped out into an empty corridor and squinted against the bright after being in dim lighting for so long. As he headed to the closest lift, he touched his PALM, reconnecting with the grid to send a message to his handler. *Mission complete. Cleaner required.*

The lift door opened, and he stepped into an empty car. The doors closed with a swish behind him, and the lift descended. A second later, the acknowledgement of his completed assignment came through, along with a notification of creds delivered into his account.

He turned to face the door when new orders appeared at the bottom of his ocular implant.

Carver inhaled a deep breath. *So much for a rest period.*

Chapter Six

Wynn woke with a start, like a pulse rifle fired next to her ear. She jerked upward, sitting straight, her heart hammering in her skull. The bedcovers slid down her body to pool at her hips, and she fisted them in her hands, trying to catch her breath.

A rumble of thunder made her look up. Rain splattered against the narrow window, the light level fractionally brighter than it had been when she'd fallen into bed.

She'd worked for hours in the greenhouse, allowing exhaustion to seep into every bone before attempting sleep. Her mind had only wanted to hyperfixate on the man dying in Foster's quarters. When her eyes had barely stayed open, she'd called it quits. The rumble of thunder had soothed her like a lullaby, with an occasional boom disrupting the constant purr.

She glanced at the door, dread swirling in her stomach. Another person died here, only meters away, while she did nothing.

Her insides twisted, and the room spun. She reached up and settled her hand on her forearm, the feel of the lines against her palm grounding her. Turning her head, she stared at the washroom door. The urge to get up and retrieve the kit she had stashed there was making her twitchy.

No. She didn't have time for self indulgence when there was shit she needed to do. She had to check the body. If comms were back up, she would report the incident to her superiors at the Science Academy. She also needed to find out how long this storm was going to last, and if any of her fields had survived the night.

Pushing the covers aside, Wynn rose. The carpet felt cool against her bare feet. She padded to the wall compartment and pulled out a set of CORE-issue comfort wear, a long-sleeved shirt and loose fitting pants. Quickly, she swapped out her tank and shorts for the clean set, and pushed the dirty ones into the laundry sluice.

Her door slid open when she stepped close, the lights in the hallway set to half-luminosity for night. She paused, swallowing. She didn't want to do it, didn't want to have another dead person haunt her dreams.

Taking a deep breath, she stepped into the corridor. Nausea swirled in her stomach as she walked to Foster's door. She stopped in front of it, lifted her hand to touch the control, then paused.

The sedative she'd given him would have allowed him to pass away in his sleep, but how would he look after bring ravaged by radiation all night?

Get it over with.

Wynn swallowed the bile climbing the back of her throat and pressed the control to open the door. She expected the stench of death to have already started because of the rotting of his organs from the inside out, but there was nothing.

And no one.

"Lights full," she whispered, and everything brightened.

She sucked in a sharp breath. The room was empty, the bed unoccupied. Rumpled sheets mussed the bed where he'd lain, but he was nowhere to be found.

Heart in her throat, she spun around and scanned the hallway up and down. Had he somehow dragged himself out of the room and died elsewhere?

Two steps took her to the door of the lab. It opened as she approached, and she darted inside, eyes scanning everywhere. It was empty too.

She continued on, past the door to the greenhouse and through the short hallway that led to the living room. Her bare feet screeched to a halt. Her chest seized. She gripped the door frame to remain standing.

The man stood at the window naked, looking out into the storm.

He stood. Upright. Alive.

She flexed her fingers against the door frame. His back was to her, and he lifted his arms slightly away from his body, his palms facing forward. His spine was straight, tall, his buttocks taut, and his shoulders wide—unlike the hunched, stumbling posture of when he'd arrived.

And his skin... it no longer appeared bright red and blistered.

Smooth, *healed* flesh covered sleek muscles.

Not possible.

Her skin prickled in warning. He shouldn't look that way. Severe radiation burns didn't reverse themselves with one dose of medicine. She hadn't been trying to cure him because that would've been impossible without a whole lab and crew dedicated to the task. Given the circumstances, she'd been trying to make him as comfortable as possible for the last few hours of his life.

None of this was right. It defied logic. It defied science. That prickle turned into an itch, and she took a step back.

He twisted his head, dropping his hands against his thighs. Wynn froze in place. He still wore those glasses. They wrapped around enough that she couldn't see his eyes at all.

She retreated another step, her hand dropping away from the door frame, then stopped again when he faced her fully.

His front was as perfect, as *undamaged*, as the back of him. Pectorals, biceps, abdomen—defined muscles swathed his body like the sculptures of old. His cock hung between corded thighs, a light dusting of hair thickening as it traveled downward. The storm behind him highlighted their size difference.

A dying man held little threat, but this large, naked man?

Her mind raced to figure out how he could be well and whole. He'd walked from the direction of the research station with nothing with him. No case, or luggage, or... anything. He couldn't have some ground-breaking drug that cured radiation sickness overnight, and she certainly didn't have one.

And again, familiarity struck her. Something she couldn't place, but urged her to step forward as much as retreat.

"Who are you?" The question snapped out of her, combative. "Why are you here?" She clenched and relaxed her hands, trying to grab hold of anything that would make her understand.

Was he Tellusian? That didn't make sense either. Where were his tattoos, then? He wasn't wearing a warrior's uniform, or even what she'd seen of Tellusian styles on media reports. His clothes and boots weren't like anything she'd seen before.

In answer to her question, he tilted his head, the jerky movement sending more fear down her spine.

Retreat. Get to safety. Run.

She took another step back. He tilted his head the other way, almost animalistic.

Another shiver raced through her body, over her scalp and down her arms. Her thoughts disconnected, like someone yelled at her through the decontamination room's door. She could see the shouting, but didn't understand the words, her mind and gut telling her two different things at the same time.

Frozen in indecision, Wynn jumped when he stepped toward her. A sensation of otherness washed over her at the motion. Despite his appearance, something told her he wasn't human.

Icy realization cascaded over her body, shortening her breaths. *No.* It wasn't possible. *No no no no no.* There had to be another explanation, something that made sense and didn't threaten her very existence.

She kept telling herself that, even as all the pieces fell into place, everything from his unusual healing ability to the clothes he wore.

"Take off your glasses." The words passed her lips in a tortured whisper.

She didn't want to find out if she was right—what her whole body had been telling her since she saw him standing at the window.

He didn't move except to tip his head oddly.

"Take off your glasses!" she yelled, panic gripping her throat.

A moment in time stretched between them, punctuated by her shallow breaths.

He reached upward slowly with one hand and grabbed hold of the side of his glasses. A swipe, and they were off. He lowered his arm until they dangled from his fingertips at his side.

Wynn exhaled a long breath. His eyes appeared normal, just a lighter shade of brown than usual. Perhaps hazel.

A relieved shiver passed through her body, and she almost laughed aloud at herself. Of course he wasn't Calypson. They didn't leave their area, just lured people to their doom with some sort of immortal promise.

Then he turned his head, and the overhead lights caught in his irises. For a second, his eyes *glowed.* Cat's eyes. That was what she'd heard the effect called.

All the blood rushed from her head. He *was* Calypson. And he stood before her. In her living room. In her outpost. On Earth and not in Sector Ten like he should be.

Protect yourself.

She spun around and ran, through her lab, out into the hallway, toward the exit and the pulse rifle waiting in the clean compartment of the decontamination zone.

Shaky hands punched in the code. Where the hell was her PALM? She could've just swiped her hand instead of getting the code wrong on the first try.

She glanced over her shoulder and screamed.

He was *right there*, not a meter away, each of his features as clear as day: his full lips, sharp nose, and high cheekbones. And those disturbingly reflective eyes accented by a furrowed brow.

She hadn't heard him move over the noise of her heart pounding in her head.

His hands were empty, the glasses gone. She couldn't tell his age, maybe upper twenties like her, but being Calypson, who the hell knew how old he was.

Her hand reached out toward the compartment, slapping the compartment's panel. When it didn't open, she tore her gaze away and punched in her ID code again.

It opened, revealing her sanitized suit from yesterday, as well as all his clothing. She grabbed a handful of the flexible material and threw it at him, one garment at a time. Then came his boots. They hit his body, but he didn't react.

Wynn swallowed and touched the barrel of the pulse rifle.

A quick movement froze her in place. He took a step forward, over the clothes and boots she'd thrown at him, then took another.

She dropped the rifle in her haste to back away, her gaze riveted to those reflective eyes.

Don't let him touch you.

That was how they did it, wasn't it? They touched a person and changed them into Calypson too. No one really knew. Maybe Calypsons ate the pilgrims, because most weren't seen or heard from again.

But she'd helped him inside yesterday, skin to skin. She'd touched him many times while bandaging his wounds. And she was still... Wynn.

He stopped beside the clean compartment and stared down at its contents. She shuffled backward, then paused in her retreat, startled by the confusion on his face. He reached inside.

Shit. Shit. Shit.

Why had she dropped the pulse rifle? Why was she such an idiot?

All her muscles bunched to run, then she froze. It wasn't the rifle he held in his hand, but the white fabric of her UV-suit. It hung from his fingertips like he'd never seen one before.

Hadn't he? His trip across Earth's terrain had been UV-suit-free. Maybe he hadn't known he should wear one.

"What do you want?" Fear and frustration laced her words. What could a Calypson possibly want with her outpost? The only thing they did here was try to get plants to grow on this dying planet.

She took another step back, then stopped when he let the UV-suit fall into the compartment and turned his attention back to her.

"Why are you here?" she asked, her hands clenching on nothing at her sides.

Maybe she'd been misinformed. Maybe everything she'd ever heard about Calypsons had been a lie. Maybe they traveled freely throughout the system, but the CORE government thought it prudent to keep it hidden. She wouldn't put it past them.

Her blood froze in her veins when he finally spoke, his voice a raspy, unused sound.

"I have come to collect you."

Chapter Seven

The color drained from the woman's face, alarming him.

Was she hurt? Ill? She looked ill.

He did not know how to fix an anomaly if they became ill.

Perhaps The Four had sent the wrong person for this job.

Instinctively, he reached with his mind, past the storm that continually rumbled around them, searching for those who would know better than him, who knew human anatomy and had medical expertise.

His mind swept outward, farther and farther, then encountered... nothing.

Alone.

He kept forgetting how alone he was.

A sickening sensation invaded his chest and stomach. He did not like that his was the loudest voice in his head.

It had started soon after leaving Sector Ten, a yawning discomfort, an endless silence when constant chatter filled most of his life.

An off-balance prickling developed over his skin. He did not like that either.

"No, you didn't," the woman, Doctor Wynn Lambdin, whispered.

He reeled his mind and thoughts back into himself as a wave of *something* crashed over him.

He could not name it, but it had been bombarding him ever since he had arrived.

All he knew was that it came from her, and it repelled and drew him at the same time.

He studied her from head to toe. Her clothes hugged her curves, a white shirt that covered her arms, and tan slacks that fell straight.

But her feet were bare, and his gaze focused there for a moment.

Had he ever noticed someone's feet before? He could not recall.

Lifting his gaze to her face, he examined her features: her pink lips, her flushed cheeks, and how her eyes, so different from his own, flashed with fire.

What created that fire? He wanted to learn.

Then he realized her quiet words were in response to his statement.

Her denial did not change his purpose, so he repeated, "I have come to collect you."

The words physically hurt his vocal cords as they strained with disuse.

He tried to recall the last time he spoke aloud, but a muddle of images and unwanted sensations cascaded through his body, followed by an unfamiliar ache in his stomach.

He abandoned the task before the images and sensations could dominate his mind.

Another wash of *something* surged toward him and crashed over his head and body while the woman's visible distress grew. Her hands clenched and released at her sides.

He often searched for words, but out here he was alone. *So alone.* The ones who had been human longer that him did not supply him with ready answers. His own internal voice was now the loudest.

But he needed to help her somehow. He took a step forward. That *something* continued to grow, more potent now. She screeched, jumping backward.

"Stay away!" she shouted, the sound assaulting his eardrums.

Never had he experienced such loud sounds coming from an adult. A newborn, yes, their shrill noises something he always avoided, but not a fully grown person.

The sound stayed his movements, freezing his feet in place.

She scurried backward to the end of the hallway until her back hit the opening to the next room and she stopped. A deep breath shuddered through her body.

He had walked this way earlier, knew it was the place where she prepared her meals.

A small, slender window ran the length of the room above the counters and cupboards, revealing a glimpse of the world outside.

The storm raged, one to which he had no comparison. Its violence mesmerized.

As soon as he could rise from his slumber, he had sought it out, staring endlessly into its churning ferocity.

It transfixed him as much as the woman who regarded him with the most dynamic expressions he had ever seen on someone's face.

Her life force pulsed just below the surface, separated and untouchable, but there.

Again, he attempted to connect with her psyche, but there was no joining of minds, only the vast emptiness of *alone.*

The lack of communication, the absence of a bond, created a sweeping sensation through his body, one that settled uncomfortably in his stomach.

No wonder The Four had avoided this. A confined, singular existence made little sense.

A strange scent enveloped this place, sterile but also green. It was not unpleasant, but so very different from where he came from, and contrasted with the arid scents he had experienced before it rained.

A louder crack of thunder resounded overhead.

Doctor Wynn Lambdin jerked, her knees looking like they would buckle beneath her.

He stepped forward again, to help her regain her balance, but a small, distressed sound emerged from her throat, stopping him.

"Can't you put on some damn clothes?" she shouted, the shrillness slapping at him differently than the sounds of the storm. That *something* flowed toward him again, an invisible wave amongst visible ones, just as vexing as when he had arrived.

His gaze returned to the compartment behind him and the items it held.

Her white suit intrigued him.

He had not understood the usefulness of such a garment, as it would impede his ability to stretch his senses into the world around him, but after the natural defenses of this planet relentlessly attacked him, he agreed with its benefits, at least for long durations within the hostile elements.

But it was his nudity she referred to.

He turned and strode to where she had thrown his clothing. One boot lay on its side, the other stood upright.

He bent over and grabbed the top of his pants with his fingers.

A small sound emerged from the woman behind him, and he straightened to regard her.

She had not moved, but the color that had leached from her face earlier had returned in force, her cheeks bright red as she stared at him.

Another wave of *something* followed in its wake.

This something tasted different, a headier, hotter flavor coating his mind.

While he tried to decipher the sensation, she jerked her chin forward, to the garment he held in his hand.

The gesture urged him to continue the task, though if he lingered on the thought, he did not understand why he knew that.

His gaze shifted to his hands. With a flick of his wrists, he shook out the rumpled material, lifted his foot, and pulled the pant leg up his calf.

He did the same with the other, all the while keeping his awareness of Doctor Wynn Lambdin open.

Once he had fastened his pants, he pulled his shirt over his head. A softer *something* washed toward him, more comforting than not.

He picked up his jacket and laid it over the edge of the compartment next to her outerwear, then slid his feet into his boots. He left his gloves where they lay beside the long weapon at the bottom of the compartment.

While his back was turned, Doctor Wynn Lambdin shifted a little, pushing off the wall in small increments.

He refocused on her with a tilt of his head.

She froze, her breaths accelerating, echoed by the quick rise and fall of her chest.

That more toxic, abrasive, *something* pulsed toward him.

She stood that way for a very long time, one foot braced forward, the other back. Then she shifted, transferring her weight to her front foot.

Perhaps she thought that if she moved slowly, he would not notice.

That would not be possible.

Since coming to this place, he had noticed everything about her.

How she was both so similar and so foreign.

How she drew him, but that *something* pushed him away.

His mind reached into the memories of the past, where he did not tread often, searching for the thing that would explain the *something* that changed so steadily on the heels of her actions.

Emotions. That was what kept washing over him, distracting him in unpredictable ways.

He had experienced many unnamed emotions since he had arrived, most sharp and stinging, but others soft and giving.

Those were the ones he liked best.

Her kindness. She had braved the elements to assist him when this world had waged its battle against his natural defenses. She had shouldered his weight despite the strain to her body.

Her apology. The pain he had experienced affected her, though she was not the cause.

Her sadness. She had thought she could not help him, though she did so anyway.

There was more sadness, but something deeper that welled upward in a continuous flood.

It weighed her down, and that made him... *feel* as well. And he was not sure what to think about that.

Beneath her skin and bones, her heart beat a quick rhythm in her chest, almost frantic. It was unlike those he was used to spending time with, their steady presence similar to his own.

Thunder cracked above him. It startled her enough to jump, though the lightning and rain had been constant since the sun rose.

The sun. Another oddity.

This was the closest he'd been to the star in a long time.

While in space above the planet, it had bombarded him with unhelpful radiation, but it had been breath-catching to see up close. More so than he would have thought.

He turned his head to track its progress through the clouds, noting how much time had passed since he had lain inside the automated life pod that had brought him here.

As soon as his focus shifted, Doctor Wynn Lambdin darted through the kitchen to the living area, light and quiet on her feet.

He tipped his head, his gaze focusing in her direction.

This building was laid out in a circle of sorts, and he adjusted his eyes off the visible spectrum to follow her path through the walls.

She tapped at her terminal, then cursed under her breath, giving it a punch before shaking out her hand. Then she was lifting and moving items on the work surface as she searched for something.

He followed her, curious about her purpose.

A gasp of satisfaction left her lips when she found an item. She glanced over her shoulder, like she could see thermal signatures through walls like him, though he knew she could not.

Perhaps The Four had been wrong about that.

But her eyes went to the door of the living area, not where he walked through the kitchen.

She tapped at the terminal, her hands shaky. A soft *beep, beeping* carried through the building between the rumbles of thunder outside.

His glasses lay where he had dropped them in front of the window. One of his directives had been to conceal his eyes, that humans would react badly to them. They had been right.

He left the accessory where he'd abandoned it and stopped at the edge of the doorway leading to the lab, hesitant to reveal himself when she appeared to be... distressed.

The word appeared to him in his mind, a description of the emotion she had been sending toward him ever since she found him standing by the window.

"Come on, come on," she muttered, casting another quick glance in his direction.

Her fingers traveled over the slick surface of the terminal, and more *beeps* intermixed with the rolling thunder.

His gaze went to her left hand, and he adjusted his sight again when he noticed a thin film covering her skin. Its heat signature denoted an active piece of technology.

He knew what it was, a PALM device that connected an individual to the main grid this solar system used for their data collection and sharing of information.

She stopped pressing buttons, braced her hands on the edge of the terminal, and hung her head.

An unfamiliar emotion swept toward him, one that tightened his chest. It tasted sour in his mind, but a description did not immediately emerge.

He took another step forward, then stopped when she inhaled a deep breath and cast another glance in his direction.

She pushed away from the terminal and scurried to the door that led to the hallway. Her feet stopped when the door slid open with a swish. She poked her head out, then back in again.

Her shoulders relaxed a fraction before she scurried toward the decontamination zone.

Refocusing on the terminal she had accessed, he walked through the short hallway to the lab, past the greenhouse doors to pause where she had stood.

He adjusted his eyes to the visible spectrum. The panel was lit up in sections, one red light flashing beside a CORE insignia.

He pressed his hands flat against the terminal, allowing his essence to flow freely through his skin and into the technology. She had been trying to send a communication, but it did not look like it had worked.

But one last message had made it through, beginning with: *Hurricane of unprecedented strength.*

There was much more to learn from this system, even cut off from the larger grid. Years of research and personal data on the people who worked here, including Doctor Wynn Lambdin.

A surge of *curiosity* burst through him, an urge to learn as much as he could about her, but his attention shifted away from the terminal when he heard a thump and a rustle beneath the sounds of the storm.

He called his essence back into himself and turned. With a slight adjustment of his eyes, he found her thermal signature, the flutter of her pulse, and her soft breaths.

She bent at the waist, her hands shaking as she pulled the protective suit up her legs. Then her arms went through each of the sleeves. She fastened the front closures until secure and took a deep breath.

He tilted his head, considering her actions. Why would she prefer to leave the safety of the building to venture into lethal weather?

He did not like the sensation of not understanding. Logic should influence decisions.

As the seconds ticked by, he could only conclude that Doctor Wynn Lambdin did not share the philosophy.

When she reached for the neck of her suit to engage her helmet and visor, he moved in a burst of speed. He did not stop until he stood in front of the door controls to the decontamination zone.

She screamed when she turned and saw him standing there, only centimeters from touching her. She jumped backward, stumbling.

He reached forward to help, when she shouted, "Don't touch me!"

She scurried backward until her spine pressed against the door frame that led to the kitchen—both of them in similar positions as they were only minutes ago.

Her distress, her *fear*, washed over him, making him pause.

He lowered his hand, unbalanced by her words and emotions. "Why can I not touch you?" His throat hurt from speaking, though it held less sting than earlier.

An odd sound emerged from her lips, a puffy one that ended on a guttural noise from her chest. Her hands clenched and relaxed at her sides.

"Because you did not ask, and I did not give you permission," she said, her words passing her lips in a tumble.

He allowed her answer to sink inside him. His urge to help had caused her more distress, and the intense emotion coating her face created uncomfortable tightness in his chest.

He found himself saying, "I will not harm you."

"Good." The word was short, stabbing like the new emotion that darted toward him. "Now let me leave."

Her eyes pleaded with him, then shifted to the violent storm raging on the other side of the two sets of transparent doors.

"I cannot do that." A sound of denial left her lips, so he added, "It is not safe."

Her barked laugh startled him.

He held still, waiting for another outburst, but she seemed to curl into herself, deflating.

He did not like that, but could not explain why.

Her chest rose and fell in gasping breaths. Her hands continued their clenching.

She shifted her weight fitfully from one foot to the other, then the movement slowed.

Her mouth opened and closed, but no words came out.

Questions crossed her face, but he could not see into her mind to search them out, could only experience the emotions she shot toward him, their strength and ferocity an attack on his mind and body.

They stood that way for long minutes.

"Are you going to change me into Calypson?" she finally asked, her words barely above a whisper.

"No." She would never be like him.

He could never touch her mind or share her thoughts. A chasm would always separate them, larger than the space that spanned between their bodies in this moment.

Her shoulders slumped, like his words saddened her, and he agreed. To never experience the solar system the way he could was a dispiriting thought.

But he could possibly give her some comfort.

"You are already Calypson."

Chapter Eight

"**B**ullshit." The word spewed from Wynn's mouth.

Confusion-wrapped terror replaced the relief she'd felt after he'd said he wouldn't hurt her or change her.

There was no way she was Calypson. She didn't live in a nebula, or have glowing eyes. She'd never traveled to Sector Ten like those who revered Calypsons, those who wanted to escape their lives.

Her heart pounded in her ears. She couldn't hear anything else as she stared at him, frozen in her indecision to run or fight.

Run where?

There was nowhere to go. The storm raged outside. He blocked both the pulse rifle and the exit.

She'd already tried to call for help. The storm was too severe for the grid to connect to this area. Wynn flexed her hand, the PALM she'd donned feeling tight and restrictive against her skin.

One last message from Asia Prime had imported before everything went offline, and it hadn't been good.

This storm was the biggest the planet had seen, a hurricane that covered most of New Asia and the Pacific Ocean. A certain tone laced the beginning of the message, a "Well, we hope we've built all the outposts sturdy enough to survive this." No help was coming because everyone was in danger. *Shelter in place.*

She was on her own.

And she was certain there were meteorologists back at the Science Academy shitting themselves with the opportunity to study the phenomenon. They wouldn't care that she was stuck out here with a person whose eyes glowed and who moved with a speed she could barely track.

Inhuman. The word bounced around in her head, reinforced by the way he held himself, so still the air between them held its breath.

A fresh surge of panic swelled in her throat. Her gaze swept to the outside world, then back to the man. How unhinged was it to get in that hovercart and try to make it to Research Station 214 for help?

What were her other options?

Her thoughts emptied except for what he'd told her. Would believing him be the most idiotic decision of all?

"I want to leave." She hated how her voice wavered.

He tilted his head, strange eyes glinting, but otherwise remained motionless.

"It is not safe."

A shiver raced down her spine. When he'd first spoken, his voice had been rough and scratchy. The jagged edges had smoothed some, leaving a deep, gravelly timbre in its wake.

That sense of familiarity rippled through her again, but she was certain she did not know this man. This *Calypson.*

"I want to leave," she repeated, her teeth gritted.

"It is not safe."

Her hands flexed in frustration at her sides. "I'm not safe in here with you. I want to leave."

His head tilted sharply, like he was surprised. *How would I even know that?* Did Calypsons experience emotion? What she'd seen of them, of *him*, made her think otherwise. She swallowed around the dryness in her throat.

"I will not harm you," he said after a moment.

A disbelieving breath puffed from her lips. "I can't trust you."

His spine straightened. "I have done nothing to harm you."

"You're stopping me from leaving. That harms me."

"It is not safe."

A growl of frustration escaped her, and he tilted his head in the other direction.

"If it weren't for the storm, would you allow me to leave?"

"Yes. We would both go. I have come to collect you."

She shook her head in denial. "Not happening. No way in hell. I'm not going anywhere with you."

His chin tilted at that, but he did not respond. Seconds ticked by while they stared at each other.

"So, what?" she croaked when her skin itched with the need to say something. "We just hang out until it passes, and then you'll try to make me go, and I'll fight you tooth and nail so you don't?" His chin lifted, and she swallowed against the dryness in her throat. "If you force me to go, it doesn't really follow along with the 'no harm' mentality, does it?"

He rolled his shoulders back. "I will not force you," he said finally.

A snort left her nose, unbidden. "You won't convince me to come with you."

He didn't react to her statement, didn't tell her she was wrong, or become more confrontational. They stared at each other, motionless, while rain splattered against the outer decontamination zone door.

Second by second, some of her terror seeped from her body. The clenching of her fists relaxed, and her heart rate slowed.

Could she believe anything he told her?

Boom. A crack of thunder ripped through the building, rumbling the floor beneath her bare feet and making her heart leap into her throat. Every time she thought the strength of the storm might be lessening, it proved her wrong.

He looked upward, as though he could see the violent sky through the ceiling.

"It will be some time before the storm abates," he said, his voice smoothing out more.

Her jaw flexed as she tried to decipher the statement. "Is that your way of saying there's enough time to convince me?"

His eyes glinted as he refocused on her. "I do not understand your question."

She huffed a breath. "No, of course not." Everything he'd done or said so far was literal. She shook her head. "Never mind."

Light flashed against the clouds, and another rumble of thunder rippled through the outpost.

He was stuck here like her. No matter who he was or what he was doing here, they couldn't stare at each other for the duration of the storm. After a day in the fields yesterday, and spending most of the night in the greenhouse, the stiffness in her muscles told her she needed to stretch and move.

And thoughts of her greenhouse made her fidgety. All the work that was meant for two people now landed solely on her. She needed to *do* something, not just stand here and worry about how he was going to "collect her."

He'd said he wouldn't harm her, and he hadn't.

He'd also said she was Calypson, but that was impossible.

A slow exhale passed between her lips, and she pushed off the wall. He twitched. She froze.

When nothing else happened except more thunder and lightning, she stepped backward into the kitchen.

He stayed in place.

She kept her eyes on him as she took another step, then another. His chin angled downward, but he didn't advance.

Wynn's butt hit the kitchen island, and she gripped the counter with both hands by her hips to keep steady.

"How about this?" she said, hating that her voice still shook. "How about I agree not to leave the outpost and you agree not to touch me, or hurt me, or do anything to me at all?"

He tilted his head, then nodded once. "Agreed."

"And," she continued before he said the entire word. "You can't lie to me."

He straightened. "Agreed."

"And," she rushed ahead again, needing this in order to keep her sanity. "Once the storm has abated enough, you will leave, and there will be no more talk about collecting me."

His quick agreement didn't come, and her hands tightened on the counter, the edge biting into her skin.

"I cannot agree to that," he finally said.

Her fingers flexed. "Why not?"

"I have already agreed not to lie."

A strangled noise emerged from her throat, her heart leaping at his words.

"Then I guess I have time to convince you to leave without me." She wouldn't go anywhere with him. Not in a million years.

She thought he would say he couldn't agree again, but he nodded once. "Agreed. You may try to convince me."

Even though it seemed irrational, those words relaxed her shoulders and lowered her heart rate. Wynn stared at him, waiting. She didn't know why, maybe for some sign he would go back on his word, but he didn't move.

The longer they stared at each other, the more the tension eased from her spine.

"All right," she said aloud. "Okay."

She swallowed, making the final decision to trust him at his word, though she might be a fool to do so, and gave him her back to face the kitchen.

The need to do something skittered through her arms and legs. Lifting her shaky hand, she touched the closures of her UV-suit, unfastening the front, then pulled the neck over her head and back to shimmy out. She slipped out of the boots, then gathered the bulky material, tossing it on the counter. It would be fine there for now.

Her gaze went to the dispensary on the left. She wasn't hungry, even though she hadn't eaten anything yet this morning. *Tea.*

Ignoring the man whose gaze burned into her spine, she skirted the counter and stopped in front of the dispensary. "Cup of water, hot, teabag number seventy-six on the side."

A beat of time passed, then the dispensary door opened, shoving the steaming cup on a saucer, the bundle of tea sitting beside it.

Movement rustled behind her, and she tensed. She turned her head and saw him stop at the entrance to the kitchen, but he advanced no farther.

Tossing him a scowl, she grabbed the saucer and headed out of the kitchen, cut across the living room, right past his glasses on the floor, then through the short hallway to the entrance of the greenhouse.

The doors slid open with a *whoosh*, and the scent of green and dirt washed over her. She aimed for where she'd finished last night, four partial pots of dirt, the germination chamber sitting beside them, its hard silver exterior glinting from the strips of lighting from above.

She probably shouldn't even be in here because of the chance the glass might crack due to the extreme weather. But if transparent aluminum could withstand conditions in space, then it should withstand this storm.

At least, that was what she kept telling herself as she refocused on her plants. If she didn't have them to take away that itchy sensation, then she'd fall back on her other source of comfort.

Her hand reflexively went to the scars hidden beneath her shirt, her hand cupping her forearm. She curled her fingers inward, then forced herself to release the pinching sensation.

Not now. Not today. She focused on the germination chamber and opened it up with a swipe of her thumb. The seal released, and the lid popped open, revealing the rows of preserved seeds inside.

She lifted the first transparent packet and separated four seeds to plant in the waiting pots. Fertilized dirt stuck to her fingers as she pushed them into the loose soil. Even if the seeds out in the field didn't live through the storm, at least she had this—months, *years*, of work she and Foster had accomplished together.

The itchy sensation returned on the heels of thoughts of her friend. Wynn tapped the surface of the counter, found a spaceball game to listen to as she worked, then centered her gaze on the next seed, the next pot.

With all four planted, she set them in their spots on the rotating shelves, pressed the control on the terminal beside her, and they rose in the air, presenting a new row empty of pots.

The door to the greenhouse slid open with a hiss, and Wynn tensed. She didn't look toward the entrance as soft footfalls headed her way, but focused on retrieving empty pots and a container of soil from beneath the counter.

They clunked onto the work surface a little too hard. She winced, then took a sip of her tea. The heat was perfect, sending a little pain across her tongue, but not enough to scald. Setting the cup back on its saucer, she unstacked the pots until she had six.

The announcers' voices fell into the background as those footsteps came closer. Her heart pounded louder and louder. Wynn kept her eyes on her hands, on the dirt, on the seeds, and didn't look until a pair of boots stopped right beside her.

Her fingers stilled, bits of dirt falling to the work surface. She tipped her chin and scanned upward, along the path of his black-clad legs, past his waist and chest, to his face. She expected him to be looking at her, but he stared at the worktable with a furrowed brow. At first she thought he was staring at the spaceball game, but then she followed his line of sight to her tea.

Wynn pursed her lips. Had he never seen tea before? Why wouldn't he have? What did Calypsons eat, anyway?

Annoyance followed in the wake of her thoughts. She didn't want to be curious about him. She didn't want him here, period, but that didn't make her mind any less inquisitive. Her fingers itched for a scanner, to run it over his body to see if his insides looked as human as his outsides.

Shaking off the urge, she focused on her seeds, planting one, then another, until six pots sat on the shelf and she pressed the button to swap it upward for the next.

She sank into the repetitive nature of the work, allowing her mind to blank. But always after a time, another question would emerge. How old was he? How had he arrived? Why did he want to collect her?

Eventually, he moved off, looking at something else. He paused, then reached toward one sapling. She tensed, about to shout at him to be gentle, but she didn't need to. His fingers stroked the leaf so gently, it barely moved. A few more steps and he did the same to another.

The farther he walked, the more the tension eased from her shoulders. But even as he left her alone, she kept her ears open for any sound of him through the clamor of the storm above and the recorded game playing from her work surface. His footsteps faded to nothing as he reached the far end of the greenhouse, then became louder again as he walked up the other side.

Wynn touched the control to swap out the next row of pots and watched him through the gaps in the shelves. He examined the pots like he'd never seen such a thing, his lips parted and his eyes wide. And perhaps he hadn't. She knew nothing of Sector Ten. No one did.

The barrier of the work surface and shelves made her bold, and she examined him as thoroughly as he did her work.

Though his eyes glinted in their disquieting way, they appeared kind. Or gentle, at least. She'd thought him expressionless at first, but now she gauged him to be full of curiosity, perhaps even wonder.

Again, a sense of familiarity assaulted her, but in the wake of it surfaced another thought. *He's handsome.* An internal curse followed. She didn't want to find anything about him appealing. If he meant to take her off world, then he was a threat.

A threat who hadn't yet broken his promises, and looked at a sapling like it held the secrets of the universe.

Her shoulders slumping, she admitted defeat and met his gaze square on.

"What's your name?"

Chapter Nine

Across the solar system

It wasn't often that assignments happened one on top of another, but it wasn't unheard of either. Except just this once, Carver could have used the time to clear his head. Maybe at one of the border stations where the laws blurred, and he could lose himself in strong alcohol and a willing body.

The lift door opened, revealing a bustling hub. He merged into foot traffic. CORE citizens went about their day, voices subdued, their clothing in pastel shades. The fashion trends on this station were ridiculous, including the light blue, two-piece suit he currently wore.

Carver nodded to the person next to him in polite etiquette and headed toward the transport hub.

With a touch to his PALM, he accepted the assignment.

Information scrolled across his ocular implant—a new handler, new contacts, a choice in transport options—erasing his previous assignment like it had never existed. The last item was an attachment, a portfolio with a massive file size. There was no name for the target or a location.

His eyebrows rose. Usually that was the first thing they sent him.

The last part of his new orders, the portfolio, was sealed, to remain unopened until he was off grid, an ultimatum order stamped on the file, along with a bonus creds package. His acceptance meant he would see this new mission through to the end, whether that meant his success or his death, and he wouldn't be able to open the file until he guaranteed zero failure and a seven-day completion.

His mind whirred as he took the next right toward the docking bay that catered to public transportation. With a touch to his PALM, he pulled up the flight plans for all imminent departures. There was one heading straight to a station where he housed quarters. It left in thirty minutes, but direct paths were easier to track.

Another transport, scheduled to depart in fifteen minutes and already boarding, required him to transfer ships midway. Accessing the passenger manifest with a swipe of his fingers, Carver swapped one of his identities for someone who hadn't checked in yet, a seat at the back where no one would sit behind him.

And just like that, he had a ticket.

He took another right and stopped at a bank of wall compartments. Swiping his PALM, he opened one up, dropped his bag inside, then marked it for pickup by the resident handler. Once sealed, he continued walking, got onto another lift, and descended two more decks. A short walk toward the docking bays, and the crowd slowed and clogged as he neared the departure gates.

The announcement of his flight echoed above him. Carver hung back, his eyes on his PALM like everyone else, minding his own business, until the bulk of the crowd for his flight had boarded. When only a few people remained, he made his way toward the gate.

"What do you mean there's no room on this one?" The masculine voice cut through the lower murmur of everything else. "I bought my ticket weeks ago."

As Carver neared the check-in terminal, he turned his head until the reception desk was in his peripheral vision. The agitated man touched his PALM, probably ordering himself a calming dose.

"I'm sorry, sir." The other person's tone placated. "There was a glitch in the system, and we're overbooked."

Carver swiped his PALM, and the security field allowed him through.

"I've been authorized to comp you…"

The argument faded as Carver and the rest of the pastel-clad passengers entered the boarding tube.

The massive transport was packed. It took forever for Carver to arrive at his seat, his jaw clenching with every polite smile, or "excuse me," or "sorry, ma'am," he had to dish out as he wove his way aft.

A jolly-looking older woman, her hair done is stripes of pink and gray, occupied the seat beside his. The sight of her welcoming smile created a band of tension across his shoulders.

He gave her a short, polite bow and slid into his seat.

"Well, aren't you a handsome young man," she said, turning her body toward him. "Are you traveling for business or pleasure?"

"Both," he muttered with a tight smile, already regretting his seat choice.

"Oh, what fun. Do you have family on *Jupiter One*? I might know them."

"My father just died," he said to stop that conversation.

"Oh." The woman leaned back a little, her interest in him changing. "I'm sorry to hear that." She paused, brow wrinkling. "But you said…" Her voice trailed off, confused.

Fuck, he hated traveling by public transport. And this last assignment had left him off-balance and unsettled.

Closing his eyes, he leaned back against the headrest, and counted the seconds until departure. Hopefully the woman took his contradictory answers as being riddled with grief. Otherwise, if she started paying him too much attention, she would remember his face, and he'd have to make sure she found her way out an airlock after they docked. He really didn't have any extra time with that seven-day limit.

The woman turned away from him, conversing with the person on her other side.

Carver expelled a slow, measured breath, laced his fingers across his stomach, and listened to the civilians around him as the last settled into their seats. A few minutes later, the ship sealed and uncoupled.

The hum of the transport rose in volume, eliminating most of the casual chatter, including the woman's conversation. A few minutes passed, and he didn't move or twitch, analyzing everyone around him, what they discussed and how they interacted. No one tweaked his senses, and he became certain he was the only agent on board.

He leveled his breathing, like he slept, and waited. The woman's interest returned to him for a time, but he ignored her. She eventually settled, her posture slumping as she indulged in a nap. Carver didn't open his eyes until a soft snore tickled the side of his neck.

Shuddering in disgust, he straightened. The woman startled, but resettled in the other direction. He gave it a few more minutes, making sure she stayed asleep before he opened his eyes and accessed his PALM.

The ultimatum order on the portfolio blinked at him, waiting for his confirmation. He wouldn't find out anything more about the job until he'd agreed to its completion-or-death terms. After this last assignment, he needed a palate cleanser.

Or would this assignment be even worse?

Curiosity won out. He swiped his bio-signature to accept the mission.

Terabytes of data downloaded onto his PALM, nameless and encrypted files compressed one on top of another.

His heart rate picked up speed. Why would they be sending him so much information? It was usually a name, location, and preferred method of death along with an end date.

He disconnected from the grid, changed the setting on his PALM to display on his ocular implant only, and opened up the first folder in the portfolio. Files were stacked within, alphabetically sorted and dated.

Where the hell were they sending him?

The location finally flashed up on his readout along with a current weather update.

What in the ever-loving fuck?

CHAPTER TEN

Earth

What's your name?

The question bounced around in his head, refusing to land.

He stared at Doctor Wynn Lambdin through the spaces between the rotating shelves. Her dark eyes caught his, the color entrancing—a rich earthy tone, similar in shade to the soil she piled into the pots. A pink flush brightened the paleness of her face.

Her emotions battered against him in waves, imitating the rain that continued to ravage the terrain. It was becoming increasing difficult to brace himself against the deluge. A part of him did not want to, intrigued by the way her moods affected him. Her gaze felt heavy, and a foreign sensation swept over him in its wake.

He did not understand that part of himself, as strange to him as naming her emotions, but it grew in purpose and need. He did not understand how to cope with that either.

Why had The Four not warned him it would be this way?

She touched the control beside her, and the shelves rotated upward on her side and down on his. This sort of mechanism could be useful back at home, and he stored the visual memory of it inside his mind to tell the others later.

Her body bent at the waist as she pulled more pots from beneath the cupboard and set them in front of her with a *click clack*.

"Are you not going to tell me your name?" she asked, her voice husky, the sound doing things to his insides he had not experienced before.

What was that sensation, that *feeling*? He did not have a name for it.

Her brow pinched, her eyes moving from him to the pots in front of her. "Or don't you have one?"

Her question brought a memory, a time when others called to him without touching his mind. A time when arms wrapped him tight and kind eyes filled with tears and worry.

The memory settled inside him, and with it, a name surfaced.

"Iax," he said, the word tasting odd in his mouth. When was the last time he spoke it aloud?

So many years ago, he could not remember a specific day.

Her head snapped up, her eyes meeting his again, and his heart thumped heavily in his chest. He realized he liked having her focus, her full attention.

"Iax?" she repeated.

The sound of his name from her mouth created a cascade of shivers across his shoulders, a pleasant sensation he wanted to experience more.

"That's your name?" The sharp emotions she had sent him earlier morphed into something calmer, though no less potent.

"Yes."

"Iax," she said again with a nod. "Okay." She returned her attention to her pots. "It's a nice name." Her eyes met his briefly. "Did someone name you? Or did you name yourself?" She shook her head a little.

He searched backward in time, the answer existing in the same place as past emotions.

"Someone named me," he answered while old memories surfaced.

A woman hummed a song.

A home filled with laughter.

"Who?" Her hands stilled. "Who named you?"

He did not understand why she asked this question, but he again searched for the answer he needed.

A man who carried him on his shoulders.

A hospital bed and whispers of concern.

"My parents."

Her shoulders relaxed slightly, and a strained chuckle escaped her lips. "I thought maybe you all grew from pods or something." She concentrated on her task for a while before asking, "Were you always Calypson?"

He tilted his head, considering her question.

"Or were you changed?" she added, clarifying. "Did you travel to Sector Ten?"

More memories surfaced, a ship filled with sick people. A stranger with kind, concerned eyes.

"I was a child when I arrived in Sector Ten."

Her expression slackened; her lips parted. Then her brow furrowed.

"Were your parents pilgrims?" Her words were harder now, biting at him like her emotions. "Did they journey with you?"

Other fragmented memories surfaced, ones steeped in pain and fear and confusion. Of being squished on a transport, others sick like him. Of an unfamiliar woman holding his hand. So much fear, but the sickness weakened him.

The feelings mimicked what he had felt from Wynn since arriving here, tugging at a point in his chest he did not know could move.

"They did not." And sadness, so similar in flavor to hers. He remembered that the most.

"Bastards." The words whispered from her lips, much quieter than the emotions cascading toward him. Why would she be so angry? Not at him, but on his behalf?

"I'm sorry." Her emotions slumped along with her gaze. "I'm sorry that happened to you."

The emotions shifted in his chest, blooming into something softer, parallel to her own. "What are these words you say?"

"I'm sorry?"

He nodded.

She stared down at her hands for a moment, then continued on with her work while she spoke. "It's an apology. I'm expressing that I feel regret about what happened to you. Showing empathy, because it must have been a horrible experience."

Her words struck him speechless. He tried to understand this empathy she spoke of, but his mind grabbed onto logic, on reason, and he could not voice either his confusion or his acceptance of her words.

They remained silent while she worked, her hands scooping dirt, filling pots, and adding seeds.

Lightning flashed in an arc, followed by a rumble of thunder loud enough to mute the voices she played from beside her. It was a game, one he had learned of a long time ago but hadn't followed since his initial voyage to Sector Ten. A gust of wind stronger than the last splashed rain against the pane behind her.

She twitched at the sound, then paused in her work. Her fingertips pressed against the edge of the pot, and her eyes jumped to his.

"I'm Wynn."

He nodded his agreement. "Yes. Doctor Wynn Lambdin."

She sipped a quick breath. "How do you know that?"

"They told me your name before I came to collect you."

Her entire body went rigid, and the emotions that had calmed turned sharp once more. "Who? Who told you that?"

His memories returned to when he had embarked on his journey to this planet. He had been told many things, some he was not supposed to divulge. Other instructions had not shared that decree.

The answer to her question lay in a mix of those instructions, but he had also promised not to lie. "They are The Four."

Her lips parted. "Who are they?"

"They lead us."

"Why would they tell you my name? How do they know me?"

"I was told to collect you."

An emotion shot out at him, one very similar to when she shouted at him to take off his glasses. Her mouth parted, then her lips formed a word. But she stopped herself from speaking, only making a slight sound, cutting her question off before she asked it.

He tilted his head, trying to decipher the action. When she had asked so many questions prior, why would she stop herself now?

She turned her gaze to the work surface, eyes blinking, then refocused on the objects in front of her. A hum passed her lips, then her hands were moving again, filling soil into the pot, and adding a seed from the small container beside her.

He watched, mesmerized, as she repeated the action over again. And again. Her emotions calmed, and another feeling emerged inside him.

The lack of her eyes on him created a disconnect, a need. She did not lift her gaze to his as she worked on one pot, then another, only glancing at the game playing on the work surface from time to time. She filled shelves and rotated them upward until she tended the last of the rows. The pots she had started with sat in front of him on his side of the counter.

She gathered her bag of dirt and shuffled down to the next section. The game's feed moved with her.

He followed too, but found the rows of pots distracting, a barrier he no longer wanted between them. He continued to walk all the way around the row of moving shelves, then toward her again.

Her emotions shot outward, then settled when he stopped beside her beverage. The deep brown color of the liquid contrasted with the pristine white of the cup.

As her emotions calmed, she raised her gaze to his. "Have I met you before?"

He considered her question. "No." There had been no point in time when their paths had crossed before this.

Another emotion welled inside him, one that did not seem appropriate to the situation. Why would he feel... a loss at never having met her before?

She stared at him at length, her eyes expressing things he could not name, but her emotions rolled over him in appealing waves.

"You're so human." She shook her head. "But you're also... not."

She refocused on her work, and his gaze returned to the cup on the counter. The aroma rising from its surface was unfamiliar, both moist and bitter. He leaned forward and inhaled deeper, trying to decipher its contents.

"Do you want to try it?"

His eyes jumped back to her. She stared at him with an odd pinch to her lips and her eyes crinkling.

"Yes," he replied, only realizing it was true after she had asked the question.

She jerked her chin forward. "Go on then."

He assessed this new, lighter expression a moment longer before regarding the cup on the counter. Picking it up, the outside warmed his skin, and the wafting scent increased in strength as he lifted it closer to his face.

Her eyes burned into him as he took a sip. Bitter flavor exploded on his tongue, making him twitch. He had never tasted anything so pungent, and could not decide if he liked the flavor or loathed it. He took another sip.

The second taste did not inspire him to take another, so he set the cup back on its saucer.

When he turned toward her, she glanced away to refocus on her tasks. "I don't usually eat breakfast. I should have asked if you wanted anything."

He did not respond to her statement, uncertain if she waited for an answer. Silence descended between them. The longer it grew, the more fidgety she became, her emotions pulsing toward him in small bursts, until she returned to her task.

She finished her row of shelves and moved on to the one with larger pots, jade-colored stems punching through the soil and reaching toward the stormy sky above. The greenery reminded him of home, and his chest panged—another feeling he had not experienced before and did not know how to handle.

Her fingers lightly stroked the leaves, then pressed into the soil. She pulled out another silver cannister from beneath the counter, this one filled with packets. She tore one open, then sprinkled the contents around the slender stem before setting it back in its place on the shelf.

He enjoyed watching her like this, content in her world—no fear or distress overtaking her. Another novel sensation filled him the longer she relaxed in his company, a feeling that warmed his skin, his head, and his heart.

He had never thought much about his heart, except that it pumped blood through his system and beat with a regular rhythm. Now it sped up as hers had done, emotions tangling inside him in ways he did not understand and could not decipher. What was it about Doctor Wynn Lambdin that affected him?

Instinctively, his mind reached outwards, searching for answers from others around him, but there was no one, no connection to ease his disquiet. Why did his breaths speed up when he watched her tuck a strand of black hair behind her ear, leaving a smudge of dirt in the wake of her actions? Why did he have the urge to touch her, to brush his fingers against that smudge to see if her skin felt as soft as it looked?

His fingers twitched at his sides. He would not go against her wishes and touch her without permission, no matter how these desires swelled the longer he watched her.

She placed the next completed pot on the shelf, and retrieved another, the material of her clothing stretching over her curves.

None of the parameters of his mission included concessions for the scenario he now found himself in, this waiting period with no objective but to examine his charge and question his purpose. But he could not find it within himself to be disappointed that the weather delayed their return journey if it meant watching her perform the tasks that gave her joy.

And that was what it was, he realized, this new throbbing emotion from her that rolled over him in pleasant waves. *Joy. Happiness. Peace.* A state of being opposite to fear.

He wished to experience this combination of emotions *with* her.

The shelf hummed as it rose upward, then it jerked and clattered. Iax looked up in time to see one pot not quite in line with the others tip as it caught in the mechanism.

Crack. It splintered, and Iax moved before he could think twice.

His one hand on her stomach, his chest against her spine, he spun her out of the way of the falling debris.

And in that one second, that one breath, his cheek briefly touched the flesh of her forehead. He inhaled sharply, the sensation akin to the moments when his essence returned to his body. His skin tingled, and the feeling spread along his face and down his neck, reaching all the way to his fingertips. His heart thudded hard in his chest, once, twice.

Thwack, thud. Ceramic pieces and lumps of dirt landed on the countertop and the floor.

Wynn's body curled inward, her heart beating rapidly against his chest, her emotions rising in a surge to crash over him, that fear, but something else too that he had not yet experienced, a shocking sensation that made him release her on a breath, their bodies disconnecting.

"Ah!" she cried out.

He thought her distress a reaction to their proximity, but she dove toward the mess of broken pot and dirt. She cradled the curved sapling, its bright green shoots contrasting with the dark of the soil.

He moved again. In a breath, he reached for the stack of pots on the countertop, then the container of fresh soil. On an exhale, he crouched beside her, new soil already in the pot and waiting to accept the bruised plant.

She jerked straight, her eyes widening at his appearance in front of her. A breath left her lips in a puff, and color rose high on her cheeks. Her eyes jumped between his, then landed on the pot in his hands.

"Thank you," she murmured, her shoulders relaxing as she took the offering. She shook the dirt from the sapling's roots, then gently settled it in the new bed of soil.

The middle bent in a depressed state after its fall. She brushed her fingers over its leaves, then stood to turn her back on him. *Clack,* it went on the counter, her hands now free to deal with the rest of the mess the incident left behind.

Iax stood too, watching her while a defeated sensation spread through him. Just as easily as the pot shattered, he had broken his promise of not touching her without her permission. He did not know how to fix the error.

So he spoke the only words that might help.

"I'm sorry."

Chapter Eleven

W ynn's breath caught in her throat at the earnest expression on Iax's face. Another sense of familiarity wove through her, but he'd said they'd never met, had even seemed regretful about it.

And how the hell could she tell that? His expression rarely changed.

I'm sorry.

She stared at the wilting sapling in her hands, then looked up at the confusing person in front of her.

"What are you apologizing for?" He'd helped her with a speed that had stolen her breath, both when he had plucked her out of the path of the pot, and when he'd assisted with saving the plant.

"For touching you without your permission." His gravelly words made her shiver.

Her hand lifted toward where their skin had connected. The small spot on her forehead tingled, an electrifying sensation that traveled down to her throat.

"You were trying to help me. I get that." His head tilted like he didn't understand her words, so she added. "Apology accepted."

And because she couldn't bear to stare at those glinting, inquisitive eyes any longer, she turned away. Walking farther down the central work area, she stopped at a different cupboard, bent down, and pulled a robocleaner from beneath.

Iax remained in place as she knelt and placed the robocleaner on top of the broken pieces and dirt on the grated flooring. The beetle-like robot hummed and whirred as it did its job between her and her unpredictable guest.

She stood to tend the bruised sapling, hoping it lived despite its fall. After making sure it had enough soil and fertilizer, she set it on the opposite workspace to monitor it instead of returning it with the others of its age.

And through it all, Iax watched her.

It was confusing, the sensation of calm that slowly replaced the dread and fear she'd experienced over the past few hours. Like he'd promised, he hadn't harmed or changed her. He'd *helped* her. He'd even apologized.

And she had until the storm abated to convince him not to take her with him.

Her stomach clenched. How was she supposed to do that? She'd wanted the chance to persuade him to abandon his task, but didn't know how to approach it.

And this storm wouldn't last forever. With her fields drowning in acid rain, she didn't want it to.

She worked for a long while before Iax moved, walking through the space to stop every now and again at another part of her germination process. She remained aware of him, listening to each footfall. Then always, he would return to where she planted.

His scrutiny should have bothered her, but it didn't.

She worked, he walked, and she didn't call it quits until her stomach grumbled.

Wynn set down her trowel and placed the last pot on the shelf before rotating it upward. She knew exactly where Iax had stopped, examining the damaged sapling a few meters away.

Brushing her palms against her pants, she turned to him. "Are you hungry?" What did Calypsons eat?

His head lifted, and he stared at her for a long moment. "Yes."

She nodded once, then turned away from his probing gaze.

The moist air of the greenhouse changed to the drier air of the lab as she crossed the threshold. She passed through the small hallway into the living space, then stopped.

Iax's glasses lay on the floor. Another dual urge surged up inside her, both to crush them beneath her feet, to deny what they represented, and to pick them up and return them to him.

Movement rustled behind her, and tension stiffened her shoulders. She remained in place while Iax strode past her, stooped, and swiped the accessory from the ground. Then she was off again, heading toward the kitchen.

She stopped again when she saw the UV-suit sitting on the counter. Without dwelling on her derailed need of escape, she snatched it up in her arms, moved to the hallway, and shoved it inside the wall compartment before returning to the kitchen.

Her plan had been to order a pasta dish from the dispensary, but the need to act, to *do* something made her jittery. She could return to the greenhouse, throw herself into work again, but she'd already promised herself she would eat. That she would feed Iax too.

New purpose rose inside her. Wynn stepped up to the dispensary and ordered a collection of vegetables instead of a complete meal. Next came the largest cooking pot from beneath the cupboard. She filled it half full of water before setting it on the burner at the far end of the kitchen island.

Thwack. She dropped the cutting board beside it and was already slicing into a potato by the time Iax crossed the threshold from the living room. He stopped on the other side of the counter.

Chop chop chop went her knife. The slice and thud against the board soothed the turmoil inside her. She turned the pieces in the opposite direction. *Chop chop chop.*

With one swift movement, she used the flat of the knife to scoop the cubes off the surface and tossed them in the pot beside her. *Plop plop plop.* They sank into the water. All the pieces went inside, then she grabbed the next potato.

"What is it you do?"

She twitched at the question, his gravelly voice sending shivers over her arms. Her fingers tightened around the knife.

Blinking, she refocused on the cutting board. *Chop chop chop.*

"I'm making soup," she said after her continued silence felt like intentional rudeness. *Plop plop plop.* She dropped more pieces into the pot.

"Your machine would make soup."

When she lifted her head, she found him staring at the dispensary on the back wall. That meant he knew how it worked, that it was pre-programmed and could synthesize thousands of recipes from the bio-matter stored within its mechanisms.

It was how most CORE citizens ate.

"Doing it myself is relaxing, focuses me. Foster—" Her voice cracked. It hurt to say his name aloud. She cleared her throat, concentrating on her potatoes again. "My colleague liked to make soup from scratch. I helped him sometimes." She didn't want to forget her friend, no matter how disturbing the memories of his death.

A shrug lifted her shoulders as she dropped more pieces into the pot. "He and I would cook together at least once a week. He always said that things tasted more delicious when done by hand, and I think he was right. Nothing from the dispensary ever tasted as good as one of his soups."

It helped thinking of him like this instead of the way he'd died, the images that haunted her nightmares. "Everything done by hand, that's what he always said." She resumed her chopping. "It's why we plant all the seeds ourselves instead of using machines."

Swallowing that thought down, Wynn pressed the control beside the burner, and a padded seat extended next to Iax. He stepped back, his eyebrows raising at its appearance.

"You don't have to stand if you don't want to," she said, jerking her chin at the seat.

He stared at it a long while before he awkwardly parked one butt cheek down in a way that made her think he didn't use chairs often.

Did Calypsons ever sit?

The question created an itchy sensation across her skin. She refocused on her vegetables, willing it to go away. A carrot, a turnip, and an onion. She chopped everything up and slid it into the bubbling water.

Her stomach grumbled again, reminding her she'd promised him food, and a soup made from scratch wasn't fast.

"Here," she said, moving away from the counter to the dispensary. "I'll get you something to tide you over. What would you like?"

She glanced at him over her shoulder, but her hand hovered over the controls when she saw his pinched frown. "What do you like to eat?"

He stared at her for a moment, then said, "Anything that provides sustenance."

The vague answer uncovered buried pettiness. *Bland it is.* She pressed the button for soup, then chose number ten. The door slid open, and a bowl of steaming broth slid out a moment later.

She set the soup in front of him and stared. He took a deliberate moment to examine the food, then picked up the spoon and slurped it.

His eyebrows shot up. "This is good," he declared.

"It is?" The only time she ever ordered the plain broth was when she had an upset stomach.

He nodded once and took another bite, then another, the movement speeding up until he was practically shoveling it in his mouth.

She could have gone back to her soup preparation, but watched his subtle expressions instead. How old was he?

Her thoughts returned to what he'd told her about himself already. "They say Calypsons don't die."

His hand stopped halfway to his mouth.

"That they live forever," she added.

He lifted his gaze to meet hers, and that silver glint didn't scare her as much.

"How old are you?" She lifted her chin. "Do you know, like in Earth years?"

He lowered his hand, the soup in the spoon dripping back into the bowl. He tipped his head before answering. "The Earth has rotated around the sun twenty-nine times since my origin."

She gripped the countertop. "Your origin? Your birth or when you became Calypson?" He'd said he was a child when he'd arrived in Sector Ten.

His head straightened. "I became Calypson after six rotations of Earth around the sun."

They were close in age.

"I can't believe your parents sacrificed you like that," she muttered. "You were so young."

His head tilted again, and his eyes became distant.

"It was an attempt to save my life," he said after a while.

The two of them remained frozen, staring at each other, as seconds passed them by. Emotion welled in her throat. "You were sick?" It wasn't unheard of for a new disease to develop in a colony, one that spread faster than doctors could cure.

"Yes."

She swallowed. "Have you spoken with them, seen them, since?"

He blinked, his gaze unfocused. "No."

"Then they're still bastards," she muttered.

With a touch of her hand, she ordered a packet of spices from the dispensary, added it to the boiling water, then continued with her vegetables.

Chop. Chop. Chop.

Plop. Plop. Plop.

She didn't stop adding ingredients until she noticed Iax's bowl was empty.

"Are you full?"

He met her gaze. "Full of what?"

A stilted laugh erupted from her lips. She smothered it quickly.

Foster would have followed that with *full of shit*, but she shook her head at herself as said, "Did you get enough to eat?"

A silent beat passed before he replied. "It will sustain me."

Didn't really answer the question, but she wouldn't quibble over word choice.

But as soon as she refocused on her repetitive chopping, her mind obsessed over what he'd told her. His parents may have been trying to save him, but not going with him? Of sending him out to Sector Ten without knowing what would happen to him? A little boy completely alone?

Cowards.

Her temperature rose, and it had nothing to do with the boiling soup.

She scooped up the pieces of the carrot and dropped them in the pot before grabbing the last potato. Her knife came down with a little more vigor than before. *Chop.* It split the oval root vegetable in half, and she turned it sideways.

Chop. Chop. Chop. Thud.

"Shit." She dropped the knife as stinging pain shot through her hand. Her knuckle burned where the knife nicked her. *Stupid. Stupid.* How dumb to get so caught in her head that she stopped paying attention to what she was doing.

She reached for the towel hanging against the counter, then jerked backward when Iax stood in front of her, inside her personal space. A startled noise emerged from her throat.

"You are hurt," he said, a frown furrowing his brow as he stared at the towel covering the wound.

"Just nicked myself." She stepped backward, but he followed.

Wynn swallowed at the way his eyes narrowed, like he could eradicate the injury with a thought. She kept walking backward until her ass hit the counter that ran the length of the back wall.

"Allow me to see. I can help."

She shook her head. "It's fine. I can grab a regenerator."

The frown on his face intensified. "I want to help you."

A disbelieving laugh erupted while her hand throbbed where she clutched it against her chest. She'd told him it had been okay to touch her earlier because he was trying to help. Now he wanted to justify another touch?

The longer he stared, the more shivers crawled up the back of her neck and over her head. Fizzy anticipation bubbled in her stomach. That brief contact in the greenhouse was burned into her skin, and she wanted to know if it would feel the same if he touched her again.

The tips of his boots stopped a fraction away from her bare toes, but he didn't reach out. Her skin buzzed with awareness while her thumb throbbed in pain. She had to tend to it, or it would scar.

Another laugh wanted to surface at the irony, but she swallowed it down.

He didn't back off, and she found she didn't want him to—as much as she should. Tentatively, she lifted her towel-covered hand off her chest and extended it to him.

His shoulders lowered as he took her hand in his, carefully unwrapping it. A bright red smear stained the white towel. Her knuckle throbbed in time with her heartbeat, but she'd never been averse to a little pain. A surge of blood rose when he removed the pressure. He cradled the towel beneath her wrist, a barrier between their skin that she frowned at.

"How are you going to do anything without a regenerator?" she murmured, then lifted her gaze.

A wrinkle of concentration marred his forehead. It was... sort of adorable.

You're losing it.

She'd believed he would change her into a mindless zombie only hours ago, and now she thought him adorable?

He stole away that thought when he lifted his other hand and placed it over hers.

A gasp ripped out of her as their skin connected. Tingles burst across her flesh where his fingers brushed her wrist, then exploded up her arm and over her shoulders.

Then came the uncomfortable heat. It raced through her, beginning with her thumb, chasing away the tingles. She inhaled a hissing breath. Her internal temperature rose, becoming hotter where her injury lay beneath his hand.

His gaze lifted to hers, and her breath caught in her throat at the way he looked at her. She should run screaming, but couldn't move as the heat slowly ebbed away, and the tingles returned.

Chapter Twelve

B right spots of color dotted Wynn's cheeks the longer Iax held her hand in his. Her pupils dilated, the appealing brown of her irises shrinking to a slender ring.

Those eyes held him captive while the tingling connection continued between them, his essence speaking to hers in a way he had not been sure it would.

But he had wanted to try.

And it worked. Despite not being able to touch her mind and taste her thoughts, he could stimulate the foundational makeup of her cells. In its wake, a new and pleasurable sensation rippled through him. He yearned for more, his body responding biologically to a need that, for most of his life, had remained dormant.

His eyes skimmed downward over the thin material of her top. Her chest rose and fell in rapid bursts, nipples puckered beneath, but it was not fear that crashed over him. It was a warmth that matched the one simmering in his chest and stomach, and even lower. His internal temperature increased along with his heart rate.

The urge to explore this emotion pushed at him. He needed to see how hot he could make her burn if he touched her elsewhere.

But she was bleeding. He broke their stare and concentrated on the life force that hummed below her skin, speaking essence-to-essence to heal the damage.

Her lips parted, and she tipped her chin to focus on their joined hands. Beneath his palm, he concentrated on sealing the laceration in increments. Her emotions swooped toward him, crashing over his head in waves, then receded.

When he was certain he had healed all the damage, he removed his hand, keeping her wrist supported underneath. Blood marred her skin, but she was no longer injured.

She gasped and snatched her hand from his. "How the hell did you do that?" She opened and closed her fingers quickly.

He was about to answer when her entire body stiffened, her eyes flying to his.

"No," she whispered, then stared at her other arm.

She took hold of the cuff of her shirt, and yanked it upward, revealing the smooth skin hidden beneath. The three thin white lines he had noticed on his arrival, the scars, were gone.

She rubbed the skin back and forth, and her eyes welled with moisture. Then her shock morphed into something more volatile, the wave of anger surging against him so violently, he took a step back.

"What did you do?" She swayed, and he reached to catch her.

She straightened, stumbling sideways out of his grasp. "Stay away from me."

At her words, he remained by the counter. She spun around to face him, one foot in the kitchen, and the other in the hallway. Her hands clenched at her sides, the one sleeve rolled up over her elbow, exposing her unblemished skin.

"What did you do?" she repeated through gritted teeth.

He did not understand her upset, why she reverted to her original hostility in the wake of him healing her injuries.

"How did you heal me so fast without a regenerator?" Her voice shook, and he found he did not like the sound of her uncertainty.

He would give her the answers he could. "You are Calypson."

She shook her head, and crossed her arms over her chest. "That makes no sense. Explain better."

He noted how her eyes flicked down the section of healed skin, then back at him. "You are Calypson, and I encouraged your cells to heal your cut." It was the clearest way to describe it.

"There's no way I could be Calypson and not know about it until now."

His eyes roved over her face, then to where she crossed her arms. "You are Calypson. Your blood is Calypson. You have the capacity to heal yourself just as I do."

She shook her head again. "I'm not. I don't have your super speed or eyes that glow. You and I are not the same."

"You are correct." The pot beside him sputtered its water, some splashing over the edge to sizzle on the element.

She dropped her arms, rocking back on her heels. "But you said I was Calypson."

"It is true. You are Calypson. You are also an anomaly."

"An anomaly? What the hell does that mean?" She tugged the sleeve of her shirt down until it covered her entire arm.

Her question verged on the area of his mission he was not supposed to disclose. He combed his mind, the directives The Four had given him, searching for a way to explain without going against their wishes. Iax found none.

Wynn gritted her teeth the longer he remained silent, but he had promised he would not lie.

"There is no way I'm Calypson," she asserted, and crossed her arms over her chest again. "You can't prove it."

"I can."

Her arms dropped, and her jaw when slack. "Then do it."

He stepped toward her.

"Ahhhh!" The cry of alarm stabbed at him as she jumped back.

He stopped his advance and tilted his head to consider her reaction.

Wynn's throat bobbed in a swallow, her hands clenching and releasing at her sides. "What are you doing?"

She glowered at him, words passing through her eyes that he could not taste. But he could freely sample the emotions pressing against him.

He straightened. "You asked me to prove it."

"I should have asked for specifics before making such a demand." She inhaled a breath through her nose, then exhaled slowly. "Explain how you will prove it before proceeding."

Caution battled her curiosity. Something else lived there too, a warmer emotion that simmered below the other two as steadily as the cooking pot of vegetables. He could not name this emotion, had no history of it in his former life.

"I will escort you to your lab space where you will analyze your blood."

"I don't need escorting. I can get there on my own. Don't touch me without my permission."

His eyes skimmed over her hair, her face, the way the material of her garments clung to body. She was curvier and more appealing than anyone he had known, eliciting new emotions deep in his stomach and a need to connect with her in more than one way.

"I will not touch you without your permission."

Her shoulders relaxed at his agreement. "Okay, let's go to the lab." She backed up one step, then two, then turned to stride down the hallway.

Before she was out of sight, he bent to retrieve the towel where it had fallen on the floor. He traveled in the opposite direction, through the living room, to meet her in the lab.

She had stopped inside the doorway, looking over her shoulder with a frown on her face. When she turned to find him already there, she jumped, her hand flying to her chest.

"Shit, you're fast." Her gaze dropped to the towel in his hand. "What are you doing with that?"

He extended it toward her. "You can analyze it."

She shook her head as she took small steps toward him. "I've analyzed my blood before, for school, many times. That won't prove anything."

He did not respond to those statements because he had nothing to add. The only way to prove she was Calypson was for her to perform the task herself.

Eyes narrowing, she crossed to the secondary terminal and gestured to the flat surface in the middle. "Place it there."

He moved toward her, and she tensed, her eyes flicking up to his, then down to the towel as he set it on the glossy black surface. She tapped the terminal, and the panel lit up beneath the towel.

A moment later, data streamed above the terminal, breaking down the makeup of the towel and any liquids within its fibers, including her blood. She enhanced that portion, the white blood cells now as large as his hand, traveling in a sea of red blood cells.

"It's human blood. Nothing unusual about it," she stated, waving her hand at the information scrolling beside the holographic reconstruction.

He stepped closer, and her spine straightened. Emotions shot toward him, then mellowed when he did not get any closer, a half meter separating them.

"Change your analyzing filters to the following," he said, then listed filter adjustments that would allow her to see the truth.

"Hold on, hold on," she said, holding up one hand. "Repeat them again."

He started at the beginning and spoke slower the second time. Tiny bumps developed across the back of her neck. A sudden urge to brush his fingers over those bumps overwhelmed him. His fingers twitched, but stayed at his sides. He would not touch her without permission.

She changed the settings as he spoke, until the images hovering over the terminal shifted, revealing an entire spectrum of color. He was about to tell her to magnify a portion of the white blood cells when she did it on her own.

"What in the...?"

Red fissures cracked along the surface, snaking like fingers.

She drew back at the sight, then shook her head. "You could have put that there. It isn't a clean sample." Her fingers flexed on the edge of the terminal. "With your own blood or something."

He had not tampered with the sample, but he did not want her to think he had lied when he had promised not to. He took one step backward. "You can provide a fresh sample."

She stared at him for a long while, a multitude of emotions crossing her face, and along with it, echoing waves. His own rose in response, and he was not sure how to process it all. These emotions felt ancient, a distant memory that he could not fully grasp. So much of what he had experienced in his life since had replaced those sensations.

"Fine," she huffed, reaching underneath the terminal to open a cupboard.

Many items crammed the small space. Pushing some of the larger containers aside, she grabbed a small one like she had used in the greenhouse for her seeds.

Standing, she closed the cupboard with her foot and set the container beside the bloody towel. It opened with a *click*. A flick of her gaze to his, and she swiped the dermal syringe from its place nestled in the foam that protected it.

She turned her body slightly, lifted the sleeve of her shirt, and pressed the syringe against the vein on the inside of her elbow. It hissed quietly. She pulled it away from her skin and set it inside the analyzer cradle beside the towel.

The image of the new sample took the place of the old one. Red blood cells spun around in a vortex, white blood cells interspersed among them. All the data showed regular human blood. Her shoulders lowered.

"You must change your settings," he reminded her.

She twitched, then shook her head slightly before doing as he said, resetting the terminal for a modified analysis. Her heart rate accelerated as the image shifted, revealing the same darker red substance coating the white blood cells.

"What is it?" The question was a whispered plea, matching the shock that washed over him in waves.

"You are Calypson." It was the only explanation he could give her that encompassed everything.

She seemed to want to deny the evidence in front of her, because she kept shaking her head.

He tried out the movement, back and forth, wondering if it was enjoyable. It did nothing for him.

"Oh, you don't shake your head at me."

At her harshly spoken words, he stopped, uncertain why she took exception.

"Your answer neither provides more information," she went on, "nor makes sense. I can't be Calypson. You came here for a reason. You must have more of an explanation than 'you are Calypson.'" Her eyes searched his face. "Why don't you actually tell me the truth?"

A sensation raced through him, surprising in its potency. She stared at him with those large brown eyes, and he *wanted* to tell her more, but these questions verged on the territory of the untouchable.

A crack of thunder filled their silence. He turned his head. The volume of the noise was less than that of its predecessors. Was the storm finally dying down? The following display of lightning dispelled that hope.

When the thunder ebbed, a sizzling sound echoed from the other side of the building. He jerked his line of sight toward it, changing his vision to see through to the kitchen.

Wynn's eyes jumped to his. "Shit. The soup." She darted out of the room as fast as he had seen her move, heading to the hallway.

He turned his head to follow her path, his gaze lingering on the empty doorway a moment before he followed her hasty exit.

"Not Calypson. Not Calypson."

The repeated words led him toward the kitchen. He paused in the doorway and watched her turn off the heat beneath the pot. Moisture dotted the surface of the counter, and she didn't look up as she wiped it up with a matching towel to the one that remained in her lab covered in blood. Her jerky movements continued beyond where the liquid had bubbled over the edge of the pot.

"Not Calypson. Not Calypson," she repeated, the rhythm of her words matching the strokes of her hand as she wiped down the counter.

A small laugh left her, one high pitched and tinged with instability. A chaotic swirl followed, crashing over him. Along with it came the urge to leave, to spare himself from the emotions of this situation.

He stayed where he was, accepting the chaos into himself. He could not taste her thoughts, but he could experience this. The longer he spent in her presence, the easier it was to digest these feelings, and he realized they were more appealing than stroking another's mind, even when volatile.

"I'm losing it." She continued wiping vigorously. "I'm losing it," she repeated.

Another small laugh escaped her, but this one she smothered with a sniff of her nose. Her hand paused, but her chest rose and fell in rapid breaths. She stared at a section of the counter that did not seem to be significant, but held her rapt attention.

A shuddering breath shook her body, then she let go of the towel to cover her forearm with her hand—the same place where the three lines used to mark her skin.

He had thought she was not aware of his presence, but then she straightened and said, "I just..." She cleared her throat, then looked him in the eye. "I need a moment alone." Moisture welled in her eyes right before she stumbled past him and headed toward her sleeping quarters.

Another sniff resounded down the hallway. The sound cut off when the door closed behind her.

Need rippled through his body—a need to help. She demanded space, but he could not leave her in distress.

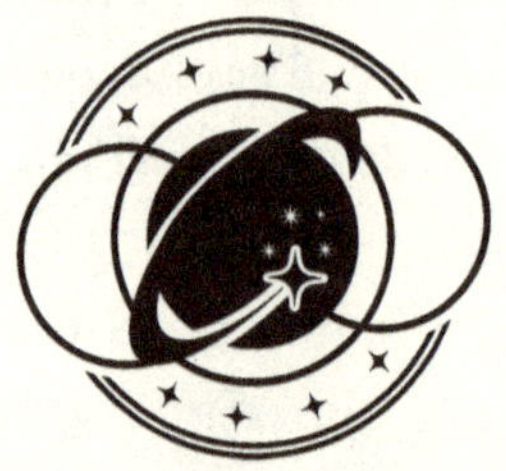

Chapter Thirteen

Her quarters spun around her. Wynn stumbled, reached out, and caught her balance on the wall.

They're gone. They're gone. They're gone.

The floor shifted beneath her feet. Sips of air passed her lips, but she couldn't get a proper lungful. Head bent, she braced her hands on her knees.

It hadn't really hit her at first. The disappearance of her scars had shocked and angered her, but now the truth settled deep inside her, forcefully shoved there along with the knowledge that she wasn't fully human.

Both truths battled for dominance while the room spun. Her skin itched, feeling too tight on her body, like she needed to take it off and replace it with another.

That spinning, out-of-control sensation had plagued her through her teenage years, culminating in the loss of herself when her parents had died.

Before Foster's death, it had been so long since she'd given in to the urge to stop that spinning sensation with self-inflicted pain. A slice here, a cut there. It helped to calm her thoughts and focus her mind. She'd always healed the cuts after giving them to herself, removing all evidence of her weakness.

Until her parents died during a Tellusian raid on their long-distance transport.

In their honor, so she wouldn't forget, she'd marked herself, one line for each of them, and allowed them to scar.

It hadn't made the spinning sensation disappear altogether, but it had helped. Every time she'd felt her control slip, she would place her hand over the marks, and the world would calm. Eventually, she'd stopped needing to cut herself. Being accepted into the Science Academy had helped with that. So had landing her dream job at this outpost.

She'd only added the third line a few weeks ago. After Foster died.

Grief flooded her. The removal of her marks felt like Iax had erased the existence of her parents and friend.

The narrow entrance to the washroom called to her. She staggered toward it, the floor beneath her feet listing to the side. Her shoulder slammed into the doorjamb, and she welcomed the pain, needed it to keep the world from spinning.

Her knees buckled, and she collapsed onto the lid of the toilet. Fumbling hands reached for the compartment under the sink. It hissed opened, and she grabbed her kit.

It hit the counter with a *bang*. She clicked it open and swiped the laser scalpel from its place on the side, then yanked on her sleeve, exposing her forearm.

Shallow breaths filled the small space of the washroom. The sight of those missing lines clenched a tight band around her ribs. Stars dotted her vision. She flicked her thumb over the control, and the laser scalpel hummed softly, the head glowing a bright blue. She brought it closer to her arm.

"You are distressed." His voice came from right above her.

She yelped and jerked straight, hitting the kit with her elbow. It slid off the edge of the counter, everything tumbling to the floor in a clatter, including the laser scalpel she held. The regenerator, the synthetic bandages, the blades, the topical ointment—it all sprayed across the shiny white floor.

Wynn's heart raced with shame. *Caught. Exposed. Raw.* She was an ulcer open to the elements, unprotected and festering. Mortification burned through her so hot it felt like her skin blazed red from head to toe.

"Get out!" she screamed, standing.

He didn't move fast enough, and she pushed two hands against his chest. "Get. Out." The flexible material shifted beneath her hands; his heart beat beneath her palms.

She shoved him. Hard.

There was no give at first, like she tried to open blast doors with her bare hands, but then he backed up a step, then another. She gave him one last shove, and he continued his retreat, unaided, until he stood in the corridor. Not fully, though, because the door didn't close.

She spun around, and dove back into the washroom. As soon as the door closed behind her, she locked it.

Ignoring the mess on the floor, she grabbed the laser scalpel. The toilet lid squeaked when she sat on it. She placed her elbow on her knee, forearm up, and flicked her thumb against the scalpel's control. It hummed, glowing blue.

But she didn't lower it to her skin because the world had stopped spinning.

She stared at her arm, unsettled. The itchy sensation had receded too. She gasped a breath, heart rate slowing, then flicked off the laser scalpel.

"Your marks."

Her fingers tightened on the medical tool at the sound of his voice. It echoed from a distance, like he stood where she'd left him.

"They were important to you?" he called.

Another sob escaped her. She hadn't cried in so long, and it hurt. She hurt everywhere.

"Yes," she whispered, not loud enough for him to hear, but loud enough to acknowledge the pain. She set the scalpel on the edge of the counter.

"I—" He stopped speaking.

She wiped her eyes on her sleeve and listened.

"I regret that I have distressed you."

She snorted. "Distressed" didn't begin to cover the emotions she was feeling right now.

A wet sound bounced off the walls when she snuffed her runny nose. Realizing what a mess she was, she grabbed a towel out of the compartment near the steam shower, and wiped her face. The towel dangled from her fingertips as she stared at the door, trying to make sense of what had happened.

He'd healed her, helped her, but in doing so had fixed everything about her skin. Not just her scars, but her cuticles too. Where she sometimes picked at them was now smooth and unblemished. Her lips too. They were always dry, but when she pressed them together, they squished together with plump moisture.

What else had he done to her with that touch? Were there things he'd healed she couldn't see?

If only he could fix all her deeper issues as easily.

It was what everyone had been told to fear—the touch of a Calypson. That just stepping close would change you into one of them. It was one reason the CORE government left them alone, the fear that any contact, even in battle would change everyone. That, and Calypsons kept to themselves, hidden from sight in their nebula. There were whispers that some group somewhere planned a siege of Sector Ten, but it hadn't happened yet.

That they lived a peaceful, solitary existence protected them from the CORE government.

Her eyes drifted to the door. But that wasn't exactly true now, was it? Calypsons were supposed to stay in Sector Ten to remain safe from invasion. The CORE had made it an unbreakable ultimatum.

But now one stood in her outpost.

What did that mean for Sector Ten? Why would they risk retaliation to send someone here to *collect* her? Why did she matter?

Wynn stood and braced her hands against the counter. "Viewer on," she rasped, and the glossy surface became more reflective, revealing her in high-definition color.

She winced. Red, puffy eyes stared back at her. Her skin was splotchy on her forehead, cheeks, and throat. Her black hair stuck out in all directions.

She leaned forward and examined her irises. There was nothing different about their brown color. She twisted her head one way, then the other. They didn't glint or do anything unusual at all.

Straightening, she frowned at herself. Iax hadn't changed her, but he'd done *something*.

With her shirt sleeve still rolled up, she turned her arm toward the mirror to reveal unblemished skin. She stroked up and down, stiff fingers over warm flesh.

For a second there, when he'd taken her hand, she'd thought something had passed between them, something special. There'd been this strange energy when he'd touched her skin, like nothing she'd experienced with someone before. Was it because he was Calypson? Or the healing process? Or was it something else entirely?

"Viewer off," she whispered, and the detailed image disappeared, replaced by the slightly warped reflection of the black terminal.

Wynn turned around and grabbed the counter, allowing the edge to dig into the backs of her thighs and palms, centering her.

She wasn't Calypson, no matter what the blood test said. She was born on *Lunar Six*, a colony on the far side of the moon. Maybe that was why she'd jumped at the chance to work on Earth, despite its lethal conditions.

And I have work to do.

With a tip of her chin, she stared at the closed door, inhaled a deep breath, then unlocked it with a swipe of her hand.

One step into her quarters, and she paused. Iax was where she'd left him, not quite in her quarters, not quite out, the door ajar. He stood still and silent, his brow wrinkled. His fingers twitched at his sides as he scanned her from top to bottom.

Maybe he searched for something, because his gaze lingered on the sleeve of her shirt. She resisted the urge to cover that section of arm with her hand.

She stepped forward.

He didn't move.

"May I leave?" Her words came out scratchy.

He straightened at her question. A beat later, he retreated a pace, allowing her escape. But he didn't give her much space, and she felt his body heat as she passed.

Ignoring the lure of another's warmth, she headed through the hallway and into her lab. The ferocity of the storm hit her again. Unbelievably, it hadn't abated. How long could this go on?

She crossed to the main terminal, tension spreading across her shoulders as her eyes landed on the towel sitting on the analyzer plate. Before she could think twice, she snatched it up along with the dermal syringe, and crossed to the other side of the lab to the reclamation unit.

Tossing both inside, she hit the destroy and recycle control. She stood there as it hummed and whirred, then when silent. Her chest rose and fell like she'd just completed a strenuous activity, and she didn't know why.

A sound rustled near the door. She turned to find Iax paused on the threshold. *Those eyes.* He stared at her in a way that made her entire body pay attention. She didn't know how to handle it. Swallowing, she tore her gaze away, and returned to the main terminal.

She tapped on the glossy black surface, turning it on, then touched her PALM to activate her ocular implant. The terminal glowed, but didn't update, still not connecting with the grid. The main computer system had collected weather stats from the central hub, and she downloaded those. Wind speed, moisture collection, acidic content—it all scrolled in front of her and connected with her ocular implant.

Lifting her hand, she rubbed her temple, annoyed by it immediately. No matter how many times she'd brought it up to tech support, they always said both were working perfectly. And drugs never worked to rid her of the mild pain.

A shift in the air behind her, and she knew Iax walked farther into the lab. He stopped at the window on her left, just in her periphery about two meters away.

Tap tap tap went her fingers against the terminal. Her data was all a muddle, a couple of her sensors not reporting, probably because of the storm taking them out. The work helped to settle her mind.

The hub continued to send her data. Miraculously, the fields' shielding was surviving the storm. The concentration of acid had diminished some, which was also good. Were her seeds surviving, or had the wind and rain washed them away? She wouldn't know until she could get back out there and scan them by hand.

She processed data until there was nothing left to analyze. Throughout it all, Iax barely moved, just stared at the storm.

Her fingers paused, and she pressed her hands flat on the glossy surface. A heavy sort of responsibility hung over her because of him. Her duty to report his presence to the authorities weighed on her, a physical burden across her shoulders. But she couldn't warn the research station, or anyone on this planet, until she reconnected with the grid. Did she even want to? A solid answer refused to form.

On an exhale, she left him there, and returned to the kitchen. The pot of soup had cooled, and she retrieved a stack of containers out of the wall compartment beside the dispensary.

Setting the stack beside the pot, she found a ladle in the drawer and portioned it out one container at a time.

His footsteps stopped in the doorway, but Wynn didn't look up. He remained there while she finished packing everything up.

She hesitated a moment, then left one container out before taking the rest to the refrigeration unit. Only when they were all placed neatly inside did she turn around and meet his gaze square on, using the wall compartment behind her for support.

His stillness, the glint in his eyes, took her breath.

"That's for you," she said with a jerk of her chin toward the container of soup.

He looked between her and the container, then his gaze resettled on her.

She shivered and pushed away from the wall. "You can use Foster's room again."

And she left him there, staring at soup.

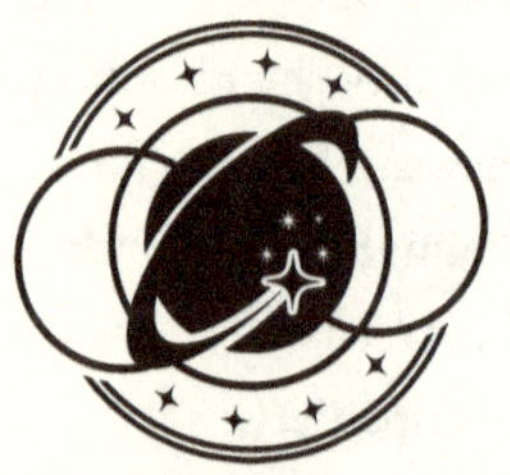

Chapter Fourteen

The door to her quarters shut with a soft *snick*, and Iax felt her absence poignantly. He knew not to follow this time, no matter how much his insides urged him to do so.

He adjusted the spectral wavelength of his eyes instead, watching her movements as she strode deeper into her space. She stopped in the center of the room. Her shoulders rose and fell in a long breath, then her head lowered a moment later. She wrapped her arms around her middle.

Her defeated posture tugged at him. He took a step forward, then stopped himself.

She stood that way for a long while, then crossed to her washroom. Hesitation coated her, then she was moving again, cleaning up the items on the floor, using the toilet, then washing her hands and face.

Out of the washroom, she changed her clothes, swapping out her long pants and shirt for shorts and a top without sleeves.

But she did not lie in her bed to sleep. Instead, she paced the width of the room back and forth. Her lips moved, but no words came out. She continued the activity until she stopped, took another one of those long breaths, and finally retreated to her bed. She covered herself completely, her back to the door.

Iax remained in place until her breaths evened out and she fell into a fitful slumber.

He wished he could help her with that too, that there was some way to calm her mind and ease her distress. He would give it some consideration. Perhaps something would occur to him the longer he spent in her company.

Lightning flashed, and a low rumble of thunder followed. The sound dragged his gaze to the narrow window at the end of the hallway and the weather outside. He had used the addition of the storm to land on this planet undetected, but the progression of its intensity threatened this structure. His return home had always been ambiguous, with many paths open to achieving his goals. But this storm added a layer of difficulty, lessening his options. Adaptability and stealth were key.

He adjusted his eyes again, examining the molecular construction of the support beams. It should hold as long as the storm did not become exponentially worse.

He turned back to the kitchen and stared at the food she had left him. He had already eaten today, and would not have needed more sustenance for some time, but she had left him more.

Two steps, and he stood next to the counter. He stared down at the golden liquid. It looked different from what she had given him earlier. Chunks of vegetables floated in the thicker broth. She had cut all of those with her own hands.

Intrigued, he grabbed the container by its sides and lifted it to his mouth. It was room temperature, but flavors exploded in his mouth, much more when compared to the one-note liquid from earlier. He drank it down in greedy gulps until the container held only drops.

He set it on the counter and licked his lips, tasting the lingering spices. If sustenance tasted that good when done by hand, he wanted to learn.

Turning, he scanned the hallway to Wynn's quarters, and found her in the same position. The urge to go to her raced through him again, but he kept his feet planted, standing guard.

It was some time later when a beeping noise from another room called his attention. He strode across the living space, and through the short hallway to the lab. A light flashed on the main terminal, and he strode toward it.

After a cursory glance, he noted it was a report Wynn had been running. The terminal beside it was black, turned off, and he pressed his hands flat against its shiny surface, infusing it with his essence. It lit up as he connected, his consciousness extending beyond himself to slide and coalesce with the technology. The report did not relate to his purpose here.

He delved deeper. Massive amounts of data bombarded his mind, almost too much to process. Most of it was data from the scientists' research and the fields they tended, years of study observing delicate balances as they attempted to grow edible food on Earth's surface. Many of the logs were entered by Wynn, the others by Dr. Foster Kish.

Iax searched further, knowing there must be more. He stretched his abilities, then hit a wall, a security barrier that tried to keep him out. He pushed past it, accessing the data Dr. Kish had hidden there.

Time passed slowly as he examined each folder, each file, then tried to piece it back together on the far side of the encryption. The dynamic encoding made it challenging.

The storm raged on the other side of the window, but he did not see it as he focused inward and searched for hidden answers.

Much time passed before he abandoned the task. He recalled his essence into himself, left the terminal as it was, and straightened. He refocused on the outside world, on the rain, and mud, and wind, and lightning.

He had vague memories of a similar event, but they were hazy, from a disconnected life. Images filtered in and out of his mind. He had seen Earth through a large window, so close it looked like he could touch it. He remembered a hospital, and doctors, and his mother crying.

They could not help him there either.

Turning away from the view, he crossed to the other side of the lab, and to the door that opened near Wynn's quarters. He would stay there, and watch over her, and make sure she slept.

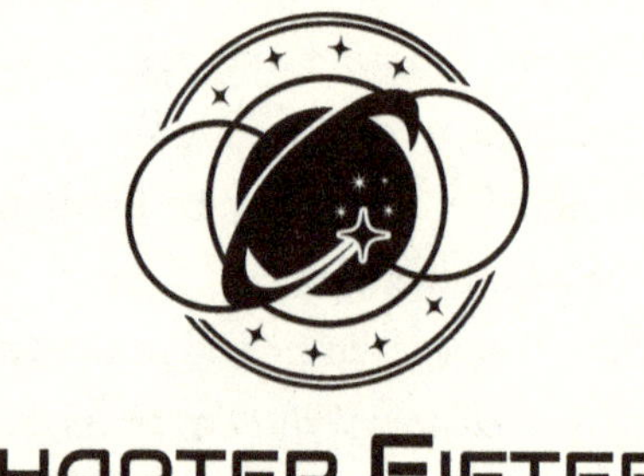

CHAPTER FIFTEEN

Earth?

Carver hated the fucking place. A dying rock with no purpose.

People acted like it was the center of the universe when it was a reminder of humans' complete and utter failure. His species couldn't even keep a planet alive. He didn't know why the CORE government didn't just pull the plug on the pointless conservationist efforts, extract whatever resources remained, and never look back.

The doors to his quarters opened, and he stepped inside the sparsely furnished suite—one place of many he called "home." A functional, disposable room he may return to at some point. Or not. Nothing in his life was ever guaranteed. Nothing was solid.

He crossed to the reclamation unit, stripped, and stuffed everything he wore inside, including his PALM. The end of a job meant hitting the restart button on his life. A new mission, a new identity.

Except they hadn't given him a new identity in the packet. He mulled that over as he took a steam, cleansing himself of his last job. He had only read through the first file by the time he'd arrived at the next station and needed to reconnect to the grid. There'd been no point of entry in a political setting or an assassination target.

The more he read, the more his objective eluded him. They'd given him information, more than he ever had on a job, and it made little sense.

"Off," he said aloud, turning off the steam shower. "Dry maximum." Air flowed around his naked body, drying his skin in seconds.

He exited the washroom and grabbed a clean PALM from the top drawer of his desk. He slid it on, and it connected to the grid a second later. Media updates and reports streamed across his ocular implant.

He strode to the wall compartment that held his uniforms. A spectrum of professions confronted him in colors of tan, and white, and navy blue. He hesitated, not knowing which one to grab, when a new directive passed in front of his eyes.

Possible target: Dr. Wynn Lambdin.

Finally, he had an objective, but it didn't state whether they wanted the person terminated or apprehended. The code to wait for more orders blinked beside her name.

This is bullshit. He'd never accepted a job to be denied the full details. The unbalanced feeling returned.

He closed the wall compartment and stepped to the next. It opened to reveal all-black attire. If he didn't need to play a part for this one, then he would wear whatever the fuck he wanted.

While dressing, he scanned through the files he'd already downloaded, searching for anything attached to the doctor's name. A personnel file surfaced, tagged with over a hundred media reports. He opened the file, and an image of her flashed in front of his eyes.

The picture was from the personnel file at her current post. She wore a tan science officer's uniform, her black hair cut to her chin. Sad brown eyes stared at him from a face devoid of any other expression. Her location tag said Earth, and she had one of the million pointless conservationist positions on the shitty rock.

But her image gave him pause. This was his target? A grunt worker? She wasn't like anyone he usually disposed of, but appearances could be deceiving.

And for the hundredth time over the past day and a half, he reminded himself that it wasn't his job to ask questions.

Sitting on the edge of the bed to pull on clean boots, he opened the media reports attached to her file. Multiple newsreels streamed in front of him, all depicting an event that had happened a few weeks ago.

He remembered it. A new species of animal had mutated on Earth's surface, and an unfortunate scientist had died making the discovery. Dr. Foster Kish was Dr. Lambdin's colleague.

Another sign that everyone should abandon the conservation efforts on Earth. The animals that could exist on its toxic surface didn't want them there either.

Each media outlet covered its own version of the death, trying to outdo the others in hypotheses of where the animals came from, and how they'd stayed hidden for so long. None of them came up with straightforward answers.

Then there were the clips of reporters trying to get comments from Dr. Lambdin as she navigated the halls of Asia Prime's Science Academy days after the incident. They shouted questions at her like rabid dogs, ignoring her pain. Her posture curled inward as defenders escorted her to the administrator's office.

Carver clicked to the next reel, the one official interview sanctioned by the Science Academy. Lambdin sat in a chair across from the interviewer, her spine straight and her hands clenched in her lap. Earth's dead terrain spread out behind her through the window.

The interview had all the earmarks of Lambdin repeating a predetermined script. Whenever the reporters asked something off-topic, the doctor clammed up.

Carver tried to remain unaffected, but her disadvantage, her inability to answer the way they wanted, tugged at him. He pushed the sensation aside, and moved on to the next clip, then the next.

The news stories were still coming from that event. The animals were being studied at the Science Academy, and the media hadn't tired of the updates.

More files were attached to those reports, ones marked with a government seal. He opened the packet. These encompassed the official investigation at the doctor's outpost, an autopsy of her colleague's remains, and a deeper dive into both doctors' lives.

Carver read for a bit, then shook his head at the useless knowledge—useless until his orders firmed up and he knew what they wanted him to do with the woman.

He slapped his knees and stood, then signaled the handler they'd paired him with to await his instructions. He wouldn't know what the hell he needed for the assignment until his final orders came through.

Like the thought materialized them into existence, live orders downloaded to his PALM.

Target confirmed: Dr. Wynn Lambdin. Retrieve alive. Final destination: Corvus, *General Cazin. Immediate dispatch.*

This was what they'd called him off for? A time-sensitive pickup? They could have asked a defender to perform the task.

And if Lambdin was a threat to CORE security, he would eat his left boot.

The really fucked-up thing was that they saw fit to send him terabytes of data, but his orders were one line. Besides Earth's live weather update, no other details about what he'd find downloaded to his PALM—only that her probable location was a remote outpost.

He grabbed a short jacket out of the wall compartment, shrugged it over his shoulders, and zipped it up. Tapping his PALM, he messaged his handler to prepare his cruiser, and received confirmation a moment later.

Carver returned to the initial package of files and read the first of them as he exited his quarters. None of them had anything to do with Lambdin. The files were from a hundred fifty years ago: the details of Operation Odyssey and the *Calypso's* doomed mission to Epsilon Eridani, a solar system over ten light years away.

Why the fuck were they sending him this shit? He could have accessed library banks and read the same thing.

He stepped on the lift closest to his quarters. "Level sixty-seven."

The lift descended, humming around him, then stopped, but the door didn't open automatically, waiting for his security clearance. He swiped his PALM, and the lift continued its journey downward.

When it stopped, he swiped his ID again, then stepped out onto a military-controlled level, the corridors empty. He passed by unmarked doors, the shiny black surfaces of the inactive terminals in between reflecting his image back at him.

He was skimming the files scrolling across the bottom of his ocular readout when he noticed a tag on the first file. He slowed his steps. They'd attached another file, this one topped with a government seal.

After entering his ID code, another massive file downloaded. Hundreds of security reports were attached to the data he'd just skimmed, including sealed generals' logs from every action with the *Calypso* when it returned to their solar system, and a wealth of secure communications between high-up officials.

What in the ever-loving fuck? Did every download have a secondary packet? Reading and listening to all of this before he reached Earth was impossible. His seven-day completion promise ticked away.

Carver picked up his pace, then stopped at the second last unmarked door on the left. He swiped his PALM on the control panel, and it opened into a docking port. He strode through the dark passage lit only by running deck lights, then swiped his PALM on the outer panel of his cruiser.

The airlock opened, revealing the interior of the customized ship. He stepped inside and inhaled deeply, the scent of his preferred cleaning fluid filling his lungs. His eyes skimmed over the sleek black interior, highlighted by beige upholstery. A two-seat cockpit spread out on his left, and a combination kitchen-living space lay on his right. Behind that, a slender door led to his sleeping quarters.

Out of the very little he owned, he was most attached to this ship.

He swiped the panel, and the airlock closed, sealing him inside. He passed the bank of wall terminals and slid into the pilot's seat. With a swipe of his bio-signature, the ship began the pre-flight process. A moment later, the engine purred beneath his feet.

His departure clearance scrolled across the main terminal. No further orders came in.

The docking clamps released with a *clank*. He pulled away from the station and set a course for Earth.

Chapter Sixteen

Consciousness trickled in a little at a time. An unsteady sensation followed.

Since Foster died, there weren't many days Wynn didn't wake up with a tight ball of nausea in her stomach, or a knot in her throat. Today it felt a little different, and her brain hadn't caught up.

She rolled onto her back and stared at the ceiling. A slice of gray cloud-covered sky shed dreary light through her quarters. A distant rumble of thunder broke the silence.

How could a storm last so long? She wished she had access to the grid if only to see how the system traveled over New Asia. It rarely rained, which was why she needed her irrigation system for the outdoor fields. Storms were rare, and usually short and violent.

Not long *and violent.*

Thoughts of the storm brought on images of her visitor. She'd left him alone, unsupervised, for way too long. Who knew what he could have gotten into.

Wynn leaned upward, swinging her legs over the edge of the bed. A chill permeated the air in her quarters. She frowned, eyes scanning to her PALM to check the building's ambient temperature, when she remembered she'd removed it again.

Maybe Iax had been messing with the environmental settings.

She swiped her hand over her face. Her temples throbbed in time with her heartbeat, the pain migrating behind her eyes. For the millionth time, she wished she could just take a painkiller like everyone else and have it work. Not that she hadn't tried.

Her gaze moved to the skin of her unblemished arm. Another wave of embarrassment shuddered through her at being caught in the washroom. She swallowed it down, not even sure if Iax had understood what she'd been about to do.

How could he not?

Cool air swirled around the exposed skin of her arms and legs. She only ever wore shorts and a tank top to bed, but the chill of the room made her wish for sweaters and long pants. Shivering, she hopped out of bed, then paused at the threshold of the washroom.

She waited for it, the falling, out-of-control sensation, that itchy need to crawl out of her skin, but it never came.

"Steam, hot," she said, stepping fully inside.

The shower compartment filled with a fine mist. Wynn undressed and stepped inside, allowing it to wash away everything from yesterday and heat her bones. The floor was cold beneath her feet when she stepped out, but at least her body was warm.

Her morning rituals complete, and dressed in an identical set of clothes as yesterday, Wynn slid on her PALM and paused at her door. What would she find? *Not a dead man.* She'd been certain of that the day before and had been so very wrong.

Unease and eagerness battled equally with each other. Wynn inhaled a fortifying breath and pressed the door's control panel.

An empty hallway greeted her. Her shoulders relaxed a fraction, but then worry seeped in. Where was Iax?

She stepped into the corridor, the low pile of the carpet pressing against the soles of her feet. A glance toward the kitchen revealed the empty container of soup on the counter. *At least he'd eaten.*

Hand trailing along the wall, she closed the gap to Foster's quarters, then hesitated. Could Iax be sleeping? She raised her hand and swiped her PALM across the control panel. The door slid open, revealing an empty room, unchanged from yesterday. The bed looked slept in, but not any different from that first night.

Wynn turned and moved toward the lab. Her feet stopped when she caught sight of Iax in front of the window. His glasses lay atop his jacket, which hung over the back of one chair. Broad shoulders filled out the material of his shirt, narrowing down to trim hips that made her mouth water in a wholly inappropriate way.

Why him? Why was this the first time she experienced genuine attraction?

She pushed that shit down, not wanting to examine it this early in the morning, but couldn't tear her gaze away. Iax stared into the storm like he needed to memorize it.

One tentative step, then another, she crossed the room to stand beside him. He didn't acknowledge her except for a slight twitch of his body.

Centering her focus where he stared, she inhaled a surprised breath. Was it just her, or was the storm subsiding? The rain seemed thinner, not the thick buckets it had been yesterday; the wind had died down too. Maybe it was finally on its way out.

Casting him another glance, she accessed the terminal, checking on what the central hub had recorded over the night. Continued rain and wind, but yes, it had died down in its ferocity while the temperature steadily dropped.

With a touch of her hand, she accessed environmental controls, raising the ambient temperature and the in-floor heating. The carpet beneath her bare feet warmed, chasing away the lingering chill.

"What are you staring at?" The question popped out of her mouth, scratchy, her first words of the day.

He didn't answer right away, and she stared in the same direction, examining the gray-on-gray horizon.

While she watched, the rain slowed, but it also changed. Hints of white intermixed with the moisture, first just one here, one there. Then more bloomed, catching the dull light of the cloud-covered sun, and the rain disappeared altogether.

It took her a minute to process the glints. *Snow!* She'd never seen snow before, and her heart leaped at the sight of it. It was unreal and magical, swirling in little vortexes to float lightly to the ground. Mesmerized, she couldn't look away.

"Something approaches."

Iax's gravelly words snapped her attention back to him. His gaze remained on the storm, but a thoughtful furrow puckered his brow.

Her heart thumped twice as hard. "What do you mean by 'something'?" A surface vehicle? Or a ship? Was someone here to take her away from this bizarre waiting period?

The thought created a dual sensation in her chest, one that both rejoiced at being rescued and another that tugged her insides, rebelling that Iax might get in trouble for being here.

Trouble. What would that even entail? What would the CORE government do to a rogue Calypson?

Her throat clicked in a dry swallow.

"They are primitive creatures," he finally replied.

A swooping sensation took over her insides, making the floor feel like it disappeared from beneath her feet. Only one type of primitive creature survived in this area.

Her vision blurred as she focused on where he stared. He couldn't mean the beasts because they'd been captured and taken far away, to one of the wildlife reserves on the coast of New Asia. Scientists had either kept them alive for study or put them down. She hadn't cared which.

But two dark shadows formed in the distance. The smudges solidified into slender shapes as they neared, contrasting against the white of the snow.

Terror weakened her arms and legs. "No," she whispered. "Not possible."

The beasts were back.

The urge to scream welled in her throat. Why were they back?

They prowled forward, their shoulders as tall as her chest, snow coating their spines. Tongues lolled out of their mouths, dripping strings of saliva into the wind.

Her breaths shortened; her heart pounded between her ears.

The view tilted. Wynn braced her hands against the terminal to remain upright and focused on the readout in front of her. There were two of them instead of four. Why were there only two of them? She tried to take a deeper breath so she wouldn't pass out.

Out of the corner of her eye, Iax stepped toward her, his arms lifting like he thought he might need to catch her. She shook her head, then met his gaze.

"Why?" she whispered, not even understanding what she was asking.

His arms lowered. "These creatures distress you?"

Distress. She almost laughed at the word, but nodded over and over again. There was nothing more terrifying than those beasts, even being locked up with a Calypson for days. She'd seen what those beasts could do, up close and personal.

All the images she'd tried to erase since Foster's death resurfaced: The four beasts circling them while they were in the field, of Foster sacrificing himself so she could make it back to the outpost, of how they'd dragged his body to the door like some sort of sick sacrifice, then ate him in front of her like they'd known how much that would disturb her, how much it would fuck her up.

She could hear his screams when she closed her eyes at night.

Iax turned his body toward the window. "I will converse with them." He grabbed his glasses and jacket, then shrugged the garment over his shoulders as he left the lab.

What?

Her lungs froze. His words didn't settle fully in her mind until the decontamination door opened and closed.

She blinked once, then twice, then ran after him in time to see the back of his jacket disappear around the edge of the building.

"No," she choked, a new well of panic rising in her chest to strangle her throat.

On soupy legs, she stumbled back toward the lab until she fell against the terminal. Her eyes scanned the horizon for any signs of the beasts, but in the time it had taken her to follow Iax, they'd disappeared.

Her hands flexed and clenched against the slick surface of the terminal while the landscape stayed disturbingly empty, filled only with blowing snow.

Iax rounded the corner of the building, boots crunching in the ice that had formed over the mud. Snow covered his head, and his jacket whipped about his legs. *No UV-suit.* His first bout of radiation sickness hadn't been enough? He'd almost died, his skin trying to melt away from his body, and he wanted to repeat the experience?

His glasses shielded his eyes, his attention fixed ahead of him where she'd first seen the beasts.

"Come back inside," she whispered, hands pressed flat against the terminal. Her gaze bounced over the terrain, never stopping. "Stupid. Stupid. Stupid."

Why was he doing this? She didn't even understand *what* he meant to do. How the hell was he going to "converse" with wild, rabid, homicidal beasts?

A shadow skulked to the left of the building. Wynn sucked in a breath, holding it. One beast emerged from the blowing snow. Its faceted and mutated flesh, like armor, lifted around its spine and shoulders in warning. Razor-sharp tines lined its jaws, the front six elongated, curving over an angular mandible.

Iax raised his hands away from his body, palms facing the beast, and stopped.

She gripped the edge of the terminal, preparing for the beast to pounce. She wouldn't be able to watch. *Not again.* With its head lowered and teeth bared, it paused two meters away, as motionless as a statue.

If it weren't for the snow and the way Iax's jacket pressed against his legs, she would have thought she viewed a still image. Neither the man nor beast moved for what seemed like an eternity.

Her heart pounded between her ears. She kept waiting for something to happen, for blood and death, but everything remained as frozen as the breath she held in her lungs.

Where's the other one? Her vision blurred, and Wynn exhaled, taking another quick breath to dispel the faint sensation consuming her head.

Icy goosebumps spread across her skin when the second beast cleared the opposite corner of the building. Low to the frozen earth, it stalked Iax.

Wynn slapped the windowpane. "Behind you!" Her hand stung from the force of the smack.

Iax twitched, his chin jerking to the side like he'd heard her through the transparent aluminum, but he didn't turn around to confront the threat.

The second beast stopped, its head down, mimicking the posture and distance of the other.

The three forms stood there in the snow, motionless. Was he really conversing with them?

There was so much guessing with Calypsons. Some people said they could read minds. Others said they sucked people's brains out through their ears. Since they'd created the nebula that hid the *Calypso* and *Omega Station* from sight and scans, no one knew much of anything about them except that some worshiped the race because of their apparent longevity, wanting that for themselves. People pilgrimaged to the nebula, never to be heard from again. *Like Iax.*

Her throat clogged, and Wynn swallowed, mesmerized by the inconceivable tableau. Everything was stuck, static, until the beasts twitched. Wynn inhaled sharply, braced herself, but they tucked their tails between their legs, and backed away one slow step at a time.

Her vision blurred again, and she forced herself to exhale. It did nothing to dispel the turmoil seething inside her. They'd eaten Foster but only *talked* with Iax? Memories of Foster's desecrated body flashed in front of her eyes. Blood. Flesh. Muscle. Bone. A living, breathing, intelligent person downgraded to a piece of meat.

An invisible band squeezed her chest so tight she couldn't breathe. Her vision blackened around the edges. Rage and relief mixed a terrible cocktail in her stomach.

The snow swallowed the beasts as they retreated. Iax didn't move for a long while, then turned, his alert focus aimed toward her.

Wynn stumbled away from the window, and wheezed, staggering toward the hallway. With one hand braced against the wall, she tried to inhale, but it was like breathing through a clogged straw. She bent at the waist, but it did little to help the way her head felt like it was about to explode.

The building spun around her. Stars speckled her vision. The need for pain, for *something* to focus her, cascaded over her head, and she reached for that section of arm that should have three lines etched into the skin, but remained smooth. More panic swelled.

The sound of the decontamination process pierced through the buzzing in her head. Her throat burned; her heart pounded.

Hissss. The inner door to the decontamination zone opened, and a full breath expanded her lungs for the first time in minutes.

The texture of the carpet sharpened. She inhaled a breath, and another, then lifted her head to find Iax naked before her, skin pink and eyes glinting.

A new familiarity shot through her, one she hadn't connected yesterday. But after seeing the beasts again, she realized their eyes glinted, caught the light similarly to his, almost glowing.

Her mind rejected that new insight as she choked out, "What *the fuck* was that?"

Chapter Seventeen

Volatile emotions speared toward him, assaulting his senses. Wynn clutched at her arm, her face twisted like she was in pain, but he did not see an injury, even when he adjusted his eyes to look deeper.

"What the fuck was that?" She repeated her question, softer, but no less distressed.

He stepped forward to help, but paused when she lifted her hand from her arm and held it up flat.

"Don't," she gritted between clenched teeth. "I can't—" She shook her head and dropped her hand, her eyes expressing something he could not name, but tugged at him to move closer, to put his arm around her though he did not know what that would accomplish.

"Please get dressed." She turned her head away to stare vacantly toward the kitchen.

Iax looked down at himself. A flush covered his skin where Earth's radiation had affected him. He continued to feel its impact on the cells in his body as his essence repaired the damage.

Turning his head slightly, he focused on the mechanism hidden behind the walls that cleansed his garments of radiation. It whirred and hummed, almost inaudibly, using a similar solution to what had misted over his body.

Iax returned his attention to Wynn who hadn't moved from her spot, her chest rising and falling in quick breaths. Her distress had not diminished despite his sending the animals away.

He walked toward the control panel beside the transparent door, pressed his hand flat against its surface, and sent his essence inside to accelerate the process. The humming increased in volume until it waned abruptly.

The compartment opened, revealing his garments folded and stacked along with the outerwear Wynn had used earlier, and her weapon lying neatly at the bottom. He dressed, starting with his pants. His healing skin scraped against the material despite its softness. Next came his shirt, then boots, but he left his jacket and glasses within the compartment.

When he turned, he found Wynn staring at him, lips parted. A breath shuddered through her body, and she leaned against the opposite wall.

"Did you really talk with them?" The words whispered between haggard breaths.

Iax considered her question and tipped his head toward where the animals had disappeared. They had only left the area after his continued encouragement.

"We communicated." Their existence was troublesome on many levels, but the one that preoccupied his mind the most was Wynn's fear of them. He could not force his mind away from the matter.

She leaned heavier on the wall, her knees bending. "What did you *communicate* about?"

He had promised not to lie, but hesitated to divulge everything he had learned from the animals. He did not want to cause Wynn more distress when she stared at him in a way that constricted his throat.

He spoke around the obstacle. "I learned where they originated, and their directive, then told them not to return here."

A single tear rolled down her face. Watching it fall cut something inside him, a rip through his chest. He reviewed his experiences since coming here, about the emotions he felt and what Wynn projected to him, searching for a way to help her.

"Their directive," she repeated. "They were following orders?"

He hesitated, searching for the best words to describe his interaction with the animals. "Not orders. They do not have words, only impressions and impulses. They follow those."

And there were similarities between him and them he needed to examine, but her next question pulled his thoughts away from the task.

"Where did they originate?"

He refocused on her face, which had gone alarmingly pale. "A lab."

She sucked in a quick breath, then shook her head in denial. "You're saying they were engineered?" Before he could answer, she shook her head again, the movement frantic. "The investigators told me they'd mutated naturally. They didn't say anything about a lab."

Her breaths accelerated, and her hands opened and closed against her thighs.

"Where is this lab?"

He searched through the conversation, but could not deduce a specific location from the impressions he received from the animals. "I do not know," he replied a moment later.

Her chest continued to rise and fall. "There were only two of them," she said, her jaw tight. "There were four last time." She pressed a hand flat against her stomach.

"These two had not been here before. They searched for those missing of their kind."

She shook her head again, her lips pressed tight together. Moisture welled in her eyes, threatening to spill.

He had thought conversing with the animals would help her, but her distress rose. *I have made it worse.* The need to help her impelled him, and he could not stop his feet from moving forward.

"Wynn," he said, her name soft in his mouth.

She lifted her head, her eyes unfocused as she stared up at him.

"I want to help you." The need was so great, it burned through his chest and throat. He outstretched his arms, not entirely sure why.

But she seemed to know. After a brief hesitation, she tucked her body against his.

His arms instinctively closed around her, and the hallway, the outpost, the storm, it all faded as he focused on Wynn and held her close.

A ragged breath shook her, the vibrations transferring to him. His arms tightened, and she expelled a longer breath.

"I thought they would kill you."

Her words were quiet and tortured, ripping through his mind like a weapon.

"I thought I would watch another person die." Her breath hitched, her shoulders shaking.

An emotion welled inside him and tasted bitter on his tongue. By speaking with the animals, he had caused her harm, but he could not fix it. He could not reverse time and make a different decision.

"I am sorry." He said the words even though they did not feel like enough, because he was apologetic for more than his conversation with the animals. He was sorry her colleague died, for the trauma she went through, and for all the secrets hidden beneath the systems of this outpost.

She stiffened, then turned slightly within his arms. Her gaze met his, and he saw so much in her eyes. They shimmered with questions and pain, and he felt acute regret because he had caused it.

The longer she stared at him, her eyes searching his, the more her body relaxed into him. His blood surged. They connected from chest to hip. He could not remember a time he had ever stood this way with another. It was both foreign and natural, his muscles sinking into the position like he belonged.

Her fingers flexed against his arm, gripping him tight, fingernails biting through the material. He liked that too, but could not say why.

He lifted his hand and cupped her jaw. "I am sorry," he said again.

She inhaled sharply, stilling, then leaned into the touch. Her cheeks bloomed with color. The shimmering moisture in her eyes morphed into something else when she blinked. Her lips parted.

Beautiful. The word came from far away. From the past. From a voice he had almost forgotten. The person had been speaking about a flower hanging high in the air in a green space, below a dome of stars.

Wynn was more beautiful than that flower, the expression in her eyes more poignant, her face full of life. He did not want to look away, not for all the flowers in the solar system.

Slowly, she reached toward his face. Fingernails skimmed his jaw, then gripped the back of his neck. He felt every digit, each length of her fingers against his skin. Tingles spread downward, over his shoulder blades and spine, then lower to settle in places that heated and yearned.

His breath stalled in his lungs as new emotions surged within him, ones with elusive names and definitions. The embrace held his body captive just as much as the emotions in Wynn's eyes, which darted lower for a moment, focusing on his mouth before returning.

Her fingers tightened on the back of his neck, then she tugged his head downward. Closer and closer his face drew to hers. She closed her eyes with a sigh, and their lips met.

His mind blanked.

Then an explosion of feelings spread through him, both hers and his. They wrapped around his essence, his mind, his body, then everything focused on one location—where his lips joined with hers.

Soft. Supple. *Perfect*. He closed his eyes, basking in the pure pleasure. Though he could not taste her thoughts, he could taste *her*. He inhaled her flavors, vibrant with life: water, and green, and earth. They settled into his mind, calming and exciting him in equal measure.

Wynn's fingers flexed on his nape, tugging him closer, but he was as close as he could get with their bodies pressed against each other and their lips connected. Moving. Opening.

When her tongue swept inside his mouth, he realized he was very wrong. They could get so much closer. The stroke of her tongue was paradise. A sound emerged from his chest and throat, something between a growl and a moan.

In echo, she groaned into his mouth. Shivers broke over his scalp, traveling everywhere.

How was he feeling these things? The few times he had observed coupling, the interaction had been impersonal. Calypsons expressed a need, and both parties took care of that need if they were agreeable. There wasn't this heat that now spiraled inside him, mimicking Wynn's emotions as they bombarded his senses.

Along with his need also rose a new emotion whose name eluded him, but it urged his hands to explore down Wynn's arms, to her waist, then around her body. His hands shook when he pressed her harder against him, her breasts squishing against his chest.

She groaned again, fingernails digging into his scalp as she continued her mouth explorations.

He had appreciated her slight form earlier, but now he wanted to memorize it. To admire and *savor* her.

He did not remember moving, but they had shifted their positions until the wall was at her back, his knee between hers. His shoulders crowded her body, casting her face in shadows. His cock strained against the front closure of his pants.

This bodily reaction had never been so painful.

The burning need inside him did not quit, and he had to touch more of her to ease the ache.

Chapter Eighteen

Wynn didn't know what the hell she was doing, and she didn't care.

All she wanted was *more*.

More of this kiss, more of the feel of Iax against her, more of all her worries and pain being swept away by the incredible sensations flooding her body.

And underneath it all was wonder.

For her entire life, she'd had superficial relationships and watched others connect with each other, all the while feeling like there must be something wrong with her.

Because no person had ever stirred her blood enough for her to become physical with them. And adding a mood enhancer to the mix had never been an option. Drugs just didn't work for her. She'd resigned herself that romantic relationships weren't for her, and she'd been okay with that.

But even friendships had been hard. Foster had been the only one to truly know her, and even he hadn't known everything. He'd teased her about her love of spaceball and her need to closet herself away for hours at a time with a good book or just listening to music, instead of trying to understand her. Connections were forced, not natural, and she'd always preferred her own company.

None of that seemed true anymore. Her head was a whirl of disconnected thoughts, while her heart thumped painfully in her throat. Her lower stomach expanded with heat and need. The apex of her thighs ached.

No person had ever made her feel this way, and he wasn't even trying.

She could tell by the awkward movements, the fumbling, the erratic tempo of his breathing. The hard-on pressing against her abdomen should have freaked her out, but she tilted her hips, thrusting against him to relieve the pulsing need between her legs.

She couldn't keep hold of her thoughts.

His groan lit her insides.

She just wanted to *feel*.

His hands explored her body through her clothing, leaving trails of lava in their wake. She leaned into his touch, reveling at how much sensation she experienced through a layer of fabric, her skin pebbling, yearning.

How much better would it be without her clothes?

Amazing. She knew it would feel amazing.

She rocked against him, wanting more, and his leg drifted upward until his thigh nestled between both of hers. Another groan ripped out of her as she found pressure and friction by tipping her hips. Her heart thumped harder between her ears with each movement. Heat spread over her skin.

She finally understood what all the girls in her dorm used to giggle about late at night.

Her hands drifted to face, over his jaw and cheeks. She marveled at its smoothness even as the action sent more shivers down her arms. He'd been here two days and, as far as she knew, hadn't shaved. She stroked his scalp, fingernails scratching, and received a tremor from the touch.

I like that. Liked being the one who elicited these reactions and made him unravel. *What would he look like when he comes?* The thought spread heat downward to settle at her center.

She repeated the action, then stroked downward, over his shoulders to his biceps. She squeezed, admiring the thickness and strength of his muscles. Then her fingers trailed lower, down his arms, over his wrists to his waist, where she circled her hands and pulled him closer.

He broke the kiss with a groan, tucking his face into the place where her shoulder met her neck. He inhaled deeply. More shivers exploded over her skin. She tilted her head back, allowing him better access. His lips teased her skin, then he paused and lifted his head.

Glittering eyes searched hers. "Do I have permission to touch you?"

She laughed. She couldn't help it. "You're already touching me." Her throat was so clogged with desire, her words tumbled over each other.

The corner of his mouth quirked, like he needed to smile but didn't know how. "I want to touch you everywhere."

"Yes." She nodded, a frantic edge to the movement. "Yes, I want that too. You have permission. All the permission."

Then she was pulling him down for another kiss, their teeth clacking. It was messy, and primal, and she couldn't get enough. She wanted to drink him up. His scent and taste mixed in her head, a combination she didn't have a name for, but contained some sort of citrusy, herbal note.

His hands fumbled with her shirt, tugging it from her pants. When his fingers connected with her stomach, she inhaled a shocked breath. Electricity rippled through her body, feeling like she'd just received a surge from a malfunctioning terminal. He explored higher, brushing against her ribs, then the side of her breasts hidden beneath a layer of underwear.

She inhaled sharply, loving his hands on her skin. But it wasn't enough.

"Backward," she rasped, giving him a shove.

He complied, but kept her against him, their footsteps in time with each other. One step was followed by more until the door to her quarters opened at their approach. They passed through, and the lights turned on, brighter than those in the hallway.

She squinted against the glare, then froze. Everything came into focus. Iax's eyes glinted down at her, holding an untapped wildness. His fingers flexed against her skin.

Panic swept away the haze of her lust. *I was about to do it with a Calypson.*

Wynn retreated. He followed for a step, then his hands dropped away from her body.

"Um." She cleared her throat around the hard lump of regret lodged there. "This probably isn't a good idea."

She braced herself for his reaction, waiting for him to convince her to continue down this path. So many times, she'd put on the brakes with a guy because she felt nothing, and he'd try to change her mind, urge her to take an enhancer. It was only intercourse, after all.

This time she put on the brakes because she felt too much.

Iax only blinked at her, his chest rising and falling in gasping breaths, the rhythm mimicking her own.

Questions flooded her mind. Did he even understand where this had been headed? Did he feel this burning need the same way she did? Was this all as new to him as it was to her? His expression revealed nothing.

No, that wasn't quite true. His parted lips, the focus he gave her, the way his fingers twitched at his sides like he wanted to grab her again, and the bulge straining against the front of his pants—she reacted to his needs as much as her own.

"I..." She ran a hand over her hair and surveyed her room, if only to break his intense stare. "I have some work I need to do."

She hadn't checked on the central hub's reports since the snow began, and she needed to make sure there were no adverse effects in the greenhouse with the drop in temperature. There were the new seeds she'd planted too, and the damaged sapling.

A list built in her mind even while her body hummed with frustration. She wanted to continue where they'd left off, needed it with every cell in her body, but she also knew how absolutely unhinged giving into that would be—even if she'd never achieved the sensations currently rioting in her body.

You don't have sex with a Calypson.

It was idiocy at its highest. She needed to get her head on straight.

Wynn took a step backward, then paused. Her body and heart told her not to leave him, an unfamiliar ache forming in her belly that tugged her closer, almost like a power cord connected them and she'd rather have it slack than pulled tight.

One step forward, then another, she stopped when their chests almost touched, staring up at him. She took a deep breath, inhaling his comforting scent.

"This might sound weird," she said, examining his face, "but I'd like to keep you close."

A beat of silence thrummed between them, then he tilted his head, nodding once. "I would like to stay close."

Her shoulders relaxed, a warm sensation filling her chest. "Come," she said, taking his hand in hers.

Tingles spread through her hand and up her arm at the connection. She inhaled a quick breath, regretting that she'd put a stop to things.

We could continue.

No! All the reasons she'd just given herself remained, and there were so many more that simmered below the surface.

Tomorrow. Hope laced the insistent thought. If the storm continued to rage, if they were stuck here longer, then she had more time to come to terms with these raw, untried feelings inside her.

And if not...

She swallowed. As far as she knew, he was still determined to take her to Sector Ten. She hadn't tried to convince him otherwise. And why was that?

But if the CORE government found him here, it wouldn't end well. The best she could do would be to convince him to leave on his own when the storm died down, before anyone arrived to check on her.

Clearing her throat, she tugged him forward and led him through the hallway to the lab. A white haze enveloped the world outside, stealing her breath. The wind had picked up, blowing the snow sideways. Thick swaths of it fell from the edge of the roof.

She kept hold of Iax's hand as she rushed toward the terminal, and he willingly followed. Then she needed both hands, tapping on her systems to get a better read on what was happening to her fields.

The heat of Iax's body warmed her arm as she worked, and she found herself leaning into him more than once. So strange that this was happening to her now, with a Calypson, when she'd felt numb inside with romantic partners for so long. Could it be because of what he'd told her? That she was Calypson too?

She pushed the thought aside—needed to if she wanted to keep her sanity—and tried to focus on her work.

Wynn analyzed the data streaming from the central hub. The probability of her seeds surviving any of this extreme weather was next to zero. She had to accept that, but wasn't letting it beat her down. There would be a day soon when she would be out there again, planting.

The data kept her in place while the snowstorm worsened. She shook her head at it. The wonder she had felt at seeing those first flakes turned into worry for her planet. None of this was normal. She hoped people were being safe.

But no matter how much she tried to concentrate, with Iax so close, questions kept surfacing—more than she could contain. Especially over what would happen after the storm abated. She needed to use this time to convince him to leave her here.

Her chest squeezed at that thought, but she cleared her throat, trying to shake it off. His head turned toward her.

"How were you able to heal so fast?" she asked, her fingers moving over the terminal even though most of her focus was on him. "After being exposed to so much radiation?"

She sensed his hesitation and lifted her gaze. When it looked like he wouldn't answer at all, she added, "How am I going to trust you enough to go with you if you don't share information?"

His facial expression changed, the frown on his brow softening. "I have a natural ability to regenerate cells because I'm Calypson. It is the same thing you saw in the enlargement of your blood."

Wynn rubbed at her forehead. "Yeah, but I can't heal like that."

"Because you are an anomaly."

She huffed out a frustrated breath and refocused on the data in front of her. "What new information can you tell me about that subject?"

When he hesitated again, she paused. "How about this," she said without looking at him. "How about with every truthful answer you give me, I'll give you one too?" She lifted her chin to meet his gaze. "How does that sound?"

"It sounds fair," he replied, but he didn't look like he enjoyed that fact.

She couldn't help the little quirk her lips made at an expression she could only call disgruntled. Refocusing on her terminal, she tapped to the next batch of data. "The healing thing?"

"Even the smallest of my cells are intelligent," he said after a time.

Interesting. She really wanted to get a sample of his blood to analyze and see how it differed from hers. But before she could ask, he made good on their bargain, freezing her in place with his first question.

"Why do you cut yourself?"

Her lungs seized, and she felt heat crawl up her throat. That raw, exposed feeling returned. *But fair is fair.*

"It focuses me." Tense, she regretted this game already. "Makes the world stop spinning. Your turn," she added before he could follow up with another question. "Why didn't you wear a UV-suit when you walked here?"

He paused before he responded. "I underestimated the effect of this planet and how far away I would land."

"Wait. Where did you—"

"My turn," he cut her off. "Why did you leave scars?"

Her breath left her in a sputter. "They were a reminder of what I'd lost. A badge of honor."

His brow furrowed in confusion. *That makes us even.* She didn't allow him to take a full breath before she asked, "How did you arrive on the planet?"

"In a pod disguised as a meteor. I had to adjust my landing parameters because of the storm."

She stiffened in realization. *The meteor.* The one she'd seen fall while she was planting. It had been his pod.

He stepped toward her, and she tipped her head back to meet his gaze. "Why does your heart accelerate like mine when we are close?"

She sucked in a sharp breath and answered honestly. "I don't know." Because she really didn't understand what was happening to her—what was happening between them.

The rest of the questions she'd had lined up in her head vanished.

Chapter Nineteen

The urge to kiss Iax again kept Wynn's nerves humming while she analyzed, tagged, and filed the data from the central hub. Each of his slight movements—a tilt of his head here, a step of his feet there—skittered across her awareness, titillating her senses. It took as much energy to focus on what her fingers were doing as it did to ignore the memory of how it felt to taste his lips and have his body pressed against hers.

When it was time to move to the greenhouse, she took Iax's hand without thinking, tugging him along. He followed, docile, and she resumed their bargain.

"Why do Calypsons live so long?" The door swished closed behind them.

"In the same way we heal: regenerative cells."

She stepped up to her newly planted seeds when he asked, "How do you achieve contentment?"

The question gave her pause. What made her happy? For so long, nothing had brought her joy. Even before the death of her parents, she'd found it hard to seize happiness for herself. She'd gained her love of spaceball from her father, and her enjoyment of learning and puzzles from her mother.

Now it felt like she only had her work.

"I guess I feel most content when I can turn off my thoughts," she said after a time. "Here in the greenhouse, or listening to music." She turned to him. "What about you? How do you achieve contentment?"

"I still search for the feeling."

His quiet answer shifted something in her chest. Were Calypsons ever happy? Something stopped her from asking the questions aloud.

Wynn moved on to check her saplings, then spent a good section of time tending the one that had taken a tumble the day before. A diagnostic of her mechanical systems followed to make sure it didn't happen again. All the while, Iax remained close enough for her to feel his body heat. She'd never been one to allow the hovering of another, but with him, it didn't feel intrusive. In fact, every time he strayed more than a meter, she waited until he caught up before she moved on.

Over lunch, where she reheated the soup from the day before, their game of questions tapered off. Sitting side by side at the counter, she kept watching him and tried not to obsess too much over how much she liked how his thigh pressed against hers.

After cleaning up the dishes, they spent the remainder of the day in her greenhouse, tending to one section at a time. She started showing him what to do, first planting seeds, and examining the saplings, seeing if they needed more fertilizer. Eventually, she would plant some outside too, hoping they could withstand the elements.

She and Foster had gone through so many genetic modifications, so many variations, and she would continue to do so until she, or whoever the CORE sent to take her place, was successful.

The work was only interrupted by their questions.

"Are there plants in Sector Ten?" She pushed another seed into the soil.

"Many." He copied her movements with his own pot.

She followed up quickly with another. "Are they like these?"

"No. Very different. You will see them when you travel with me."

Her hands stopped moving, her heart leaping in her throat. "You have yet to convince me."

He tipped his head slightly in acknowledgement, then asked, "What would have happened if we had gone to your bed together?"

A strained laugh erupted from her mouth, obliterating her fear of his previous answer. She wasn't sure if his matter-of-fact tone made it harder or easier to answer a question like that. Did Calypsons have sex? They had to if they procreated, and the history logs could attest to that.

"Um," she began, feeling heat climb up her throat. "I guess it could have gone a few different ways." She cleared her throat. "It would have depended on how we were feeling and what we both wanted."

He nodded once, agreeing. Her shoulders relaxed.

After a while, she asked, "If we go to Sector Ten, how are you taking me there?" If he'd arrived in a pod acting like a meteor, then it was unlikely they could leave that way.

"Multiple modes of transportation."

She faced him fully. "Give me an example," she demanded, even though she knew she'd asked more than her fair share of questions.

"Confiscated ships, shuttles, and transports."

"Wait." She gripped the edge of the counter. "You were going to steal to get us off world?"

"Adaptability is key to the success of my mission." He said the phrase more monotone than his previous answers, like he was repeating someone else's words.

That halted her questions for a while, her mind filled with fear for what would happen if she traveled with him.

When he stroked a leaf, she said, "You seem to like it in here."

There was a pause before he answered. "Yes. This section of your outpost reminds me of home."

"You have greenhouses?"

"Something similar, yes."

And that was the first thing he'd told her that made Sector Ten not sound as scary. Of course they would have plants. Every station and ship needed bio life for the people to survive, for food and fresh air. Thin layers of leafy plants were built in between decks for oxygen, and depending on the size of the ship or station, it would have dozens of hydroponics bays to feed the inhabitants. Arboretums too, along with smaller green spaces, all fed by a network of synth lights to feed the plants.

Refocusing on her plants, she continued her work, pruning dead leaves, turning the pots, and making sure they had the right amount of fertilizer and water. Beside her, Iax mimicked the process, making the work go twice as fast.

She flicked her gaze from the pot in front of her to Iax.

"How big is the habitable section of Sector Ten?"

"Very large. Many live there."

She wasn't surprised. Hundreds of people had comprised the original crew of the *Calypso,* and many more had pilgrimaged to the nebula since.

The structure of their game had evaporated, so she asked another. "How many hydroponics bays do you need for food?" Maybe that would give her a more tangible grasp of their population.

"Our food sources are not like yours, but we sustain ourselves."

She searched his face, getting the sense he didn't want to expand on the answer. *What was really hidden inside the nebula?*

Wynn didn't ask the question aloud as she set the pot in its place on the rack. They moved to a different section, these plants some of the largest in the greenhouse.

"You want to return, don't you?" she asked after fertilizing another plant.

He nodded once. "Very much."

Her fingers rested on the edge of the pot as she stared at him. Backlit by all the plants sitting in their rows, his pale skin glowed. Like he belonged among the greenery.

"What do you miss the most?" The volume of her voice had lowered, almost reverently.

His head tilted. "The noise."

Without music playing, she supposed this place was rather quiet, but if her thoughts were calm, she'd found the silence comforting.

She refocused on her plant. "What kind of noise?" Maybe she should find another spaceball game to listen to.

"Voices."

Her fingers stilled, and she lifted her head. "A bunch of chatterboxes, huh?"

His eyes softened, and her chest squeezed. "Yes."

They completed rack after rack while the snowstorm raged outside and the light dimmed. Weariness settled into her bones, telling her she needed to rest. Emotional turmoil had taken up most of life over the past days, weeks even, and her body was done with it.

But the darker it grew outside, the more nerves assaulted her.

She didn't understand why at first, until an odd panic gripped her at the thought of Iax sleeping in Foster's room again. Not because it meant invading Foster's space, but that they would separate. How had the warmth of his body beside hers become a necessity?

Her hands settled on the edge of the work surface dotted with dirt. Iax placed the last pot on the rack, then touched the button to raise it to the next level. It hummed, followed by a weighted silence.

She turned a little and found him studying her with his head tilted to the side. "Do you always sleep alone?" she blurted.

He blinked and straightened. "Yes."

She nodded, then let her head drop back. "Yeah. Me too." This was dumb. She didn't even know what she was asking, and stared at the snow accumulation on the roof of the greenhouse without really seeing it.

"Do you want to sleep alone?" His question came after several beats of silence.

Straightening, she turned. An inquisitive frown puckered his brow.

"I guess I don't." Her body flushed hot at the admission. She didn't want to be left alone with her thoughts, her memories, but it was more than that too. Her very skin yearned for closeness.

There was another beat of silence, and another. The wind howled outside the windows. She'd had to increase the temperature inside by ten degrees to protect the plants.

"You want me to sleep with you?"

A strained laugh sputtered out of her mouth at the question. "Not like *sleep*, sleep." Not that she hadn't been thinking of how he tasted, how he'd felt against her all day, but despite her body being on board with the make out session *and more*, her brain was definitely glad she'd stopped them when she had.

"But yeah," she admitted. "To actually sleep." A shaky sensation had entered her limbs at how much she really needed to rest.

His head tilted. "All right."

Tension oozed from her shoulders, and before she could re-examine any of that exchange—or second guess herself—she took his hand and led him from the greenhouse to her quarters.

The door opened with a swish. "Lights dim," she said before they could brighten to full and bombard her with common sense.

Because she definitely shouldn't be inviting a Calypson into her bed.

Wynn dropped his hand and hurried toward the wall compartment, grabbing a clean set of sleepwear. With a glance over her shoulder, she headed toward the washroom to clean the dirt from her skin, take off her PALM, and change into her sleepwear.

When she stepped out, he was in the same position as she'd left him, his eyes fixed toward her.

"You can use it now," she said, her voice tight with nerves.

He didn't move for a moment, then passed her by, the door closing quietly behind him.

Taking a deep breath, she crossed to the laundry sluice, and shoved her clothing inside. She paused beside her bed, stared at it, and wondered what the hell she was doing.

The door to the washroom opened. She tensed, then turned to find Iax stalking toward her.

"Did you want to get more comfortable?" she asked in a high-pitched voice when he stopped beside her.

His head tilted in question.

"I don't have sleepwear in your size, but you could take your shirt off if you like."

Stars above, it sounded like she was trying to get him naked. Her lower extremities thrummed, loving that thought, but the rest of her? She barely resisted the urge to cover her face with her hands.

Iax turned a little, then took hold of the hem of his shirt, pulling it over his head.

Her mouth went dry. What did Calypsons do for exercise? Because this one was *built*. Sculpted flesh spanned his chest, defined abdominals disappearing into the top of his pants. She'd felt those muscles beneath her fingers this morning, and now she wanted to both look and touch.

Shaking her head, she lifted her gaze to his face. She wouldn't suggest that he remove his pants too. From experience, she knew he wasn't wearing anything beneath, and that would open a whole other cargo container of trouble.

She gestured to his feet. "You should take off your boots, too."

His head tilted, then he sat on the edge of the bed, reaching down to pull them off. *Thump. Thump.* They settled on the floor.

She stood in front of him, gawking at this beautiful man while her heart raced. He returned her gaze, eyes glinting in the low light. Even those were alluring to her now, and she marveled that her perception of him could have changed in such a short time.

"Scoot back," she murmured, her throat tight.

His hesitation made her trust him even more.

"So I have room to lie in front of you," she qualified.

He did as she asked, keeping his eyes on her the entire time. She swallowed, then climbed onto the bed, tucking herself in front of him until her spine met his chest. He held himself stiffly, his body only touching hers in unavoidable places.

And she realized he didn't know what to do, didn't know how to cuddle.

"Like this." She reached back and grabbed his wrist, wrapping his arm beneath her breasts.

He was tense for a moment, then his body relaxed into hers.

She sighed, loving how her cheek felt against his bulging biceps, and how his chest cradled her head. How the backs of her thighs aligned with his legs, their feet a tangle. With their size difference, he cocooned her.

Since she'd never really done this before, she expected to feel claustrophobic, but her heart raced with pleasure. One more deep breath, and tension eased from her body.

Despite her restless thoughts, she drifted off to sleep.

Chapter Twenty

Iax could not stop staring. Not at the tousled hair on her head, or the gleaming softness of the skin of her shoulder and arm, or the way her chest rose and fell with each breath.

The longer he stared, the more a new emotion bloomed and solidified. It was such a curious feeling, one that was hot, but also hard and unyielding. He wanted to hold her tight, to squeeze, and to never let go. He did not understand it, but the longer they lay there together, the more it took over his mind.

His arm flexed around her, echoing his thoughts. She had given him permission to touch her, and he had not squandered the opportunity. For the forty-fifth time since assuming this position, he tucked his face into the back of her neck and inhaled deeply. The scent of her was doing things to his head, altering him. She smelled of tranquility, and he could not get enough.

He understood something was happening to him, but did not know what. His mission at the outset had been simple: travel to Earth, retrieve Dr. Wynn Lambdin, and bring her to Sector Ten by any means necessary. That last part had been the only uncertain portion, and why they had chosen him—for his unique way of adapting to any situation.

But this? The feelings Wynn evoked in him were not within his mission parameters. He felt her everywhere. Not just physically, but in other ways too. Her voice affected him. The way her eyes traveled over his body altered him. Her ever-changing emotions wrapped around him and would not let go.

His arm flexed around her again. *He* would not let her go. The stirring emotions were too addictive, too perfect, too *real* for him to do anything except hold her tight.

A slice of light pierced through the window above them, the angle cutting across Wynn's face. She twitched, then opened her eyes. Her soft, relaxed body stiffened.

"The sun," she murmured, the mellow emotions she had attained while sleeping, changing into something sharp. Then she was moving out of his arms, pushing out of the bed to face the window.

He mourned the lack of her warmth against him.

She swayed, and he was on his feet beside her in the next moment, waiting to see if she required assistance. Her eyelashes fluttered as she blinked up at the window.

"I need to see." She spun around and dashed toward the door without bothering to change her clothes. It barely had time to open fully before she was out in the hallway and racing toward the lab. Iax quickly grabbed his shirt where he'd dropped it the day before, tugged it over his head, slid on his boots, and followed.

The lab's door closed just as he stepped outside, then reopened again as he neared. Sunlight lit the entire space, making him squint against the brightness. He walked forward, his gaze fixed on the landscape. A sheen of water froze across the dirt, reflecting the sun like glass, and highlighted the melting mounds of snow that had collected overnight.

But beyond the patch of blue sky roiled more storm clouds. He considered them with a tilt of his head.

With a new device adhered to her left hand, Wynn's fingers tapped against terminals. Weather updates streamed above its surface, then an environmental diagram rose in front of her. A storm cell spread across most of New Asia, a vortex of clouds, thick and gray, giving way to a wider ring around it, heavy with torrential rain. The sun broke through the center, almost a perfect circle of clear sky.

Right above the outpost.

"It's not done," she whispered, her jaw slack as she stared out the window. "It's the eye of the storm."

Then her fingers were flying again, the readout changing to something else. He tipped his head at it.

"I've reconnected with the grid." She pulled up another menu, this one full of relays and communications. "But this won't last long." She said the words absently as she pulled more and more data from the grid. "I can..." Her voice trailed off, her gaze meeting his.

Confusion clouded her expression, but the emotions that wrapped around him were something else. *Wariness. Hesitation. Dread.*

Her throat bobbed in a swallow. "I need to contact my superiors."

She stared at him for a long moment before turning back to her terminal. Her worry grew, washing over him, then she tapped on the surface, slower than before.

He assessed the situation. If she contacted her superiors, the result might be detrimental to his end goal. Leaning forward, Iax pressed his hands flat against the terminal's surface.

A second passed, then his essence infused the systems, accessing the same files.

"What?" Her hands stopped moving, then lifted away from the terminal. "What are you doing?"

He did not answer but dove deeper into the lab's systems, accessing the communication array. She had not yet sent out a message. Should he stop her ability to do so?

The question pulled him in different directions, the ones that needed to fulfill his mission, and the ones that did not want to hurt Wynn in any capacity.

"Iax?"

His name came out of her mouth tentatively, laced with more worry.

Before he could decide which path to take, a new sensation crawled up his spine. A distant voice nearing at a quick pace.

Tipping his head, he changed his focus from the communication array to the outpost's sensors.

"Someone approaches," he said after a moment, receiving confirmation of what this unknown voice was telling him.

"What do you mean?" Her hand settled on his arm and gripped him tight. "The beasts?"

"No." He tilted his head to the side, the mind so close now he could taste it. "Someone in a ship."

As soon as he spoke the words, a cruiser buzzed above the building, shaking the roof.

"What the hell?" Wynn yelped, squeezing his arm tighter. "This is restricted airspace." She dropped his arm and tapped at the terminal. "No ships are allowed this close to the fields. The grid broadcasts warnings everywhere."

His essence entwined with the system's, he felt what she was doing, scanning the ship for the cruiser's ID and access code. There were none.

It was like the ship wasn't there at all, though they could both see it circle with their own eyes.

Wynn's volatile emotions swooped out toward where the cruiser lowered, then changed to something sourer. Worry for him.

"Who are they?" She did not need to voice another question for him to understand her meaning. *Were they here for him?*

Since the ship was closer now, he could dive deeper into the man's head.

"His name is Sawyer Knox."

Iax reached his mind and twisted around the man's thoughts and desires, around secrets and lies, to find the information he searched for.

"And he is here for you."

"What?" The word exploded out of her mouth. She turned her head until she stared at him, her hands braced against the terminal. "You can read his mind?" She inhaled quick breaths as she looked toward the ship.

The passenger door released, then slid open to reveal a slice of darkened interior.

"Yes."

She gasped and diverted her attention away from the ship to him. "Can you read my mind?" A flush brightened her cheeks.

"No."

"But you perceive something from me." It was a statement, not a question, rushed out frantically.

"Yes," he agreed. "I experience your emotions, but cannot taste your thoughts."

Confusion furrowed her brow. "Why not?"

"You are an anomaly."

A strangled sound left her just as Knox emerged from the ship dressed in a flight-suit, helmet engaged. Clad all in black, his physique muscular, he wore two large guns strapped to each of his thighs. After a brief pause to survey the icy terrain, he advanced toward the outpost.

Wynn's distress mounted, and her breaths quickened with each step Knox took toward them.

Iax did not want Wynn distressed. It hurt the empty spaces in his chest. "I will speak with him."

He turned on his heel and headed toward the decontamination room.

"Wait. What?" Wynn's breathless words bounced inside the lab, then her bare feet slapped against the floor as she followed. "Like how you spoke to the beasts?"

He stopped where his jacket lay inside the compartment and put on his glasses first. "I believe I will need to rely on verbal communication." Though he could taste the man's thoughts, Knox was not aware of his presence in his mind.

Iax slipped his jacket over his shoulders, then slid his hand upward to fasten the closures.

Wynn stared at him, her jaw slack and her body still, until he touched the control to open the inner decontamination door. Out of the corner of his eye, she snapped straight and stepped forward.

"Get back in here and put on a suit, you idiot."

The door closed on her words. They wouldn't reopen again since the second door was already opening. Sunlight spilled inside the last section of the decontamination room, illuminating the grated floor.

He did not look back as he advanced toward the last door, though he felt Wynn's emotions tumble toward him in a toxic combination of fear and dread. All the more reason to deal with Knox quickly. Iax *hated* to feel her distress.

Just as the second door closed, she shouted something else, the words muffled by the transparent aluminum. He could not stop now. Knox drew closer, and Iax had tasted the darkness of his mind.

The last door opened, and Iax stepped out into a frozen, sunny world.

Chapter Twenty-One

Everything about this place was a shithole.

Carver scanned the horizon, his helmet interface sending streams of data. The desert of cakey dirt had turned into an icy mess, each step hard and uneven. There were no trees, no rivers, nothing to make the surface of Earth anywhere he would want to spend time. Just an ugly building attached to an even uglier greenhouse, both on stilts, like even it knew better than to allow its belly to touch dying filth. A surface-to-station tether shot up in the distance, the returning storm already obscuring its slender shape.

Thick clouds swirled in a foreboding circle. He didn't have much time before he had to get out of here. He'd waited long enough to land, gauging the span it would take to retrieve the doctor and exit the atmosphere.

Movement grabbed his focus, and his hand went to his gun. His steps slowed as a person strode around the edge of the main building.

There had been nothing about a secondary target in his package, but during his short flight across the surface, his sensors had picked up a single-person pod, one that had self-destructed after landing.

The man heading toward him was definitely not Wynn Lambdin.

He was dressed in black.

He wore glasses.

He didn't have a protective suit of any kind.

His skin was vulnerable to the elements, his body exposed to lethal levels of radiation.

Everything Carver had just read on the way here, why his superiors seemed fit to load him down with terabytes of data, clicked into place.

He hadn't been told this was a rescue mission.

Carver pulled his gun and fired. His shot hit nothing but air.

He blinked, then the fucker was in front of him, delivering a punch that stole his soul. Carver flew, and so did his weapon. He landed with a *thud* and a *crack,* and his breath abandoned his lungs the moment he hit the ground.

A circle of blue sky rimmed his vision. His visor interface displayed data: wind speeds, temperature, and a helmet diagnostic after receiving the hit. It tracked the fucker as he neared at five kilometers an hour.

A shadow blocked the sun, then a tall form.

A disquieting sensation traveled over Carver's body at the fucker's perusal. He waited for another attack, his senses attuned to the other's movements.

But then the man took a step back.

Not today. Carver's hand shot out, and he engaged the shocker embedded in his PALM, its intensity level set to maximum.

The charge connected, and took the fucker down like a charm.

Carver lay there for one breath, then another before he rolled to his knees and stood, his eyes never leaving the prone form. *Shit, that hurt.* His entire body throbbed from the hit and fall.

He stared at the unconscious man. His glasses were askew, his eyes closed and jaw slack. The beginnings of radiation burns etched his cheeks a pink color.

Was he what Carver thought he was? He had short hair like a defender, and didn't look different from any other man he'd met in his life.

Not taking any chances. Carver aimed at the man's forehead and fired. Brain matter and blood sprayed across the ice, crimson on white.

The back of his neck prickled, and Carver lifted his head to peer toward the main building, a hovercart parked out front. If Dr. Lambdin hadn't been changed into a Calypson, then she was probably dead.

Unwanted dread swirled in his chest. He'd signed up for a life-or-death deadline. Hopefully, the footage of the Calypson walking on Earth without a suit would be enough of a consolation prize to keep him alive.

He glanced up at the sky. He didn't have much time before the eye of the storm passed. Might not take off and get clear of it if he wasn't quick here.

Keeping his gun in hand, he trudged toward the outpost. He left his other gun where it fell, not wanting to waste time. It was programmed to his bio-signature anyway. No one else could use it without some major re-programming.

The closer he approached the building, the less ice covered the ground, making it easier to walk.

Kerclunk. The sound made him pause, fingers twitching. Metallic shutters descended over a large section of windows, covering them completely. He squinted. Someone was alive in there. He stalked toward the steps leading to the main entrance, then climbed them two at a time.

He pressed his hand to the door's control, his PALM interacting with the outpost's systems. *Interesting.* The building was under lockdown. Someone wanted to keep him out.

Lifting his hand away, he tapped on his PALM, then pressed it against the control panel. The contact allowed him to access the outpost's security systems. Then, with a tap of his fingers, he overrode it using his universal codes.

Kerclank. The shutters retracted. The outer door to the decontamination zone opened.

With his weapon loose in his hand, Carver stepped inside. As soon as the doors closed behind him, a sheen of cleansing fluid covered his body, then trickled through the grating beneath his boots. Air swirled around him, the sound loud enough to mute everything else.

While the process continued, he scanned what he could see through the transparent doors. A basic hallway led in two directions. His eyes caught on a bundle of white on the ground, a UV-suit.

Carver turned his head slightly, toward where he'd left the body. He couldn't see it from this angle, but he now questioned whether he'd killed a Calypson or someone else. The man hadn't been armed.

Seconds ticked by, and his annoyance at the decontamination process grew. Finally, the light beside the door turned green, and the doors slid open. He stepped into the second portion of the decontamination zone.

Nothing moved on the other side of the door.

A wall compartment hissed open, waiting for him to disrobe. *Not likely.* He wouldn't step into a building without protection, especially when that fucker had come from inside.

Carver pressed his hand to the panel, circumventing the process. It took too long, but the light turned green on the panel. The interior door slid open with a hiss of pressure.

Silence throbbed in contrast to the hum and hush of the decontamination process. He touched his PALM, adjusting his view to partial infrared. He scanned left, then right.

A heat signature pulsed, a slight smudge of red against the dead materials of the building. The hunched form held a weapon. The data streaming along the bottom of his visor told him it was a long-distance rifle, an older model that was prone to malfunction.

His finger flexed on the trigger of his gun, then he checked that his autonomous shielding was set to maximum. Not that a rifle like that would do much damage.

Keeping his eyes on the person on the other side of the wall, he touched the controls on his weapon, changing the setting to stun. His orders hadn't altered since he'd received them. He was supposed to bring them the doctor alive.

The door on his left opened automatically when he approached, revealing a lab. Carver stopped out of the line of sight, and scanned everything he could see from his position: wide windows revealing the sunny landscape beyond, and a bank of terminals, their shiny black surfaces reflecting the light.

He refocused on the person, noting her feminine curves within the scope of the thermal imaging. Her slight form shook, the weapon jiggling in her hand. She stood with her back to the wall, her head moving back and forth between his location and an exit on the other side of the room.

Her behavior was the opposite of the fucker outside.

With a flick of his finger against his PALM, Carver adjusted his helmet settings so she could hear him.

"Doctor Wynn Lambdin?"

Her body stilled, her focus returning to his position. She raised the weapon a little higher, her head tilting to aim over the sight, but her arms shook.

"Who's there?" Her words were tight, like she was being strangled.

"Your escort. I have orders to take you off world." He stepped forward, just enough for her to see him, but kept his gun tucked behind his thigh. "Lower your weapon."

She appeared to have her wits about her, fully human, exhibiting none of the characteristics that he'd seen in the files he'd reviewed on the journey here.

That made things easier.

She wore skimpy undergarments, a pair of white shorts and a top held up by thin straps. Tears tracked down her cheeks, her expression twisted with fear and anguish.

Despite the gun in her hand, Dr. Wynn Lambdin was not a threat. The fear on her face—that was real. No one could fake that.

What had the bastard done to put that fear there?

And he shouldn't give a fuck. He had a mission to complete—take her to General Cazin on the *Corvus*. Carver had staked his life on it.

"Doctor Wynn Lambdin," he repeated, though he knew it was her. Except for the puffy eyes, blotchy skin, and lack of clothing, she looked the same as her picture in her personnel file and the newsreels he'd watched. "ID confirmation required," he ordered.

She stiffened, then her throat bobbed in a swallow. "Four seven one six two four." The words sounded automatic, pulled out of her from years of working with the CORE government.

Confirmation materialized on his interface, along with the same picture from before.

"Put the weapon down."

Eyes wide and red, she stared at him, unwavering, and for a second it felt like she could see right through his tinted visor, though he knew it was impossible. Then she turned her head, her focus shifting to the outside world.

He followed her line of sight. The wall of black clouds swelled toward them, and with it a thick belt of blowing snow. They needed to get out of here before it hit.

Her shoulders settled with a deep inhale. Then she refocused on him, raised the rifle, and aimed at his head. "No."

Disbelief ricocheted through him, and he had the urge to laugh. No one ever told him no. They begged for their lives; they died before he even knew he was there; they shat themselves in fear. But they never told him *no*.

He filtered through the information he'd received, what he'd expected to find at this outpost, and how he'd misjudged the situation.

Dr. Lambdin didn't want to be saved.

He stepped forward, and she twitched. "I've been ordered to take you off planet," he said, his tone heavy with order. "Gear up."

She shook her head. "I'm not going anywhere with you," she gritted, her jaw tight and her fingers flexing on the rifle. "You can't make me."

"Oh! I see," he said, keeping his tone light. "Not a problem."

Her brow furrowed, and the rifle wavered.

Then he was moving, firing his gun before she could get a shot off. It hit her square in the chest. Her eyes widened a moment, then she dropped to the floor like he'd turned off the gravity.

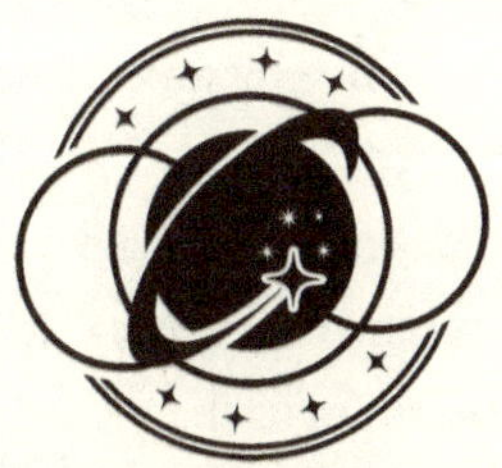

Chapter Twenty-Two

A thick wedge dug into Wynn's stomach, and the need to vomit crawled up her throat. *Omph. Omph. Omph.* The repetitive movement made each motion worse than the last. Blood rushed to her head.

Wynn groaned, trying to get away from the pain, when something tightened around her legs. She stiffened. *Where the hell am I?*

Sunlight pierced the visor of her helmet when she forced her eyes open, adding to the ache in her head. She was upside down, and the way the world spun brown, white, and blue around her made the contents of her stomach surge.

Visor? She wore a UV-suit, but didn't remember putting it on.

Omph. Omph. Omph. The movement and pain continued. *I'm being carried.*

The man who wore a flight-suit.

His shoulder dug into her stomach with every step. His name eluded her for a moment, but then she remembered what Iax had told her.

Iax! Her struggles increased, her body thrashing. She searched for him on the horizon, her skin breaking out in a cold sweat.

He'd killed Iax. She'd watched the entire thing, stood frozen in horror, screamed when Sawyer shot him in the head. He hadn't even hesitated. Iax had been unconscious, defenseless, and this man had shot him point-blank.

He hadn't needed to do it. Profound sadness and rage shimmered through her body, her limbs shaking.

Evil. Evil. Evil.

She squirmed again, using her hands to push against his back and helmet, trying to break his hold.

"Settle down, or I'll do more than stun you." His voice came through her helmet interface, right into her ear.

The threat dried the moisture in her throat. She couldn't get the sight of spraying blood out of her mind, couldn't get a grip on the spiraling world around her. It morphed with her memories of Foster's death, becoming one grotesque scene of red and white and teeth and terror.

Pressing her lips together, she stifled the sob bubbling up her throat.

Sawyer Knox wasn't a defender. His flight-suit was all black instead of their silver and white uniform, and she hadn't been able to see his face through the visor of his helmet. He'd appeared more inhuman than Iax.

Where was he taking her? She swallowed against twisting fear.

The sun beamed through the empty space between the clouds, highlighting the icy, wet ground. A bulky black mound contrasted with the melting snow, catching her eye. She stilled. *Iax.* A sob burst from her lips.

He'd been living and breathing not an hour ago.

Sawyer's arm tightened painfully around her legs. "What is he to you?" The helmet's interface warped his voice, giving it a mechanical quality.

She didn't have an answer.

Each painful step brought them closer to the cruiser. A knot of nausea reformed in the pit of her battered stomach. She couldn't stop staring at where Iax lay, while pressure built in her chest. Sawyer hadn't needed to kill him, no matter what his orders were. Iax hadn't carried a weapon.

The black mound twitched. Her breath caught in her throat.

He's moving. He's alive.

Those two sentences formed a mantra in her head, her heart beating so hard it felt like it would burst from her chest. She didn't look away from where Iax lay, afraid she had imagined it.

But no, he rolled to his side, revealing the spray of blood beneath him.

Her ribs tightened painfully. Wynn turned away and saw they were way too close to Sawyer's ship. The door slid open at their approach.

It felt imperative that she didn't get on that cruiser, but if Iax might have a chance at getting away, then the man carrying her couldn't know he survived. She forced her body to slump even though his shoulder dug into her more.

The sound of the wind diminished as he pushed her through the door. Wynn's legs gave out, and she found a bench beneath her ass, stopping her fall.

The instinct to escape fell upon her, and she pushed herself up on wobbling feet. She hadn't taken one step toward the door when a hand pressed beneath the edge of her helmet, closing around her throat.

"Do you want to get stunned again?" His harsh question stabbed her between her ears.

Automatically, her hands pulled at his, trying to gain space to breathe properly, but he held her too tight. The door closed behind him, blocking out the sunlight. A haze shimmered around her vision, then stars sparkled and disappeared in flashes.

I'm going to pass out. Blackness crept in little by little. *He's going to kill me.*

His fingers tightened for a moment, then he gave her a small shake and let go. Wynn collapsed on the bench, gasping for breath, and rubbed at the pain lingering in her neck.

By the stars, this guy was a fucking asshole. Worse even. She just couldn't think of a better insult.

As her vision cleared, the cruiser's details came into view. From the outside, it had looked like a regular cruiser, something someone could rent if they had enough creds. Inside told a different story. It was sleek enough to transport the Chancellor himself. Plush upholstery, shiny terminals, lush carpet from bulkhead to bulkhead—it all spoke of an out-of-reach wealth.

She turned her head, refocusing on where Sawyer had gone. He sat in front of the main terminal, with an empty seat beside him. The viewer showed familiar terrain stretching as far as the eye could see, those ominous clouds advancing so quickly that she couldn't see the tether in the distance.

But Iax was out there, and he wasn't dead.

Two desires warred within her, one that wanted to protect Iax, the other for her to escape. She bent her head, desperation giving way to hopelessness. How was she supposed to get out of this? Did this man's arrival have something to do with Iax? The timing couldn't have been a coincidence.

She thought of those blood tests in her data banks and would have given almost anything to erase them—to erase everything that had happened over the past few days to protect both her and Iax.

Wynn wrapped her arms around herself and breathed through the dread in her chest and the pain in her throat. The air in her UV-suit tasted stale and dead despite the readout saying it was normal. She couldn't take a proper breath, wanted to retract her helmet, but since he hadn't removed his, neither did she.

The sound of the ship powering up hummed around her. Wynn's heart raced, panicked breaths slipping between her lips.

"Where are you taking me?" Her voice didn't sound right.

"Buckle up," was the only thing Sawyer said.

The ship hovered before she could follow the order. Wynn lurched to the right, bracing her hand against the bulkhead. The angle of the ship changed sharply before the momentum stopped.

"No fucking way."

Sawyer's stunned statement dragged Wynn's attention to the front viewer.

It was Iax. Standing in front of her outpost. And he held a weapon in his hand, the muzzle pointed at the ground.

Vision blurring, she braced a hand on the bulkhead beside her to stay upright while her heart surged with joy. She *hadn't* imagined him moving out there. Somehow he'd survived a shot to the head. She couldn't believe it.

Her heart thumped hard in her chest, and she swayed. He'd been outside too long. He needed radiation medicine, regeneration gauze, and whatever she could do for his head injury.

The stillness that had gripped the interior of the cruiser broke when Iax lifted the weapon.

"Motherfucker." Sawyer spat the word, his hand accessing the tactical display on the control panel.

A sound hummed from all around her, weapons charging.

Wynn's vision darkened. "No!" she screamed and dove forward.

His elbow shot out, connecting with her tender stomach. *Oof.* Her body snapped backward, all the air leaving her lungs. She stumbled back, then fell on her ass, gasping for breath.

Two shots pulsed from the ship. *Divvd. Divvd.*

"No," she shouted again, lurching to her feet, using the bulkhead for balance.

"Shit," her escort growled, then fired again. *Divvd divvd divvd.*

Her eyes froze on the viewer. It seemed impossible, but Iax dodged out of the line of fire. The shots hit her outpost, first near the entrance, then their quarters, turning it into a smoking pile of rubble. Her stomach swooped, then rose in her throat.

But Iax was running, still alive.

He spun abruptly. A shot pulsed from Sawyer's discarded weapon.

Tuvvd. It hit the hull, and the ship listed to the left. Wynn braced her hand against the bulkhead. It wasn't enough to keep her balance. The world upended, and she fell to the side and rolled. She didn't know which way was up. She braced herself against the deck when her gaze landed on the main terminal at the front of the ship.

The control panel glowed red with warnings. Lights flashed.

"Shit. Shit. Shit."

Sawyer righted them, then tracked toward where Iax stood in front of the greenhouse, the ship's engines purring as it tilted.

Another weapons lock, and weapons surged. *Divvd. Divvd. Divvd. Divvd.*

He fired continuously. She couldn't see Iax within the torrent, but her greenhouse shattered into a million pieces. Shards, and green, and metal, and dirt.

"Stop!" she screamed. "Please stop!" She dove at Sawyer again.

His hand shot out and landed dead center on her chest. Wynn struggled, trying to free herself from his grip, then her entire body shook. Her vision hazed to black.

He'd used a shocker on her. She wondered why it surprised her.

Out of the corner of her eye, the ship tilted, and so did her world.

Then her vision blackened to nothing.

Chapter Twenty-Three

The doctor's limp body dropped to the floor. He hadn't killed her, didn't have orders to do so *yet*, but he didn't have time to check her vitals to see if the two stuns and falls had done any permanent damage.

Carver had bigger things to worry about.

Somehow, with only one shot, that motherfucker had disabled key systems. He shouldn't have even been able to punch through his shields, but his ship didn't seem to know that. He shouldn't have been able to fire his bio-coded weapon at all.

The cruiser whined in distress, as shrill as the doctor's screams had been moments ago. The ship lurched, something wrong with the altitude controls. It wouldn't allow him to ascend any higher than what they already flew. The terrain tipped at an angle as he tried to level out the ship.

The outpost lay in a smoldering mess of metal composite and broken computer terminals. Greenery and transparent aluminum stuck out at odd angles where the greenhouse once stood, the plants now exposed to the elements.

He couldn't see the Calypson fucker anymore. If he'd somehow eluded an entire barrage of weapons, then this planet—hell, the entire system—was in serious shit.

Carver's scans showed heat patches where the building burned, but besides the smoldering innards, nothing else moved. He didn't trust the scans. He'd shot the guy in the head, and he'd somehow survived.

For good measure, Carver cracked off a few more shots, leveling any area that stood higher than a meter. Then he waited again.

While he continued to scan, Carver ran diagnostics, trying to figure out what the fucker hit to unbalance his ship. A readout scrolled across his PALM and helmet's interface, each detail worse than the last. But the last item on the list was the most tragic. The ship was no longer space-worthy.

"Fuck!" He smashed his hand on the controls.

There was no way he could fix all the issues on his own, not when the clock on his orders kept on ticking. And he couldn't wait for help with that storm about to blanket this entire region for days.

His eyes jumped to the tether in the distance. The clouds and snow almost obscured it completely, but it was there, connecting the research community to the orbiting station. Unless another ship materialized in the next minute, it might be their only option to get off world.

He returned his attention to the destroyed building, scanning and waiting. When nothing moved but flames, he tapped the controls, and accelerated away from the destroyed outpost, heading straight toward the tether.

The sun disappeared the farther they traveled from the wreckage. The wind picked up, battering against the hull of the ship. Then the snow started. It coated the ground in a layer of white, hiding the ice that had formed across its barren surface. Nothing during his time here had changed his views on this waste of a rock.

Would the terabytes of data he'd downloaded for this mission tell him what was really going on here? His superiors hadn't told him he would encounter a hostile. Maybe they hadn't known, but instead of giving him a heads-up on their suspicions, they'd thrown him headfirst into something that could have ended him.

Agitation skittered across his skin. He didn't like being jerked around.

Kilometers disappeared as they neared the research station. Lights glowed, speckling the landscape in tiny life-saving beacons—something to aim for in this cloud-drenched world. Then buildings dotted the horizon, squat and on stilts like the doctor's outpost. The tether solidified, a straight line dividing the snowy sky in two.

He glanced over at the doctor and noted she hadn't budged. *Good.* She'd regained consciousness too quickly after being stunned the first time.

Focusing forward, he circled the outer buildings. The research station itself spread in a massive compound to the north of the port with interconnected labs, housing quarters, and greenhouses—larger versions of the doctor's single outpost. Heat signatures dotted the inside of the buildings.

He aimed the cruiser at the tether port and landed in an open space beside it. *Thunk.* He hit the ground a little too hard, his descent ruined by the cruiser's malfunctioning systems. He powered down, locking key systems as he did so. The viewer deactivated, revealing the strip of transparent aluminum that served as a window. Snow splattered against it, distorting his view of the tether.

Carver pushed out of his seat, stepped over the doctor, and headed to his bedroom at the back of his ship. The door slid open, revealing his pristine space. Before he could dwell on leaving everything behind, he opened the first tall compartment with a swipe of his PALM and grabbed a hard-sided case, his go-bag.

The door closed behind him, and he approached the doctor. Her chest rose and fell in even breaths. He squatted down, giving her body a quick scan. Vitals appeared on his visor. She was a little battered, but alive, and that was all that mattered at the moment.

He scooped one arm under her legs, the other under her back and stood, hefting her over his right shoulder. A step toward the door, and he slapped the controls with his PALM. Wind slammed into them as soon as the door opened. One slice of sunlight lit up a portion of the landscape in the distance, but disappeared in the next gust of snow.

Keeping the doctor balanced on his shoulder, Carver jumped down to the icy ground. He touched his PALM, sealing the door tight, then modified the security measures to the highest possible settings. He hated to abandon his ship, but it would be here when he was done with this assignment.

Carver turned, adjusted his footing, and set off toward the tether port's entrance. He kept his free hand next to his weapon as he neared the hexagonal building. A passageway connected it to the research station on the opposite side.

A red light flashed above the double-wide door, and realization dawned. "Motherfucker." The tether cabin was at the top, parked at the orbital station, and he needed to recall it before they could leave.

More wasted time.

The minutes were ticking down on his deadline, and every second mattered when his life was at stake.

The sound of his footsteps changed as he stepped onto the platform that spanned the port's doors. Keeping the doctor over his shoulder, he pressed his PALM against the control panel and overrode the system.

It took a minute, but the doors released with a hiss, opening up into a decontamination zone. Transparent inner doors revealed a narrow corridor that encircled the space where the tether vehicle would settle when it arrived.

He strode inside. The doctor twitched, then groaned. Carver hefted her weight forward, setting her on her feet against the wall by the control panel. Her knees buckled, and he pressed a hand against her sternum to keep her upright. She slumped forward, her body weight pressed into him, her head lolling to the side.

When he was sure she wouldn't fall down, he touched the control to recall the tether cabin. The port hummed, and numbers appeared on the panel, counting down the minutes until the tether would make it to Earth.

The doctor jolted, then straightened, her head moving back and forth. Her hand shot out to brace against the wall. She remained that way, frozen, then turned toward him.

Her gaze landed on him through the visor of her helmet.

He'd thought her eyes sad when he'd first seen her profile image in his files. Now they burned, hot emotion aimed right at him. Her chest rose and fell in quick breaths. Her gloved hands clenched and released. They stood that way, the control panel counting down in his peripheral vision, until his visor beeped with a contact.

Someone approached the research station. He turned to face the outside world. No, more than one—something from the east and something from the west. He looked toward the west, where they'd come from, and gritted his teeth. A vehicle approached at a slow pace. *A hovercart.*

"Son of a bitch." It was the same hovercart that had been parked in front of the doctor's outpost.

He dropped his go-bag beside the doctor, knelt, and unlocked it with his bio-signature. The largest of his guns lay on top, and he yanked it out, checked the settings, then shut the case with a loud *snap.*

"Move and I'll shoot you," he said before standing and striding through the open door.

He stepped out into the blowing snow. The intensity had increased since they'd arrived. Wind slapped against his body, so fierce he swayed with it. A thick coating covered his cruiser on the right, and he couldn't see more than a few meters beyond that.

But his visor kept sending data, able to scan more than he could. The target to the west—no, it was two targets—advanced at almost the same pace as the hovercart.

His sensors also told him the doctor hadn't listened to his last order. He turned and fired a warning shot. *Pop.* It connected to the platform in front of her feet, melting the metal composite in a circle. She'd been reaching for his go-bag, but his warning shot froze her movements.

"The next one will take your head off."

It would really piss him off if she didn't listen. This day was going from bad to worse, and taking the time to alter all his recordings to justify her death would delay his schedule.

Snow obscured the hovercart, but it slowed as it neared. The other two targets kept their speed, while the fucker stopped the cart just out of sight. He hopped out, well and whole.

"Unfucking believable," Carver muttered.

Then the Calypson faced where the other two targets advanced, his arms lifted slightly away from his body. Through Carver's infrared, they looked like animals, and all the articles he'd watched and read on his journey resurfaced. Those mutated canines, the ones that had killed a scientist, were they about to attack the Calypson?

But they skidded to a stop before they pounced.

"What are you staring at?" The doctor whispered her question, her tone fearful.

Good. She should be terrified of him. It would keep her compliant.

Carver's blood curdled as all three forms turned toward him in unison. Was the fucker controlling the animals? It sure as hell looked like it. He lifted his weapon and aimed over the barrel.

Dark shadows solidified into sharper forms as the trio emerged from the snow, a canine on either side of the Calypson.

Behind him, the doctor gasped.

The closer the fucker walked, the clearer the damage to his head became: cheekbone, flesh and muscle. Beneath the disfigurement, the calm Carver had observed on his face during their first encounter was now replaced with twisting rage. *So the fucker could feel.* Then Carver would do his best to facilitate his descent into anguish.

He fired at the beast on the left a half second before firing at the one on the right. Then he aimed dead center of the group. *Pop. Pop. Pop.* A trio of shots pulsed toward them. The first connected with the animal's shoulder, sending it flying backward. The second animal dodged, the shot disappearing into the snow, sizzling through the moisture as it traveled.

Carver didn't see if the third shot connected, because the animal veered and charged.

A strangled sound, a warning, emerged from the doctor's comm connection in his helmet. He had no time to think about it because the canine barreled toward him.

Pop pop pop. Three shots hit the animal's center mass. Muscle and tissue flew, but the beast didn't stop, leaping toward his throat with a snarl. Carver used its momentum, ducking, then jamming his gun into the animal's belly. *Pop pop.* The bulky, bleeding mass flew over his head. He rolled, following it over, and fired again, aiming for its head.

The shots obliterated its face and skull, halting its progress. It skidded to a stop in the snow, leaving an arc of red behind it.

Gulping breaths ricocheted inside his helmet, the sound of the doctor's panic filling his head through their helmets' interface.

Carver turned. The Calypson stood directly in front of him, his eyes glinting silver, confirming all of Carver's suspicions. He'd moved fast earlier too—too fast to clock. That rage remained, and it intensified when the Calypson's gaze flicked to the doctor behind him for the briefest of seconds.

Carver reacted on instinct. *Smack.* He punched him in the gut, then followed through with a roundhouse kick to his head. *Thud.* The Calypson bent with the force, but otherwise kept his feet. When he straightened, his expression darkened further. Carver swung his weapon, intent on taking his head off like it was a club, but the fucker grabbed the muzzle in one hand and crushed it like it was made of bio-matter instead of metal composite.

Fuuuuuuuuck. The human race was in serious trouble.

Carver reached for the gun strapped to his thigh and yanked. The Calypson slapped it away before he could fire a shot. It skidded to a stop in the snow.

His fist slammed upward in the next instant, connecting with the fucker's jaw. He received a jab to the shoulder for his trouble. Every punch and kick resulted in an equally intense block. It felt like the Calypson knew what he was going to do before he did it.

Purposefully, Carver emptied his mind.

A low growl vibrated from his right. He turned in time to see the animal leap. Carver dropped to the ground, then rolled until he reconnected with his gun. He rotated onto his back and fired.

The shots caught the animal in the chest, and it howled before twisting out of the line of fire. Carver kept shooting in an arc, aiming for the Calypson who hadn't gone far. Two headshots, and the fucker dropped to the ground. *Thud.*

Everything went silent except for the wind. Carver lay there for a second, catching his breath and listening. The second animal had run off somewhere, but he couldn't hear it. *Off to lick its wounds.*

He kind of felt like he needed to do the same. Carver hadn't had his ass handed to him in a while.

The thought got him moving. He rolled to his knees and stood, his gun loose in his hand. The Calypson lay motionless where he had fallen.

A loud hum made him look up at the tether. The cabin descended, then slowed as it neared the port. He watched for a minute, marveling at its slick construction, then it disappeared inside the structure. *Kerclunk.* The sound echoed as the cabin attached.

He peeled his eyes away and focused on the body. He'd given the Calypson another two headshots, but Carver wasn't taking any chances. Hell, if he had the time, he would decapitate the fucker.

"Shithead," he muttered, stepping closer. *Pop.* He gave him a third shot to his face.

A swallowed scream penetrated his eardrum. He turned his head and looked toward the doctor while he repeated the process. *Pop. Pop.* This time he aimed for the fucker's chest.

Carver tipped his chin when he realized she was trying to get into his go-bag again.

Straightening, he strode toward the port while adjusting the settings on his gun.

"Bad doctor," he muttered as he stepped inside the decontamination zone.

He aimed and fired. The blast stunned her for the third time, and she dropped to the ground as the door sealed behind him. A fine mist covered his body.

Fuck, he would be glad when he was off this doomed planet.

Chapter Twenty-Four

With only one eye working, Iax watched the tether cabin disappear into the clouds as he lay on the hard, frozen earth. And with it, something in his chest fractured, a physical hurt worse than the ones on the outside of his body.

Hot emotions spread through him in contrast, and a burning need climbed his throat. Sawyer Knox had taken Wynn against her will. She had not wanted to go with him, but he took her anyway. Sitting in the entrance to the tether port, she had been listless, harmed. Then Knox had stunned her with his weapon before leaving.

The heat inside Iax grew. He did not know the name of this emotion, but it flamed through him, aiding in the healing process. It fueled his determination, his extremities twitching.

A dim consciousness pulled at his own. Iax could not turn his head, but knew it was an animal, its life force leaking from its body. The other had retreated, though Iax did not know where.

And the tether vehicle continued its path upward, Knox stealing Wynn away from her home. From *him.*

That hot emotion took hold of his throat and squeezed. He searched deep inside himself, as deep as the analysis had searched Wynn's blood. There was so much there working, healing at the cellular level, but there was also so much damage. He had not yet fully healed when Knox attacked a second time. Now, his body paid the price.

Each layer of repaired tissue stung more than the last. The radiation thrumming through his body and the snow settling on his exposed skin did not help. Beneath it all, that burning need grew brighter, demanding he heal faster.

Seconds ticked by, then extended into minutes. Progress allowed him to first move a finger, then a hand, then an arm.

At last he could shift his weight, brace his elbow against the icy ground and lean upward. A groan ripped from between his lips as his newly reconstructed muscles shifted and strained. He curved forward, sitting up fully. A large hole gaped across his chest, exposing skin, muscle, and bone. He watched as his essence repaired the damage one cell at a time.

Iax braced a hand against the ground and pushed himself up to his knees. The blast had burned away most of his clothing. What remained stuck to his skin. Another moan rippled through him as he balanced one foot beneath him, then the other.

Snow swirled around him in a gust. Determining he would stay upright, he stared toward where the animal lay dying. Its consciousness trickled out of him, his thoughts focused on where the other of its kind had gone. Iax turned his head, seeing the heat signature disappear in the snow.

Their existence... there was something happening on Earth that The Four would want to learn. The animals' thoughts were disjointed and unclear, but the beasts wanted him to find something on this world, an important place.

Before he reached the animal, a final shudder convulsed through its body. The animal's consciousness faded to nothing, leaving Iax alone in this world.

A hollow pain formed in his chest, different from the injury Knox had given him. The sensation pulled at Iax in places he had not known existed until he met Wynn. He tore his gaze away from the corpse to stare at the tether reaching toward space, obscured by clouds and blowing snow.

What connection did these animals have to her? Why had they been so intent on her outpost?

Determined to find out the truth, he turned his attention to the ship Knox had left behind.

Iax took a step, then another, displacing snow. Ice crunched beneath his boots. He stumbled, barely catching himself before he fell, then pushed forward, keeping the sleek ship within his focus. It bobbed and tilted on the horizon with each stride. Snow pelted against his face, abusing his healing skin.

His last few strides stumbled, and he lurched, his body slamming into the side of the ship. Fresh pain exploded through his chest and head. He waited until the stars cleared from his vision, then pressed his hand against the access panel.

It did not open.

Keeping his hand flat against the surface, Iax closed his eyes, and allowed a portion of his essence to infuse the ship's molecular structure. He passed the outer layer of protection and breached the inner workings of the control panel inside. It released with a hiss, then slid sideways to reveal a dry interior.

Iax leaned heavily against the exterior of the ship to guide himself inside. The door sealed behind him. Protected from the elements and radiation, his body experienced immediate relief, the continued healing of his cells accelerating.

He stumbled past a bench to the front of the ship and slapped both hands against the main terminal. What essence he could spare surged inside, investigating, reporting, fixing. The one blast he had delivered earlier had damaged more than he would have liked, but he had not wanted Knox to take Wynn off world.

Concentrating, he sent his essence to fix the damage, then turned his attention to the rear of the ship. Beyond a small kitchen space equipped with a dispensary, a door sealed off the back section. He advanced toward it with a steadier gait. It slid open on his approach.

A wide bed fitted with black sheeting took up the central section. One more door was behind that, then wall compartments encircled the room. Iax stopped in front of the first section and touched the panel. The door slid open to reveal hanging garments in different shades. He stepped to the next one and opened it. This one had more of the same, but with different designs.

Iax tilted his head, recognizing some uniforms from his preparations before traveling to this planet.

The next section held flight-suits similar to the one the man had worn, and other suits in the same style as Wynn's outerwear. Iax now understood the benefit of wearing such a suit in this climate.

He left everything as he had found it and touched the control for the slender door at the rear of the room. It slid open, revealing a washroom and toilet, similar to the ones in Wynn's home.

An emotion surged through his chest, one he could not name, but hazed his vision with red. Knox had destroyed her home, everything she cared about, and the things that had brought her joy. She had felt so fondly and strongly about her place of work, and it had connected her to her deceased colleague as well.

Knox had leveled it like it meant nothing.

A new need rose in Iax, the urge to end Knox's existence because of what he had done, but repairing the ship would take time. Iax clenched his fists and stepped inside the small space, allowing the red clouding his vision to ebb into determination. He stripped. The washroom housed decontamination buffers and would cleanse him of radiation and other contaminants.

Once finished, he stepped out of the small room and paused in front of the compartment filled with protection suits. He grabbed a black one identical to what Knox had worn. He slid it up the newly healed skin of his legs and chest, then over his shoulders. By the time he secured the flight-suit at his throat, and engaged the helmet, his body was almost fully healed. He finished by securing new boots to his feet, the size slightly snug.

Exiting the sleeping quarters, he strode toward the front of the ship and pressed his hands against the main terminal. He infused more of his essence into the ship to help with repairs. The cruiser was not space-worthy yet. It would not be a good idea to attempt leaving the atmosphere, only to implode before reaching the cold of space.

The urgency within him grew. He needed to get to Wynn.

Iax settled in the pilot's seat and initiated flight controls. The ship might not be space-worthy, but it could fly. The engine activated, and the ship hovered a moment later. He adjusted his eyes and found a fading heat trail for the last animal, the imprints of its paws quickly disappearing in the cold.

Snow assaulted the outside of the ship, obscuring the viewer's readout. Most of the terrain was flat, but a visual scan revealed a mountain range in the distance.

He kept the ship low to the ground, avoiding the worst of the wind. Kilometers sped by, then the trail stopped abruptly at a rock face, almost as though it went inside.

Iax circled once to make sure the heat signature did not resume at an alternate location, then lowered the ship near where the trail ended. He powered down the engine, but left a portion of his essence to continue repairs.

With the touch of a button, he engaged the flight-suit's helmet, then stood to access the door. As soon as it opened, wind and snow knocked against him. He pushed against it to jump onto the frozen soil, then sealed the door with a thought.

He walked toward where the animal's heat signature abruptly ended. Confusion set in until Iax refocused his eyes, probing deeper. A void existed beneath him, the construction long and deep. It looked to have been there for some time.

Shifting his weight, he crouched, took off a glove, and placed his bare hand against the ice and snow. Essence exited through his fingertips to infuse the ground. It surged downward, searching for weaknesses in the design or technology he could exploit. He found it amongst wires and metal, traveled even farther into the construction, and accessed a terminal running on emergency power.

The ground shifted, then a dull *bang* resounded, vibrating against his boots. The circular platform beneath him lowered into the structure. Donning his glove, he stood and surveyed this new world through the cylindrical tube surrounding him.

It was a utilitarian room, full of compartments. Another circular platform sat a few meters away, like the one he stood upon. Above him, an identical piece of earth slid into place, sealing the room from the elements.

The platform stopped, and a decontamination process started. Since part of his essence was already within the system, Iax stopped it with a thought, and opened the cylinder to step off the platform. Silence greeted him.

He extended his mind outward, searching for life, but came up empty. He was alone.

He advanced toward the central door and opened it with a command of his mind. The technology in this place was flawed, low on power, and every mechanism needed encouragement from his essence to complete its given function.

A long corridor extended in two directions. He glanced left, then strode to the right, following a lingering heat signature. He passed by many lab spaces equipped for different tasks.

His feet slowed when one door remained ajar, something blocking it. He analyzed the scene and realized it was a hand—a detached hand. He stopped in front of the door and looked inside. It was another lab, this one filled with equipment covered in dried blood. Streaks of it coated the floor.

Leaving the severed hand behind, he kept walking until he reached the last lab at the end of the corridor. He opened the door with his mind and stepped inside.

This lab was bigger and contained dismembered body parts—most unrecognizable. He stepped over a piece of a leg, then a piece of... something else, and stopped in front of the main terminal. Leaning forward, he took off his gloves and pressed his palms flat against its surface.

The panel brightened as he infused his essence inside, a smaller amount than if he had not been repairing Knox's ship. He accessed key systems, memory banks, and project details. Files upon files opened up to his mind, a chronological map of all the research and experiments the people in this hidden bunker studied and analyzed, everything centering on creating viable life on this planet—an unsanctioned counterpart to Wynn's purpose here.

One word kept repeating within the data: Strata.

A distant memory tickled the back of his mind. It originated with a person who had traveled to Sector Ten and coalesced with his kind. But the idea did not fully form, and Iax could not access others' knowledge to confirm the memory. But The Four would be very interested to learn what was happening here.

These people were taking creation into their own hands in a much more drastic way than Wynn's work.

Another name surfaced, one he recognized from his perusal of Wynn's systems: Dr. Foster Kish.

He was the one she thought of with tears in her eyes, the one who had died before Iax arrived. A slithering sensation trickled through his chest, one he set aside in order to probe deeper into the data banks. The Four would not be the only ones interested in this information. Wynn would also want to know of her colleague's involvement.

Iax sank his essence deeper into the programming, recording details in his mind to revisit later, when a sound caught his attention. He recalled his essence into himself, then turned, alert. A double-wide door led off into another large space. He strode toward it, signaling for the door to open. Once wide enough, he stepped through.

Cages stacked three high lined the narrow room, most of them empty. A few had prone forms lying inside, animals like the others he had conversed with, all dead.

Except for the one lying outside a cage at the far end. Her weak life force pulsed in a slowing rhythm. Iax advanced toward her, between the stacked cages. The animal blinked at him, her eyes glassy as he stopped and crouched. She jerked her head, and her eyes glinted. After digesting the data banks of this place, he was no longer surprised by their shared trait.

Deep pain racked her body, both physical and from the loss of her mate, the one locked in the cage in front of her.

He took off his glove and reached to touch her jaw. *What happened here?*

The animal responded with images and surges of emotions—impressions steeped in pain, and horror, and blood.

He could not fix the past, nor help the other animal, but he could help heal her.

Focusing, he sent his essence inside her, but she protested. Confused, he halted the process and waited. Images bombarded his mind. She did not want to live without her mate, and she would not leave her mate's corpse behind to escape this place.

Iax's mind turned to Wynn. He would not leave her either. Everything inside him told him to hurry, to find her, and to keep her from harm. This ran parallel to the animal's emotions, though primitive.

But he had a word for it now. *Mate.*

Such a unique concept compared to what he had known since arriving in Sector Ten. Most of his kind did not burden themselves with monogamous relationships, though some did, like two of The Four.

But the animal was in agony. He could not leave her this way. Instead of healing her broken and battered body, with permission he sent his essence to her heart and stopped it.

Those glassy eyes clouded, the light inside them going out a moment later.

A waste. These creatures did not deserve the pain they had been born into. They did not deserve to be treated as commodities instead of living things.

Iax recalled his essence into himself. With her body cooling, it was a similar experience to retracting his essence from a terminal. Once the process was complete, he pulled his glove back on and stood.

That hot emotion resurged inside him. He took in his surroundings with a more discerning glance than he had upon arriving now that he had seen it through the animal's eyes. All the warnings The Four had given him before his journey came to the forefront of his mind. Humans carried the capacity to do much harm. They were selfish in their search for power and pleasure. They hurt others for their own gain.

Nothing Iax had seen so far disputed that.

Except Wynn. She was the only deserving one, and he would not leave her to her fate.

A venomous sensation boiled in the pit of his stomach and continued to grow the longer he stared at the dead animals. Iax spun on his heel and returned the way he had come. The ship he had left above needed more of his essence to finish repairs, to be space-worthy once more.

Sawyer Knox should not have touched Wynn without her permission.

Chapter Twenty-Five

The kilometers disappeared beneath his feet, Earth's surface now hidden by clouds. It would take a while to get to the orbital station. Carver tapped on the controls, urging the cabin to go faster, but they were already at max speed, and he couldn't override it with his universal commands.

And every second that ticked by brought him closer to when he should reconnect with the grid.

Bracing his hands against the terminal, he hung his head and took a deep breath. His last minutes on that fucking planet kept playing through his head.

He'd been fighting a Calypson. After seeing the fucker's eyes glow, after he'd come back to life twice, there was no doubt what he was.

Had he killed him for certain? The agitated sensation crawling up the back of Carver's neck told him not to assume so.

There was more going on here than he understood. Usually, he didn't care about that kind of shit. He'd get his orders, complete his task, and move on to the next one.

But for this job? All he had were questions.

What was a Calypson doing on Earth?

Why hadn't they warned him? He would have come more prepared—with a pulse cannon and laser saw.

Why Wynn Lambdin? What did she have to do with anything? Why did the Calypson have an interest in her?

And what the fuck were those beasts? He'd seen reports of them, but up close? They shouldn't exist. The mere sight of them made his skin crawl with *wrongness*.

And the fucking Calypson had controlled them somehow.

Carver shouldn't be asking these sorts of questions. They would get him terminated, but there was far too much shit he didn't know.

He turned slightly and stared at the doctor's slumped form. She herself was an oddity—the fact that she'd been in the news recently, then apparently worked alone at that same outpost. Then she'd tried to defend the fucker.

And she shouldn't be able to shake off a stun that fast. Not just once, but twice.

His eyes narrowed. There was one way to keep her down.

Turning, he knelt next to his go-bag, and opened it up with his bio-signature. There was a lot more space inside since he'd abandoned his big gun. Carver gritted his teeth. His *favorite*. That fucker had crushed it with his bare hands.

Carver pushed his smaller weapons aside to pull out a compact med kit. He popped the lid open, revealing rows of medical nodes and dermal syringes. He swiped the node at the back, clicked the case closed, and locked everything else inside.

Straightening, he strode toward his charge, then knelt beside her. With a touch to her UV-suit, he forced her helmet to disengage.

Her eyes fluttered, and he slapped the node onto her throat. She twitched, then jerked forward, her fingers shaped like claws. Carver tapped his PALM, dosing her. She slumped down, still as death except for the rise and fall of chest. He waited for a beat, then two, making sure the sedative kept hold.

When she didn't move, he stood and accessed the massive amount of data his superiors had sent him. It was becoming clear that he should have read more of it before arriving—not that they'd given him enough time to do so.

Maybe that was the point.

File names materialized on his visor's interface, and he had the urge to shake his head at the sheer volume of it. There was no way he could have gone through all of this before arriving, especially with the termination time limit they'd given him.

Maybe they had set him up to fail.

But there had to be something in there that shed light on what the fuck he'd encountered on the planet.

Where to start? Carver strode to the bench seating along the bulkhead and sat sideways, so his legs stretched over three of the butt-shaped impressions, and his back leaned against the bulkhead.

Still off grid, this was the first time he'd looked at these files where he didn't feel like the CORE peered over his shoulder, watching what data he accessed.

He tapped his PALM, accessing the oldest files, the interactions the CORE government had with the *Calypso* during its journey. Routine updates, personal letters to friends and family, astrometric data—none of it would help with his current circumstance.

Carver skipped ahead to the files that correlated with the *Calypso's* return to their solar system. Again, there was so much data as to be debilitating in volume: every communication from *Omega Station* before it went dark, recordings of conversations between generals, and all the data from ships in the area during that time.

He'd learned most of this at school.

Carver jumped ahead again, scanning file names and searching for something he could use, or what parameters he should narrow down. A familiar name caught his eye. His chest squeezed tight: *Captain Milo Archibald.*

An image materialized in his mind's eye of what that man looked like only days ago: bloody wrists, defeated expression, glazed eyes.

Shaking off the agitated feeling that ran up his arms, Carver clicked on the folder. The top file on the mountain of data consisted of compiled recordings. He selected the first one with a touch to his PALM, initiating playback.

The line of data scrolling across the bottom of the feed identified it as the ocular recording of Captain Archibald in Sector Five, aboard a civilian cargo vessel twenty-seven years in the past.

Carver was about to see what the captain had all those years ago and went oddly breathless.

It started with a view of an airlock, nothing unusual about it, its circular construction similar to any of the cargo vessels Carver had traveled on.

Archibald turned his head, revealing a man and a woman on the left. The woman looked older, and the recording identified her as Miranda Archibald, then listed a bunch of useless data below her image: age, place of birth, permanent residence, known affiliations. It did the same for the man, Toro Valcon. Nothing in his information stood out either.

Then the view changed to show one more man on his right. This guy was big, bulky in a way that most people weren't able to achieve, and looked like he could crush a man's skull with his bare hands. The name below listed him as Brock Goodwater, a former defender, only serving his mandatory five years before cutting the CORE loose. He would have made a terrible agent. Too big meant too noticeable.

This crew was typical of cargo runners. They moved things for a price, lived a nomadic lifestyle, and did their best to stay out of the cross-hairs of Tellusian pirates.

And they were all listed as deceased.

On the recording, they held weapons in front of them, uneasy expressions on their faces. Miranda in particular looked like she was about to vomit.

A loud *kerclunk* resounded. The recording jerked, then another softer *clank* followed. The airlock rolled open, revealing the interior of a second ship, but no people.

"Is there anyone on board?" the captain called out, his voice sliding directly into Carver's ear, a younger version of the ravaged voice from days ago.

He gritted his teeth.

Silence met the question. The captain looked at his crew again, hesitation on their faces.

No one moved at first, then Goodwater ducked, stepping inside. The light on his weapon led the way. The captain followed.

Two more feeds popped up on either side of the captain's. One was Goodwater's, the other Valcon's, who took up the rear behind Miranda.

The recordings showed sleeping pods on either side of the narrow corridor, and Carver frowned. This was a long-distance transport, but a private one, the finishings too lush for a government ship. Plus, the location tag on the recording said Sector Five. There were no public transports in that area; it was too close to Tellusian space.

Why would a cargo crew fly that far out to begin with? *Probably smuggling.*

No civilian cargo carrier would pass up the opportunity to make extra creds with unsanctioned loads.

Carver paused the recording to access the initial assessment again. It listed their cargo at the time as being cloned livestock. That made him snort. "Livestock" was a great place to hide people. And that close to

Tellusian space? He would have bet his entire bank of creds that there were passengers on that ship who weren't supposed to be there.

Shaking his head, he continued to watch the recording. The group moved past the closed doors of the sleeping pods, and into an empty living space. Each view swept the entire area, lighting every corner. There was no one there.

Carver focused on Goodwater's feed as they approached the closed door of the cockpit. He looked back at his captain, got a head nod, then touched the control panel to open the door.

They all froze as they took in the sight of a small boy sitting on the floor between the two seats, his head bent and his palms facing forward. From his size, Carver would guess his age to be ten or so. There was no additional information under his image. No name, no nothing.

Archibald took point, advancing to kneel in front of the child. "Are you okay?" he asked, his hand reaching toward the boy's shoulder.

It stopped mid-air when the boy lifted his head. His irises glinted silver in the low light.

Someone gasped. Someone else swore.

Carver swung his legs over the side of the bench and gripped the edge of the seat with both hands.

There was jostling among the team as they tried to back up all at once in the narrow space.

Archibald dropped his hand, but hadn't moved otherwise. The moment stretched while they stared at the small boy who did nothing but stare back. He had short hair, and his clothes appeared odd, as if fabricated off center.

Finally, Archibald stood and said over his shoulder, "Get the government on the comm."

The last thing on the recording was Valcon reaching over the pilot's seat to turn off an active distress beacon.

Carver blinked at the dead feed, his mind racing with more questions than answers. How was it that Milo Archibald, the man who Carver had killed not even a week ago, was the captain who discovered a Calypson child on an abandoned ship?

Why had they sent him to torture and kill that man? His superiors had wanted a number. A number of what?

Archibald asked what had happened to the boy. He'd been asking about *that* boy.

What had happened to the kid? Could it be the same person he'd just fought?

No. Their facial features hadn't been similar. And as soon as the CORE had gotten a hold of that boy, he would've never seen the light of day again.

Swallowing, Carver tapped his PALM, scanning for files related to the kid. They would have sent those too, right? They had to have if his superiors had known what they were throwing him into.

But every file after that one had nothing pertaining to the kid.

A sick sensation swirled in his stomach. Even without having access to those particular files, Carver knew what would've happened to that boy. *Dissected and analyzed.*

The doctor stirred, and he touched his PALM, dosing her. She slumped back into a heap. Carver shook his head. She shouldn't have been able to wake from that either.

The doctor continued to be full of surprises.

He hated surprises.

With a touch of his PALM, he watched the recording again. And again. He didn't know what he was searching for, but studied every second of that video like his life depended on it.

Maybe it did.

Watching it for the tenth time, he became breathless when he realized there was a discrepancy. The time on the terminal when Archibald turned off the distress beacon didn't line up with the time the CORE government received their call. They should have contacted the CORE *after* turning it off, but it was the other way around, the contact time an hour before the creation of the recording.

The tether cabin's terminal beeped, pulling his attention away from the paused recording. Carver pushed off the bench to stride toward the primary controls. The cabin had broken through the stratosphere, and the trip was now counted in minutes.

He sent a communication to the administrator of the tether station, a list of requirements for their arrival.

A moment later, a communique from the *Corvus* appeared on his ocular implant—the first since he'd breached the atmosphere of this fucking planet. It demanded an update on his retrieval and the status of Doctor Wynn Lambdin. General Cazin's personal insignia marked the directive.

Carver's fingers hovered over his PALM, ready to deliver the recordings of his time on Earth.

Not quite yet.

He wouldn't debrief until he got more answers. And the doctor had them.

CHAPTER TWENTY-SIX

The world hummed loudly around her. Wynn's entire head buzzed with the noise, her temples throbbing. Stale air swirled up her nose.

She forced her eyes open and focused on a metallic deck. She didn't remember getting here. *Where is here?*

The hum changed, the pitch lowering, and she tried to place the sound, knowing she'd heard it before. Wynn turned her head, and something tugged at her throat. She reached toward it.

"Touch that and lose your hand."

The distorted voice came at her from the right. Wynn froze, her hand hovering near her neck. A chilling sensation crawled up her spine as she remembered the events of the past day. *I'm in the tether cabin.*

Those last few moments before she'd gone unconscious muddled in her head. She remembered seeing the two men fight, and the beasts so close to her. *Too close.* She remembered the need to help Iax, but also to defend herself if the beasts neared.

She closed her eyes. Her last memory of Iax played against the back of her eyelids.

Her fingers twitched where they'd stopped near the throat of her UV-suit.

"They told me to bring you in," Sawyer added. "They didn't say it had to be in one piece."

Nausea swirled in her stomach, realizing he must have attached a node of some type. What had he given her?

She dropped her hand and pushed herself to sit straight. The cabin spun in a never-ending streak of gray and black. Pressing her thumbs to her forehead, Wynn waited until the world stabilized before turning toward the voice. She found him near the main terminal clothed in his flight-suit, his helmet engaged.

What did a monster look like? She couldn't decide if she wanted to know.

The main viewer in front of him revealed stars and the bright glow of nearby stations. The cabin's humming lowered again as they slowed toward orbital level.

"Engage your helmet," he ordered without looking at her.

Hopelessness and rage swirled together in a heady mix. She needed to get away from him, to hell with whatever orders he obeyed. Her every cell screamed *danger*, even more so after what she'd witnessed on the surface.

Iax. Was he alive or dead? She swallowed around the large lump in her throat, the skin of her neck tugging with the motion and reminding her of the node. Her fingers twitched to take it off, but Sawyer's threats rang in her head.

He turned his body until he looked in her direction. "Engage. Your. Helmet."

Wynn hated this man with every fiber of her being.

Glaring at the reflection in his helmet, she reached and pressed the control on her suit. The visor slid into place with a *snap*. Behind him, the viewer blacked out as the tether cabin inserted itself into the orbital station. Her heart raced, a foreboding itch crawling over her skin. *Clank*. The docking clamps engaged, the sound echoing twice more before everything fell silent with deafening finality.

"Up," he ordered without looking at her, grabbing his case off the deck and slinging it over his shoulder.

Tension surged through her body, her limbs stiff with the need to flee. She stared at him for a long minute, waiting to see what other threats he would throw her way, then pressed her hands against the deck to push herself to stand.

The cabin swayed, and she tried to focus on the blackened viewer to regain her balance. But there was something wrong with her, like whatever he'd given her remained in her system, making the bulkheads undulate.

Strong fingers encircled her upper arm, holding her in place. She jerked, trying to get away from the vise-like grip, unnerved she hadn't heard him move.

He tugged her closer and bent his head until the only thing she could see in the reflection of his visor was the warped image of her pale face behind hers.

"If you try to talk to anyone," he said, his voice sliding directly into her ear now that the comm interface was engaged, "I'll start shooting indiscriminately, and their deaths will be on your head."

"What the hell?" she choked out, her throat feeling like he still squeezed it.

He had to be bluffing.

"Do you want that? Blood on your hands?"

She stared at him with a slack jaw, disbelieving he would actually follow through.

He must have seen her skepticism, because he said, "My superiors don't care as long as I get you to your end destination. They'll blame it on some extremist attack and call it a day." He stepped closer. "So I ask again, do you want blood on your hands?"

She swallowed, unable to move, but whatever he saw on her face must have appeased him. He straightened and yanked her toward the exit.

Wynn tugged on her arm, trying to free herself, but when he loosened his hold a fraction, the bulkheads swayed. She stumbled. The grip on her arm tightened, and he jerked her forward.

The inner decontamination doors opened with a swipe of his hand. Sawyer pulled her inside. As soon as the doors closed behind them, the process started, a fine mist covering their suits.

Keeping hold of her, he pressed his PALM to the outer control panel. Wynn leaned as far away as she could get from him. The need to curse at him, to kick and punch, burned through her blood. But it was all she could do to keep her balance.

"Make your visor opaque," he said without looking at her.

She fumbled a moment, then tapped her PALM to obey.

The decontamination process stalled before it could go through a full cycle. The moisture on their outerwear evaporated in a gust of wind. He dropped his hand from the panel, and the inner doors opened.

A woman stood there, backed by two defenders in uniform. A superintendent's emblem graced the left side of her pristine white uniform, with the CORE insignia above that. She frowned at them, her gaze bouncing from one to the other.

She opened her mouth to say something when Sawyer spoke first. "Is the ship I requested ready?"

More tension climbed Wynn's spine as the woman's scowl deepened, a red flush traveling up her throat. "I could not obtain the exact vessel. You didn't give me enough time."

"Then you'll take us to the fastest ship docked."

His anger whispered into Wynn's ear through their comm connection, twisting her already nauseous stomach.

One perfectly groomed eyebrow arched with skepticism, then the superintendent snorted and turned on her heel. "This way. We have one ship you can *commandeer*, as you put it, but that's all. You'll need to make do." The defenders stepped to the side, their backs to the bulkhead, and waited.

The grip on her arm tightened a moment, then relaxed. Sawyer guided Wynn forward, and they followed the superintendent down the typical corridor of a space station, the bulkheads lined with shiny black terminals, some turned on, but most off. The footsteps of the defenders thumped behind them, adding to the anxiety growing in Wynn's head.

The superintendent tossed them a look over her shoulder. "Chancellor Fearing is my uncle. I'll be sure to tell him about this encounter."

Sawyer stopped walking, and so did everyone else. "Make sure you do." He stepped to the terminal beside the superintendent, dragging Wynn along, and pressed his hand against the dead surface.

It lit up at the touch, then data scrolled across the top. The superintendent's face lost all its color. Wynn tried to read the information by adjusting the angle of her body, but Sawyer jerked her back.

The superintendent's eyes narrowed the longer she stared at the terminal, then she snapped to attention. "Like I said, this way."

Two corridors and one uncomfortable lift ride later, the five of them entered a cavernous docking bay filled with ships. Open blast doors revealed a chunk of space, the dark side of Earth a slender slice.

Wynn couldn't tear her eyes away from it. Iax was down there somewhere. Was he even alive? Did he heal as before? Her stomach clenched while the questions choked her.

The superintendent's clipped pace stopped beside a small shuttle.

Sawyer looked at the ship, then at the superintendent, then back at the ship. He laughed, his fingers flexing on Wynn's arm tighter than they had been before. Her skin stung under the pressure, focusing her.

His laughter cut off abruptly, and he straightened. "No. Unacceptable." He yanked Wynn forward, past the little shuttle and the shocked expression of the superintendent, toward a yacht docked two ships down.

It was three times the size of the cruiser they'd abandoned, and bright white instead of black. Wynn had to tip her head back to see it all as they neared.

"We'll be taking this one," he declared, stopping in front of it.

A gasp, then the slap of shoes as the superintendent caught up. "That's impossible. That ship belongs to Administrator Jannex."

"Even better." Sawyer jerked her toward where the ramp extended from its belly, guarded by a two-man security detail. "Is the administrator aboard?"

The superintendent scoffed. "No, not currently—"

"Send him my regards."

The guards drew their weapons at their approach. Wynn sucked in a breath, feet skidding.

Pop. She hadn't even realized Sawyer had let go of her until the shot pulsed out of his gun. The wave of the stun caught both guards in one fell swoop before either of them could get off a shot. They crumpled to the ground.

Wynn's heart pounded as she took in their slumped forms, her feet frozen to the deck. They weren't defenders, but they might as well have been since Administrator Jannex, one of the ruling class, employed them.

Swallowing, she glanced back at the superintendent. She'd frozen too, her hands out at her sides, the two defenders behind her holding their weapons, one aimed at her, the other at Sawyer. Wynn braced herself, ready to get stunned again, but no one moved.

Except for Sawyer, who had returned to her, grabbed her arm, and led her toward the ramp.

Wynn cast another glance at the trio. Why was everyone letting him do this? What had the superintendent read on that terminal?

During her dazed shock, he'd dropped the security field protecting the ramp. They passed by the motionless bodies of the guards and stumbled up the ramp, their hollow footsteps echoing loudly in the unnerving silence of the bay. Reluctance dragged at her feet, but Sawyer yanked her up the rest of the way.

They entered a darkened space, a cargo hold filled with crates and containers. Sawyer dropped her arm to access the control panel near the door. The ramp whined as it lifted, and her heart pounded harder and harder. Automatic lights brightened as the cargo hold dimmed.

The ramp closed with a hissing *clank,* and she turned her head to find Sawyer standing right beside her, though she hadn't heard him come closer.

He touched his PALM. "Sleepy time."

"No—" The word stuck in Wynn's throat as her knees gave out.

Chapter Twenty-Seven

The ache in her wrists woke her. It stung, then burned, then morphed into searing pain. A low hum vibrated from all around her, the sound of a ship traveling quickly.

Wynn's shoulders ached too, but the pain in her wrists overrode everything. She gasped for breath, trying to get away from it. Her feet flailed while she tried to regain her balance, but she kicked into nothing, then swung back and forth.

It took her a moment to realize what that meant. *I'm hanging.*

Her pounding head felt heavy on her shoulder, too heavy to lift, but she cracked her eyes open. The undulating view down her body revealed a grated deck. She wore her sleepwear and no shoes. The tips of her toes brushed the floor, just enough to make her sway, but not enough to give her grip. A sheet of plastic beneath her crinkled with her efforts.

She forced her head to look up. Tight bindings encircled her wrists and attached to the overhead beams of the cargo hold. The more she moved, the more they chafed, almost all of her body weight resting on the tight bands. A line of blood trickled down her arm.

The drugs in her system evaporated at the sight of that blood. Her heart pounded in her throat, her eyes attaching to the red with single-minded focus. Panic clawed up her throat and hazed her vision, making the cargo hold spin.

No. She wouldn't get herself in a more compromising situation by passing out. Wynn inhaled deeply, then exhaled, concentrating on the pain in her wrists like she would a laser scalpel to her flesh, allowing it to settle her. She did it again and again until the room stopped whirling.

Boot steps bounced off the stacked containers. She snapped her head toward the sound. Sawyer rounded the corner. He still wore his full flight-suit, and the closer he neared, the more she saw her distorted reflection in his visor, an elongated white smudge amid gray and black.

"What the fuck?" she croaked, her throat tight with the need to scream.

He stopped in front of her with something held tight in his hand.

She struck out with her feet, trying to kick him, but he was out of reach. Her effort rewarded her with more pain in her wrists and her body twirling in some macabre dance.

"What did you do to me?" she asked when she faced him again.

He paced in front of her, back and forth. "Gave you a sedative." The mechanical quality of his voice was subdued. "Removed your tracker."

Her eyes darted down to his hand, and she focused on the objects he held: a laser scalpel and a regenerator. Her rage swelled. She rolled her shoulders, the skin twinging where he'd surgically removed her CORE tracker, and realized the node remained, too.

"What else?" she ground out between clenched teeth. "You took off all my clothes."

He paused, his head turning her way. "I'm not a psycho."

"Yes. You. Are," she gritted.

He cocked his head. "Not that kind of psycho." He resumed his pacing.

A sob of frustration wanted to escape her mouth, but she swallowed it down. Now that she'd seen what he was capable of, she wouldn't show weakness. Not if she wanted to survive this. Whatever *this* was.

She stared at him, the back of her eyes burning.

"We're going to have a chat," he declared.

Her jaw ached from clenching her teeth. "Fuck you."

"No thanks," he said with a shake of his head. "We're here for business, not pleasure." Four steps to the left, he spun on his heel, then took the same four steps to the right. "I'm going to ask you some questions, and you're going to answer them honestly."

"Like I said," she growled, straining against the bindings until more warmth tricked down her arm. "Fuck. You."

He stopped and turned his body toward her. "It's easy. I ask a question, you answer, and nothing else needs to happen."

With a flick of his thumb, he turned on the laser scalpel. *Hummmmm.*

She jerked back, trying to get away from him even though she was bound in place. A fresh wave of panic crashed over her head.

He turned it off, then resumed his pacing. "It's just some questions."

Anger and hate welled inside her. "You destroyed my home. You *abducted* me. I'm not answering your questions."

She couldn't swallow for the toxic emotions clogging her throat. *Nothing left.* Not one thing left of the outpost. The greenhouse lay in a heap of shattered rubble. Every plant she'd nurtured from a seed that might have survived the blast would have died in the elements.

Her work meant nothing. *Pointless.*

Her entire life was pointless.

That spinning sensation started in her stomach, though she remained stationary. The cargo hold swirled around her in shades of gray.

"That is unfortunate," he said in response to her denial, his words focusing her attention. He stopped again, his body squared off in front of her. "That person who was with you, you knew what he was, didn't you?"

Iax. This was all about him, wasn't it? Everything started the day he arrived. And Sawyer had left him dying on the surface, his body broken in the snow.

She pushed those images aside to remember him as he was at her outpost. His curiosity. His strange innocence. The way he'd touched her. The way he'd made her *feel*.

"You know where he came from, right?" Sawyer paced left, then right, his hand tapping the tools against his leg.

She closed her eyes. An image formed of Iax approaching her outpost. How he'd walked across the surface unaided, incurring so many radiation burns his skin had blistered. If he'd healed from that, then a weapon's blast, he could survive anything.

He's alive. He's okay. If she said it enough, maybe she would believe it.

"Why was he at your outpost?"

Her eyes popped open. Sawyer had paused across from her, still tapping his thigh, the image of her stretched arms reflecting in his visor. What remained of the moisture in her mouth evaporated as she remembered what Iax had told her. *My blood.*

They stayed that way, facing off, the trickle of blood from her wrists trailing down to her elbow. Her heart pounded in her throat.

"Do you know Captain Milo Archibald?"

Her head snapped back at the question. *Who?* She'd never heard the name before.

"Why does General Cazin want you?"

She shook her head to clear it, not recognizing that name either.

Sawyer resumed his pacing. Back and forth. Back and forth. "The Calypson." He practically spat the word, though his helmet distorted the effect. "How long have you known him?"

The question elicited an involuntary scoff. She'd only known Iax for days, but it had felt like much longer. Why else would she have been contemplating sleeping with him? *You did sleep with him.* Another scoff, because it was only *sleep*, though the best sleep of her life.

No monsters had invaded her dreams.

"How did that fucker survive shots to the head?"

The question froze her thoughts while a replay of what this man had done to Iax traveled through her mind's eye. More reason not to cooperate.

"How was he healing himself?"

Her breath caught in the back of her throat, and the cargo hold spun. The rampant sensation escalated the longer she thought about all Iax had said, how he'd told her even his cells were intelligent.

"What did he want with you?"

Panic swelled in her chest. She hadn't realized it, her vision hazed in memory, but Sawyer had stopped right in front of her.

The question felt loud and echoed in her head. It knocked against the truth, rattling her. Iax had called her Calypson and had encouraged her cells to heal. If someone correctly analyzed the data from her blood sample, it would prove Iax's words true. But it had been destroyed with the rest of the outpost. For the first time since Sawyer had leveled her home, she was glad of it.

He stepped closer and wrapped his hand around her throat. Her heart pounded hard in her head. The room spun faster.

"Answer one of the fucking questions." He squeezed slightly, restricting her airway. "Pick one."

"Maybe I'd answer your questions if you took off that stupid helmet." She spit. The lack of moisture in her mouth diminished the effect, but small dots sprayed across his visor.

His fingers flexed on her throat. A noise escaped Wynn while helplessness swirled inside her chest, her skin feeling tight and itchy. She couldn't make it stop.

Her legs flailed futilely. She tipped her head back, the only way she could get away from his grip, but it only served in exposing her throat more. The out-of-control feeling intensified until she hung in the middle of a storm as intense as the one ravaging Earth. His other hand grabbed her elbow.

Hummmmm. She barely heard the noise above the sound of blood pumping in her head.

Everything around her stilled as a new pain emerged through the haze. She snapped her chin down, his hand around her throat restricting the movement.

In her peripheral vision, he sliced a line in the flesh of her inner arm with the laser scalpel, red blooming across pale flesh. The familiar pain overrode everything else, even the ache in her wrists, her entire focus targeting the incision. Her breath stalled in her throat as the haze obstructing her vision dissipated. Blood dripped down from the wound to her armpit.

Her breaths accelerated as she breathed through the pain. The cargo hold stopped spinning. Everything *cleared*.

Sawyer finished the line and paused, waiting. She sucked in a breath, feeling like herself for the first time since he'd landed near her outpost.

With a tilt of his head, he started a second line above the first.

He thought this would make her talk?

A soft breath left her mouth, and the need for pain she'd left in her past returned with full force. She'd gained a small taste of that comfort when she'd added the last line to her trio, but she hadn't returned to her kit in the washroom until after Iax arrived.

The line scored her flesh, and a breathless inhale expanded her lungs in the wake of the addictive sensation, the allure of control.

Sawyer flicked the laser scalpel off, his hand tightening on her elbow. "What the hell? You're getting off on this?"

She laughed. She couldn't help it. It was so damn funny. He'd stripped her, intended on doing harm, and *this* was how he thought he'd get her to talk?

His chin tilted down, then up, scanning her body, like he was truly looking at her for the first time. Maybe he searched for evidence of past cuts. But he wouldn't find them. Not after Iax.

Iax had healed her marks out of kindness, and this man returned them to her out of anger and perversion.

She laughed harder.

The fingers flexed around her throat.

His confusion made her heady with power. She knew the feeling was false, a trick because she hung there at his mercy, but it didn't dampen the boldness that rose inside her.

She jutted out her chin. "Let me see the eyes of the man who wants to kill me." Her voice rasped the more he squeezed. "Or are you that much of a coward, Sawyer?"

His head jerked back like she'd struck him, his one hand dropping away from her elbow but the other tightening around her neck.

"What did you call me?"

"Sawyer Knox," she gasped between clenched teeth. "That's your name, right?" Stars dotted her vision as her airway closed up.

She wouldn't let him knock her out again.

Using every last bit of strength inside her, she smashed her forehead against his visor.

Smack. Snap. Pain bloomed across her face as he stumbled back. But her effort tripped his helmet to disengage.

She sucked in a breath and held it, her head aching from the hit. She couldn't regret it. Not when she stared into his shocked brown eyes.

Wynn didn't know what she'd been expecting. Perhaps a face as grotesque as the beasts of Earth, one to match the state of his soul.

Sawyer Knox was not scary to look at. Some might even call him attractive. His dark, almost black, hair was cut right to his scalp. A dusting of facial hair covered his jaw.

He looked normal. Unimpressive. If he wore the same uniform as her, she would have taken him for a scientist.

Until she stared deeper into his eyes and saw the taint of his soul. This man had done many horrible things in his lifetime. She could taste it in the air as easily as she could smell her blood.

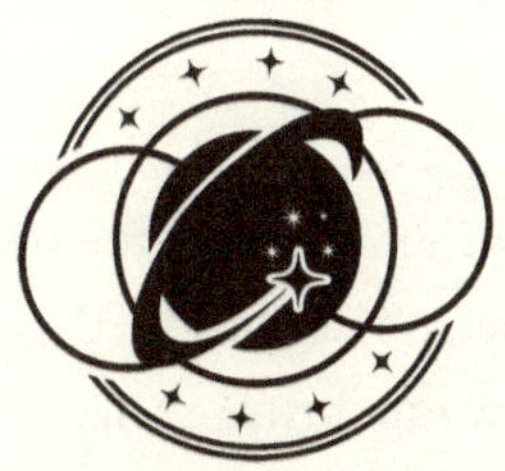

Chapter Twenty-Eight

Hearing his real name aloud for the first time in decades froze every part of his body and stole the words from his mouth.

Sawyer Knox. Blood pumped between his ears as he glared at the woman hanging from her wrists.

That's your name, right? Her words echoed hollowly in his head.

The agitated sensation he'd experienced during Archibald's interrogation began at the back of his neck and spread throughout his body. Not only because she'd said his name, but she could see the face attached to it. The scent of dust and metal invaded his nostrils.

Remove the threat. She knew too much about him, and that meant she needed to die.

Except, he had to follow orders. And for some reason, he didn't think he would enjoy killing Wynn Lambdin.

That agitated sensation turned into an all-out burn. His gaze went to the two bleeding lines on her arm. She'd accepted those cuts like she enjoyed them, and he only knew one person who would've done the same. *Me.*

During his training as a kid, he used to get overwhelmed, panicked, and the only thing that would bring him back to himself was pain. He'd become addicted to it. Egged the other kids on to fight him because hits would bring clarity, then beating the shit out of the other little snots would bring satisfaction.

He'd thought he'd left that all behind—along with his name.

"How do you know that name?" he asked, disgusted that his voice came out weak, choked, the raw parts exposed now that his helmet was disengaged.

She stared at him with parted lips and curiosity-filled eyes. He hated it. She wasn't begging or pleading for her life. She wasn't crying or blubbering. In fact, she looked the calmest he'd ever seen her.

Frustration replaced the disbelief, and his senses returned to him like someone poured them back into his body. He stepped back toward her, pulled his gun, and pressed the muzzle against her temple. "How do you know that name?" he ground out.

He'd had so many since he started working for the CORE government as a child, but not that one. *Never* that one.

She shook her head once, her forehead pink where she'd hit him, but white under the pressure of his weapon. The blood from the cuts he'd given her dripped onto her top, some falling to the plastic sheeting in quiet drips.

Fuck the government. He would start cutting off body parts if she didn't start giving him some answers that made sense.

No, you won't.

He pressed the gun harder against her head. "How do you know that name?" he repeated.

"You're not going to kill me," she said instead of answering, her eyes flashing fire. "You would have done it already if you could."

"Then how about we see how you feel if I blast off your toes? Would you like that?" He pointed his gun at her feet. "How do you know my name?"

A battle waged behind her eyes, indecision and defiance. She licked her lips, then said, "Cut me down and I'll tell you."

"Tell me, then I'll cut you down."

"I can't trust you."

"No, you can't," he agreed with a nod. "Doesn't look like you have many options." He made a show of scanning the cargo hold, empty except for them and containers left for storage.

She swallowed, then lifted her chin in defiance. Her neck was red from where he'd gripped her. "He called you that."

"Who?"

"Iax."

It took him a full second to realize she meant the Calypson. The fucker had a name? Sawyer didn't know why he found that odd, but he did.

"How did *he* know my name?"

Her eyes narrowed. "I answered one question. Now cut me down."

Sawyer didn't realize he was pacing again and stopped in front of her. The two lines on her arm bleed steadily, hitting the plastic at regular intervals. *Drip. Drip. Drip.*

He stepped closer, and she tensed. Raising the regenerator, he turned it on with a flick of his thumb. It hummed as he brought it close to her wounds.

Her eyes rolled in the back of her head, like he gave her the greatest pleasure, though he knew the healing process stung.

Fuck, this was weird seeing it from the other side.

With the last cut healed and residual blood drying on her skin, he swapped out the regenerator for the laser scalpel. A gasp caught in her throat, a look of betrayal crossing her features.

He scoffed. After everything, she expected him to follow through on his word? *Fool.* She should know by now not to trust anyone in this system. *No one will look out for you except you.* A lesson he'd learned early in life.

He stepped back and reached above her hands, slicing through the bindings with one swipe. The action set her on her feet, then her knees buckled. *Splat.* She fell forward onto the sheeting; the plastic crinkled. He reached down to help her before he caught himself. Clenching his jaw, he moved off the drop sheet.

"You're going to answer more questions, or I'll string you up again." At least he knew she didn't like that part.

Her hand covering the newly healed cuts, she glared at him.

"For your wrists," he said, tossing the regenerator in front of her.

When the hell had he gotten so soft? He didn't understand what was wrong with him. First Archibald, now her. Why couldn't he just get the fucking job done?

Buzz. The noise of the regenerator took up the silence while she healed her chafed wrists.

"You're an agent, aren't you?" she asked without looking up.

And that wasn't how this was going to work. He left the question unanswered and paced back and forth.

"What else did that fucker know about me?"

She shook her head, and his hand tightened on his weapon. Would he have to resort to threats again? *Not like that worked.*

Then she said, "He only told me you were there to collect me. That's it. Only your name and that."

He couldn't hear a lie in her voice. How would the Calypson have known his name and objective, though? Sawyer thought of ways his communication stream could have been hacked and came up empty.

There'd been moments during their fight that he'd thought the fucker was in his head, predicting what he'd do before Sawyer did it. He'd blanked his thoughts on purpose and had come out on top because of it.

The doctor cleared her throat. "He didn't say much at all," she added.

There it was, the tightness that told him she withheld information. He narrowed his eyes at her and continued to pace.

"Why does Cazin want you?"

A huff of breath left her, her focus on her wrists. "I don't know who that is. You should know more than I do. You were the one sent to *collect* me."

He couldn't detect a lie there either. And if she didn't have some personal connection with Cazin, then this entire thing circled around the Calypson.

"How did the fucker control the beasts?"

The regenerator stopped, and so did he. Holding her forearm, she stared up at him with an uneasy expression, then shook her head.

His hand tightened on the scalpel.

"Silently," she said a second later, her voice quiet. "Somehow." She shook her head again. "I don't know."

She refocused on her wrist, most of the redness gone.

"Why was he at your outpost?"

Her entire body stiffened, the regenerator jerking against her skin. She didn't look up when she said, "I don't know."

"Lie," he spat, resuming his pacing. "You do know, and you're going to tell me." He had the urge to turn on the laser scalpel for emphasis, but knew the effect would be lost on her.

"Same reason as you," she finally murmured. "He said he was there to collect me."

There was truth there, but something else too. He didn't have the time to explore it more. "Where was he going to take you?"

She tensed and shook her head.

Sawyer stopped and kept his voice even. "Where was he taking you?"

She kept her head down when she said, "Sector Ten."

He heard the terror in her voice, the uncertainty. She hadn't wanted to go with him—the first reaction he could relate to.

"Then why help him?" It was a pointless question when he had so many more to ask, but it burned to be answered.

Why did she help a Calypson? Why did she try to stop him from attacking one of the biggest threats in the solar system? Everyone knew what they could do to a person, what they were capable of if you got too close, though the *how* of it remained a mystery. Which begged the question, how was she still human?

She lifted her chin and met his gaze. "He treated me with more respect than an asshole like you." Her jaw flexed. "And I would do it again if given the chance."

They stared at each other for a long moment, more questions needing to be answered, but their time together was short. On cue, his PALM beeped, letting him know the timer he'd set had run out.

Turning on his heel, Sawyer left the good doctor on her knees staring after him, and made his way to the bow of the ship. A slender spiral staircase punched upward, and he took the steps two at a time to the upper level. Plush carpet dampened every stride as he passed through the sitting area toward the cockpit.

With a swipe of his PALM, the door slid open, revealing a four-seat setup that would rival any ship out there. The creamy smooth texture of the upholstery contrasted with the black of the shiny terminals that wrapped around the entire bulbous cockpit. Above them, a viewer showed the unending vista of space.

He slid into the pilot's chair, the upholstery squeaking as it rubbed against the material of his flight-suit. A flashing red light on the main control panel drew his attention. He tapped it to turn it off—a summons from Earth's orbital station, and another from *Jupiter One*, Jannex's home base.

The administrator would have lost his shit when he found out about his commandeered ship. Sawyer relished the thought. Any time he could stick it to the ruling class, he would.

Ignoring both summons, he adjusted their course. He hadn't wanted to go straight to the *Corvus* without first interrogating the good doctor and had plotted an arched route that would take them there eventually. But his time for detours was over.

Another communique appeared, this one sent to him directly. Cazin's signature scrolled across the bottom of his ocular implant. With only a short span remaining on this trip, it was time to send his update.

His fingers twitched. *Not yet.* He couldn't send the past days as raw data.

He started with the last hour in the cargo hold. The radiation down there was always a bitch for sensors, making it easy to erase how he'd strung her up by the wrists. He went all the way back to the moment they stepped on this ship and he'd knocked her out.

I don't have time for this. A rushed job meant a messy job, and he'd done this twice in the past week.

Maybe it was time to cut himself loose from the CORE before they decided he was worth the termination order. He could use his extensive contacts to disappear and never resurface on the government's radar.

A problem for another day. He was already short on time.

He continued to scrub anything that revealed the doctor's resistance in coming along. Adding some personal but benign facts to the brief, he concluded with, *She's been an absolute delight,* before sending the package to the *Corvus.*

He didn't know why he'd lied. She'd been anything but cooperative, but he also knew what reception she'd garner on a Guardian if he marked her as a hostile.

And he definitely didn't mention that she'd helped a Calypson.

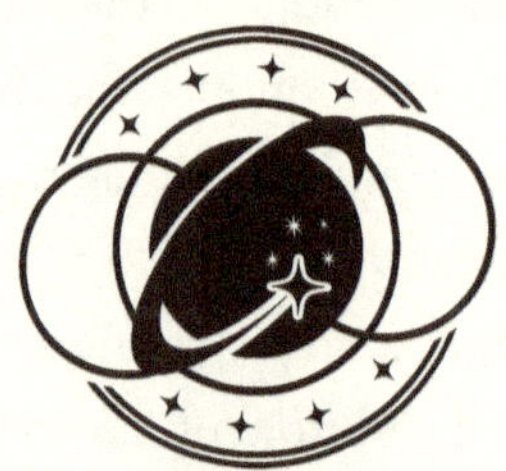

Chapter Twenty-Nine

The regenerator went silent with a flick of her thumb. Wynn gulped a breath, trying to settle her racing heart. She didn't understand what just happened, why he'd cut her down instead of continuing his interrogation, but she wouldn't tempt fate by asking.

With the hard surface of the deck pressing into her kneecaps, she stared where Sawyer had disappeared. She couldn't comprehend his questions. Except for the one about why Iax had been at her outpost, they'd made little sense. Who were Cazin and Archibald?

She shifted her weight off her knees, and the plastic beneath her rustled. Drips of her blood smeared in an arc in front of her. Her heart skipped a beat. She couldn't leave it here. Not after what Iax had shown her.

Keeping the regenerator tight in her hand, she moved off the plastic and pulled it toward her, bundling her blood inside with crinkling fistfuls. She wadded it into the smallest ball possible, then searched for a reclamation unit. Every deck had one.

There. At the back. Wynn stood on shaky legs. After hanging so long, each step took an effort, her bare feet protesting at the cold deck. She stopped in front of the reclamation unit and flexed her left hand. He'd taken her PALM. She also didn't know where her UV-suit went.

Manually opening the compartment with a press of her hand, she stuffed the plastic inside with sudden urgency, like if she didn't get it in fast enough someone would stop her. A scrape of her fingers against her throat, and the node followed. The small door closed, and she pressed the destroy and jettison control. Her shoulders relaxed a fraction when the light went green, signaling completion.

Wynn rotated her throbbing wrists. She might have healed the damage to the outside of her skin, but she felt bruised beneath.

Swallowing, she scanned the cargo hold. Behind the crates, a slender staircase led to the next level above, like the one where Sawyer had disappeared. Wynn cast one last glance at where she'd hung, then headed up, her hand tight on the smooth railing.

She stepped into a sitting room that stretched long one way and turned into a kitchen in the other. Plush carpet squished beneath her feet. By the stars, the ruling class lived well. If this was how Administrator Jannex traveled, what was his home like?

He might live in luxury, but she also knew he wasn't immune to tragedy. Months before Foster's death, a different news story had gripped the system by the throat. A Tellusian attack on a medical station resulted in the disappearance of a ruling class member—Administrator Jannex's only daughter.

Wynn hoped the woman was dead, a mercy compared to the hundred scenarios she could imagine for women taken captive by Tellusians. Wynn's parents had received a gift by dying during the attack on their transport instead of being forced into servitude.

Swallowing around the sudden lump in her throat, she walked through the sitting room to the kitchen. The carpet changed to shiny black decking, and her feet protested again.

The door to the next room opened as she neared. She stepped into a corridor lined with doors. Sleeping quarters, if she had to guess. Wynn passed them by to the next set of double doors. These opened up into a stateroom with an oversized bed at its center. The luxury of it all hit her again.

Everything felt wrong on this ship. The air tasted wrong. The color of the deck was wrong. The hum of the vessel sounded wrong.

But she needed something to wear, and drying blood covered her arms.

The thought spurred her forward. She opened the first wall compartment, then the next, looking for clothing. She found feminine garb in the third one, most of the clothes too lavish for someone like her, but there were some more casual outfits too.

Get clean first. She didn't want her blood to transfer onto anything.

Wynn moved to the slender door on the right, and it opened into a washroom with the biggest steam shower she had ever seen. It probably could have fit ten people.

She stripped down to nothing, then stared at the bundle of clothing in her hands. It had blood on it too, but there'd been a reclamation unit in the stateroom. She hurried back out and shoved the bundle inside, hitting the destroy and jettison button again. All the while she glanced over her shoulder, thinking Sawyer would walk in on her naked.

He didn't, and the light turned green.

Dashing back into the washroom, she indulged in a quick steam, scrubbing the blood from her body until her skin turned rosy, then made sure every last drop of red washed down the drain.

Clean and dry, she approached the clothing compartment again. Whoever these belonged to, probably the administrator's wife, they were made for someone taller than her. The underwear would fit, though.

She dressed quickly, half expecting Sawyer to come find her, to threaten her again or tell her to stop what she was doing, but he didn't. She rolled up the pant legs and sleeves of the basic beige outfit, exercise wear. Socks and shoes were next, but the black flats were too big, and she ended up just putting on the socks.

Staring at the door to the kitchen, Wynn took a deep breath to settle herself. It didn't work. Should she stay here? Just wait until something else happened that was beyond her control?

She shook her head. She wouldn't hide from what happened next. Sawyer said he was taking her to General Cazin, and she needed to figure out why, even if he didn't know either. And from what he'd asked her, she could only assume he didn't.

Her empty hands clenched and unclenched as she walked through the exit and paused in the kitchen. Even though she'd dressed, she felt naked and vulnerable after what he'd done to her in the cargo hold.

Adrenaline pumping hard, she crossed to the first cupboard and opened it, finding bowls. She opened the drawer underneath it and found cutlery. She moved to the next drawer and found knives.

Snatching up the biggest one, she shut it, then continued her route to the front of the ship. The handle felt heavy in her hand as she approached the cockpit door. It opened at her approach, revealing a curved area with four seats, everything designed with luxury in mind.

Sawyer sat in the pilot's seat, his back to her, and his helmet disengaged. Wynn remained in the doorway, waiting for him to say something, to tell her to fuck off or worse. When he didn't, she gripped the knife tighter, and stepped inside.

The urge to slam the knife into his skull overwhelmed her for a split second, chased away by common sense. She'd seen him in action, knew she wouldn't get away with it despite his back being turned, and retaliation might be worse than what he'd already done.

With the knife held firmly in front of her, she walked forward and slid into the co-pilot's seat, keeping her eyes on him the entire time.

"Feeling better?" he asked without looking at her.

"Fuck you," she spat, her fingers flexing around the knife.

He scoffed in response, then glanced at what she held. "The first thing you need to learn about weapons is that anything you bring to a fight can be used against you."

Her breath caught in her throat. Was that a threat or a warning? When he faced forward again, she decided it didn't matter as long as she got to keep the knife.

The stars stretched before them on the viewer, endless and vast.

A ration tube obscured her view and made her jump. She turned her head.

"Eat it," he ordered, his hand wrapped around the thin cylinder.

"Not hungry," she lied, because she couldn't think of food right now, even a ration.

He shoved it closer to her face. "Eat it, or I'll shove it down your throat." His dark eyes narrowed with promise.

"I hate you." Wynn swiped it out of his hand just to get it away from her eyeballs.

"That's fine. Wasn't asking to be besties." He faced forward again.

The urge to disobey, to just throw the thing over her shoulder, taunted her. She also didn't doubt he would force-feed it to her, but why did he even care?

Refocusing on the static view in front of her, she transferred the knife to her left hand and ripped off the top of the tube to suck down the gooey paste. The acid in her throat and the rumbling of her stomach settled almost immediately. *Know it all.* Not that she would admit it aloud.

She threw the empty tube at his head. "There. Happy?"

A small streak of green goo marked his temple where the tube connected. Wynn sucked in a sharp breath knowing she'd gone too far and braced herself.

He tilted his head slowly, until his narrowed gaze captured hers in a death grip. She tensed.

He lifted his hand.

She flinched, the knife lifting in preparation.

He paused, then continued the movement until he wiped the smear from his temple.

"Ecstatic," he murmured, then extended his hand toward her until he wiped the goo on the shoulder of her clean shirt.

When he faced forward again, she let out her breath so slowly it whistled.

He turned his chin slightly, but didn't comment.

The longer she sat there, and nothing happened, the dumber she felt holding the knife. Her hand started to sweat, then cramp. Huffing out a breath, she gave up, and set it on the terminal in front of her, then pulled her knees up to her chest and wrapped her arms around her shins.

"How long is this trip?" she finally asked.

He was silent for so long she didn't think he would answer.

"Not long now."

Another silence descended. She broke it after a handful of minutes. "Why do they want me?"

Even though she was looking straight ahead, she saw him glance at her from the corner of her eye.

"I don't know."

She squeezed her shins tighter and rested her chin on her knees. A surging panic rose inside her, one she couldn't stop with breathing alone. The blade of the knife glinted at her, tempting her to grab it and give herself some clarity with one nick of her flesh.

Not an option. As alluring as it had become during this psycho's torture session, she wouldn't allow herself to succumb to that need again. She'd promised herself.

Shutting her eyes, she squeezed them tight to remove the sight. But her breaths didn't slow as she gasped filtered air. Hell, she was going to pass out.

Thwack. She jumped as something cool hit the back of her neck. Her eyes popped open, and she turned her head to find Sawyer staring at her, his brow furrowed as he held something above the collar of her shirt.

"What are you doing?" she croaked, and lifted a hand to touch what he held against her. A ration, but a larger, square one.

"Lowering your temperature," he said, then dropped his hand to face forward. "It helps sometimes."

The question of how he would know that was on the tip of her tongue, but she swallowed it. However he knew, it worked. The panic faded as she concentrated on this new point of contact.

She kept it there while staring out the main viewer and that endless span of stars. Then, something on the screen changed, and she blinked. A glint reflected up ahead.

The glint enlarged when Sawyer touched a control on the terminal, changing into a full-fledged Guardian.

She let go of the ration at her neck, and it dropped to the deck with a soft *splat*. "What were your orders?" she whispered, her panic growing again.

He hesitated, then said, "To pick you up. To take you to Cazin on the *Corvus*. That's it." He pressed his PALM to the terminal when a message materialized at the bottom of the viewer.

The closer they drew, the more her heart beat in her throat and her head pounded. The ship's details became more defined: the gray exterior, the massive amounts of decks, the cannons dotting the hull. Her stomach swirled with dread. She dropped her feet to the floor and gripped the edge of the terminal.

Sawyer circled them aft. The hangar doors were already open, the lights within welcoming them inside. Tiny dots on the left and right of the landing lights formed into defenders standing in rows. Another group at the rear of the hangar wore bio-suits, and two med beds hovered close by.

"Sawyer...?" she murmured, her chest seizing tight.

"The welcoming party," he muttered, never taking his hands or eyes off the controls.

"What are they going to do to me?"

"I don't know."

"Not good enough. Why are you bringing me here?"

"I don't know."

"Not good enough!" she shouted, but it was too late. The ship settled on the landing pad.

The control she'd regained over her breathing left as rapidly as bio-waste in a reclamation unit. Wynn opened and closed her hands, trying to keep hold of her sanity.

What did they know?

Sawyer powered down the engine, and the ship fell silent while the screaming in her head rose in volume.

"Up," he ordered when he stood.

She found her legs moving even though everything in her told her to get away.

"Let's go." He led her to a spiral staircase and made her go down first. She almost tumbled the entire way down from the shaking in her legs.

His hand gripping her upper arm, they passed the spot where he'd tortured her, and headed to the cargo hold's doors. He lifted his hand to the controls, then hesitated.

"Get your hands on your head."

She turned slightly and blinked the panicked haze from her vision. "What?"

"Get your hands on your fucking head," he barked, then muttered, "Scientists and their questions." He hit the control that opened the door and lowered the ramp. It whined loudly, echoing inside the cargo hold.

"And don't make any sudden moves." He interlaced his fingers behind his head.

Swallowing, she did the same, and watched as the ramp lowered to the deck. Defenders clogged the space around the ship, their weapons aimed at them. The ration she'd just eaten surged up her throat.

Sawyer stepped ahead, shielding her. Then the shouting started.

"Step out of the ship!"

"Walk slowly!"

"Drop your weapons!"

"On your knees!"

"Face down!"

Each confusing command layered the next. Wynn flinched as they echoed inside the hangar, each like a physical blow.

Movement blurred, then Sawyer was gone. A firm hand gripped the back of her neck and pushed. Something banged into the back of one knee.

With her hands on her head, she couldn't catch her balance and fell forward with a shout.

Her cheek slammed into the deck. Stars dotted her vision. Through the haze, she saw Sawyer with his face pressed into the deck too, a hand behind his head and a knee in the middle of his back.

Someone wrenched her arms behind her. She whimpered.

Her eyes watered, blurring the sight of someone in a bio-suit reaching for Sawyer's neck, a dermal syringe in their hand.

Something cold touched her throat.

Then all went black.

Chapter Thirty

Consciousness trickled in through a haze of drugs and pain. Sawyer's nose twitched, then he froze when he realized he didn't know where he was, or why.

A throbbing ache resonated through half of his skull. Memories followed, ones of being slammed into the deck in the hangar, and of the good doctor receiving the same treatment.

The fear on her face wasn't something he was used to. He'd scared a huge number of people, sure, but there was something raw and unsettling about her pleading expression.

He'd been expecting the reception, knew from what he'd sent the general that there would be questions: how neither of them were changed into Calypson and how they'd gotten away.

Right before he'd gone under, all he'd wanted to do was fight them off—and that would have led to his death. And hers.

Keeping motionless, Sawyer assessed where he was without opening his eyes. He lay on his side, with something soft beneath his shoulder and hip. No injuries except for the throbbing in his head. Air touched his skin, his flight-suit removed. It wasn't an enormous space, maybe the size of crew quarters.

And though it was silent, he didn't feel like he was alone.

"Ahem."

The deep sound of a throat clearing bounced off the walls. Sawyer's eyes popped open. Across from him, a man with pale skin and a dark goatee leaned against the door frame, someone he'd never met in person before: General Cazin. His white CORE military uniform was pristine, its silver trim gleaming in the overhead lights. Emblems adorned the space beneath the CORE insignia, denoting his rank and commendations.

An important man.

Sawyer had killed many important men, quietly, and in the name of the CORE.

Bracing his hand, he sat up in one smooth motion, his legs swinging over the edge of the bed. His head spun for a moment, and he gripped the bed's frame tight to keep from tilting.

He stared down at his bare legs, the blood rushing to his toes. They'd removed everything except for his underwear, no shirt, and he wasn't even sure those were the same shorts he'd put on at the onset of this mission. A new pair of CORE-issue boots sat tidily near the door. He mourned the loss of his old ones. He'd just broken them in.

He lifted his head. "Sir," he said, meeting the general's narrowed gaze.

Bushy eyebrows shrouded deep-set eyes, his mouth pursed. "You cut it a little close."

"I got the job done, sir."

Cazin tipped his chin. "Congratulations. You're not Calypson."

Sawyer ran a hand over his face and across the thick stubble of his jaw. "Didn't think I was." How long had he been out?

He reassessed his body. They must have fed him something, because he wasn't hungry. And they wouldn't have brought him here first thing, would've taken him to a lab, or a medical facility, to have him checked out in a controlled space.

He ran a hand over the back of his head. "And the doctor, sir?" The question came out before he could think better of it.

Cazin's one eyebrow lifted. A moment passed between them where Sawyer kept his expression fixed with mild curiosity, and the general stared, assessing.

"She checked out too." He pushed off the wall, straightening. "But enough of that." He glanced at his PALM. "I have your report here. Is there anything you'd like to add?"

The urge to tense, to think about everything he deleted from the official record, rode him hard, but Sawyer kept his gaze level and his breathing even. "No, sir."

A pregnant pause filled the silence following his answer, and Sawyer's mind went over anything they could use against him. The abandoned torture session, the unsanctioned research, the voids of missing time. Could they have discovered any of it? He didn't think so, not with the untraceable programs he'd used, but technology was ever-changing, always advancing.

The general shifted his weight. "Your mission is complete. I'm here to discharge you officially. You'll need to remain aboard for forty-eight."

"Do I need to stay confined, sir?" As quarters went, these weren't bad, especially on a Guardian. At least he wasn't in a cell.

"No. You'll have restricted access to the ship. Colonel Biggs will see to your needs. I've sent the information to your PALM."

The name and image of a defender scrolled across the bottom of his ocular implant.

A babysitter. Of course. Because generals knew that if you let an agent loose on your ship, secrets were bound to escape.

Busy work for another day. Sawyer had more important things to figure out first.

"Do you have regeneration baths on board, sir?" His fight with the Calypson still ached in his bones.

Cazin tipped his head. "Deck Sixteen. There's a long waitlist." He turned to face the door. "I'll see you're bumped ahead." He raised his hand and swiped his PALM. The door opened.

"Thank you, sir."

Cazin hadn't moved fully into the corridor when Sawyer asked, "What will happen to her?"

Cazin paused mid-step. The air between them shifted and charged. *Fuuuuuck.* Sawyer didn't even know why he'd asked, but it would earn him a marker on his file. He was in no position to ask questions.

His back tense, the general turned slightly and met his gaze over his shoulder. Sawyer kept his expression bored. Their stare lengthened, Cazin's eyes assessing and Sawyer forcing himself not to look away.

Nothing to hide. The CORE knew everything about him. Controlled everything about him. He knew nothing. *Nothing. Nothing.* An empty vessel. A tool. A means to an end.

The general didn't ask him to clarify the question, or ask anything at all. He broke the stare and headed down the corridor. "Stay out of trouble," he said, the last of the words muffled as the door closed.

"Yes, sir," Sawyer muttered. A wave of something similar to embarrassment rolled through him.

Bracing his hands near his hips, Sawyer rose. His legs twitched beneath him, watery in a way that meant he hadn't used them for some time. *How long have I been here?* He looked down at his PALM and noted the time. Two days.

Sawyer turned away from the door and flexed his stiff shoulders. *Need to get dressed.* The compartments would have something, either an off-duty uniform or some sort of civilian garb.

When he'd first received this mission, he'd hoped the general's termination order would come across his schedule at some point, and the sentiment hadn't shifted.

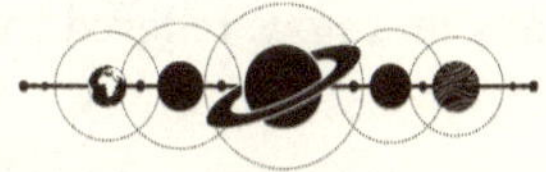

Viscous regeneration fluid suctioned against his skin. Sawyer inhaled through the breathing tube attached to his nose and mouth, then let it out slowly again. A strong antiseptic scent filled his nostrils, clearing his nasal passages with every breath.

He should feel claustrophobic in here, but never had. It was more like what he thought a hug might feel like. Only a muffled murmur penetrated the fluid, the world ceasing to exist. He enjoyed the idea that everyone else had disappeared, and it was just him surviving in this suspended reality, comfortable.

But when his mind emptied of his usual thoughts, the unusual crept in, things he shouldn't be thinking about.

What are they doing to the doctor? Why had they wanted her in the first place? Besides the fact that those beasts had killed her colleague, she'd led an unremarkable life.

He shouldn't care, but found his mind returning to those questions over again.

And what had the Calypson wanted with her?

Beep. Beep. Beep. Beep. The bath's timer echoed hollowly through the thick fluid, telling him his session was over.

It hadn't been long enough. When inside a bath like this, he had the urge to disappear, to just sink down inside and melt, to let the goo fill his mouth, nose, and throat, and to drift away.

Could he ignore it? The defender supervising the baths hadn't been overjoyed Sawyer had skipped the line, but with the general's insignia on the order, there was little he could do about it.

Beep. Beep. Beep.

He reached a hand to the side panel and slapped.

Beep. Beep. Beep.

He tried again and missed, was about to hit it for a third time when it halted. He exhaled long and slow, relieved to have the grating noise out of his head.

On his next inhale, the fluid around him lowered, a whirring, gurgling noise filling his head.

Motherfucker. That defender was on a power trip.

Sawyer sat up, thick fluid running off his head and shoulders. His ass settled onto the built-in seat in the center of the bath as his buoyancy disappeared. He curled his shoulders forward, stretched his neck, and opened his eyes to see the last of the pink fluid glug down the drain. It covered his feet and clung to his dick, groin, and the hairs of his legs.

Bracing his hands on the side of the tub, he stood. A pair of CORE-issue boots filled his vision, and a small towel dangled between them. He tilted his head back until he met the eyes of the defender on the other end.

"Colonel Biggs," he said, recognizing her from the general's communique.

She stared down at him with a narrowed, distrustful gaze. The white of her defender's uniform contrasted with her medium-brown skin. Like most defenders, she'd cut her hair to the scalp, but had bleached it blonde. Displeased lips pressed into a hard line.

Grabbing the railing on the side, he yanked himself up onto the deck with a hop, then turned to face her with his arms loose at his sides.

Her eyes skimmed him up and down, eyebrow raised. When he didn't grab the towel, she tossed it at his chest.

He caught it and dried his face and neck. "To what do I owe the pleasure?"

"I was told to keep an eye on you," she replied, tone flat.

He tipped his head when her eyes followed the path of the towel to his junk. "Taking your duties a tad literally, aren't we?"

"I take my job *very* seriously," she said, her unamused gaze meeting his again.

"I can see that." He strode away from her, his damp feet slapping against the black tile between the rows of baths, all filled to the brim with pink fluid, leaving a trail of goo behind him to be swabbed by maintenance.

The space was as big as a hangar, but the overhead was a third of the height, giving it a cave-like feel, especially with the shiny deck reflecting the strips of lighting from above. Biggs's boots smacked against the deck as she followed, disturbing the natural hush of the place. They passed the power-tripping defender at the intake desk and moved into the lockers beyond.

Sawyer finished wiping down his legs and tossed the towel into the laundry sluice. When he turned around, the colonel blocked his path.

"I don't trust agents, and I don't want one on my ship," she said, eyes flinty. "You shady shits would stab your own mothers if you were ordered to."

"Can't." He stepped around her to open his locker with his ID code. "She's already dead." He pulled out clean underwear and pulled them up his legs. "The CORE doesn't like parents interfering with its agent-training programs." One of the little tidbits he'd learned from snooping where he shouldn't.

He should feel *something* about the fact that the CORE killed his parents before he'd really known them, but they'd trained him too well. He hadn't known them and didn't experience a loss.

It wasn't a unique story. The CORE did what they wanted when they wanted. Laws were for the common folk.

He finished dressing in his off-duty defender uniform by sitting on the bench to slide on his uncomfortable-as-shit new boots. Once fastened, he stood, confronting the colonel, who hadn't moved since entering the locker room.

"I'll help you out," he said, stopping in front of her, fingers twitching for the comfort of a gun. They wouldn't give him one here. "I'm going to the galley, then to my quarters to get some much needed rest. Good work on the babysitting job. Well done."

He gave her a hearty slap on the shoulder, then passed her to the exit. It would have been too much to ask for her to leave him alone. He heard her follow and felt suspicious eyes burrowing into the back of his head.

Even though he wasn't hungry, he checked the location of a galley on his PALM and headed there.

He had to figure out a way to ditch the babysitter. Because the burning urge to learn what they were doing to the good doctor and why had only grown.

Chapter Thirty-One

Neverending dirt stretched before her. Wynn pumped her arms and legs, trying to run faster.

He'd told her to run, but betrayal slashed through her chest. She shouldn't have left him.

Don't look back.

Don't stop.

Her heart pounded in her ears. Her visor fogged from her breath, making it almost impossible to see.

She tripped on a clump of dirt and stumbled. Unable to catch her balance, she landed face first in a row of seeds.

The visor cracked, then shattered, the sound so loud it felt like her ears bled.

Then she wasn't wearing a UV-suit at all. She lay in the dirt in her underwear, her skin exposed to Earth's radiation.

She tried to scream, but her lungs were already burning, her throat closing. Ugly burns spread across her hands, and arms, and face. She clawed at her skin, ripping the pain away. Then something howled in the distance.

Wynn's eyes flew open. She closed them again when bright lights stabbed at her from the overhead. Sweat coated her body from her forehead to her knees. She lurched forward and found her arms and legs held down by restraints.

Panic speared through her chest. She opened her eyes again and looked down at herself, realizing she wore a patient's two-piece garb. A sense of violation swept away her panic, replacing it with rage.

Clenching her jaw, she turned her head. She was in a lab. Terminals lined the wall, interrupted by analyzers similar to what she'd used at her outpost. A movable machine sat close to the bed, one arm extending over and blocking some of the light from above.

She turned her head the other way and found a one-way window glaring her reflection back at her. No doubt there were people on the other side.

That rage turned white hot.

"Hey!" she shouted, flexing against the restraints. "Let me out of here!"

Schzzzz. From the corner of her eye, a metal band extended from the table by her ear and rose upward. She struggled against the restraints around her wrists, then twisted her head back and forth. The band lowered over her forehead, keeping her skull in place.

"Stop it! Let me go!"

She couldn't move with this new restraint in place, forced to stare up at the overhead.

"You're going to regret—"

Another buzzing sound drew her eyes to the side. A dermal syringe extended from the bed, aimed at her throat.

"No! Stop it! Just let me talk to someone."

She fought to remember the names Sawyer had told her, but came up empty as the syringe neared. It pressed against her neck and hissed as it injected fluid into her bloodstream.

I'm so done with being knocked out.

Then all went dark.

Cool air whispered against hot cheeks. Wynn tensed, then opened her eyes to find white upon white stretching before her. Pain pulsed through her temple, and she winced when she tried to sit up. Her hands connected with a padded floor.

She froze. A brief memory of being restrained slammed into her head. She pushed herself up, the steady breaths of slumber morphing into sharp inhales. Her feet propelled her backward, scrambling, until *smack.*

Her spine hit something firm. She turned to find more white. It extended upward and over her head. *Nothing but white.*

She braced her hands beside her hips and faced forward. Her impression of endlessness shifted, the white in front of her forming into another wall, four of them becoming a room smaller than her quarters, the ceiling barely high enough to allow her to stand.

"What is this place?" Her words croaked out of her, then disappeared abruptly into the walls, muffled.

No one answered.

Her mind raced with memories. She and Sawyer had landed on a Guardian, a warship. They'd removed her uniform, she remembered that, and she wore the white garb of someone awaiting surgery—a loose-fitting long sleeve top that opened in the back, and baggy pants, but bare beneath.

Bile welled in her throat. What had they done to her while unconscious? Heart thundering, she ran her hands down her body, assessing, then back up again. Her hand shook as she touched her neck and felt where the dermal syringe had injected her.

"Where am I?" The question rasped between dry lips. She licked them, needing a drink of water.

How long had she been unconscious?

Wynn pressed her hand against her stomach. It clenched and churned. She felt empty, like she hadn't eaten in days, but hunger was a long way off.

"State your name and ID number." The robotic voice came from all around her, assaulting her senses.

She shook her head and picked a point to stare at in the white nothing. "I've done nothing wrong. Why am I imprisoned?"

"State your name and ID number."

She fisted her hands. "No. Let me out of here."

The soulless instruction repeated, and she shook her head again. "I won't participate in whatever this is until I have some answers."

"State your name and ID number."

"Where is Sawyer? Did you put him in a box too?"

Stupid question. It had been his job to bring her here.

The voice from above didn't speak, and a gaping silence ricocheted around the small space in the wake of her question.

She felt the wall behind her, searching. They had to have gotten her in here somehow, through a door or hatch. The rubbery material passed seamlessly beneath her fingers until she arrived at the corner, turned, and explored more.

The voice echoed again, this time louder. She flinched, pausing in her search when it repeated the same command. "State your name and ID number."

Swallowing, she searched her memories for the name Sawyer had given her, the person who had given the orders. "Where is General Cazin? I need to speak with him."

The voice only repeated the order.

Wynn opened her mouth to tell it to fuck off when the walls rippled with color. She pushed away, not wanting to touch them. Heart pounding, she watched as the cube morphed into an orb, no longer solid, but liquid, like she stood inside a room-sized bubble.

Wynn. Wynn. Wynn. Wynn.

Her name vibrated from the walls, attacking, then retreating. She hadn't spoken, but it came from everywhere.

Then, faces formed in the warped surface of the bubble, emerging like ghosts. Wynn gasped, trying to get away, but they solidified into people. People she recognized. People who had been a part of her life enough to imprint on her soul. Her childhood best friend. Her mother. Her father. *Foster.* Her heart ached as each face formed then vanished, speaking her name like they'd snatched it directly from her memory.

"Wynn! Wynn. Wyyyyyynn. Wynnie!"

Fragmented voices echoed. Her old teachers, fellow students, they all shouted her name until she covered her ears.

"What is this?" she whispered, horrified. How was it possible?

The bubble burst around her, replaced by a fully formed setting. She sat in the cockpit of the stolen yacht, her arms wrapped around her knees, with Sawyer beside her. A glint of the Guardian sparkled in the distance.

Her mind revolted, rejecting what her eyes told her. This couldn't be happening, not exactly how it once was.

Was she lying on the med bed, connected to something? Or was she actually standing inside a sphere? *Or a cube?*

The image froze, then reversed. She was stumbling through the ship. She showered. She walked backward to the cargo hold. She hung from her wrists while Sawyer interrogated her.

Everything slowed again, then went forward.

"What did he want with you?"

Sawyer's distorted voice came from right in front of her, the reflection in his helmet revealing her pale face.

Panic surged in her memory and her present, the things Iax had said to her surfacing too fast to stop. *They can't know.* She couldn't reveal what he'd told her, or they would dissect her piece by piece.

She glanced downward and noted the medical garb covering her body. *None of this is real.*

Heart in her throat, she extended her hand behind her and took a step backward. Her fingers met the padded material of the cell, even though she couldn't see it. Swallowing, she continued her search of the walls, looking for an escape.

Everything went in reverse again. Sawyer stole the administrator's yacht, they walked backward through the orbital station, and onto the tether cabin.

Panic made the surrounding images swirl. The world became a cyclone as she lost control of her calm, her skin feeling too tight. Desperate, she lifted her right hand to her left forearm and found the space beneath the sleeve of her medical garb. For a moment, the smooth flesh there confused her, stalling her erratic breaths.

She dug her fingernails into her skin, trying to control the chaos enveloping her head and body.

Everything went black for a moment. She blinked against the change in lighting, hope swelling that this was the end, that giving herself pain tempered her memories, but then she saw her outpost in ruins, her rage surging as she fought to stop Sawyer.

The scene shifted, then jumped backward to a point before Sawyer had landed his ship. Before she'd known Iax as gentle and considerate. She stood in her kitchen, and the storm raged around the outpost.

She froze, still as a statue. The cutting board lay before her, surrounded by vegetables. She held a kitchen knife in her hand. It felt as real as any knife, and she knew that couldn't be possible.

I'm in a white room.

But she wasn't, and watched as the knife slid into the potato, slicing it in half before chopping it into cubes.

Thud. Thud. Thud. Thud.

Each stroke was sure and precise. She lifted the small pieces with the flat of the knife and slid them into the boiling water. She tried to resist the movements, but the need to do something with her hands overtook her, along with the need for a distraction from... something.

No. Someone.

"What is it you do?" Iax stood in front of her, his reflective eyes glinting in the overhead lights.

Her heart pounded. She shouldn't be here. She needed to keep this part of her life a secret because... because...

The thought became elusive, replaced by the immediacy of the moment.

"I'm making soup," she answered, continuing to chop and drop the bits into the pot.

"Your machine would make soup."

"Doing it myself is relaxing, focuses me. Foster—"

Thud. Thud. Thud. Thud went the knife. She knew what came next. The lab. The blood test. Her lips went numb with horror.

But then the scene reversed. She couldn't stop it, and it landed somewhere even worse.

Iax stood in front of her, only a meter away, exactly as he had the morning after he'd first arrived.

Pure terror crawled across her skin. Her heart lived in her throat and pounded in her head. They would see it all. Everything. They controlled her mind like a media feed, and she had no way to stop it.

"Are you going to change me into Calypson?" she asked him.

"No," he replied, his voice monotone.

No, no, no! Wynn choked on the memory. She couldn't go down this path. Her life depended on it.

They can't know. She looked upward, wanting to see the roof of the box, but she saw the ceiling of her outpost instead.

"You are already Calypson," he added, and Wynn's heart dropped.

This can't be happening. They shouldn't be able to dig out her secrets this way. There was too much he'd told her that even she didn't understand.

She dug her fingers into her arm. Anything to stop where this vision headed.

The images swirled and sped backwards again. She knelt in her fields, watching a meteor careen toward the surface, its vapor trail a mark against the coming storm clouds. Time moved backward further, to when she was at the Science Academy, being interviewed. It lasted only a moment, then she returned to her fields.

A snarl and a howl echoed all around her.

"No," she whispered. She couldn't live through it again, especially in this mockery of her memories.

A sob of frustration escaped her. She closed her eyes and dug her fingernails in deeper, wanting to draw blood.

The scene settled, and she stood in her outpost. A growl snapped through the surrounding space, and she jumped. Sunshine beamed through the transparent doors of the decontamination zone. The stillness made the fine hairs on her arms stand on end.

Another growl rattled around her, followed by a howl. Her heart surged into her throat. She knew this moment in time, saw it continually in her nightmares, and never wanted to be here again.

She tried to think of something else, anything else: her parents, her favorite color, the first boy she kissed. She dug her fingernails deeper into her skin, gasping at the pain. Tears pricked her eyes, then spilled over.

She ran toward the outpost, stumbling between the rows of dirt. Her heart pounded, her lungs straining with each breath. Tossing a quick glance over her shoulder, she searched behind her. There was another form in a UV-suit out there, too far to distinguish.

Foster. The four forms that blended so well with the brown landscape obscured his body. His screams echoed in her helmet while she ran until she heard nothing but her own sobs.

He'd sacrificed himself so she could get to safety.

Wynn's knees buckled, and she collapsed to her knees, but the scene continued.

Safely ensconced in the decontamination room, she watched as one beast dragged his decimated body closer. Like it wanted to mess with her.

Intelligent monsters. A sour taste filled her mouth.

Wynn turned away and closed her eyes. Her breaths left her lips in short bursts, anxiety and panic climbing through her chest. She covered her head with her hands, and the howling gave way to silence.

She didn't move for a long moment, too fearful of what she would see if she looked. When the quiet echoed between her ears, she lifted her head.

Her life continued to play, but it had reversed past the point of Foster's death. It slowed, and she was making soup with him. Her heart caught at seeing him well and whole, a smile on his face when he looked at her while dicing an onion.

Everything sped up again. She arrived at the outpost for the first time and warmed at the welcoming smile on Foster's face and the kind crinkle of his eyes. *Everything is going to be okay.*

More movement, and she returned to the moment she found out she landed the position on Earth, a swell of elation making her heady.

The colors and shapes sped up, then slowed once more.

"Dr. Wynn Lambdin."

She was back on Asia Prime on the day of her graduation. The ceilings of the auditorium soared above her, light spilling inside from the skylights to cast a golden glow over the hundreds of spectators.

The ceremony commentator stood beside her, and she saw herself decked out in her graduation gown and hat.

"Dr. Wynn Lambdin. Advanced Sciences. Biology, Botany, and Genetics." Hand extended, she accepted the digital diploma from her professor into her PALM, and shook his hand.

The world around her swirled, and changed. She no longer stood in an auditorium, but a familiar corridor with two doors on the right and one on the left—her childhood home.

"Wynn!" someone shouted from behind her.

She spun around, and her breath caught in her throat. Her father strode toward her. *Alive.* Her heart thundered in her chest. It turned to panic when he didn't stop, but walked right through her body.

"Wynn! Where are you?"

She spun in the other direction and watched him walk into her old room. There was a squeal of delight, like she'd been hiding on purpose. Wynn barely remembered this moment. How would she see it now?

Her feet moved to follow, to see what she looked like, how long ago it was, but the scene shifted and morphed. The ground beneath her remained solid, but she swayed while the images spun.

The swirl of gray changed into smudges of viridian and turquoise, then solidified into a green space. It took her a second to recognize it, an atrium in the middle of four levels of classrooms, the school she'd attended for her primary education.

The scene changed again, dragging fragments of her memories along with shards of locations she barely remembered: a friend's house, a restaurant, a vacation destination.

Everything spun together, then slowed.

Singsong voices echoed. "Wynn. Wynn. She has no kin. Wynn. Wynn. Put her in the bin."

She stood in a place she didn't remember, a room in a station that gave an institutional feel—not quite a school. Something else. Something colder.

A small girl sat in the center of a group of children. *So small.* A baby, really. She was curled into a ball, arms around her shins, and head tucked into her knees. Short black hair crowned a hidden face.

The children around her, six of them, all older, skipped around, shouting the same line repeatedly. "Wynn. Wynn. She has no kin. Wynn. Wynn. Put her in the bin."

That's me.

But she was so young she had no memory of this.

Was it real?

With everything else she'd seen, she had to guess that it was. Except if she couldn't remember it, how was this box reconstructing it?

She flexed her fingers against the wall. *Not right.* The gray, institutional carpet spread before her, but beneath her feet she felt the padded material of the box.

Nothing here was right.

Why would she be here? It felt like an orphanage, but she wasn't adopted. Her parents had never told her that. She had baby pictures. They'd told her the story of her birth, how they'd almost had her in the shuttle because her mother's labor had developed so quickly.

Had it been a lie?

Wynn reached up and swiped a stray tear from her cheek.

An adult, a woman wearing light pink civilian clothing, entered the room, breaking up the children and their taunts. They scattered, racing out into the corridor. The woman bent down, picked up the toddler and left through the same door as the rabid children.

Wynn stepped forward, intending to follow, when everything accelerated in reverse once more.

There was a ship she didn't recognize, children she didn't know. They were all squished together, holding each other. A feeling of fear swelled inside her, so poignant Wynn knew she must be reliving the experience. But she didn't remember being here either. A boy looked at her, and his eyes glinted.

Wynn's breath stalled in her throat. Who was he? She didn't know. Though his eyes glinted, he didn't look like Iax, or anyone else she'd ever met in her life.

Then the scene reversed again, so fast she could hardly catch it. An eerie blackness enveloped the cube, a hazy sort of image. She squinted to see better. Light emerged in a narrow sliver, amid sounds both muffled and loud. Pain. Fear. Confusion. *Too bright.* A piercing wail made her cover her ears with her hands.

A face emerged through the chaos. Eyes glinted. Wynn's breath caught in her throat. She knew that face from the history banks. Briar Galloway. Leader of the Calypsons. Another familiar face filled her sight, then another. She was in a lab of some type, being passed from one emotionless face to the next. The wailing continued, and she realized she was the one doing it.

My birth?

Wynn's skin went hot and cold at the same time.

No. No. No.

She wouldn't believe it. This couldn't be the place of her origin, even though it continued to play in front of her like she was part of a newsreel.

If the CORE didn't kill her for this, then they would lock her up forever.

Terror choked the breath right out of her until her vision spotted.

The memory paused, then sped up in fast forward. Wynn gasped a breath as she sat in the shuttle with other children; she curled into a ball while others taunted her; then she was in her house, being tossed into the air by her father. Squeals of delight echoed so loudly, her chest ached.

Further she traveled, to grade school, secondary school, and beyond. Her post-secondary education whirred by in a blink, then everything slowed.

She was right back at her outpost, everything as crystal clear as the day she'd lived it the first time. Muttering to herself, she frantically pulled on a UV-suit, her hands shaking. Rain splattered against the decontamination room's doors like someone threw buckets against them.

And she was going out in that, to help the stranger to the outpost.

A cold sweat broke out across Wynn's skin. *Stars above.* Whoever was in charge could watch everything that transpired between her and Iax in real time.

She didn't think her terror could increase even more, but in this moment, her dread for him exceeded her worry for herself. The damage was already done for her, but for him? They would hunt him down.

She had to do something.

The memory kept playing; the doors opened to allow her outside. She didn't understand how she'd completed the task the first time, with the wind and rain slapping against her body so violently.

Everything accelerated a moment, past where she tucked her shoulder under his armpit, then helped him to the door. It slowed again as they went through decontamination, stripping as they went, then sped up again to where she lowered his naked body onto Foster's bed. Then she was back again, treating his wounds as best she could, and making him comfortable.

Events jumped ahead, and she woke the next morning, went in search of him. When she found the bed empty, the memory jerked erratically, then paused. Wynn stood on the verge of the lab's door, not moving forward or back.

"What's happening?" she whispered, not sure she wanted the answer.

The memory jerked forward, then back, then forward again.

Then, all at once, the memory stopped. The images faded away.

And Wynn stood alone in a small white box. Her arm throbbed where she'd dug her nails in, blood beading on her skin.

Now that they'd discovered the truth about her, she knew the worst was yet to come.

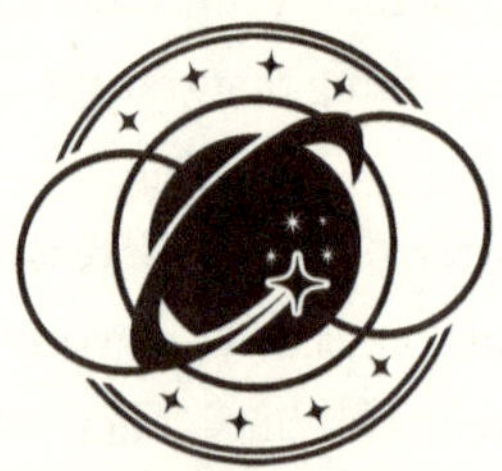

Chapter Thirty-Two

A low murmur of voices pulsed against Sawyer's back. The galley wasn't full, but enough defenders and other warship personnel occupied the space to give him a buffer of anonymity. His off-duty uniform blended in with others, even when he took a little longer at the terminal than he should.

"What are you doing?" Colonel Biggs's question rolled over his shoulders.

He'd lost her two decks above, choosing to use one of the smaller galleys aft of the ship instead of the main ones fore, but he'd known his alone time wouldn't last long.

Without turning around, he tapped twice on his selection. "Ordering breakfast." The dispensary hummed while it worked, then the back panel opened to reveal his steaming pile of proteins mixed with the ideal amount of greens, and a cup of water. He picked up both and turned.

Biggs blocked his path, her hands loose at her sides and her eyes narrowed. "You were trying to access our main systems."

He lifted his plate and cup. "Nope. Getting food." He skirted her with a step to the side, and slid into a seat near one of the starboard portholes, the view a curtain of stars.

It took her a moment, but Biggs followed, sitting opposite him and crossing her arms over her chest.

"You should grab something," he said, gesturing to the dispensary with his fork. "You look hangry." He took a bite of the hot mess that was his meal.

She glowered as he ate.

Shaking his head at her, he flipped over his hand and touched his thumb to his pinkie to activate the local newsreels while he ate. There was nothing about his trip to the planet, even in passing, though one weather report surfaced above the rest when he searched for news on Earth specifically. That monster of a hurricane continued to ravage New Asia, disrupting travel, sensor data, and routine activities. Missing person reports followed.

Bored with the same old news, he set his fork down and took a swig of water.

The colonel hadn't moved, even her eyes, in the entire time he'd dedicated to ignoring her.

"Wouldn't your day be better spent doing something else?" he asked.

"Definitely. But the general says you're one to watch, and I'm inclined to agree."

He took another bite, returning her scowl with a placid expression.

During his brief span on his own, he'd noted this Guardian had more security than most, scribes installed in the overhead at regular, one meter, intervals. The weapons lockers had double the protocols too, difficult to hack without his go-bag—which they hadn't returned to him, and probably wouldn't.

Getting rid of the tail for good would be difficult. Short of shoving her out an airlock, which he didn't have the clearance for, he was stuck with her until she abandoned the task.

With a scrape of his fork, he scooped the last bite off his plate and shoved it in his mouth.

"This has been fun," he said, standing. "We should do it again sometime." He turned toward the reclamation unit on the back wall and strode between the other tables. Eyes lifted when he passed, taking in his uniform, then jumped to Biggs, who followed close behind.

Because of her, he was being *noticed*, and he hated that. His job, *his life*, depended on him blending in. The urge to take out everyone who'd seen his face in the past fifteen minutes bit at him.

If he couldn't get away with one murder on this ship, then he definitely couldn't get away with twenty.

The small door of the reclamation unit opened at the swipe of his PALM. He slid his dishes inside and strode casually to the exit without looking behind him. The soft thump of the colonel's footsteps followed as he walked through the corridor, the scribes recording his every move.

His neck prickled at the feeling of the colonel's eyes boring into his head. Defenders, both on duty and off, passed them by. The ones who had their visors transparent assessed him in a way that made Sawyer clench his jaw. He really needed to ditch her.

They passed by airlock accesses, and the murder scenario teased his thoughts again before he pushed it aside. He turned another corridor, one that led to a bank of lifts, then stopped.

Sawyer took a breath before he turned to confront her. "This really is a waste of your time, Colonel."

She stopped in front of him, out of reach, her hand hovering over the AL-22 strapped to her thigh. "Not from where I'm standing. You were trying to access the ship's systems using the galley's interface."

He gave her nothing. Not an answer or a twitch of expression. "Do you really think if I wanted to start some shit you could do something about it?"

She lifted an eyebrow. "General Cazin has the utmost confidence in my ability, or he wouldn't have given me this assignment."

True. But Sawyer wouldn't give her the satisfaction of agreeing with her.

"He doesn't trust you, and neither do I," she went on calmly. "If it weren't for the mandatory forty-eight, I would have you off this ship immediately."

"You and me both." He relaxed his posture and ran a hand over his head. "Look, I'll make your life easier. I'll stay in my quarters for the rest of my time. No babysitter needed."

He didn't wait for a response, but turned around and headed for the bank of lifts at a quick pace. When the door opened, he stepped in, hoping this was where he would leave the colonel behind. But she was only a half-step behind him and slid inside before the door closed.

He regarded her with a blank expression, and she returned it, unruffled.

"Deck thirty-two," he said aloud, keeping her gaze.

She tipped her chin downward and crossed her arms over her chest.

So much fun. He bet she was a riot during the after-hours team-building regimen.

He glanced down at his PALM, calculating how many hours he had left of his false freedom, when the regular lighting in the lift abruptly dimmed. Red lights pulsed overhead.

The colonel's shoulders tensed, and she lifted her PALM. Sawyer looked at his own, but was getting nothing other than a standard warning to return to quarters—a civilian-level message.

Standing this close to her, his eyes automatically skimmed the words materializing above her PALM. In the next moment, she engaged her helmet. He wouldn't be seeing anything now, all data and intel displayed through her ocular implant inside her visor. But he'd caught enough.

Single vessel approaching.

Presumed hostile aboard.

All defenders to battle stations.

Biggs slapped her PALM against the lift's interior panel, overriding the system. The lift stopped, then reversed direction. Sawyer's stomach swooped at the change in momentum.

"What ship was it?" He stepped forward, seeing his reflection in her visor, the scruff he'd left on his face giving him a buffer against the world. "The specs?"

Her head turned to him, but she didn't answer.

"If it's the fucker from Earth, then I need to know."

She twitched, then held up her PALM.

An image of a ship, *his ship*, formed above her hand. Weapons fire targeted it, the pink shield rippling against the black of space. Sawyer knew his upgrades could withstand even the largest weapons from a Guardian—for a time.

How the fuck had the Calypson gotten it space-worthy? It had only been a couple of days, and Sawyer's last diagnostic had predicted weeks of repairs.

"That *fucking* thief." He tore his eyes away from the feed. "I need a battle-suit," he said. "And a weapon."

A burst of orange erupted from his ship. They both braced, but it didn't even make the Guardian shudder.

It should have. Sawyer knew his weapons, and they were fierce.

Maybe the Calypson hadn't fixed everything. Even with that thought, an itch of unease traveled up his spine.

The door to the lift opened on deck ten, and Biggs stepped out without acknowledging his requests. She marched aft, to battle stations and tactical.

"Probably a pulse cannon, too," Sawyer called, following behind. He'd need a bigger gun to take that fucker down. Not even his cruiser's weapons had kept him dead.

Biggs didn't acknowledge the demand, swiped her PALM on a security panel of a restricted area, and strode inside. It closed before he could get to it, and swiping his own PALM did nothing.

"Fuck." He really needed some sort of protective suit if he was to get off this ship alive.

And that was what he needed to do. If that fucker landed, Sawyer wanted to be as far away as possible. His job was done. He had nothing invested in this ship except his mandatory forty-eight. They could all burn for all he cared.

Not quite true. Not everyone.

He ignored that little voice as the lights continued to pulse down the corridor. More defenders rushed to where Biggs had disappeared. He thought about following despite his lack of clearance.

But then he took a step backward, and another.

He'd lost the babysitter. He was on his own. Just what he'd asked for.

I need to get off this ship.

He'd always thought of himself as a smart man. Leaving right now might feel cowardly deep in his bones, but retreating, getting as far away from the *Corvus* as possible, was the smart thing to do.

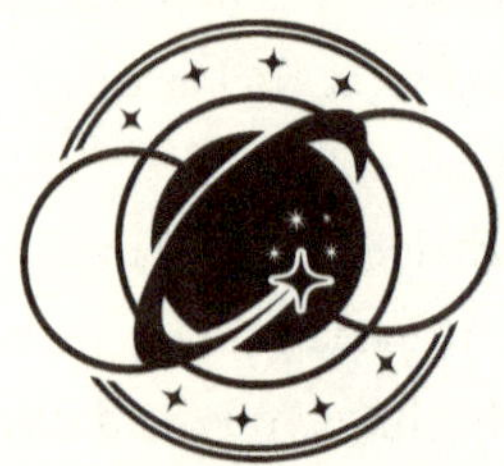

Chapter Thirty-Three

F ar past Mars, the Guardian formed as a speck on black, just another star, until Iax drew close and the speck grew into a sleek warship.

He had learned many things about Sawyer Knox's vessel while traveling. About its enhancements, its defenses, its camouflage capabilities, and its weapons.

After hours upon hours of repairs on Earth, Iax had left the atmosphere. Well-timed too, because more ships had been about to arrive at both the research station and Wynn's outpost as the storm ebbed in strength. He had engaged those camouflage capabilities to slip past them without incident.

And while on his journey, he had taken the time to converse with the ship fully, to integrate himself until a thought opened a door, or adjusted his trajectory. And he sent his essence into the belly of the cruiser, to the four unique weapons, shells, hidden within. He infused all of them with a portion of his Calypson self. They waited, as expectant and eager as he, for the hulking mass of the warship to come into range.

Even more interesting, he had learned more about the man who owned this vessel. His secrets, the data he digested, the rules he liked to break.

That such a man had touched Wynn Lambdin, and had forced her out of her home, created a haze over Iax's vision he could not clear. He was fixated on her, and relentless in his need to find her.

Voices echoed over the comm system, instructions, orders to identify himself. To stop, stand down, and prepare to be boarded. Along with the orders came the drone of thousands of new voices in his head. Relief shimmered over his shoulders.

Ever since he was a child, he had heard others. But since being so far away from Sector Ten, he had known only silence and quiet, except for the animalistic thoughts of the beasts, and the brief contact with Knox.

With his hands pressed flat against the main terminal, Iax ignored all the voices, both inside his head and out.

Weapons fire pulsed toward him. With his shields raised, he waited, ready. That was the other thing he had analyzed and improved on the journey. The shot connected, and the shields rippled with the force before absorbing the energy. No need to deflect when he could power his torpedoes with free energy from the warship.

The Guardian remained locked down. They would not voluntarily allow him to land, but Wynn was on board. His stomach clenched, and pressure built in his chest with his need to find her.

Another shot pulsed toward him. It hit, rocking the vessel, then absorbed into the ship's systems, stored as harmless energy.

My turn.

He fired from main tactical. *Divvd.* An orange pulse burst from the ship and connected with the Guardian's shields. The payload dispersed on contact, analyzing its frequencies. Iax adapted his systems to match.

On the next attack, Iax aimed his adapted torpedoes. *One. Two. Three. Four.* They pulsed from the depths of the cruiser to hurtle toward the warship.

A rapid burst of weapons fire sprang from a different part of the Guardian than the original blasts, these trying to take out his enhanced weapons.

One hit his fourth torpedo. Iax gasped as his essence scattered into the void of space between him and the warship. Another hit torpedo number two, and he gritted his teeth. It stung, losing that little piece of himself. But already he was healing, moving on to the next task.

Two of the modified torpedoes made it through the barrage. They slammed into the outer hull of the massive ship in separate locations, then burrowed inside.

Shots continued to rain on the cruiser, and the reserves of energy topped up to full. His scans, and the information Knox had saved within the computer systems, revealed all the hangars where a ship this size could land. With just a thought, Iax aimed for one on the port side.

His essence stretched, then connected to the ship's systems. He interrupted the conversations the ship had with itself and opened the hangar doors. He passed through the SNAP shielding using the codes he had digested and entered the hangar.

Defenders lined the interior, their weapons aimed at the ship. They fired, the pulses making the pink of the shields ripple around him. Iax concentrated on landing beside a bright white vessel three times the size of what he flew.

The defenders continued their assault, the shields undulating. He stood and strode toward the sleeping quarters, where he had laid out supplies. With a thought, Iax lowered the ship to the deck. *Thunk.* He touched down just as he stopped at the foot of the bed.

He already wore one of the black flight-suits Knox had left behind, but kept his hands and head bare. His essence needed free rein if he were to take over this domain. But he could not sustain similar injuries as he had on the planet. It slowed him down and put Wynn in danger. He would do everything in his power to remain well and whole, his abilities at full strength.

He swiped an autonomous shielding device from atop the covers and attached it to the shoulder of his flight-suit. Then came the weapons he had found in the locker beneath the bed, one gun on each thigh. Lastly came the knife holster he strapped to his hips.

Fully armed, he strode to the hatch. It opened as he neared. The defenders' rounds continued to bombard the ship, the world a blur of pink beyond the door. Iax reconfigured his autonomous shielding to match the frequency of the ship's defenses and stepped through.

Every gun aimed toward him. If not for the autonomous shielding, he would have fallen. Instead, his body swayed with each contact while a recurring thought looped in his mind: any of these people could have hurt Wynn.

Anger propelled him as his shielding absorbed the blasts, then deflected excess energy. At this distance, there was little he could do to deter their attacks except return fire. He pulled the weapon at his thigh. *Pop. Pop. Pop. Pop.* His four shots connected, hitting center mass, but with their own shielding, it did insignificant damage, only disrupting their formations.

He knew Tellusians liked knives for that reason.

Iax strode forward, bracing for every blast, and pushed ahead. The defenders closest to him broke their lines when he continued to advance.

With a burst of speed, Iax charged the person closest to him. He struck out, punching the weapon from their hands, then gripped the back of their neck tight. They struggled, their hands reaching to dislodge Iax's grip while the surrounding defenders fired, the area brightening with weapons fire.

Smack. Iax slammed the person's head into the ground. Their visor remained intact. In one movement, Iax unsheathed the knife at his hip, grabbed the control panel on their sleeve, and sliced through the fabric of their uniform.

His essence swept inside. The man screamed, the sound muted inside the confines of his helmet. Iax froze as the coalescing took hold. A surreal euphoria, a gratification he had not expected, warmed his skin and calmed the chaos of the hangar.

This was the first time he had initiated a coalescing on his own. In Sector Ten, he had not been assigned to the bay where pilgrims docked, but he had felt their minds merge with all others, that faint growing sensation as new people integrated with the collective consciousness.

There was skill involved. Those who succeeded in coalescing were the ones left in charge of such matters. There was an element of chance, that the joining might not take hold, that the newly integrated mind might reject the connection, leaving the person unresponsive.

With Iax being new at this, there was more of a possibility of that happening. But here, it was necessary, unavoidable, to coalesce with others if he wanted to find Wynn and return to Sector Ten unscathed.

The soldier's consciousness merged with his own. Iax's breaths shortened as their minds entwined and Shay, the defender, accepted the Calypson essence into himself. There was always resistance at first, but they soon understood the contentment of being *one*.

The power of it. The freedom of it.

Shay released a haggard breath, and with it, the initial pain vanished from his body. His helmet disengaged, revealing eyes that glinted in the low light.

With a hand around his wrist, Iax assisted him to his feet. Arms clasped, they stared at each other, their purposes coiling. Shay understood what needed to be done and why. It took only a moment, a half breath, and their minds aligned.

More. They needed more Calypsons to help with the cause. More coalescing.

They turned in sync to face the defenders shouting and firing at them nonstop. Orders came through Shay's comm, and Iax heard them too, alerting them to the crew's next plan of attack. The soldier also knew this ship well, and could guess what General Cazin's next orders might be even before they came through the comm.

Together, they charged forward and took hold of the closest defenders. Weapons knocked to the deck, clattering. Shouts became screams.

Two became four. Then four became eight. Eight became sixteen. Slowly, the chaotic cacophony ebbed into quiet, and Calypsons filled the hangar. An entire squad worth.

And as the last of the defenders joined them, Iax finally learned the information he had been searching for.

Wynn. She was being held captive on deck seven, under heavy guard.

Then that is where we will go.

They all agreed.

Chapter Thirty-Four

Turned out, he wasn't a smart man after all.

The silent alert continued to pulse down the corridor. Defenders ran in both directions, heading to battle stations. Sawyer had taken a quick trip to the regeneration baths and found a spare on-duty uniform, but no weapon. Helmet engaged, he kept urgency in his steps like everyone else.

When a lone defender headed down the corridor toward him, Sawyer's mind calculated the risks, the outcomes, in the space of a few seconds. The odds of success weren't in his favor with the security on this ship as it was, even with the distraction of the Calypson, but a growing part of him didn't care. He would deal with the scribe feeds later.

The moment the defender passed his peripheral vision, he grabbed hold of their nape and slammed them face first into the bulkhead.

There was a moment of confusion, of struggle, before Sawyer threw them to the deck. One more slam, and the person stopped moving.

Sawyer looked up and down the corridor. When it remained empty, he disengaged the defender's helmet. A pale man with blond hair lay prone beneath him, his jaw slack and eyes closed. Sawyer took off the man's PALM and swapped it with his own. He needed to know what was going on—direct orders from the bridge.

Sawyer slid the man's AL-22 free of its thigh holster and popped open the side panel. With a quick adjustment, he coded it to his own biometrics.

Standing, Sawyer initiated his helmet's interface. Information streamed in front of his eyes and across his PALM. A target infiltrated the ship, their location unknown. Conflicting reports rose side by side, along with mentions of where the Calypson traveled, and that he had help. The feed flickered, went out, then reappeared with new information.

In short, everything was fucked, and the Calypson had already taken out the scribes across the ship. *Lovely.*

Sawyer left the unconscious defender where he lay and jogged to the nearest lift. It opened immediately, and he stepped inside. Red lights pulsed around him as the lift rose upward and seconds ticked away.

Getting off the ship should be his number one priority, but Sawyer's mind raced with possibilities, circling back to the same thing over again: the only reason the Calypson would board the *Corvus* was to retrieve the good doctor.

And he didn't know why he cared when he'd completed his mission.

He halted the lift with a swipe of his PALM. Another swipe, and he accessed the lift's on-board terminal to hack into the ship's schematics.

It took him a minute, but he found a void where crew quarters and ship's systems should be, listed as unnamed rooms of undetermined sizes. Labs, he guessed.

The secrets the CORE tried to hide always screamed the loudest to be found.

The lift resumed for a few heartbeats, then the door opened. Sawyer stepped out onto deck seven and paused. A different feel existed on this level, the air expectant. The height and width of the doors were more like a hospital than a Guardian.

Sawyer skulked forward, down the hallway toward the lab with the strongest shielding. Red lights pulsed through the corridor, the deck itself eerily free of defenders. He passed one closed door, then another.

He paused at a corner, turned his head to the right, then froze.

A group of defenders blocked his path. Sawyer's steady breaths jammed in his throat.

"Fuck me," he breathed.

On any other day, he would have thought they were there to arrest him because he'd knocked out a defender, stolen weapons, and hacked the ship's systems. But these defenders weren't quite right.

They held too still, their weapons loose at their sides instead of angled defensively in front of them. And their helmets were no longer engaged.

He aimed his weapon and shouted, "Stand down." They blocked exactly where he wanted to go.

The defenders didn't acknowledge the order. Didn't move. Didn't twitch. Sawyer's finger flexed on the trigger control.

A hand slapped down on his shoulder. He spun around. His gun flew from his fingers, knocked away with a force that stole his breath. The Calypson fucker stood there wearing a black flight-suit, his eyes glinting. More defenders gathered behind him, their helmets disengaged.

Sawyer reacted instinctively. The fucker deflected his first punch, and the second and third, then his kick. Sawyer stepped back, begrudgingly releasing a portion of ground.

His breaths shortened, and the power behind his strikes became frantic. The fucker was wearing *his* clothes, using *his* weapons, piloting *his* ship. Sawyer's rage fueled him, but every attack was met with equal measure. He couldn't get the upper hand and ceded another section of ground.

A sound whispered behind him, and he turned. The group he'd first encountered advanced.

He was about to be overwhelmed without a way to stop it. Desperate, he charged forward, knocking the fucker back. The others swallowed him in their mass.

The knife came out of nowhere.

He expected a jab to his torso and was caught off guard when it slid up his arm, slicing the sleeve of his stolen uniform. A warm hand met his skin a second later.

And that was all it took.

Sawyer's limbs froze as something unseen strangled him. It was a splash of cold, then hot, almost like a regeneration bath, but so much more intense. He shouted, then dropped to his knees. Fire scorched his skin, burned over his arms and shoulders and head.

Euphoria followed.

It swept through him on a fundamental level, this pleasure-pain that defied science, logic, morals. His identity blurred, and a collective will took its place.

No. Part of him rebelled against this change even as his mind boiled with new truths, facts, faces.

He understood so much now.

Yes. He was not sure if it was his thought or another's.

He heard questions and felt desires. An inexplicable calm, an emotionless resolve, replaced passion, loyalty, and anger.

We need to find her.

His curiosity combined with a singular purpose, a need so great that he wouldn't have fought it even if he could.

They were so close.

His feet moved without a thought, and he stood. Power rippled through his arms, and legs, and skin. He clenched his fists, relishing in this new invincibility. It felt right, like everything up to this point was destined.

His eyes connected with the man in front of him. A wealth of memories passed between them. Volatile emotions evaporated into structured purpose, an intentional path, both into the future and from the past. Everything connected perfectly for him to exist in the here and now.

He left the gun where it lay and turned around. The group of defenders parted for him. He knew their names. Their hopes. Their dreams. Their hidden, horrible secrets, some so similar to his own. Some so much worse.

But none of that mattered as he strode down the corridor to the medical lab.

They needed to retrieve the doctor and take her home.

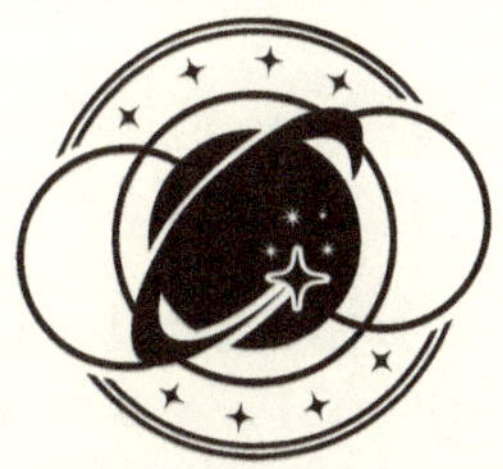

Chapter Thirty-Five

Wynn wrapped her arms around her knees tighter and pressed her forehead into her kneecaps until her brow throbbed with insistent pain.

It didn't help calm her spinning mind, but it blocked out the white glare of the room.

Any second now, the mental torture session could resume, stealing memories that weren't anyone else's to own. Her arm stung where she'd dug her nails into her skin, but even that wasn't helping settle her thoughts. Her skin itched and chafed. Small drops of crimson seeped through the thin, white material of her top. It caught her gaze and held.

A crawling sensation crept over every inch of her skin. In her mind, she bathed in blood—her demise at the hands of these people. Expectant dread settled over her shoulders. She'd tried to find a way out, but couldn't feel a hatch or door. She existed in this small space, and there was nothing else.

This was the extent of her world. A white cube and disturbing memories.

What else is there?

She couldn't remember.

Minutes passed into what felt like hours. Her empty stomach clenched on nothing. *Maybe I'll starve to death.* She would prefer that to what they'd already done to her mind.

She remained in her static existence. *Waiting.* Waiting for when they ended this game and dissected her in the name of science. She pressed her forehead to her knees harder, relishing the pain.

A hissing sound emerged from all around her. Startled, Wynn lifted her head, eyes blinking against the whiteness. She dropped her hands beside her hips, and braced, waiting for the walls to change into another memory.

They shifted, but not in the way she expected. The subtle patterning on the white walls lifted, moving upward above her head. An alternative source of light seeped in from below, then widened as the cube rose.

Wynn rolled to her knees, muscles bunching as she fisted her hands against the padded floor, ready to fight for her life. A terminal emerged on her left, another on her right.

The cube continued upward, and she stood on shaky legs. Blood pumped through her extremities, making her toes tingle. How long had she been in here? She didn't know, her sense of time suspended like the box above her.

Her breaths shortened as she took in the rest of her surroundings. Defenders, at least twenty of them, crowded the space. Red lights pulsed around the room at regular intervals while she stood on a platform in the center of a science lab. *Like a damn experiment.* Tension ratcheted up her spine.

The defenders didn't advance or point their weapons at her. Among them, two medical officers clad in black stood stock-still, their faces expressionless. They all appeared to be waiting for something.

A burning sort of anxiety seeped into her lungs. Wynn turned, then sucked in a breath when her eyes landed on the only other person wearing black. *Iax.* He held a gun, and his flight-suit outlined the width of his chest and the definition in his muscles.

She hadn't realized how uncertain she'd been about his survival until this moment.

Without thinking, she jumped, throwing herself at him. He caught her against his chest, arms holding her so tight her feet didn't touch the deck. *This is real.* He was solid and whole in her arms. The pliant material of the flight-suit rubbed against her skin.

Her lungs emptied in one long breath laced with profound relief. The buzzing in her head cleared, and the spinning of the room slowed.

"Wynn Lambdin," he breathed against her hair, the gentle tone calming her. A ragged breath shuddered in and out of his body.

Her throat clogged with relieved tears, and she pushed her face into his neck and inhaled. His scent filled her head, and his heart beat against her chest in a steady rhythm, calming her more. Wynn squeezed her eyes shut, wanting everything to disappear but them.

She pulled back a little and looked up into his glinting eyes. A red tinge colored his cheeks and neck. His expression turned thunderous when his gaze landed on her sleeve.

"You are hurt." His hands skimmed to her forearm, and his body shook, the vibration settling into her bones.

Wynn glanced down at the dots of blood. "Only a little." Her tongue darted out to moisten her chapped lips. "I did it to myself." And there were more pressing concerns than a few scratches. "They stole my memories. Of everything. Of you. I couldn't stop it."

His hands paused in their inventory of her body.

"They know who I am." And she was still processing that truth. That she'd been born in Sector Ten. That she'd been in the presence of Briar Galloway, then sent away with others.

Iax's eyes glinted from the overhead lights, his body trembling. He nodded once. "I understand." His arms around her squeezed before he set her on her feet.

She gasped as the coolness of the deck connected with her bare soles. He took her hand in his.

"I didn't want to tell them," she added, her voice shaking as much as his body. The person-sized box looked benign hanging from the overhead. "That thing somehow pulled thoughts from my head without my cooperation. I couldn't stop it."

"I understand," he said again after a beat, then turned his head to look at one defender.

Wynn sucked in a sharp breath. It wasn't a defender after all, but Sawyer. He wore a defender's uniform like the others, blending in, but she would never forget the man who had strung her up for torture.

A hard knot formed in her throat as she stared at him, his body stiff, his eyes glinting like the others. He'd been so angry when he'd questioned her, but now all she saw was detachment.

It's not right.

As much as she hated him, every cell protested at seeing him this way.

She shouldn't care. The man had forced her from her home, destroyed it, and attempted to murder Iax multiple times. She shouldn't care he'd been *changed*. That didn't stop the crawling sensation from traveling up her spine and over her scalp at the way he stared at her. Where Iax had nuance to his expression, Sawyer looked completely empty behind his eyes compared to the fire she'd seen on their journey here.

She jumped back when Sawyer lifted his weapon, her shoulders slamming into Iax's chest. Then Sawyer swiveled, aiming at the terminals surrounding the box. *Pop. Pop. Pop.*

An involuntary shout escaped her as glass and sparks flew in all directions. Next, Sawyer aimed at the box itself, and she ducked against Iax's chest as metal and circuitry shattered and fell to the floor. *Crash.* Hardware fizzled and popped.

A hollow silence rang in the wake of the destruction. Then they were moving, Iax's hand around her waist, lifting her above the glass and debris that crunched beneath the defenders' boots. He didn't set her down until they'd exited the lab.

Iax's hand tugged her along, his chest pressed against her shoulder. Sawyer remained close on her other side as they hurried down the corridor. Bracketed between them, the men traveled as one, their steps in sync.

They turned a corner, and Wynn peered up at Sawyer. He cast her a quick glance, then focused forward. Nausea swirled in her stomach.

"Where are we going?" she asked, her throat tight and scratchy.

Iax answered. "To the bridge."

Her feet skidded against the cold deck as fear gripped her heart. "What? Why?" They needed to get off this damn ship as fast as possible.

His hand was under her elbow in the next moment, herding her along. "We will all travel to Sector Ten."

She stopped, and his chest knocked into her. "No," she said with a shake of her head. "You can't take this entire ship." Scowling at him, she lifted her chin.

He tilted his head, eyes glinting. "I need to guarantee they will not pursue us."

"Then figure out a different way." When he continued to stare at her, impassive, she gritted her jaw. "If you take this ship, *this warship,* then the CORE will surely attack Sector Ten in retaliation. Do you want that?"

The entire group did not move in the wake of her question. The alertness reminded her of a computer system processing data too big for its servers. Wynn sucked in a breath and kept Iax's gaze, willing him to see the truth in her words.

The CORE government was already on edge with Calypsons and Tellusians alike. A large-scale attack, like absconding with a fully armed and staffed Guardian, would bring war to Sector Ten's doorstep. The CORE wouldn't be able to ignore it.

Stars above, they might not already because of what Iax had done.

Iax blinked, then nodded. "You may be right. We will leave instead. And quickly."

Wynn didn't have time to bask in her full-body relief, because they were moving again, switching directions to return where they'd come, Iax on her right and Sawyer on her left. They passed by the open door to the lab, then neared a junction. The group's steps slowed, perfectly in time with one another.

She heard a rustling, and turned her head to see a section of defenders at the back of the group spinning around, guns raised. They all stopped, the barrier of defenders around her making it hard to see what was happening.

Weapons fire blasted through the corridor, connecting with some defenders. Their autonomous shielding rippled with the impact, and the group closed tighter around her. Sawyer's shoulder pressed against hers. The terminals lining the walls and the overhead burst apart from the onslaught.

She gripped Iax's arm where he blocked her body with his.

"Use your gun or something," she shouted at him as he stood there unmoving.

"There is no need for my weapon here."

The commotion from the direction of the weapons fire faltered, and the deafening pops faded. Wynn shifted her position, needing to see, and caught sight of new defenders through the gaps of people. They had joined the fray, sneaking up behind those who had launched the attack.

A disturbing tranquility, an expectation, froze all sense of time. A shout rang out, cutting the silence like a blade. Another followed. The tortured sounds punched Wynn in the gut, making her flinch.

The shouts turned to screams. Someone dropped to their knees. Two more did the same. Wynn covered her ears, needing to block out the wretched sounds, but they seeped through her fingers and into the parts of her mind where she hid from beasts. Her skin crawled as the sounds crescendoed.

Then the corridor quieted as abruptly as the noise began.

Wynn lifted her head. "Are they...?" She didn't know if she could bear to see the bodies.

But the soldiers weren't lying dead on the floor. They stood with their weapons dangling from their fingers and their heads tipped to the side in question. All of them. In the same way.

Iax had done this. The person who could be so sweet to her had caused pain—transformations none of them had asked for. And she understood he would continue to do it. *For her.*

Her stomach swam with dread and doubt while his arm continued to guide her forward. They found a bank of lifts and separated into smaller groups to travel downward. The door opened, and they all poured out onto a hangar level.

With his body so close, she felt Iax stumble before his feet hitched in an uneven gait.

She reached for him instinctively, supporting his weight to help him.

"What's happening?" She scanned his face, not liking what she saw there. "Why do you look ill?" Not only were his cheeks flushed, but his entire head had taken on a pink hue.

They continued down the corridor, but his eyes flicked to hers. "I have coalesced with too many and spread my essence too thin in a short period of time."

Her fingers flexed on his flight-suit. "You mean when you change them?"

"Yes."

Her feet halted in place. "Then stop it!" She smacked his hard chest. "Stop doing it."

He shook his head once, then urged her forward. "I require more than myself for the success of this mission."

Her fingernails curled into the material of his flight-suit. That may be true, but her stomach swirled with anxiety every time she caught sight of their glinting eyes. For Iax, it felt like who he was, but everyone else? They hadn't been this way before he'd arrived on the ship.

The door ahead opened, revealing a massive hangar. A shimmer of recognition went through her when she saw the administrator's yacht through the opening. The section of defenders ahead of them filed through first, then she, Iax, and Sawyer before the rest. Some bodies lay on the deck, prone, and she wasn't sure if they were alive or dead.

The group's footfalls echoed in the quiet of the hangar, a contrast to the shouting and chaos she'd experienced when she'd arrived. A *pop* resounded, and she tossed a glance over her shoulder, noting that one of the changed defenders sealed the door shut with a blast of his weapon.

Squeezed between Iax and Sawyer, they headed to the stolen yacht. She braced her heels against the smooth deck, pulling on Iax's arm to stop their progress.

"What are we doing?" she asked when Iax acknowledged her resistance. "What will happen to them?"

The unit halted. Everyone stared at her with blank, glinting eyes.

"The ship is big enough to carry them all home," Iax replied, voice level.

She shook her head, words stalling on her tongue.

"It is where they want to go," he added.

A strangled sound left her throat at his certainty. "Maybe now. But not before you arrived." If she didn't want to go to Sector Ten, none of these defenders would. "I bet none of them would have consented to this." Especially Sawyer. His loathing had been clear.

Her fingers flexed on Iax's arm. "Can you change them back? Free them?"

His brow furrowed slightly, as big a frown as she'd ever seen on him.

"Change them all back, Iax." She squeezed his forearm for emphasis. "I demand it. Now." If she had any sway with him, and she believed she did, then he must listen to her. "I won't go willingly otherwise."

And still he hesitated.

"*Please,* Iax." How to get through to him? "You touched them without their permission."

He straightened with a nod, then stepped away from her to face the expressionless group. None of them moved, but was that fear she saw in Sawyer's eyes?

She swallowed her growing uncertainty. "Have you changed anyone back before?"

"No." He took another step away from her.

Her stomach twisted. "Will it be safe?" She licked her cracked lips.

"Uncertain." He lifted his hands out to his sides.

"Then maybe we shouldn't—"

That creepy-crawly sensation returned to her skin when Iax stopped in the center of the group. Dozens of eyes glinted as they focused on him.

A primal roar came out of nowhere, sounding as though a large animal had taken over the hangar. But there was no animal. No beast. It was all their voices crying out in pain, like Iax ripped something vital from their bodies. Or that a mutual terror had taken hold. Terror and something even worse: devastation.

Her eyes went to Sawyer a second before they all dropped to their knees, hands grabbing at their chests like they tried to stop their innards from spilling out. Blood seeped out of the corner of Sawyer's nose.

Wynn's breaths turned into rapid pants. Her fingernails dug into her arms. *What have I done?* She'd thought she was helping, and instead these people looked like they were dying.

They flopped forward, backward, sideways. Each of them fell to the deck and lay unmoving. The sounds of their shouts echoed throughout the hangar, then silence.

She couldn't catch her breath.

The tableau froze in her mind, Iax standing at the center of the circle of bodies, his hands lifted from his sides, palms forward. The scene would forever be etched in her memory.

He turned around, then headed toward her. "We must go," he said with an edge to his voice that she had not heard before, and his face more flushed. He took hold of her elbow and steered her toward the cruiser. "There is no need to take the larger ship."

Heart in her throat, she looked over her shoulder at the lumps of motionless bodies.

"Are they dead?"

"No," he gritted, his teeth clenched.

Her focus shifted to him. He looked to be in pain, but was fighting it. What had it done to him? A cold sweat broke out across her skin.

She barely felt Iax's hands on her waist as he lifted her into the cruiser. She didn't remember how she had arrived in the co-pilot's seat. No one else entered the hangar before the engine started and the ship hovered above the landing platform.

Shields rippled around them, and they punched through the SNAP shielding. The cruiser hummed as it shot forward, fleeing that awful place. Then stars upon stars extended before her.

Wynn couldn't see them through the tears blurring her vision.

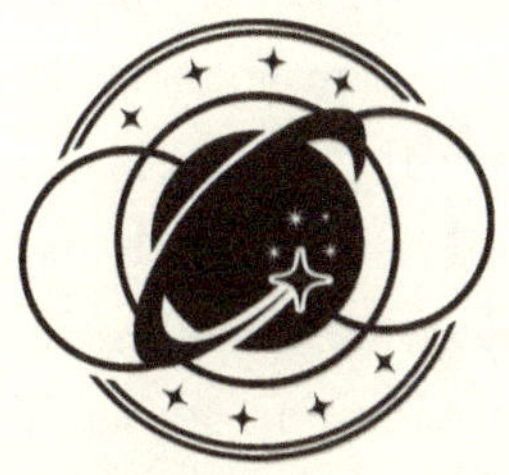

Chapter Thirty-Six

The farther away they traveled from the warship, the more Iax expected Wynn's relief, but she did not move. With her arms wrapped around her shins, she pressed her forehead against her knees, making herself into a ball.

He did not like this lifeless version of her.

Not lifeless. He experienced her emotions as they pulsed over him in waves. While separated, he had craved the sensation even more than the taste of another's thoughts.

Her emotions rose and fell chaotically, a contrast to her stillness—a stillness that unnerved him.

He put more distance between them and the Guardian, and did not relax until he knew it would be impossible for any ship in their hangar to give chase and catch up. While on board, he had made sure of that, disabling most of the essential systems before he had recalled his essence into himself.

Without the help of a Calypson, it would take the crew many days, perhaps weeks, to repair the damage he had unleashed in their systems.

The farther they traveled, the more Iax's mind emptied of others' thoughts. He understood now the heady nature of coalescing. In the beginning, he had lost some minds, but none near the end. He did not know what The Four would think of that. Would they be displeased because of his errors, or would they task him with coalescing pilgrims in the future?

Though his tension eased, he could not say the same for Wynn. Her spine hunched over her legs, her shoulders shaking while her emotions continued to churn in eddies. He could not see her face because she tucked in tight to her knees.

During their separation, she had stayed at the forefront of his mind. He could not separate his thoughts from his needs, and that had only intensified when he landed on the warship. His need to find her, to free her, had taken precedence over everything, including his mission to The Four.

He could not stand the thought of her closing herself off to him now.

Iax reached out a hand, intent on touching her shoulder, to comfort her like she had sought when he had freed her from the lab, then paused.

The day he had arrived at her outpost, she had screamed at him not to touch her. Had they returned to that place? Unsure, he dropped his hand, but his eyes went to the red stains on her sleeve.

"You are injured." His voice came out louder, harsher, than he intended.

Her head jerked upward. A watery gaze focused first on his face, then down on her arm. She covered the stains with her hand.

"May I see?" He swiveled in his seat, his hands shaking with his need to touch her.

After a small hesitation, she placed her arm in his hand. Tension eased in his chest at the contact, his fingers flexing.

Reaching with his other hand, he gently rolled up her sleeve to see what she had done to herself. Four crescent-shaped marks impaled her skin. A smear of dried blood discolored the surrounding area.

"You have four marks on your arm now." She had three back at her outpost, the ones he had healed unintentionally.

Her eyes lifted to his. "There's one for you now."

That thing in his chest shifted again, so large now it clogged his throat too.

"May I heal you?"

Almost immediately, she shook her head. "I know they won't scar like the others, but I need them for now, as a reminder."

He remembered what she had said at her outpost, that they were a badge of honor. She wore her marks like the Tellusians wore tattoos. A symbol. A tribute. And from Knox, he understood more about how pain could focus a person.

That she had added a mark for him, perhaps thinking him dead, made the space in his chest grow.

"Thank you," he murmured.

Her emotions changed again, swelling differently. She moved then, lifting herself from her chair and into his lap, the papery material of the medical garb rustling. Instinctively, his arms went around her to hold her close.

A sense of calm, of rightness, infused him as her body settled fully against his. He could hear her heart and feel her breath. Her head tucked under his chin perfectly, and he never wanted to let her go.

Her breath hitched; his grip around her waist flexed.

It took him a moment to realize he had spoken the desire aloud.

She stared up into his eyes, searching. "How did you know where to find me?"

While sinking into the deep brown of her irises, he debated the benefit of telling her the truth, that it might alienate her. But he had also vowed never to lie.

Iax lifted his hand and brushed her hair away from her cheek. "When I was in contact with you, trace amounts of my Calypson essence remained on your person." Her eyes widened, but he continued. "It provided me with a direction, then the pull became stronger as I neared your position."

She looked down at herself, a new tension straightening her away from him.

"It is not visible to the human eye," he explained. "Unless someone changes visible spectrum filters, like during your blood test."

Meeting his gaze again, her throat bobbed up and down in a swallow. "It didn't matter that Sawyer destroyed my outpost. The CORE found out about me, about what you said, from my memories." Moisture welled up in her eyes. "I don't know how it worked, but they knew everything about me. My entire past. Things *I* didn't even remember."

A wave of emotion rose inside her and washed over him, deep with a shade of grief. One tear slipped free, and he caught it with his thumb.

"I was there in Sector Ten as a baby." Her breath caught, and more tears slipped free. "Briar Galloway was there too when I was born, then she sent me away. I didn't even know I was adopted."

Another wave of that sadness crested over him just as a wealth of tears fell from her eyes. A sob rippled through her body. She tucked herself tighter into his arms, and he held her close, perhaps too tightly, but could not loosen his hold while she cried.

These truths hurt her. At the onset of his journey, The Four had given him information, knowledge, to aid in the success of his task: that she was an anomaly, that she was a Calypson, though she did not share any of the traits a Calypson usually exhibited, and that she had been sent away.

In the beginning, these were only facts to him. Now they were pain to her. A different sort of emotion rose in him. To hear her sobs, to feel her body shake—it broke pieces of him on the inside, ones he could not name, nor mend. Those broken pieces turned into aching wounds, and he found his eyes welling with moisture as well.

He closed his eyes and held her tight, feeling her pain along with his own.

Eventually, her sobs subsided into sniffles. She lifted her head, her eyes rimmed with red. "I don't know what those scientists would have done to me if you hadn't come."

"I will never abandon you," he promised, knowing it was true with every cell inside him. And along with that came another realization. "And I will never make you do something you do not want to do. Or go where you do not want to go."

With a thought, he slowed the ship, the constant hum altering in cadence. Their momentum wavered, then settled as the engines powered down.

Swiping at the tears on her face, Wynn straightened. "What are you doing?"

"I will not take you to Sector Ten if you do not wish it."

No matter what his orders were at the beginning of this mission, he could not fulfill them if the outcome harmed her. She had been through enough and deserved peace.

Bracing her hands against the terminal, her gaze flicked from the stars in front of them to his face and back again. "But—" She licked her lips and shook her head. "Where else would I go?"

"I do not know. But you did not wish for me to collect you, so I will not."

Her happiness, her contentment, had become too important to him. He would rather incur the wrath of The Four, to never return home if that was what she wished, than be another person who forced her to go somewhere against her will.

As she stared at the stars, her breaths expelled from her lips in rapid bursts. New, erratic emotions surged upward, ones very similar to what he had experienced at her outpost. With a shaky hand, she reached for the space of skin where her nails had gouged her body, covered them, and squeezed.

His chest tightened, and he reached without thinking, laying his hand on hers. It pained him to see her hurting. He'd thought to ease her stress by offering her a choice, but in doing so, it appeared he had added to it.

"Where else would I go?" she repeated as a shuddering breath expelled from her lips. "Tellusian space? Home?" She scoffed a wet sound. "The CORE will search for me everywhere. There will be bulletins with my picture, and people already know what I look like from the recent news coverage."

She shook her head again. "I don't understand how anyone could have known I was different. Why would they have sent Sawyer after me? I've lived my life according to CORE law, and I've never gone against the government. I didn't even know I was adopted." She turned and met his gaze. "How did you know to come for me?"

He went over the series of events that had happened prior to receiving his assignment, all the communications he had viewed, and those he had heard secondhand.

They had chosen him for his youth and memories of a life barely lived, as well as his willingness to follow orders and his physical capabilities. He had no strong attachments before he left either, making him a prime candidate.

They had also thought his curiosity about Earth would be an asset. Not only had he studied the planet as a child, but even after coalescing with other Calypsons, his interest in Earth remained. He had read many volumes of data about the planets in this solar system and in Epsilon Eridani.

As for how they knew how to find her...

"The newsreels," he said simply.

She swallowed. "What do you mean?"

"She recognized you."

"She?"

"Briar Galloway."

The color in Wynn's cheeks waned, and her brow furrowed while displeasure rose between them.

"I think I have a lot to say to that woman." Wynn gritted the words between clenched teeth.

A tentative hope bloomed at her angry words. "Does that mean you want to travel to Sector Ten?"

She lifted her gaze, and her eyes searched his again. "Why did you come for me, Iax? You could have left me to my fate and gone home."

"I already told you—"

She interrupted. "And you also said you wouldn't take me to Sector Ten against my will, so your mission can't be the only reason."

He held her gaze, but did not answer, his mind racing for ways to explain.

"*Tell* me, Iax. Why did you come for me?" She turned to face him fully, then gripped his arms. "Please tell me." Her voice broke.

"I needed to protect you." The words came out with such vehemence her head snapped back.

Her eyes jumped back and forth between his. "Why?"

"Because I... care about you. I *care*. So much." His arms flexed around her to keep her close. "Emotions burn inside me. They grow when I am near you and when we are apart. I cannot stop them." His fingers pressed into her skin. "I do not want them to stop."

The color returned to her face, a bloom of red across her cheeks. He followed its path with his eyes, then lifted his hand to cradle her cheek. He paused a fraction away from her skin, his breath stalling in his throat.

She tipped her head, pressing her cheek into his palm. The same tingling explosion he had experienced the first time he had touched her consumed his flesh, traveling up his arm to his scalp. She inhaled a sharp breath.

The fracture in his chest mended, the one he had experienced since watching that tether cabin leave Earth with her inside. He needed her gaze on his like he needed to breathe.

Her pupils dilated, heat taking over her expression. She bit her lip, and a strangled breath emerged from her throat. A smoldering emotion rose between them, the same that had happened at her outpost, in the hallway against the wall. The one he could not explain or stop.

Lust. Tenderness. It washed over him and lit his body everywhere. His cock jerked to life and hardened, protesting the tight fit of the flight-suit. Everything became hot all at once.

A sound wanted to emerge from his throat, but he forced it down until she lifted her hands, grabbed both sides of his face, and kissed him.

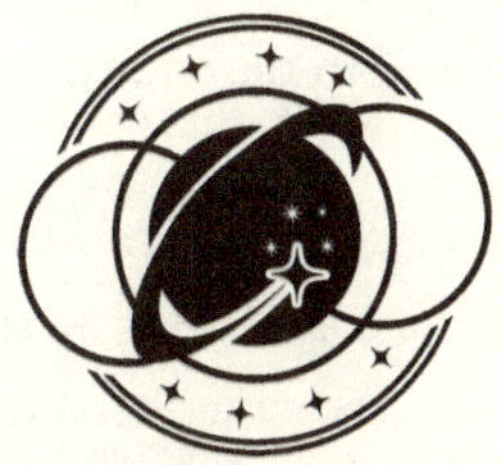

Chapter Thirty-Seven

A moan shuddered from him to her and back again until Wynn didn't know who had started it. Her head filled with the scent of him, the taste of him, and the feel of his skin beneath her palms. A pleasurable fire encompassed her entire body, her insides sighing *at last* as her dry lips drank him in.

The flesh of her cheek tingled where he touched her, electricity traveling across her face and scalp. Heat filled her chest and scorched its way to her fingertips and between her legs.

It was addictive, this feeling that she'd never experienced with anyone else. From the beginning, it made little sense that her skin shivered on contact, that her breath froze in her lungs, that when his face filled her vision, everything else faded into background noise.

Why did she burn for him, and only him?

She broke the kiss and blinked away the lust-filled fog that shrouded her vision. Iax's glinting eyes came into focus. The disquiet she used to get from the unique trait had all but disappeared. Somewhere along the line, she'd grown accustomed to the oddity, thought it beautiful—just another shade of eye color.

And she found him more expressive and wasn't sure if it was because she knew him better, or if he was showing more emotion.

"Are we safe here?" She jerked her head toward the stars without looking at them. "In this place?"

There was a moment of stillness in his body, then the ship powered up and accelerated without him moving a muscle.

"We are too far away for anyone on the *Corvus* to catch up," he assured her with an even tone.

"But what of others?"

He blinked. "We are alone out here, but I will continue to monitor our surroundings."

Without touching a single control. Even not understanding that eerie oddity, she trusted him. How could she not when he'd arrived in that lab like an avenging angel, fury coursing through his body. When he'd wrapped his arms around her, it had felt like she was coming home for the first time in her life.

Wynn dove back into the kiss. The smooth skin of his cheek melded against her palm, and she dug in her fingernails just a little. Her other hand gripped his scalp, holding him to her.

A groan vibrated through his chest. The deep sound made her insides squirm. His arms wrapped around her tight, grounding her in a way she hadn't thought possible. She reached for more, pulling him against her and shifting in his lap. He shivered, his hands flexing against her skin.

She ripped her mouth from his and gasped a deep breath. "Would it be like this with any Calypson?" Her fingers clenched against his skin. "Are you doing something to make me feel this way?"

Did she still carry his essence on her body? On her skin or clothes? The thought of carrying a piece of him didn't disturb her like it should, but was it altering her? Had he from the beginning?

"No," he stated with an emphatic shake of his head. "This is not the same." He pressed his forehead against hers. "You are important to me." He kissed her roughly, then retreated. "You make me *feel*." He recaptured her mouth, robbing her ability to speak.

His words were stilted and jerky, but she felt them all the way to her toes. *So sweet.* Emotion welled up in her eyes. Her earlier, panicked, tears turned into something more poignant: relief and affection. He made her feel too. Had she ever experienced life with this kind of sharp clarity?

A frantic need built inside her. His hardness pressed into the side of her thigh, and she shifted against the bulk, restless.

"I need you, Iax," she said against his lips.

An exposed sensation erupted over her skin at the declaration. She'd never said those words to anyone before, had never *felt* them before. But with him, she felt everything.

"I need all of you." To forget what could have happened and just focus on *them*.

But would he even understand what she meant? Reaching between them, she grabbed as much of his cock as she could through his flight-suit. "I need this." She squeezed. "Inside me." She thrust against him. "Now."

A moment of nerves almost overtook her at her declaration, but then another groan ripped through him, erasing her misgivings. He stood, cradling her body with one arm beneath her shoulders, and the other under her knees. Her medical garb crinkled at the movement.

Wynn linked her arms around his neck as his long strides carried them through the cruiser. A slender door opened when he approached, revealing a bed at its center, its covers black. Many wall compartments lined the bulkheads. He turned sideways so they could both get through without her banging her head.

Then she was floating, flying, landing in the middle of the bed with a soft whoosh of air. Iax followed her down, covering her body with his and sealing her lips in another kiss. She drank him in, her legs wrapping around his waist automatically. With a flex of her heels into his back, she pulled him closer. His bulge rubbed exactly where she needed him, fanning the flames licking up from the lower half of her body.

Her lips pulled at his, thirsty. This need came from deep inside her, and she embraced it, wanting to devour and be devoured.

He leaned back, and his eyes burned with a desire that echoed her own. There was something else there too, a tenderness that she'd only started to see at her outpost before everything went to shit. The visible affection made her lungs strain as she tried to catch her breath.

Iax reached forward, grabbed hold of the papery material of the medical garb, and tore it away from her body. A shredding sound bounced off the wall compartments.

Bared before him, cool air kissed her flesh. He paused, his eyes roving over her, lingering over the marks on her arm. A wave of nerves assaulted her as her nipples hardened beneath his thorough gaze.

Reverently, he skimmed his fingers up her ribs, across her collarbone, then downward over the swell of her breasts. Her breath hitched.

"So soft," he murmured. "I have gazed upon galaxies and nebulae, and none are more breathtaking than you."

A startled laugh stalled in her throat at his earnest words, erasing most of her anxiety. If he had been anyone else, she would have chalked those words up to empty praise. But in the brief time she'd known Iax, he had never embellished or exaggerated anything. He spoke plainly without figurative meaning, and he'd certainly never been poetic.

A hot emotion shifted in her chest. If he said these words to her, she trusted he meant them.

"That's the nicest thing anyone has ever said to me." The words felt tight in her throat.

After everything she'd seen him do aboard the *Corvus*, his cold resolve at commandeering an entire warship and changing the entire crew, it didn't seem like this level of sweetness could exist within him.

"To see this softness on your face," he murmured, "I will speak more of these truths."

The earnestness of his expression and the sincerity in his words melted her heart. Warmth spread over her skin. She wanted to be closer. *As close as possible.*

Her fingers flexed on his arms as she pulled him toward her, and the material of his flight-suit squeaked slightly. Her legs tightened around his hips. His face lowered, eyes glinting with hunger.

She paused when his lips were only a centimeter away from hers.

"I've never done this before." Embarrassment squeezed her throat, the words scratchy.

"This," he repeated, his brow furrowing.

She swallowed, her fingers twitching against his biceps. "Been with a man." Her cheeks scorched with heat.

When his expression did not clear, she added, "Like, sexually. Coupling. Intercourse. Whatever you want to call it."

His brow smoothed. "I also have not been with another."

She jerked in his arms. "You haven't?" She didn't know why it shocked her so much, but it did.

Maybe because everyone she knew, friends, colleagues, acquaintances, had been having sex since they were teens. It was mostly transactional, a way to satisfy a mutual need. Even Foster had put it on the table as an option because they were in such a remote location, which she'd refused. He'd taken quick trips elsewhere to tend bodily cravings.

Iax leaned forward and rubbed his cheek against hers. "No one has called to me the way you do." He inhaled deeply, causing goosebumps to erupt across her flesh.

Called. It was a good way of putting it. No one's body, or mind, had called to her in this way either.

"I'm nervous," she said when he pulled back and met her gaze again. Despite trusting him, anxiety swirled and mixed with the passion in her stomach.

"We only continue if we both want what is happening between us."

She nodded frantically. "I want that." Her hips thrust upward. "I want it all."

His eyes crinkled with what could only be called pleasure. "Then we will explore each other. New territory for both of us."

Yes. Equal footing. It hadn't felt like that in the beginning, but they were equals now. No matter how different they were biologically.

"Are you going to leave me, Iax? Take what you want and leave me to my fate?"

"No," he asserted with a shake of his head. "Never."

She believed him. She might be a fool, but she believed every word he spoke and trusted him with her life. Her throat tightened with emotion and need.

Consumed by it, she found the closure of his flight-suit. She ripped it downward, revealing the black shirt beneath. The flight-suit gaped, and she flexed forward to press it off his shoulders until the bulk of it settled around his hips.

Then she yanked at the hem of his shirt to find the skin beneath. "Need this off you."

He shifted, then lifted his weight, tearing the garment over his head to throw it aside.

She reached for him greedily. His smooth flesh exuded heat under her fingertips. She guided her hands up his ribs like he'd done to her, over his chest, thumbing his nipples lightly. Carved muscles and ridges undulated beneath her palms, everything perfectly honed.

"More," she demanded when she'd trailed her fingers back down and they settled on the bulky material hanging off his hips.

He straightened, then leaned backward, standing to push the flight-suit down his legs. It dropped to the deck with a quiet *thwap*. His pants came next, revealing thick thighs and an erect cock. She'd already seen him naked, but not with these feelings pulsing inside her. A rush of heat pooled between her legs. She licked her lips.

Then she was shucking off the bottoms of her medical garb, and kicking them off the bed. Up on her elbows, she lay bare before him, heated by the need in his eyes.

She reached forward, wanting him closer. One of his knees wedged between hers. The bulge of his shoulders burned beneath her palms. She urged him on top of her, needing his weight.

His chest pressed against her breasts. An incredible sensation swept through her at feeling his skin against hers. It stole her breath. Her hands roved everywhere, over the muscles flexing in his back, the hills and valleys. His lips took hers, wet and demanding. Her head thrummed while her heart raced.

Reaching between them, she grabbed his cock. Hot, pulsing, thick. It jerked in her hand. Saliva rushed into her mouth, and all she wanted to do was find out what he tasted like.

But he shifted his weight downward, and his cock slipped from her grip.

"I want to learn all of you." His mouth brushed the skin above her breasts, ghosted over her nipples, then the flesh beneath.

Each touch sent her higher, every inch of her buzzing and burning. He was so gentle, so sweet, and her mind spiraled—the opposite of panic. Desire drenched her, her head swirling with it. Her fingernails scratched into his shoulders.

His lips traveled over her belly button, and his fingers brushed the dip in her waist. Warm breath whispered against the curls of her mound, then lower.

"You're driving me out of my mind," she moaned when his nose nuzzled the lips of her sex.

"I have had the same thought." His words vibrated against her skin. Then he licked her.

Flares shot off in her head. She gripped his scalp, keeping him in place.

His fingers dug into the flesh of her thighs. She loved that, those pinpoints of pain that added to the sensual, even when he spread her pussy wider, opening her more to his onslaught. It was an invasion and homage all at once. She closed her eyes, marveling at every burst of pleasure he gave her.

"How do you know how to do this?" she panted between gulping breaths. He seemed far too experienced for this to be his first time pleasuring a woman.

He pulled away from her to say, "I have experienced the pleasure of others."

She tipped her chin to meet his gaze. "Wait. What?" Her fingers flexed against his scalp. "What do you mean?"

"I have seen many Calypsons give and receive pleasure within Sector Ten."

She pushed up on her elbows. "Like, out in the open?" She licked her dry lips. "Or, were you invited to watch?" She couldn't wrap her mind around it. CORE citizens might be free with their bodies in a transactional way, but they didn't invite spectators—that she knew of.

"In passing." Then he dove back between her legs, and her mind emptied of questions.

She stayed that way, watching him consume her like a man starved. He lapped her up with long lashes of his tongue, then short strokes to her clit. Repeatedly, he passed that place that shot sparks in her head, then retreated.

Each stroke drove her higher until a flaming tingle erupted over her entire body. With more suction to her clit, then a furious pressure, she shattered with release. Stars exploded behind her eyelids. She couldn't think, couldn't breathe, as wave after wave of euphoria swept through her.

Her fingernails dug into his scalp as she shuddered. His groan reverberated through her pussy, adding to her pleasure.

She had made herself come before, but it had never felt like this—like she'd been taken apart and put back together again.

Second by second, she slowly returned to her body and loosened her hold on Iax's head. He hadn't stopped licking her, his tongue lapping through her folds, and circling her entrance like he couldn't get enough. But every so often he would pass close to her clit again and make her jerk. She finally tugged on his scalp.

He lifted his head, his chin and lips glistening. Her heart rate had been slowing, but now it picked up again. Satisfaction and something more shone in his eyes. Goosebumps broke across her skin from the expression, and the dull ache inside her throbbed harder than ever.

She lifted off the bed and took hold of his shoulders. "More," she insisted, tugging him closer.

He crawled up her body slowly. Her heart raced, and she met him halfway, her lips connecting with his. She kissed him with everything she had inside her, tasting herself on his lips. His bare chest brushed against her nipples; his cock nudged between her thighs. She gasped into his mouth.

Every part of her felt like a pulsing nerve, sensitive and needy. She thrust her hips upward, wanting more connection. It wasn't enough. Pushing against his shoulder with one hand, she rolled on top of him, and he allowed it. Her thighs spread over his as she flattened herself on top of him. She gasped a breath, the lewd position making her feel more exposed than ever.

She liked this view of Iax, willing and wanting beneath her. Her fingernails dug into his shoulders as she lowered herself. A growling sound emerged from his chest. The wet gush of her pussy spread over his hard length, cradling him. Settled fully, she thrust her hips, riding him without taking him inside her. The movement grazed her overstimulated clit, making her twitch and jerk.

Iax's lips parted as he watched her face, rapt, while thrusting in time with the flex of her hips. His fingers gripped her ass, guiding her forward and back.

The smooth glide of his thickness between her folds made her ache more. She grabbed hold of his hands, then leaned forward to trap them beside his head. With his face so close to hers, she kissed him, an open-mouthed sloppy thing full of tongue and teeth.

"Need you inside me. Now," she demanded against his lips.

He nodded, the action infused with a frantic need that mirrored her own. "I need that too," he groaned, surging upward.

She bit his shoulder. His skin tasted like salt and something else both familiar and foreign, something she couldn't name.

"I want you to come inside me." She pulled away to stare into his glinting eyes. "It's safe." Like all CORE officers working in remote outposts or war-torn sections of the system, she had the implant that made conceiving a child impossible.

The rest of her thoughts scattered when his thickness probed her entrance. She reached down between them, guided him to the right angle, then groaned as he sank inside her that first inch.

So good. It was so damn good, her mind glitched.

Chapter Thirty-Eight

Heat and light surrounded him. He knew nothing except for the feel and taste of Wynn. He stroked up her arms, over her shoulders, then down her sides. Tiny bumps broke out across her skin in the wake of his touch. Their heartbeats echoed one another's.

He now knew why he had never coupled with another. He had been waiting for the perfection of this moment, the flawless way their bodies joined together. She consumed him, body and mind. He did not exist except for this.

Then he reached a resistance within her. He knew anatomy from others' medical knowledge, and understood this was an untouched place, and that passing through might cause her pain.

He did not like that thought, did not want this first experience between them tainted by discomfort. With his fingers laced with hers, he concentrated his essence, aiming to ease her hurt as he had healed her cuts.

Their points of contact flared with sensation: their hands, her full breasts squished against his chest, the softness of her stomach against his, her spread thighs, and the way her wet heat gloved his cock.

He focused past all those points to where his essence spoke with hers. Then, with another twitch of his hips, he sank into her more.

There was a pause, her eyes widening, then an easing and acceptance as she took him deeper. Another inch of ecstasy. He groaned again, unable to keep the noise inside. Throughout this experience, he had made sounds he never knew he could create. Her lips parted, and a bloom of color swept over her features. A fresh emotion cascaded from her to him in a thick wave. He felt it too, hot pleasure building inside him.

"Oh," she moaned, sitting up to take him deeper.

Short breaths expelled from her lips until she was fully seated. They settled together, adapting to the change in their bodies. A red flush stained her cheeks and chest; her eyes darkened.

His hands moved to her hips to hold her in place. Her warmth wrapped him like she belonged there. *She does.* An unfamiliar emotion pounded through him, something without a name, but with it came a potent dose of attachment.

He did not want to let her go. Not ever. He did not think he could, even if someone demanded it.

Swallowing, he focused on where their bodies joined. The sight stole his breath. She took him so well, stretched open and pink. It was a view he could stare at for hours. More magical than nebulae. More mesmerizing than star clusters.

But he also knew there was more pleasure to give. Hands tight on hips, he lifted her slightly, then guided her down. They groaned in unison. Her eyes fluttered closed, and she tipped her head back, exposing her delicious throat.

Had he ever paid attention to someone's body the way he was becoming obsessed with hers? He could not remember a single instance.

He lifted her again, then brought her down harder. Explosive lightning ricocheted through his body.

"Oh, stars," she breathed, her eyes opening to focus on his face.

He liked that, her entire focus on him. It caused his heart to pound like he had raced a hundred kilometers.

Then she moved on her own, and he didn't think he had ever experienced anything so profound in his life. In and out, her fevered body sheathed his in an erotic slide of flesh. Their essences fed off one another, rising in a tidal wave of pleasure. Each give and take connected them more. The yielding of their bodies made it impossible to know where she began and he ended. Emotions entwined in a concrete tangle, building until they roared in his head.

"Yes," she breathed, pushing his threadbare control right through his fingers.

Smooth motions turned frantic. He slammed upward, needing more friction. Bursts of light bloomed behind his eyelids at how good it felt. His testicles tightened.

"More," she moaned, rotating her hips. "Harder."

His vision blurred. In the next instant, he rolled, keeping himself inside her, until he was on top. Her arms wrapped around his shoulders, and her one knee lifted. He grabbed hold of it to angle himself, then snapped his hips forward again and again.

Breaths puffed from between her lips. Her fingers bit into his scalp, shooting tingles across his shoulders, and he understood how she could find pleasure or solace in pain.

She wrapped her other leg around his waist to take him deeper. Each jerk of his hips brought them closer. She cried out his name, then her teeth dug into his shoulder. Her inner walls clenched around him.

Iax was not sure how another being could be so perfect.

The heat grew inside him until he could hold back no longer. He thrust inside her and came in a hot jolt. An explosion shot off behind his eyelids. She tightened around him again, and he groaned her name into the crown of her head, his body convulsing.

He held her this way, straining, until he collapsed and his body covered hers from top to bottom. He turned his face into her throat and inhaled her scent deep into his lungs. Despite her time on the CORE warship, she still smelled of earth and warmth.

When she twitched beneath, he propped himself up on his elbows to stare down into her eyes. Though he softened inside her, he did not want to separate. He also did not want to crush her.

He rolled again, taking her with him, and settled his hands on the globes of her ass, keeping her solid and safe on top of him.

She huffed out a gentle laugh. "All right, then," she said, then tucked her face in the crook of his neck.

Iax closed his eyes and exhaled a slow breath. If they could stay this way for the remainder of their lives, he would die content.

"You know," she said, the words vibrating against the skin of his throat. "You were pretty good at that for being your first time."

"Could I not say the same of you?"

She lifted her head to meet his gaze. "I don't know. Could you?"

His chin jerked in a small nod. "You, this experience, has changed me on a molecular level. For the better."

Her eyes widened, then she licked her lips. "You really have a way with words, you know that?"

It seemed like a rhetorical question, so he did not answer, only squeezed the flesh of her bottom again.

A huff left her as she dropped her face into the crook of his neck. A hush enveloped them while his thoughts circled on how to remain secluded, just the two of them, for as long as possible, taking and giving pleasure.

Unfortunately, they would run out of air after too long.

Wynn pulled him out of his hypothesizing when she shifted away from him.

"Washroom," she murmured, and he forced himself to release her lush curves.

But he did not wish to let her go, especially as she slid off his softening length. The movement made him twitch and harden.

She looked down at him, a little smile curving the corners of her mouth. He hardened more.

A look. She could have him wanting with a look. More reason to figure out how they could stay cloistered indefinitely.

She slid off the bed, her breasts and ass jiggling as she dashed toward the washroom. Then the door closed, blocking his view of her.

His brow furrowed. Even this paltry separation seemed too much. If they were not lying next to each other, touching, then they were too far apart.

Instead of shifting the spectrum of his eyesight to watch her beyond the door, he expelled a breath and lay back on the bed to stare at the overhead. He did not know how these possessive feelings had started, but they had intensified during their separation. Now he could not stop them. He *did not* want them to stop.

And the longer he stared at the overhead, the more discontent gathered within his chest.

He turned his head when the door finally opened, revealing her naked form. The tension that had been growing inside him eased as she hopped on the bed and crawled closer. The sight of her flesh made his mouth water. Perhaps he could convince her to remain unclothed most of the time, as did some in Sector Ten.

She settled herself in his arms, and he sighed. The sensation of wholeness encompassed him. He stroked her arm, relishing the smooth skin gliding beneath his fingers.

"Have you decided?" he asked after a moment of quiet.

She lifted her chin to meet his gaze. "Decided what?"

"Where you wish to go. The ship will eventually run out of air, though the recycling system on board is much more sophisticated than usual for a ship this size."

Her eyes widened, and she leaned back to search his face. "You'd truly allow me to go anywhere I wanted?"

"Yes." Her body stiffened and her eyes narrowed, so he added, "And I would stay by your side."

Her lips parted, then she let out a small laugh.

"You do not believe me?" he asked, hurt that she would doubt his intentions. "I need to keep you safe and protected. It consumes my consciousness, as you do."

Her expression softened. "It's not that I don't believe you. I don't want to be far from you, either."

His heart flexed at those words, a lightness entering his chest. Then she went on, "But what I said about myself earlier goes for you too. They would kill you on sight if you returned to CORE space. The same goes for Tellusian space. Your eyes."

She brushed her fingers over his forehead and down his cheek. Shivers erupted through his scalp.

Her thumb paused at his temple. "You couldn't hide long anywhere with these beautiful eyes." She dropped her hand, and her throat bobbed up and down in a swallow. "There is no choice for either of us, is there?"

His mind continued to race, to search for alternatives to their predicament, but no matter where his conclusions took him, there was no safer place for her than Sector Ten, taking away the choice he wanted to give her.

The sudden urge to comfort her overwhelmed him, and he wrapped her up in his arms, holding her tight. Iax's fingers flexed against the supple flesh of her shoulder, while his mind went to the last conversation he had with The Four. They had been specific about his orders, his objectives, but not the outcome once accomplished.

He was completing his task, but wholly changed.

"I need to keep you safe," he said, though it did not accurately answer her question. "No matter what The Four wish of us."

She stiffened, lifting off him a little, until their gazes met. Her eyes jumped back and forth between his. A frown puckered her brow.

"The Four," she repeated. "Tell me more about them."

He went over his mission directives once more and found he did not care so much about what he was told to keep to himself when considering Wynn's feelings.

"The Four are the ones who... guide us with core principles: intelligence, strength, loyalty, and balance. They educate, and keep the peace, and solve problems, though we all have a say in how we achieve our own contentment."

Interest lit her eyes. "Like a government? But only four people with power?"

He tilted his chin in acknowledgment.

"Do they have names?"

"Yes. You will know them: Briar Galloway, Heath Wiseman, Leon Sweeney, and Miri Bondar."

She tensed while he listed them, but relaxed after a moment.

"You're right. I do know those names," she murmured before resettling against him. "It's so strange that they live after all this time." She set her cheek against his pectoral, her fingers creating swirling patterns against his sternum. "How long does a Calypson live?"

He thought about it for a moment, then could only answer, "I do not know."

Her fingers stopped moving. "Has anyone ever died of old age?"

"No." Death was a day of great sadness in their community, and none had yet died from living too long. "Our cells regenerate, and we have not found a limit."

She lifted her head again. "Then the rumors are true, that you can live forever." Her expression turned heavy. "How long will I live if I'm an anomaly?"

His arms tightened around her. He did not like the thought of her passing to another plane of existence. "I do not know." And he did not want to think about a life where he existed and she did not. "Many, many years, I hope. Lifetimes."

Her mouth twitched, then she resettled against him. His body sighed at the skin-to-skin contact.

She flattened her hand against his chest. "There is no place for us except Sector Ten." A new edge had entered her voice, and her echoing resolve washed over him.

He covered her hand on his chest, and a swelling emotion overtook his body. She had said "us," joining their futures together.

With a gentle tug, he pulled her up his body so he could capture her lips with his. A groan rumbled through his chest at how good she tasted. He did not think he would ever get his fill.

He rolled her over, his body covering hers from head to toe. It would take them days to arrive in Sector Ten, and he planned to give Wynn Lambdin limitless pleasure, to bury himself inside her many times, before then.

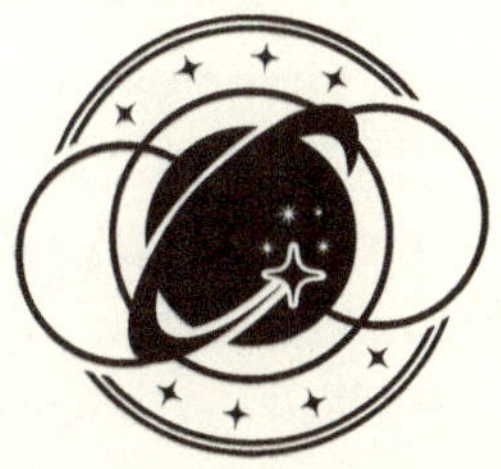

Chapter Thirty-Nine

Wynn opened her eyes and found the space beside her empty. She'd been having unsettling dreams, ones that echoed her time on the Guardian, where they'd shown her memories she couldn't recall. Ones where she huddled with other children in the dark, confusion and hunger beating at her.

Those memories sometimes morphed into the faces of her parents, her adoptive parents, and a sense of calm would replace the fear, as it did now. She stretched out her hand and touched the shiny black fabric of the pillow next to her. It was cold, and so was her exposed shoulder. How long had Iax allowed her to sleep?

As she rolled onto her back, the sheets shifted with her, and she stared at the overhead in the dim lighting. What was she getting herself into?

All night they'd explored new ways to pleasure each other. There was a tenderness between her legs she embraced, because pleasure outweighed the soreness. With each new intimacy, she fell deeper into whatever it was they created between them. Iax's glinting eyes reflected her emotional journey back at her. Whatever *this* was, they were in it together.

Swallowing the growing lump of emotion in her throat, she rolled to her side and slipped out of the covers. Cool air tickled bare skin as she went to the washroom for a steam. Once dry, she gave herself permission to explore the wall compartments of Sawyer's ship.

An unnerving sensation crawled up her spine as she opened them one by one. Along with a compartment dedicated to the color black, uniforms of every color, both CORE and Tellusian, filled the racks. Even weirder, Sawyer had one compartment dedicated to more feminine clothing in a range of sizes. Swallowing her unease, she found generic undergarments and a jumpsuit in soft pink close to her size, as well as short, gray boots that were a tad large. Once dressed, she made her way to the cockpit.

A gasp clogged her throat at the image on the viewer.

The Calypson nebula stretched from one edge of the screen to the other. The clouds were drenched in blues, and purples, and oranges, then morphed into an electric teal blue. She'd never seen it so large before, so vibrant, and that age-old question popped into her head.

What are they hiding?

In a blink, the image disappeared, returning to the unchanging view of stars. Her eyes jumped to Iax. He'd changed into some of Sawyer's clothes too, a black long-sleeved shirt, black pants with pockets down the side, and boots.

"We are a distance away," he explained. "That was an enlargement."

"Why did you remove it?" she asked, walking toward him.

He touched her hand when she was close enough, guiding her to sit on his lap. "Because it brought you fear," he said against her temple, giving her a kiss.

She turned so she could see his face. This close, she could see the hazel color of his eyes beneath the glint. "Because you sense my emotions?"

He nodded once. "Though I cannot taste your mind, I sense your emotions like they are physical things." His hand stroked her arm. "They wash over me. They curve around me. I am getting better at deciphering their meaning, but you tantalize me with new ones."

How bizarre that he could read the minds of others but only feel her emotions.

He leaned closer and rubbed his cheek against hers. "In truth, I have become dependent on the experience."

With a sigh, she melted into him, her back to his front, then frowned at the viewer. "I don't think the nebula will ever *not* make me nervous. I'd like to see."

"As you wish."

The image returned and stole her breath again. She inspected it, trying to see what existed beyond the colorful gases, but couldn't discern much at all. Her stomach twisted itself in knots. The clouds throbbed like a living entity.

And they headed right for it.

Right *inside* it.

The more she thought about it, the more she felt that familiar itch on her skin. She took a deep breath, willing the ship to stop spinning, but it didn't help. She felt that slip, that loss of control that would send her into panic.

Then warm flesh connected with hers, stalling her breath.

Iax's fingers wrapped around her wrist. It grounded her in a way she'd never thought possible from touch alone. He seemed to know intrinsically what she required, and since he experienced her emotions, it made sense. That connection kept her in Iax's lap instead of falling into an abyss of hyperfixation.

The need for pain dissipated, and the ship settled around her. Wynn turned into him, pressing her face into his throat while entwining her fingers with his.

"Thank you," she whispered against his skin, and gave his fingers a squeeze.

He nodded slightly, rubbed his cheek against her forehead, then turned so he was square to the viewer. The image changed back to the vast view of stars, but his arms remained around her.

Wynn stared at him for a moment. She wasn't a pilot, or knowledgeable about ships, but she knew he didn't control the ship the way Sawyer had, the way she'd seen others do. He never touched the console or adjusted the settings.

"How are you doing that?" she asked, keeping her gaze on his face.

"Doing what?" he asked, glancing at her.

"Piloting the ship without piloting the ship." She cocked her head toward the controls.

He blinked, then hesitated long enough she thought he was choosing his words carefully, or didn't want to answer at all.

"It is my essence," he finally said, his tone even.

"Your essence," she repeated. "You've used that term before. What does it mean?"

"My Calypson essence coalesces with the ship's systems, making it unnecessary for me to use the tactile interface."

She swiveled until the edge of the control panel supported her back, and she faced him. "Like how you do with people? You merge with the ship like you did with those people aboard the *Corvus*?"

"Yes. Merge is a good word for it. We work together."

"And it's the same for all Calypsons? This working together?"

"Yes."

She didn't know how it was possible, but she'd seen it with her own eyes. If she dwelt on what happened on the *Corvus* for any length of time, swirling panic took hold. Not because he would have merged with everyone and taken the whole warship to Sector Ten to save her, but because she should have felt guilt over that truth and was finding it hard to do so. Every time she thought about what they'd done to her, what more they'd been planning to do, bile rose in her throat. She'd thought she would die in that box. That they would keep her there and she would never be free.

Would the same thing happen in Sector Ten? Were the Calypsons just as bad? Ready to sacrifice her in the name of science?

"Your negative emotions are resurfacing." He encircled her wrist with his fingers.

"I think I just need a distraction," she said, turning to rest against his chest, her cheek pressed to the soft material of his shirt.

He remained still for a moment, then let go of her wrist to place his hand flat against the terminal. "I have something to show you. From back on Earth."

Wynn straightened when data streamed above the control panel, huge amounts of it at a rate she couldn't decipher.

"What is this?" she whispered when images of the beasts intermixed with stacked files, reports, and personnel files of scientists she didn't recognize.

As soon as she focused on something, it disappeared, replaced with some new fragment of data, making her head spin.

"After Knox took you, I found the origin of the animals. Scientists created them in an underground lab not far from your location. After years of experimentation, they turned on their tormentors."

She blinked, trying to process what he said with what she saw, but her mind was having none of it. Then Foster's face appeared, and her breath stalled in her throat.

Not possible. There was no way he had something to do with the beasts, the things that killed him.

"Where is this coming from?" Her voice sounded scratchy, wooden, in her own ears. "How are you showing me this?" He had only touched the panel with his hand, and he didn't wear a PALM.

"The files and images are from my memory."

She gasped and spun to face him. "How is that possible?"

He stared at her with a slight pucker on his brow. "I can download a certain amount of data and retain it for future use."

She stiffened at her next thought. "Is your body completely organic?" Maybe Calypsons were cyborgs.

"Yes. I have less technology in my body than you." He gently tapped the side of her temple near her ocular implant, inert now that she wore no PALM.

"Then how can that work?" Wynn shook her head in disbelief. "The process would corrupt information. No human could do that without tainting the data." But she'd seen a similar process in action with what they'd done to her memories.

Wait. Her thoughts jerked to a stop, a moment of breathlessness, then tumbled forward again, parallels forming one on top of another. Without being aware of it, she moved from Iax's lap to the seat beside him to access the files herself.

She'd already made connections between him and the beasts, the way their eyes glowed, but was it more than that?

Did the government have access to Calypson technology? How many scientists were working on this?

"Foster was in there." His face was now buried under the data that came after it.

"I found evidence that your colleague was a part of the project for many years, even before you joined him at your outpost. A group of people who called themselves Strata ran it."

The moisture in her mouth dried up. "So *not* government sanctioned."

She didn't want to believe it, but it was right there in front of her. Her mind raced to her time with him, filling gaps in with this new knowledge. Foster had left the outpost more often than was strictly necessary, and she'd always thought he'd gone to Asia Prime for R&R.

The name Strata prickled against another memory, one where Foster had been talking about a newsreel he'd just watched. She had never heard of the extremist group but now realized he must have been probing to see if she wanted in on the project.

Whatever her response had been, she must have reacted incorrectly, because he hadn't told her more. She was glad of it now. The shit in front of her was messed up. They'd kept these animals in inhumane conditions, tortured them to discover pain tolerance, submitted them to the harshness of Earth's atmosphere over and over again.

No wonder they'd killed their creators.

"Their eyes," she whispered when a new image of a beast rose in front of her.

"There is some evidence that they had been experimenting with Calypson DNA."

Her stomach twisted in knots. "How?" How the hell would they have gotten hold of Calypson DNA?

"That is what I intend to find out."

"You and me both," she muttered, her fingers tapping away at the terminal, searching for more parallels from her experience on the *Corvus* to the lab he found on Earth.

Wherever she dug, she ran into walls. The data collected about the beasts was entirely organic. It didn't begin to explain how that white box had stolen her memories. But this information could have been used to help the success of her own work on Earth, strengthening their seeds.

Her mind was a mess of questions, of worry, and of confusion. How had Foster done it? Kept these two separate lives? He'd been her best friend, her only friend, for years. Had she known him at all? It felt like sabotage and betrayal both.

She allowed her mind to wander, to ask questions, and to pull at memories from her past, re-analyzing them with fresh eyes. If this Strata group had come by the foundational scientific information through dishonest and immoral means, then she would have wanted nothing to do with it.

Foster had been right to leave her out, despite the hurt it caused.

She hadn't realized how long she'd sat there, digging into the data, until Iax stroked the side of her arm gently.

"We will eat," he said when she focused on him. "Then you can return to this if you wish."

Her stomach rumbled its agreement.

Sawyer's cruiser was equipped with a fully stocked dispensary, and they ate identical plates of balanced greens and proteins, sitting side by side in the small kitchen space.

"Your soup was better," Iax said, his eyes crinkling.

She agreed, but didn't say so aloud because sitting next to Iax redirected her focus to his throat and lips, and the way his hands moved. His glinting eyes darkened at her continued perusal, and her body warmed in response.

They found themselves in bed before either of them finished their meals, staying there for hours while they explored each other's bodies. Wynn acknowledged he might be purposefully distracting her from analyzing data, but didn't mind in the least. Not when the pleasure he gave her, the intimacy they shared, escalated with each encounter.

They fucked in every part of this ship, in positions she couldn't have dreamed up on her own.

But whenever her mind cleared, curiosity followed, and she found her feet moving to the main terminal and the data files Iax had downloaded there.

"What more can you tell me of Calypsons?" she asked during their third day of travel. "Can you upload information to the terminal like you did with the lab on Earth?"

He was silent for a long while, and she turned her body to face him. A pucker marred his brow. "I have not downloaded a dataset like I did at the lab. I can not give you continuity that way."

"But you could give me something else?" She had so many questions, but answering one created three more. "My ocular implant and PALM never seemed to fit me right. Drugs rarely work too. Is it because I'm Calypson?"

His chin jerked in a small nod. "It aligns with our origins, the discord between human cells and Calypson ones. It is a strain that is never balanced in some individuals."

A breathless sensation filled her mouth with this new information. "Can you tell me more about your origins?"

He tipped his head, hesitating again. "When we arrive, I will find you the access you require."

Her stomach swam with sudden nerves. "How far away are we?"

"Not far," Iax said, tilting his chin at the viewer. "There."

Wynn looked in the same direction. The stars hadn't changed, but the longer she stared, the more a slice of color emerged in the center of the viewer.

She straightened, setting her feet more firmly on the ground. The bright patch lengthened, then widened as they neared. *The nebula.* They were finally here, and she was seeing it with her own eyes. It grew in size with each passing second, and what hadn't been visible minutes ago, spanned the viewer from edge to edge.

A dry swallow lodged in her throat.

Her sense of time slipped through her fingers as they traveled farther inside. She kept glancing at Iax, waiting for him to look concerned, but his focus didn't waver as he piloted the ship in his unique way, taking them closer to what hid inside.

Her stomach clenched with unease the deeper they submerged the ship into the gaseous cloud, her nerves telling her this was a mistake. But it was too late now, and she had nowhere else to go.

Finally, after what seemed like hours, the clouds thinned, revealing dark shapes within. She clutched at the armrests, fingernails digging in. Her apprehension turned to confusion as the clouds dissipated into nothing.

What am I looking at?

Her brain couldn't comprehend it, though it tried. It wasn't a station or a ship. It wasn't mechanical or a plant. There was no metal composite, though a majority of the formation was as dark as a Tellusian warship.

It was none of that, but all of it at the same time.

As they neared the structure, the more it baffled her. Thick arms, both transparent and opaque, extended away from a central mass, becoming slenderer as they reached outward toward the gaseous clouds. Bulbous shapes bigger than research stations grew from senseless locations. The organic quality of the construction reminded her of the shirt Iax wore when he first arrived at her outpost.

She turned her head, taking in his placid expression. His calm kept her panic at bay, though her stomach twisted from the sight of this unusual... structure. She refocused on the parts of it that were the closest. Glasslike tubes wove in and out of the darker appendages, then twirled in on themselves. They had to be constructed from transparent aluminum to withstand the pressures of space, but she'd never seen the material used like this.

Everything she saw made more questions erupt in her mind.

"How does this exist?" She leaned forward to watch one arm disappear beneath the ship. "How are people protected? Is there shielding?"

"In a manner of speaking."

She reached and grabbed his arm. "Iax. Talk to me straight here. I'm kind of freaking out. Please explain to me how this is possible."

He turned his head and met her gaze, then stared at her a long while before he gave her a nod. "Everything you see is connected. Life. Death. Birth and rebirth. Nothing exists on its own. Everything is shared, distributed. What makes up the outer shell of our territory also makes up the outer part of me. We are stronger because of it."

She snorted. "That's a long explanation to *not* tell me what the heck I'm looking at."

His mouth twitched, then he faced forward again. "It is both organic and inorganic working in tandem."

The central mass of the structure distracted her from more questions, because she finally, *finally*, recognized something.

Within the confines of the black twisting shapes, the appendage of a ship stretched outward, its white metal composite contrasting with the organic forms. More transparent corridors existed here, all leading to the center, these mostly parallel with each other instead of twisting in all directions.

"That's the *Calypso*, isn't it?" she asked, standing to get a better look at the ancient ship.

"Yes. It is our heart. Our birth."

"Does it still fly? Or has it been altered irreparably?"

His head tilted, but he didn't answer.

Too classified? Or something else?

Movement caught her eye, and she leaned forward to stare around Iax. A small ship, something like she might see on Earth, traveled between the larger, bulbous shapes. More of them flew behind it. *So many.* She'd thought they were stars in the distance, but no, the expanse of the nebula hid the stars. Little ships buzzed everywhere, from the center of the structure and beyond.

And it extended so far. She tried to think of a station or colony that rivaled it in size, but her mind grasped no comparison. Nothing in orbit around a planet or moon.

That's it. It was like the *Calypso* had turned itself into a planet.

Its size only increased as they flew closer. Soon, the central structure's vastness obstructed everything. She focused on the one part she could identify, the engine connected to engineering, then found more. The biodome stood out among the bands of black encompassing it.

Iax circled downward, then sidled up to one of the transparent arms that spiraled from below.

Wynn had all but forgotten her fear as she'd taken it all in, but it returned tenfold when she heard the ship connect with the arm. The hollow sound reminded her of a docking clamp. She hadn't seen a docking hatch, but air hissed around the door.

The controls powered off, and Iax stood. Wynn found her feet glued to the deck, her fingers tight on the edge of the main terminal.

"They are waiting," he said after a moment.

"Who?"

"The Four."

The names he'd told her bounced around in her head, and with them, the memory of Briar Galloway's face at her birth.

Resolve straightened Wynn's spine, and she stood to meet Iax's gaze straight on. The Four had a lot of explaining to do, and she wouldn't rest until she got answers.

When Iax reached for her hand, she took it willingly. A steady feeling swept over her. She might be nervous about what she was about to find on this strange station, but she had Iax at her side. That meant more than anything.

Swallowing, they stopped in front of the exit. The airlock released, then the door slid open. She almost expected to be sucked out into space at how flimsy the corridor looked, but warm air entered, accompanied with the scent of something earthy and moist.

"No harm will come to you," he said, gently tugging her forward.

Wynn gripped his hand tight, and he squeezed hers back. The action grounded her and stalled the spinning sensation that wanted to take hold.

Inhaling a deep breath, she stepped into a silent corridor.

Chapter Forty

For hours now, the sound of other Calypsons filled Iax's mind. Though it had been only days since he had left, the empty silence in his skull had made it seem longer. The first taste of others' thoughts, the first whisper, had been as welcoming to him as Wynn Lambdin's embrace.

Those who knew him well reached out in recognition. Then others, sampling that initial connection, had reached out too. The quiet murmur had grown.

Now the chatter crashed against his skull, filled his brain in an aching way, and he could no longer filter out individual voices. A communal question rose above the rest, curiosity over Wynn and where she had been, and how she could live without coexisting mind-to-mind. Tension crawled up Iax's spine the more he listened and absorbed.

He had forgotten how loud it could become, a normal state of existence that no longer felt natural.

Layered on top of the noise, Wynn's emotions pushed and pulled at him. It eased the ache in his head and allowed him to focus on her, the volume of chatter turning into background noise. And when he focused more, he could force that noise further out of his head, cloaking it—even when The Four reached out to him directly.

His full attention on Wynn, he tugged her closer. She fixed her gaze downward through the transparent construction of the corridor.

"It feels like I should be falling," she murmured, her fingers flexing in his, then her gaze lifted, eyes full of questions.

Her curiosity pulsed at him and soothed his lingering restlessness. He focused on that, on the way she calmed him, and tucked her body under his arm.

"It is a grown material," he explained, "organic, but also manufactured." He inhaled deeply, relishing the thickness in the air.

She tipped her head to stare at him, her jaw slack, then blinked. "I'm going to need more explanation than that."

He felt the corners of his mouth twitch. "You can receive all the answers you want later." He rubbed his cheek against the top of her head, needing more contact with her body. She curved into him, and he breathed easier. "But first, we need to speak to The Four."

They were the loudest voices in his head, and the ones who were most... discontented with his continued silence.

Wynn's throat bobbed in a swallow as she stared up at him. After a long moment, she nodded, and he guided her forward.

The corridor curved upward in a spiral, then darkened as it integrated itself into the decks of the *Calypso*. Clumps of illumination hung from the overhead, glowing red to light the way. A few more steps and the solid construction of the *Calypso's* hull surrounded them.

Wynn leaned her head against him, her arm wrapping around his back. "This is creeping me out. It's too dark." Her nervous energy fluctuated.

Iax pushed a thought through the constant babble in his head, and the luminosity in the corridor brightened.

She jerked against him. "Did you do that?" she asked in a whisper, her words echoing off the walls.

"In a manner of speaking," he said with a small nod. "We all work together to accomplish tasks."

"I'm not sure that explanation helped with the creepy factor," she said, finishing with a stilted laugh that died as fast as it started.

They continued to walk upward. The deck curved gently, making it hard to see what lay ahead. He had never thought of it as creepy before this, but he could understand what she meant. He took a deep breath, reminding himself that this was his home, even if seen through new eyes.

"Why is it so quiet?" Wynn whispered. "You said that you missed the noise, but I hear nothing."

He tipped his head. "For me, it is loud."

She opened her mouth to say something, when her attention caught on a different sort of light glowing from ahead, chasing away the darkness. They climbed the last section of the incline, this one steeper, and stepped onto the shiny deck of the original *Calypso*. White light brightened the corridor, similar in design to Wynn's outpost and the warship. Calypson outgrowth poked through the metal composite in dark, thick bands, holding everything together.

It might have been the light, or the familiar corridors, but the farther they walked, the more Wynn's shoulders relaxed. Her energy shifted, a nervousness still existing within her, but the frequency changed. And the more comfortable she became, the more he could accept the voices in his head.

She slowed her steps as they neared a door, then murmured, "Engineering," as they passed the entrance.

"Yes," he agreed. Though they had not used it for that function in over a century.

She licked lips, then smacked them together. "Why does the air taste like that?"

"Like what?" He mimicked her actions to better answer her question.

"I don't know." Her brow furrowed. "Thick. Wet. And some sort of flavor I can't describe."

He could not give her a simple answer to her question, so he said, "Perhaps because we have many lifeforms living together."

She paused in her steps. "What do you mean by lifeforms?"

"Calypson adaptations, extensions, outgrowth." He gestured to where the thick band of black came out of one section of bulkhead, and disappeared into another. "We have many forms."

"Many forms," she repeated, her frown deepening on her forehead. "Are you part of that wall?" She shook her head immediately after asking the question.

"In some manner, yes." He knew it was not a sufficient response, but could not give her another at the moment.

If he could link their minds, he could explain their entire existence in a brief span of time. But being limited as they were, he felt his frustration mount at not having better words to give her.

"Sorry." She huffed out a breath. "I think I'm asking too many questions."

He squeezed her hand. "I do not believe there is such a thing as too many questions."

"Oh, I know there is. I was definitely told to keep quiet when I was an annoying little kid."

He tugged her forward. The insistent urging of The Four scratched at his mind the harder he tried to block it. But Wynn was more important than their impatience.

"I would like to see that," he stated.

She lifted her chin to focus on him instead of the bulkheads. "What?"

"Your curiosity as a child." He nodded for emphasis when her eyes widened. "I can imagine it being as captivating as your curiosity now."

She pulled him to a stop, her cheeks brightening with color. "That's a beautiful thing to say."

Mesmerized by the emotions fluttering across her face, he said, "If it is beautiful, then it suits the person I'm speaking about."

Her lips parted, and he could not stop himself from leaning down to steal a kiss from her lips. She sighed and curved into the action, her body aligning with his in a way that felt right. Her hands gripped the front of his shirt to pull him closer, and her softness pressed into him.

A moan emerged from the back of his throat. He deepened the kiss. They had spent many hours together, sharing their bodies, but it never seemed enough. He wanted *more*. His desire surged, and so did his need to bury himself in her body.

One step, then another, he urged her toward the bulkhead until he could lift her onto one of the dark arms of outgrowth. Her legs wrapped around his hips, and her fingers dug into the back of his scalp. He could not get close enough. Could not devour her enough to suit his rising urgency.

Wrapped up in their intimacy as he was, it took a moment for the shock to register. Not his shock, but others'. It was not the act itself that manifested this emotion in his fellow Calypsons, but the emotions inside him, his intense affection for Wynn, that he could not mask.

Reluctantly, Iax broke the kiss to press his forehead against hers. A deep breath calmed him, then he acknowledged the insistent presence of The Four.

They had been attempting to probe further into his mind since the cruiser had come into range. He had answered their surface inquiries, but had closed a larger part of himself away from their prying—a task The Four seemed to accomplish without effort, but that strained the edges of his own mental abilities. Even though he and Wynn were physically alone, he could not hide his actions from the rest of the Calypsons, nor mute his potent emotions.

And their horror reflected their inability to relate or understand his current state of being. Before he left, that would have been cause for change, to fix himself, to adapt, to adhere to the norm.

Right now, he found he did not care what they thought. Being with Wynn was more important than all of them put together.

And that might be the most shocking thing of all.

Her eyes searched his face, a new frown growing there.

"Come," he said, lowering her to the deck with his hands on her hips. "We are almost there." Their fingers entwined, he tugged her gently down the corridor.

He felt her eyes on him as they walked the rest of the way to the lift, felt her concern for him swell. He had not thought he outwardly revealed his growing sense of uncertainty as they traveled toward The Four, but she must have seen something for her nervousness to turn into worry for him.

Unable to resist, he tucked her under his arm and kissed the top of her head. She sighed, but her concern for him remained. *Selfless*. He did not think he had met another as empathetic as her, and it was doubly surprising when considering how and where her childhood started.

She had asked her questions, and they were warranted, but Wynn should have known these things all along. She should have grown up here as he had, despite being different. Or maybe even because of it.

When he thought of what The Four had done... a hot emotion grew inside of him, similar to what he had felt on the Guardian, but more unsettling because it was associated with Calypsons he respected. They had made the wrong choice and had admitted as much to him before he left, but after everything Iax had learned and experienced, it was more erroneous than what they had conceded.

He and Wynn neared the lift, and the door slid open. With a hand on her spine, he guided her inside. As it ascended, more inquiries from The Four pressed inside his skull. The closer he and Wynn neared, the easier it was for them to do so.

He had never thought it intrusive before, but now he fought to keep parts of himself hidden from their probing.

"What's wrong?"

Wynn's question snapped him out of his silent battle, and he realized he had pressed his fingers against his temple.

He dropped his hand. "An ache that will ease soon."

She opened her mouth, perhaps to suggest a painkiller, but the lift stopped on deck eight, the door revealing a corridor thickened in green growth.

Wynn gasped, then rushed out, her hands reaching for the plants, but she stopped a few centimeters away and looked over her shoulder at him, a question in her eyes.

"You can touch them."

She refocused on the plants. Some had leaves almost microscopically small, others were larger than her head. Reaching up, she stroked the underside of one such leaf, making it shiver with pleasure.

She gasped, then stretched her arms wide, touching the growth on both sides of the corridor at once. "This is amazing." The greenery surrounded her, making her skin glow.

His time in her greenhouse emerged in his memory, the concentration and contentment she experienced there. Lifeforms of this nature gave her happiness. *Surround her with plants.* He loved seeing her like this, wanted more of her joy, and would endeavor to make that happen.

But first, The Four were waiting.

She walked forward, arms outstretched, and he followed. A gasp burst from her lips, and she snatched her hand back, cradling it against her chest.

"What is it?" he asked, rushing toward her.

"I cut myself on something." She turned over her hand. A thin streak of red scored her finger from the tip of her pinkie to her palm. A single bead of blood gathered.

He cradled her hand, and his emotions surged. Anger joined the caustic feelings that roiled below the surface with each step closer to The Four. To see her hurt was unacceptable. He searched the foliage for what had harmed her. A barbed vine hid among the different shades of green covering the bulkheads, its spikes stretched outward.

He shook his head, slightly baffled as he returned his gaze to her hand. "It should not have harmed you. The barbs retract when someone is near." He looked into her eyes. "It must not sense you." In the same way he could not taste her thoughts?

A frown clouded her features as she tore her gaze from his to stare at the injury. "I'll be more careful in the future." She flexed her fingers, but he held fast.

"Allow me."

She nodded after a moment, and he lifted her fingers to his lips. With one flick of his tongue, he stroked the side of her hand, then pulled her smallest finger fully into his mouth, stimulating her Calypson cells.

Her breath caught in her throat, and her pupils dilated as she watched. She tasted of iron, and salt, and her distinct flavor of earth and warmth. When he let go of her pinkie with a *pop*, the skin had completely healed, with the blood removed.

"That was a turn on," she whispered, her cheeks full of color. "Can we go somewhere private for a bit?" Her throat bobbed in a swallow.

The request delivered a surge of blood to his cock, but he reluctantly shook his head. "After we have spoken with The Four." From their insistent badgering in his head, they would seek them out and interrupt them if he and Wynn were to take time to pleasure each other.

He took hold of her hand and tugged her along, being sure not to guide her too close to plants that should have been protecting her, not harming her.

They continued down the corridor, the foliage thickening and retreating in intervals. Ahead, thick bands of black and green growth kept the double-wide doors open, revealing a tall space filled with plants of all shapes and sizes, and the lifeforms who lived within them.

A small noise escaped Wynn, and he looked to where she stared, not at the greenery, but at those who waited for them. *The Four.*

They had seen his tender actions to heal her, had probed his mind enough to know they had been intimate many times now, though he had tried to keep these experiences private. They had seen what he had done on board the Guardian, knew what lengths he would go to if the same thing were to happen again.

They had seen too much. He could taste their shock and confusion.

And he found he did not care.

He tugged Wynn forward to meet them, officially completing his mission.

But the first direct thought The Four shared had him pausing mid-step.

Humans have corrupted you.

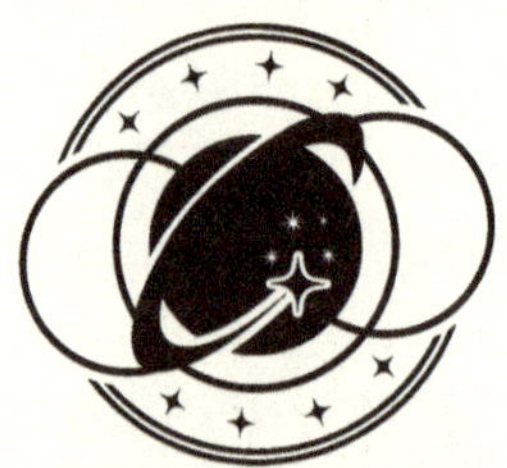# Chapter Forty-One

It was the silence that kept getting to her.

Wynn thought she knew solitude. After working at her outpost, both with Foster and alone, she knew what quiet meant. But there was something unnerving about the silence of this place.

Corridor after corridor, they encountered nothing but a quiet hush and increasingly peculiar plants. Having Iax beside her helped stave off the panic that might have wanted to take hold—him, and the continual swirl of questions in her head. Every time something distracted her, like hostile foliage, it wasn't long before she circled back to her outrage.

But the sight before her whisked it away, and she didn't know where to look. At the transparent dome above, revealing a view of the nebula that she could stare at for hours? Or at how that dark, organic-like construction material was here too, surging out of the bulkheads covered in leaves, twisting up and through the plants and trees? Or the viewers that seemed to grow out of those same trees, like heavy, electronic appendages too big for their branches? Or at the massive tree that took up the middle of the space, twisting and twirling on itself, with branches thicker than her body and a trunk that she wouldn't be able to wrap her arms around?

Or, most disconcertingly, the four people standing together near the center of the space, right next to it?

Wynn's feet halted, and she swallowed around the nerves in her throat. Not people, *Calypsons*, right out of the history banks, just like Iax had said: Leon Sweeney, Heath Wiseman, Miri Bondar, and Briar Galloway.

They all wore matching bland expressions, and clothing that resembled what Iax had worn when he arrived at her outpost, black garb in that mesh-like material. Now Wynn saw similarities between it and the bands of dark growth that had woven themselves through the bulkheads of the *Calypso*. Three of them had bare feet.

Wynn's eyes landed on the woman standing in the middle of the group and stayed there as Iax tugged her forward, his fingers linked with hers. Everything was quiet, but for the soft whooshing of air swaying the leaves on the trees, even more aggressively near the top of the biodome.

Her heart pounded in her head as the space between them and the four Calypsons diminished. With each step closer, the knot in Wynn's stomach grew and hardened. She squeezed Iax's fingers, and he returned the gesture.

They stopped a handful of meters away from the group who stood as still as statues. Briar Galloway's unnerving stare captured Wynn, freezing her beneath the warm glow of the synth lights.

Whenever Calypsons communicated outside of Sector Ten, it was Galloway who did the talking—brief though it always was. A sour taste coated the back of Wynn's tongue. This was the woman she had seen in her memories. And if Galloway was the person in charge, then she was the one who put Wynn on that ship with the other kids.

Heath Wiseman stood beside her, as he always did in those communications. Second in command, he stood taller by a few inches.

On Galloway's left stood Captain Sweeney, and like the rest of them, he hadn't aged a day since setting off on their mission so long ago. If possible, he looked even younger than his personnel records from the *Calypso's* manifest. He was the only one wearing shoes, boots like Iax had worn.

Lastly, Dr. Miri Bondar stood on the far right. She'd been the head geologist on the *Calypso's* original mission, and Briar Galloway's best friend by all accounts.

The silence between them grew as the seconds ticked by, echoing louder than weapons fire. A sense of waiting, of expectation, grew along with the emotions churning in Wynn's stomach. She flexed her hand in Iax's.

"You will speak your thoughts aloud," he finally said, the sound jarring in the hushed atmosphere. "So Dr. Wynn Lambdin can understand as well."

Her eyes snapped to him, then returned to The Four. They'd been speaking with each other this entire time?

A cold emotion bloomed in her chest. These people could say whatever they wanted to each other, about *her*, and she would never know the difference. She had never felt more like an outsider than she did right now—in the place of her origin.

She accepted it, what Iax had told her at her outpost, about what she'd seen when mentally tortured in that white box. As peculiar as this place was, there was also something familiar about it. As much as she hadn't wanted to come here, it felt like the place she was supposed to be.

And they'd sent her away. Discarded her like garbage.

Her grip on Iax's hand tightened.

Finally, one of them spoke. "Your state of mind has turned volatile," Galloway said, her voice rough and unused.

It took a moment for Wynn to realize Galloway wasn't speaking to her. All four of them stared at Iax.

"You have returned changed," Sweeney said a moment later, a hint of inflection in his voice, something close to censure. Wynn probably wouldn't have noticed except for spending so much time with Iax.

Her gaze swung from him to the others, then stayed on Iax.

"I am angry," he said aloud, his shoulders tense and his hand rigid in hers.

A length of silence followed the statement, filling the gap between them with something that pulsed and writhed.

"What creates this anger?" Wiseman asked, his head tilting to the side.

"That you sent her away those many years ago, she and others, when they deserved to be cared for. Like all Calypsons."

Wynn gripped his hand in both of hers and looked up into Iax's face. He stared The Four down like he prepared to battle, like he would fight them all for her. Wynn's own ire shifted and morphed. To know that Iax felt the same way as she, that he stood beside her, against his own people, *his leaders*, soothed some of the bitter emotions that burned in her chest.

"Being away from us has tainted you," Sweeney said with a tilt of his head.

"Humans have tainted you," Bondar agreed.

Instinctively, Wynn stepped forward, ready for a fight. "He is *not* tainted. Stop saying that." She kept hold of his fingers, and he stepped up beside her. "He *cares*."

And maybe it was the first time he had. Because he could feel her emotions, he must have experienced new ones of his own. The evidence was right in front of her the longer they spent in each other's company.

Wynn swallowed. "I don't care what weird-ass shit you've learned to grow in this place. You can't control what people *feel*, even if you want to."

Iax's fingers squeezed hers, and she stepped into his warmth. No one reacted to her declaration. The Four continued to stare at them in their disconcerting way.

"We can only hope," Galloway continued after a minute, like Wynn hadn't interjected, "the others sent with similar tasks will remain stronger than you."

"Similar tasks?" The statement slapped against Wynn like a physical thing. Her fingers tightened around Iax's. "You mean you've sent people after the others?" Her gaze bounced between them. "Did you send more people to Earth?"

Her questions rang out, then dropped like stones, unanswered. If she'd surprised them with her knowledge of the others, they didn't show it. A silence stretched and morphed into something uncomfortable. She looked up at Iax and swallowed around the lump in her dry throat. Would he explain better? If not here, then when they had a moment of privacy?

A stormy expression gathered on his face, his frown intensifying as he stared at The Four. "I requested for you to speak aloud," Iax said after a minute, the sentence harsh, reminding Wynn of his mood during her rescue on the *Corvus*. She shivered.

Another lengthy silence followed before Galloway tipped her head and said, "Leave us."

Wynn's stomach swooped with the force of the command. It took her a second to realize they meant to send Iax away. A protest rose at the back of her throat, but before she could voice it, Iax's denial shot out like a weapon's blast.

"No."

It hung there between them, resonating long after the sound faded.

Wynn's heart pounded, and she stepped closer, until the length of her arm pressed up against his.

"You once followed orders." This came from Captain Sweeney, the same censure from earlier bleeding through again.

Iax lifted his chin. "It is Wynn whom I follow now."

The Four's heads snapped back at the same time. Wynn's heart soared to hear those words. His loyalty meant *everything*.

Affection, gratitude, and love for him swelled. He'd stuck with her, rescued her, not just because of the orders these people had given him, but because he'd *needed* to. Did he understand how rare that was? Putting someone else first? Even Foster, who she would have considered her closest friend, had ulterior motives.

Wynn turned to face him fully and took his other hand in hers to entwine their fingers. He'd told her he could sense her emotions. Could he feel this too? Had he felt it even before, when they were making love? Maybe even sooner than that? She swallowed around the lump of emotions clogging her throat.

Did he feel the same way?

"That means a lot to me," she said, her voice tight. "I would follow you, too."

That was all she would say when they had an audience.

With a last squeeze of his fingers, she stepped in front of him, her back to his chest, to lean against him. His hands settled on her shoulders.

The Four's eyes narrowed in unison, glinting eerily in the synth lights shining overhead.

"Whatever your reason for wanting me here," Wynn said, her voice raised and firm. "I'm not going to cooperate if you force Iax to leave."

A silence spread, allowing the rush of wind in the biodome to overshadow everything else. Were they communicating silently even when Iax had asked them not to? Wynn lifted her chin until she could see his expression. With the way he frowned, she could only guess so.

Facing them down, she waited another handful of seconds before saying, "I've had quite the week and traveled a long way, so let's have it. Why did you send Iax to get me?"

She jerked against Iax when light flashed from above. The dead viewers held amongst the leaves and trees came to life, and the first of what Wynn saw stole the breath from her lungs.

Images, so many images, played above her: her personnel files, her schooling records, the newsreels of Foster's death and the surrounding media storm.

But worst of all, they'd somehow gotten a hold of what had transpired on the *Corvus*. There was no other explanation for how the things she'd experienced in the white box, the lost memories of those other children, the forgotten time at the orphanage, could play on these screens.

She focused on one viewer in particular, the one where the children had been taunting her at the orphanage. It looked like they'd pulled it from her head, the details were so sharp. How was any of it possible?

Panic and pain surged within her. Iax's hands stiffened on her shoulders, then shifted, until he hugged her to him, his arms under hers. She gladly accepted the embrace and gripped his hands.

"How did you get this?" she whispered, tearing her eyes away from the viewers to confront Briar Galloway. Had Iax somehow had a hand in it? He'd been able to show her those files from the hidden lab with just a thought. Was she right about this technology having a connection to Calypson abilities?

She turned slightly to ask Iax when Bondar answered the question.

"Transmissions exist as energy, and we intercept them."

"Even this far out?" Wynn shook her head, realizing the question foolish. The transmissions would have had to travel to Sector Ten for them to receive those newsreels too.

But these feeds from the *Corvus*? They wouldn't have sent them to just anyone. They would have been under layers of security and protocols. A spear of anger straightened Wynn's spine.

"Okay, so you're powerful. Very impressive. Why did you want me here?"

"Many reasons," Wiseman said with a tip of his head. "But three stand out among them."

When none of them expounded on that statement, Wynn's frustration bubbled. "And those are?" She gestured with her hand for them to get on with it.

"You were no longer safe at your location." It was Sweeney who spoke, but it didn't matter. They seemed to work as one entity, one train of thought.

The feeds above her changed, focusing on the newsreels following Foster's death. There were other things too, documents and communications with CORE insignias. Wynn squinted, but it was too far to see many details.

"I don't understand," she said.

Multiple viewers showed images of her face during the time of her questioning after the incident.

Then Wiseman spoke. "The public nature of your colleague's death brought attention to you that had otherwise remained dormant, including ours."

More files materialized, then disappeared. One comm feed spread across multiple viewers, making it easier to understand. It was between a high-ranking CORE general and a man dressed in a science officer's uniform, both of whom she'd never seen before.

We believe there is at least one on Earth, but we haven't received confirmation yet. I'll be contacting an agent for retrieval as soon as possible.

Make sure it's your best agent. If she is one of them, we can't afford to fuck it up.

Wynn's heart lodged in her throat as she realized the two men were talking about her. The Four had sent Iax to stop an agent from taking her? She guessed she should be thankful for that, as bitter as the gratitude tasted at the moment.

"And the second reason?" she asked, her hands clenching Iax's. He pulled her tighter against him, and it helped calm her some.

"We made a mistake." This came directly from Galloway.

Wynn swallowed, her throat tight and dry. "What kind of mistake?"

A long silence pulsed, and she watched The Four, who held perfectly still, communicate. That was what they had to be doing despite Iax's demand for verbal communication.

Galloway spoke again. "Twelve anomalies, like yourself, were born in a short span."

Twelve. Now she knew how many had been on that ship with her. "And you sent us away." She said it with an even tone, but her insides boiled.

"Yes. Your existence caused confusion and discord. We attempted many methods to manage you, but all failed."

"Manage us," Wynn repeated, the words tasting as dry as dirt.

There was a pause, then Galloway said with more feeling. "We admit our mistake. We are trying to fix it. Sector Ten is where you belong."

So many questions hovered on the tip of Wynn's tongue, but the next one seemed most important of all. "But why would you send us away?" Why hadn't they cared enough? Why had they discarded children like space trash?

"We did not know how to attend to you," Bondar answered.

"You were anomalies, your needs different from ours," Sweeney added.

"None of you were content." This came from Wiseman. "We failed in our efforts."

Then Galloway finished with, "We believed sending you outward would unite you with others more like yourself, humans who could understand you."

Iax's arms flexed around her.

"Some of us were just babies," Wynn whispered, the ache in her chest widening. She thought she would be angrier, more enraged to face this truth, but all she felt was profound sadness for all of them.

"Your emotions surged unpredictably." Wiseman's eyes glinted when he turned his head slightly. "It affected everyone, causing strife."

"This is not contentment," Bondar agreed. "We always strive for contentment, for tranquility."

Frustration bubbled up her throat like a fount. "Life isn't about contentment," Wynn gritted. "It's about love and loss and pain and pleasure."

Behind her, Iax rested his chin on the top of her head, and gave her a small squeeze.

Wynn swallowed and went on. "No one is content a hundred percent of the time. That's an impossible task."

"Yet Calypsons would have achieved it. Except for the anomalies."

"Sorry to break your perfect record." That feeling of not fitting in, of being different, existed here too. Wynn guessed it would never be possible to shake, but at least she had Iax at her back.

What had happened to the others? Her stomach churned with dread. "How many have you collected so far?" She needed to meet them, to see with her own eyes that they were okay.

"You are the first," Sweeney declared.

That dread morphed into a ball of terror. "But you know where they are, right? You said you've sent others." Wynn dug her fingernails into Iax's arms.

"We are searching." This came from Galloway. "We are using all our resources to accomplish the task. We sent one of our kind to retrieve you."

"Iax," she said reflexively. "His name is Iax."

The only response she received was the viewers above them lighting up again. The images were different: stars, and stations, and moons, and planets. *Colonies.* Then some interior views too, both CORE and Tellusian from the look of people's clothing.

Was this everywhere they were searching right now? There were so many. *At least twelve?*

Wynn shook her head, unable to fathom having that many Calypsons sent out in the system searching at the same time. After what had happened to her and Iax, it couldn't end well. She may have stopped Iax from commandeering an entire Guardian, but who would stop the others from making similar decisions?

One particular viewer caught her attention, an image of a baby just being born from the view of a doctor or nurse in the delivery room. It reminded Wynn of what she'd seen of her own lost memories.

She swallowed around the tightness in her throat and met Briar Galloway's gaze head on. "You were there when I was born."

The viewers flickered off one by one, their screens blank.

"Yes," Galloway agreed, the word clipped. "I am present for all Calypson births."

A momentary surge of relief spread through Wynn. It was quickly chased away when she realized she hadn't asked the correct question, the one that would ease the insidious suspicion tormenting the back of her mind since her time in the white box.

"Did you give birth to me?" She almost choked on the question. "Are you my biological mother?"

A different sort of silence hung between them now that she'd voiced it. It shifted and strained against her body until she leaned most of her weight into Iax. It pulsed and throbbed, sounding hollow in her ears. She gripped his arms tighter.

Galloway shifted her weight, then spoke. "Yes." The word was as loud as weapons fire, and as quiet as a whisper.

The wind in the space surged, echoing the emotions in Wynn's chest. Her stomach dropped through the deck. When she'd seen that memory, she had known it deep in her body, a profound truth her mind had rebelled against. To have it confirmed both horrified and freed her. For a moment, it didn't feel like she had solid mass, and her thoughts disconnected to crash into one another.

She stared at Galloway, unable to form words to express herself. *She's a sociopath.* To send a baby into space with barely anything at all, her *own* baby. Wynn couldn't grasp the thought properly, and panic welled in her throat. She couldn't control it. The foliage spun, mixing with the colors of the nebula beyond the biodome. She couldn't take a proper breath; her vision hazed black around the edges.

She reached for her marks, then paused when the memory of her adopted parents took the forefront of her mind. Those were the people who had loved her, who had given her joy. She would remember them as the amazing people they were. The thoughts grounded her, giving her something to focus on besides the ugly truth.

She didn't need scars when she had her memories.

Slowly, the haze cleared from her vision, and she stood in a room with four people who couldn't feel enough.

Couldn't *care* enough.

If she focused on that fact, she knew she would spiral more, so she concentrated on the memory of her parents' love, embraced it until everything returned to razor-sharp focus. She would find a different way to honor them than leaving scars. The room settled around her.

Wynn took another deep, cleansing breath, then turned her head to gauge Iax's reaction. "Did you know?" she asked quietly, only for him to hear.

"No." His arms tightened around her. "And I am sorry."

A defeated breath huffed out of her. It was Briar Galloway who should apologize.

Maybe this is her attempt to make amends.

Wynn pushed away that voice, not wanting to be charitable in this moment. Everything was too much all at once: the escape from the *Corvus*, this place with its freaky plants, and all these revelations. It overwhelmed when all she wanted to do was be alone with Iax, to find comfort and process these discoveries in private.

She lifted her chin, her jaw clenched. "Was that the third reason you brought me here?"

Another silence stretched, then Wiseman spoke. "No."

His answer punched her in the chest, and the sensation of spiraling resumed until Sweeney added, "We need help with the anomalies."

The statement returned her focus to Galloway. "You already said you sent people out to 'collect' them like you collected me. How can I help with that?"

Galloway tipped her head. "Not those anomalies. The others."

Wynn's heart surged in her throat, and she stepped forward. Iax's arms dropped away from her. "There are more?" She stepped forward again. "More like me? Are we related? Siblings?" Another step. "Or just mutations of the Calypson gene?" And another. "Why are we different?"

Her voice had risen throughout her onslaught of questions, and when The Four stepped back in unison, she paused. "Where are they?" she insisted when none of them answered.

Galloway spoke after a long moment. "We have them contained."

She delivered the statement with such matter-of-fact blandness that Wynn saw red. "You have them locked up? Like criminals? Like they've done something wrong?"

"It was either that, or send out another transport."

Wynn clenched her fists, the urge to scream bubbling up her throat. But she had to be satisfied with the increasingly uncomfortable expressions on their faces.

"Lady," she spat, "you're a real piece of work. Take me to them. Now."

Chapter Forty-Two

T he Four thought him corrupted, tainted, and they might be right.

So many thoughts bombarded Iax's mind, not just from those in the biodome, but other Calypsons he had known from the time he arrived in Sector Ten at such a young age, all of them questioning.

Because he had changed.

They accused him of switching allegiance.

He had countered that he had no allegiance, only life. No oaths had been sworn, though he had followed commands. He had met expectations, and now he... could not.

Because Wynn's safety, happiness, and wellbeing meant more to him than anything—above everything.

And that disturbed The Four greatly.

He presented a problem. They worried that each of the Calypsons they had sent out into the world would return as changed as him.

It was a valid worry. Once exposed to the world of humans, it was impossible not to view Sector Ten through new eyes.

He did not voice his thoughts as he guided Wynn toward where more of the anomalies existed, through the corridors where Calypson construction merged with the old CORE science vessel. Another Calypson trailed them, and Wynn kept looking over her shoulder at him, then back at Iax.

"This is Atlas," he said, realizing he should have explained earlier, but the occurrences in the botanical biodome had occupied his mind. "He is escorting us to the anomalies."

The Calypson was one of the main individuals who taught Iax how to defend himself, along with Heath Wiseman. The pair referenced their training from the days they worked for the CORE military and improved upon it in the way of Calypsons.

Wynn sent Iax a look from the corner of her eye. "Like a babysitter or something?" The stormy expression she had been wearing since the biodome had not relaxed, and echoed the volatile emotions that crashed over him in waves.

He tipped his head, decoding what she meant, then nodded. "Yes. Like that."

Her eyes narrowed, but after shooting Atlas another glance, she faced forward and said nothing more.

Atlas sent him a thought, a question, with the same taste of confusion others had sent him, but Iax ignored it, refusing to communicate nonverbally in Wynn's presence.

"This way," Iax said, tipping his head to the right and lifting his hand to the small of her back to guide her. Wynn glanced at him and leaned into the touch. A shot of pleasure rushed through his body.

After spending so much time together, their physical separation was not something he enjoyed. To touch her settled a restlessness inside him. He tugged her closer, wanting to shield her from what she was about to see and experience.

Through the open plane of communication that existed in Sector Ten, Atlas perceived the action and sent an account to The Four in the next moment. Iax would not have expected anything less, but a sense of betrayal swept through him. The Four had given Atlas orders: to watch them, guide them, and report. If Iax had been given the same task before being sent to Earth, he would have followed it without question as well. But he also knew Atlas on a more personal level, and could not stop the swell of bitter emotion.

Their eyes met, and Atlas tipped his head in confusion.

Iax would not explain himself when the infraction seemed so obvious.

"Why do I get the feeling he's telling on us?" Wynn asked, her eyebrows lifted in question as he guided her onto a lift.

"Because he is."

Her emotions swirled around them as she cast Atlas another narrowed-eye glance. "Another one to put on my shit list, then."

The door to the lift closed behind Atlas, and it descended.

Iax made a mental note to ask her what "shit list" meant later.

When the door reopened, Atlas stepped out first, leading the way to the cargo hold. They followed, Iax's hand on Wynn's spine. This section of the ship was quieter, very few Calypsons venturing deep anymore. It also had the fewest Calypson upgrades, the bulkheads mostly unblemished.

It used to have more, the dark scars remaining where the organic technology had existed, but none twisted and turned like the above decks.

A set of double doors lay ahead, and Iax reached with his mind. They opened with a soft *whoosh* to reveal a dimly lit interior.

Wynn's footsteps hesitated as she neared, and she stretched her neck forward to peer inside the voluminous space before setting foot inside.

He brightened the luminosity of the overhead lights, and she straightened, shooting him a questioning glance. He nodded once, claiming responsibility for the change in ambiance, and her eyes crinkled in thanks.

We do not need to touch minds to speak without words.

Another section of his chest shifted at the thought. Despite their limitations, they were connected.

Wynn stepped inside and swept her gaze back and forth. Storage crates towered in rows, creating temporary corridors. Iax knew from others that at the onset of the *Calypso's* mission, terraforming machines had filled this hold. Space had claimed those machines for two hundred years, some probably still orbiting Mesola and Eridu, the rest scattered to the stars.

Wynn frowned at him, opened her mouth to speak, when a soft noise echoed from within. Alarmed eyes met his, then she was off, following the sound. He trailed in her wake, matching her speed through the crates, until she stopped at where they opened up into a makeshift room.

"Oh, my stars," she breathed. Her hand flew upward and pressed against her chest while distress swirled around him.

Iax stepped close behind her to see what she saw.

Six children occupied the space. When they noticed them, they all clustered on one of the two sofas that sat perpendicular to each other in the center of the room. Double-stacked cots, bunks, were pushed to the edges where blankets lay in heaps. An array of personal items spread throughout the room, some tidy while others were more haphazard. In the corner, two angled crates made a counter of sorts. On top, a clear container held water, with six cups stacked neatly. A smaller crate lay open next to it, rations and other food set inside.

The children huddling together pulled Iax's gaze. Emotions swelled and took over the space in his chest where only Wynn had existed moments ago. Wearing clothing made of the same webbed organic material as most Calypson apparel, the two oldest, one boy and one girl, held their arms around the younger four protectively, their eyes wary.

The boy's brown hair hung past his shoulders in untended clumps, and the girl's hair was just as unruly, though a darker shade. A few years younger, the two other boys looked almost identical in appearance. The youngest girl appeared barely able to walk. She stuck her thumb in her mouth and turned her eyes away from them. The last child looked only a couple of years older than her.

None of them had the distinctive eyes of Calypsons, but all were born here.

They were like Wynn.

An unsettling emotion coursed through his body, one he could not name yet. There was affection there, but also a different sort of protectiveness than what he felt with Wynn. He wanted to help these children. They lived, but was this living when they were so isolated?

A shot of anger followed the thought. He knew the anomalies existed here, as everyone did, but he had not been a part of their care and had not understood their living arrangements. But seeing them now? Emotion settled in the back of his throat, burning.

He realized it was calculated. The Four kept this from most of the population to protect them, but also to hide their failure at taking care of the anomalies. He and the others were sent to retrieve the original twelve for that reason.

His hands fisted and clenched.

"I didn't think it was possible for me to get angrier at those people."

The little ones jumped at Wynn's harsh words.

"I'm sorry," she said in the next instant, her voice gentled. She squatted down, making herself eye level. "I'm not mad at you."

The youngest curled tightly into the older girl, but the others stared at her with curiosity.

"Can you tell me your names?" Her voiced trembled.

The oldest boy stared at her with his brow furrowed, then he looked to the older girl and gestured with one hand, grunting twice.

Wynn gasped, then turned to Iax with horrified eyes. Hotter emotions swelled and slapped against him.

Her expression cracked his chest wide open.

"They can't speak?" Wynn's breathing matched her emotions, panicked and chaotic.

A sound came from the girl.

"No, it's even worse," Wynn murmured, standing to face Atlas, who had followed them in, but kept his distance. "You didn't bother to teach them language."

Atlas only stared at her, his eyes glinting, but Iax heard one wayward thought. *It was not necessary.*

But Atlas and The Four were wrong. If Iax found solace in communicating with Wynn verbally, then these children would have benefited from it as well.

Wynn looked to Iax when Atlas did not answer. "What are they doing here?"

"This is their home." It did not seem an adequate accommodation, but it was what others had deemed appropriate.

"But why *here*? Like this? Away from everything?"

His stomach swam with distaste. "They were corralled to minimize their impact."

"Corralled?" The word expelled between her lips in a gasp. "Fucking stars, Iax, they aren't animals."

"I know this." He took her hand in his to let her know he stood with her.

"Who made this decision?"

There was only one answer. "The Four." They had the final say in all things.

Her eyes narrowed into slits. "If I ever see any of them again, I'll probably punch all of their beautiful faces." She let go of his hand and strode toward Atlas, eyes spitting her ire. "You got that? You tell them they're weak and useless leaders. And fucking twats. When I see them again, there will be violence."

The declaration, and the way Atlas backed up from the threat, should have horrified Iax, but warm pride filled his chest.

She turned toward him, her lips pressed together tightly. "Why were they left with so little?"

"They cannot access Calypson technology the way we do."

"Oh, for fuck's sakes." She threw up her hands. "A ship full of brilliant scientists and you couldn't figure out a way to make the interfaces tactile?" Her voice rose at the end, disbelief coating every word. "To teach them how to speak commands?"

She shook her head, and her shoulders slumped with what he could only call sadness. It paired with the darker emotions swirling around her body. "It shouldn't shock me. If they sent me and others away just so they didn't have to deal with us, why am I surprised they would treat these children this way?"

His chest tightened. He did not like that this situation caused her distress.

A deep breath lifted her shoulders, then an exhale relaxed them. With a determined look in her eyes, Wynn turned back to the children. She re-entered their modest space, and he followed, though he left some distance between them. Wynn drew a little closer, then sat on the empty couch. The twins stared at her with open curiosity while the older two regarded her with cautious expressions.

"My name is Wynn," she said with a hand placed against her chest. "Are you all okay? What do you need?"

The oldest boy's forehead scrunched; the older girl tipped her head.

Wynn took another deep breath and patted her chest. "Wynn."

Understanding entered their eyes at the same time. They looked at each other once, then the boys said, "Mack."

A smile erupted on Wynn's face, then she looked at the girl. "Bex," she said, touching her chest.

Wynn's smile widened, and so did the warm sensation enveloping Iax's chest.

"Mack," she said to the boy, and he nodded.

"Bex." The girl nodded too, tentative smiles curling their lips.

Wynn focused on the younger children.

"Dexxa," said Bex when she touched the littlest's head.

"Ari." The boy gestured to the girl in his lap, who was a little older.

Then Wynn looked at the twins between them.

"Mass," Bex said, with a tilt of her head to the boy closest to her. Then she jerked her head to the other. "Sam."

Wynn's shoulders relaxed, and she nodded to each of them. "It's a pleasure to meet all of you."

They gave her a confused look before focusing on him.

"Iax," he said after a moment.

They all nodded, but didn't ask the same question of Atlas. Perhaps because they knew him.

Iax sent a questioning thought toward him, and a small bit of information returned. Atlas sometimes brought them food and refilled their water.

Wynn turned toward him, the smile gone from her face. "We need to get them out of here." She gestured to their haphazard living arrangements. "They shouldn't be confined to this area when there is so much that could benefit them above."

"I agree."

Her shoulders relaxed, and she sent him a nod. "They need proper quarters, and terminals, and dispensaries, and anything else kids have access to."

He nodded at that as well. "Atlas will help. He was sent to assist in this as well as to report back to The Four."

Wynn cast the other Calypson a glance. "Well, it would be nice if he were good for something."

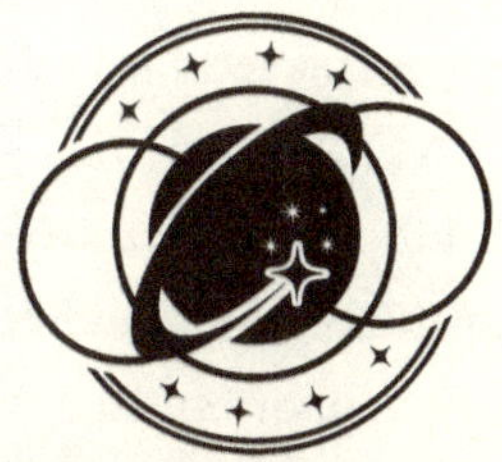

Chapter Forty-Three

Her heart hadn't stopped hurting since she'd seen those kids for the first time in that shitty little space. Speechless, she couldn't believe how the Calypsons had discarded and ignored them.

But that was what had happened to her too, wasn't it?

With the decision made that they couldn't stay in the cargo hold, more silent Calypsons arrived out of nowhere, ready to carry the kids' belongings to a new location.

The kids crowded Wynn during the process, keeping space between them and the Calypsons. To realize they inherently trusted her eased some of the ache gripping Wynn's chest.

While walking through the corridors, the kids continued to grunt and babble, using their hands to communicate. They'd taught themselves language, and Wynn was in awe of it. Everything about them amazed her. That they'd survived in such substandard living conditions. That they'd banded together to create a caring family unit.

They were smart, strong, and resilient. Pride mixed with her hurt and disbelief at finding them in such a secluded existence.

Would the same thing have happened to her if she'd lived in Sector Ten instead of being discarded to CORE territory? She wouldn't have had the love of her adoptive parents. She wouldn't have had the benefit of good schooling and excellent opportunities in the scientific community.

She vowed then and there to make those options a possibility for these kids too. They deserved the whole solar system after everything.

An odd sort of peace enveloped Wynn as they took the lift upward, everyone squishing into the lift except Atlas and the other Calypsons carrying the children's belongings. Iax had told her it wasn't acceptable for her to live anywhere else but with him, and she didn't want the kids far. They were all relocating to deck eleven, where Iax said some empty quarters remained.

"Did you know?" she asked, turning her body fully toward Iax as the lift hummed around them. "Did you know when they wanted me to take charge of these kids?"

He shook his head slowly. "They did not tell me their full intent, only that I was to collect you, to bring you home."

The growing tension in her chest eased at his words.

"They also told me it was not safe for you to live as you were," he added.

The lift stopped, and the door opened, revealing a corridor thriving in the twisting black ropes of Calypson construction, leaves and vines intertwined until it was difficult to determine where the growth began and ended.

A sound of surprise and wonder erupted from Bex.

Wynn cast her a small smile as she followed Iax off the lift.

"This way." He tilted his head to the right.

Wynn glanced back at the lift. Six faces stared at her with wide, questioning eyes. She gestured with her hands. "Come," she said, encouraging them off the lift. "We're finding you a better place to stay."

Mack took a hesitant step out with Ari on his hip, the girl's head tucked under his chin and her thumb in her mouth. Bex followed, holding Dexxa, the toddler's body slumped in slumber. Each of the twins held the back of Mack's pants, their grips twisting in the material, but they stared at her with openly curious expressions and something else that tugged at her heart. *Hope.*

Wynn swallowed around the emotion threatening to clog her throat, and waved them onward. "This way." She walked backwards a few paces, then when she was sure they followed, turned around to stay close to Iax.

"Your quarters are on this deck?"

"Yes. As are others."

He hadn't even finished speaking when a door slid open beside them, making Wynn twitch and pause.

A Calypson stood there, a man, wearing an outfit that resembled the shirt and pants Iax had worn, though these were a deep blue. He held a tool in his hand, a diagnostic device.

Though nothing about him seemed threatening, the kids all shrank against the bulkheads, and Wynn instinctively stepped in front of them.

The man did nothing for a long while, only stared at them with the same unblinking stare Iax had used on her when he first arrived at her outpost. Then he turned abruptly, passing the kids at a clipped pace to head to the lift they'd just used. The door opened with a quiet swish.

"He will not return," Iax said after the door closed.

Wynn stiffened. "He's leaving this deck because of the kids? Because of us?"

"Yes." Iax turned his head to meet her gaze.

She clenched her fists. "Everyone is going to have to get over it. I'm here. These kids are here. We shouldn't be treated like we're diseases. Especially when they were the ones who wanted to *collect* me."

Iax stared at her for a long moment, then agreed with a nod. "I will tell them." His words had taken on a hard edge.

Then he continued down the corridor, and she hurried to catch up. "Are you in trouble? With The Four?" They hadn't seemed happy with him, though they hadn't shown much emotion at all.

"I have completed my mission," he said simply.

That didn't really answer her question, but it made her say, "They might give you another mission." They could send him to collect someone else.

"No," he replied. "They won't."

She wanted to ask more, but he stopped in front of a door. It opened silently.

"These quarters are vacant," he said, stepping into a sparse space.

Wynn followed, and her shoulder relaxed at how normal it looked. They could have been quarters on any space station, dated in its style, but not overrun with those large, structural ropes that seemed to take over everything else in this place. A bank of tall windows took up the side opposite the door, revealing an unobstructed view of the nebula in all its glory, colorful and undulating.

Bex gasped, making Wynn turn around, but then the girl was rushing toward the windows, her jaw slack and her hands tight on the toddler in her arms. The rest of the kids followed. The twins pressed their faces against the transparent aluminum as they stared.

Wynn's heart clenched. "Please don't tell me you've never seen this before," she murmured, but that was exactly what she was witnessing: kids who had never seen the outside of a cargo hold, who knew nothing of the outside world at all.

Disgust welled up in her anew, followed by a fiery anger that burned through her chest and up her throat with the need to scream.

Iax stepped toward her, settling his hand on her spine.

"We need books," she said, her words thick. "And computer terminals, or tablets, or even PALMs. I need to teach them... everything." She swallowed around the sudden dryness in her throat, the gravity of what she was about to take on weighing on her shoulders.

Ari squirmed out of Mack's grasp, and he set her on the deck. She ran around with her arms spread wide. Maybe she'd seen a ship in the distance and mimicked it. The playful sight calmed Wynn a little. It made her believe these kids would be all right.

Mack put his arm around Bex and pulled her in close to his side, his hand on her hip as they stared out the window together.

Wynn's breath caught as an extra worry formed in her mind. "Are they siblings?" she asked Iax. "Brother and sister?" She gestured to the pair, who looked to be in their early teens.

He tilted his head, and she got the feeling he was asking someone who was not in the room with them.

"They are not related by blood," he said finally.

Wynn exhaled a slow, relieved breath. The way they looked at each other, it would take a lot of awkward explanation about genetics if they'd been siblings, and Wynn wouldn't have relished it.

"Genetics connect only the two lookalikes," Iax added after a moment.

Wynn nodded, but that got her scientific curiosity going. "Then it's random? The anomaly thing?"

Iax paused a moment. "No one has predicted it yet."

It was another thing she needed to study now that she was here. She wouldn't assume that Calypson scientists had explored every research path when they couldn't even teach these kids language. She would need to analyze their blood, and hers, and try to find connections. Her mind moved to how big a control group she would need.

She stiffened at her next thought. "Do I have siblings?" And who the hell was her father? Heath Wiseman?

She should have asked Briar Galloway more questions, but she was honestly so disgusted with the woman that if she never saw her again, it would be too soon. Wynn's true parents were the ones who had adopted her, the ones who'd shown her love and died too soon.

"You do. But they are not anomalies."

Wynn snorted. "I'm the black sheep, huh?"

It took him a moment, but he responded with a tilt of his head. "It would seem so. And I have joined you in that regard."

She'd feared Calypsons before coming here. Now she just disliked them intensely. Whatever advantages they gained at being a telepathic hive-mind, they squandered in their lost humanity. Segregating these kids? It was unforgivable.

Or ignorant. But how could they be so ignorant when most of them used to be human? Had they lost *all* of their empathy? It didn't bode well for those they'd sent out to retrieve the others like her.

She let out a defeated, choked breath. The CORE was no better. They'd been about to dissect her in the name of science. The Tellusians were even worse, raiding stations and ships for supplies and people. They didn't care who got caught in the crossfire. Like her parents.

What a messed up system we live in. But as she stared at the kids, who took in the room and the outside world with a fresh sort of wonder, hope bloomed in her like it had on those kids' faces. Maybe they would all make this system a better place.

The door opened, distracting her from where her mind had wandered. The Calypsons who had gathered the children's belongings, entered the quarters with their arms full.

Wynn straightened and headed to the slender door at the back of the space, assuming it was the bedroom. The door didn't slide open as she approached until she glanced over her shoulder at Iax. It opened with a silent whoosh.

"We're going to need to fix that," she said. "Make things motion activated for me and the kids."

He nodded his agreement.

Turning around, she stopped short when she surveyed the room. It was empty like the living space, except for one bed in the center and a smaller window.

"Oh, there's only one bed here. Maybe they should occupy more than one set of quarters, anyway." The space wasn't much bigger than where she'd found the kids.

She'd barely finished the thought when Bex and Mack came at her with a babble of grunts and hand gestures, motioning to the smaller room.

Wynn froze, then let out an apologetic huff when she understood the fear in their eyes. "You want to stay together. Got it." She lifted her gaze to Iax's. "Will they bring up the bunks too?"

He nodded once.

It didn't take long for the kids' belongings to be deposited and the Calypsons to leave as quietly as they'd come. The six of them poured into this new space, finding the blankets and items they knew were theirs.

It didn't seem like she'd done enough for them, but at least they had a window and weren't quarantined like they carried the plague.

Progress. It might be slow in coming, but they were making progress. She would fix this, correct the life they'd led until now, even if was the last thing she did.

Wynn's throat clogged with emotion, tears threatening to fall, and she realized just how exhausted she was. Everything that had led her up to this point came crashing down. The storm on Earth, abduction, torture, the *Corvus*, the white box, Iax saving her, the journey here, then finding out about the anomalies... it was too much.

She swayed with weariness.

A warm hand on the back of her neck steadied her.

"Come, Wynn Lambdin. You need rest."

And she did. But she also didn't want to leave the kids alone. Not after everything.

But smiles broke out across Bex and Mack's faces as they watched the younger children run out of the bedroom to chase each other in the bigger space. Set against the backdrop of the nebula, Wynn's chest constricted with a poignant pain she couldn't name.

"I will tell Mack and Bex how to find us," Iax asserted. "We are only one door down."

With that assurance in her ear and settling her mind, she allowed Iax to guide her out into the corridor.

Chapter Forty-Four

Calypsons strove for contentment, but Iax had lived here for most of his life and had not achieved it until this moment.

In his quarters, Calypson construction emerged from the bulkhead in thick bands, supporting what once used to be a bed, but was now more of a large cradle. Built for one until today, he had widened it with a thought upon their arrival.

Wynn lay in his arms, asleep, her naked body pressed against his, under a thin blanket made of the same material as most of his clothing. It had taken him a long while to relax her enough for sleep to take hold. Her worry for the children had overwhelmed her, distracting her from taking care of herself. He would not allow her to neglect her own needs in sacrifice for others.

He skimmed his hand down her face, and she turned into him. Even in sleep, Wynn's emotions throbbed against him, the sensation mellowed through her dreams. They had to be sweet ones for this warmth to exude from her body. He lapped it up and sighed. This was the only place he wanted her to be. Beside him. Touching him. Joining with him.

When they had first arrived in his personal space, she had examined everything with a slack jaw.

He had looked where she had, wondering at her thoughts. His quarters were not like the ones they had left. He had the same view of the nebula, but that was where the similarities ended. While the children's new quarters were bare, growth covered the bulkheads of his, some as thick as what they'd seen in the biodome. And between the swaths of greenery were items he'd set among the tentacles and vines.

"Aren't you full of surprises," she'd murmured, staring at the stacks of artwork and handmade items people had brought with them to Sector Ten.

"I do not think so," he said, contemplating the assemblage.

She spun around to face him, her lips curled upward, then tipped her head at the stack. "I didn't take you for a hoarder."

He glanced at the artwork, wondering at the playful emotion rambling toward him. "I do not understand this word."

"You like to collect things." She turned around again, moved toward the ancient paintings, examining them more closely. "Not just people when you're ordered to."

"Yes," he finally agreed. "Others do not find value in these things."

She lifted her eyes to his. "That seems to be a common theme in this place."

His body tensed as her melancholy washed toward him.

She picked up one of the smaller landscapes, an ocean view, and lifted it until it was a small square amid the nebula beyond the window.

Then he was there, his arms surrounding her, giving her the contact they both needed. They had shed their clothes, and given each other pleasure, and she had finally rested.

Now he held her with her cheek pressed against the swell of his biceps, and her hair flopping over one eye. He lifted his hand and tucked the section behind her ear so he could see her better. She sighed. He smiled.

He felt it then. *Again*. The curiosity of the others close by, reaching, probing. Thoughts stretched and touched his mind. As he had done earlier, he slammed down his mental barriers, enshrouding him and Wynn in privacy. An echo of their shock pulsed behind the fabricated wall, a rippling effect, but he ignored it in favor of giving his full attention to Wynn. Her happiness. Her pleasure. Their shared experiences were their own.

The tension in his body must have woken her, because her eyes fluttered open. She turned slightly, froze, then relaxed again when her gaze met his. The brown of her irises warmed, her eyes crinkling.

"Hello," she whispered, then stretched forward to kiss him.

After a light brush of their lips, she pulled away. "The kids?" Her eyes searched his face.

"They are fine. I checked on them recently." And she had been so exhausted, she had not stirred when he left the bed or when he returned.

She relaxed back into his arms, but a troubled expression remained on her face, accented by her hot and cold emotions. Iax waited for her to put her thoughts into words.

"I need to keep reminding myself I'm free," she whispered after a minute. "I thought coming here might mean the end of my life, but... it's not."

He shook his head and tucked that wayward hair behind her ear again. "No, it is not."

"I'm free," she repeated with a nod, "and I'm with you. And I have... purpose with the children." She cleared her throat. "I don't agree with how your leaders went about it, but I agree change was needed for those kids."

"Yes." He ran his hand down her arm and watched her shiver.

"And I can't help but want to study why we are different. I need a lab, and access to data." She paused. "But I won't force those kids to help me unless they want to. I'll need to work on language first." A frown wrinkled her forehead. "The organic life you have here," she added. "I want to learn everything about it."

Of course she would, because she loved plants and anything that grew.

"There is much." He pulled the blanket over her arm to keep her warm.

She let out a nervous laugh, eyeing the edge of the modified bed. "Yeah, I'm getting that picture."

He lifted his hand and gently stroked her cheek with his knuckles. "You belong here."

"I do?" The expression in her eyes revealed her uncertainty.

But he nodded once. "You do. With me. With others like yourself. You will find your happiness here, Wynn Lambdin." It was a promise he would never break. "I want you to be my mate."

Her head jerked back slightly. "Your mate?" Her brow furrowed. "Is that what Calypsons call a couple here? Mates?"

He shook his head. "It is not, but I want us to be mates, if you agree."

Her body melted into his, her lips curling into a small smile. "I'd like that."

Iax lowered his head, brushing his lips against hers. Her softness was his undoing. He groaned as she pulled him harder against her, an inferno of emotion rising inside him, needing release.

Perhaps it was a good thing the others on this deck had moved away, because he was not sure he could tamp down his emotions when he coupled with Wynn Lambdin, nor would he want her to.

When she rolled on top of him, he groaned again at how good her body felt against his. Setting his face against her throat, he greedily sucked the scent of her into his lungs.

His only mission, now and forever, was to make her happy and see her content. Nothing else mattered.

The Four were coming to realize that.

Ever since leaving the biodome, they had been setting up their own mental blocks, keeping information from him. They believed him compromised. There had always been some barriers, a pillar of secrets and commands only The Four had access to, but these new blocks were different, almost like they were protecting everyone from him, his *taint*.

But they could not cut him off completely. They needed him. He was the bridge they required to connect to the *Corvus*.

He may have left the ship, but some of his essence remained. Not enough to coalesce, but enough to watch, and wait, and listen.

Though distant now, if ever that ship neared Sector Ten, he would know.

And they would all be ready.

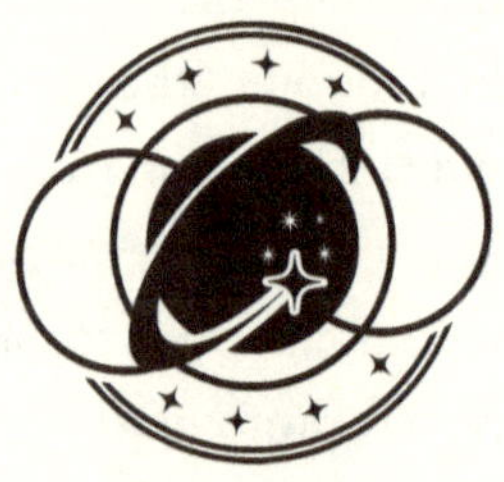

EPILOGUE

Pain. *So much pain.* It came from everywhere, inside and out, a scream in his head, in his gut, in his soul.

Sawyer knew pain. He trained for years, from the time he was a child to when he became a man, and pain tolerance was a favorite lesson of the scientists who conditioned CORE agents.

But this? This was nothing like he'd ever experienced. It felt like all the blood left his body at once, through his pores, his eyes, his mouth, his hair. His insides turned out, and his outsides turned in. The skin on his face curled off his bones, rolled down his chest and abdomen, then scraped down his legs to settle at his feet. His muscles melted, boiled, and evaporated. A breath was torture, and so was a whisper.

Then, all at once, the pain stopped.

Sawyer inhaled deeply and sat up like a shot. White light shone from everywhere, piercing his eyes. He closed them to stop the ache in his temples and rubbed at an itch on his jaw.

The pain had been a memory—a distant one, if he could believe the growth of hair on his face—the agony of emptying, of returning to his human form.

He braced his hands beside his hips, and a padded floor squished beneath his palms.

He opened his eyes to find a blank white wall in front of him. *What the fuck?* He turned his head and examined the space he'd been stuck in. There was nothing here but white walls.

The memory of saving the good doctor from a box surfaced. *We destroyed it.* It must not have been the only one on board the *Corvus*.

Unease swirled in his empty stomach. He hadn't known what they'd done to her. She'd been in one piece when she'd exited the box, though she'd appeared haggard and distraught.

Couldn't be worse than that pain.

Other memories surfaced, ones that came after. Of boots coming toward him, defenders in full battle gear and scientists decked out in bio-suits. Hands grabbed and dragged him, lifting him onto a hover bed to take him to a lab. He remembered the hum of a decontamination chamber and the buzz of a laser scalpel.

Sawyer ran his hands over his body, trying to figure out what they'd done to him, but he didn't hurt anywhere except for the ache in his head from the bright white. He wore some scratchy medical garb, the same as the good doctor, and it crinkled as he shifted to his knees to scan behind him.

He was alone. That might be the most disturbing thing of all.

Just a breath ago, he'd heard them all in his head, all the people the Calypson fucker had transformed. He would have taken the whole damn ship if she hadn't stopped him. Sawyer remembered their names, their desires, their hidden secrets.

And that meant they would remember his.

Coalesced. The word bounced around in his head. Every person they crossed, he'd had the urge to coalesce with them as well. To become more complete.

Except the good doctor. She'd been untouchable, but important.

He knew so much more about her now, but an acute frustration rose at not knowing everything.

When he'd joined the others, he'd never felt so whole, so complete, so *strong,* in his life. They'd worked together, indestructible, powered by one thought, one motivation, and he'd reveled in it. The synchronism. The *purpose.*

Now he was weak. Alone.

A fiery surge of anger followed the thought, and he fisted his hands against the padded floor. He'd had no will of his own. He'd been a puppet, even more so than being an agent for the CORE. If the Calypson had told him to lift his arm, he would have, believing the idea was his own while he accomplished the task. If the fucker had told him jumping out of an airlock would have benefited the group, Sawyer would have done that, too.

A crawling sensation prickled over his skin. He'd been used, forced to act, but while changed he hadn't wanted to lose the power he'd gained.

The dichotomy of it warred inside his head, making his heart race. *None of that.*

Taking a deep breath, he opened his fists and placed his hands flat against the floor, grounding himself.

What happened to the others? Those who had experienced the same pain?

He took another deep breath and tried to stretch his mind outward. When nothing immediately happened, he scoffed at his own stupidity, and shook his head. Of course he couldn't reach them. The Calypson fucker had reversed everything, emptying them all.

But that didn't explain why Sawyer's mind was playing tricks on him, how a strange murmur in the back of his head told him General Cazin stood close by.

Sawyer lifted his head and narrowed his eyes at the white wall. It rippled, and he gritted his teeth against the need to react while his heart beat a hard rhythm in his chest. The rippling increased until it settled into a live image—like he would see on a viewer.

General Cazin took up the center of the feed, standing at a terminal in a lab with two scientists. The space looked exactly as it had when they'd saved the good doctor. Either he was still on the *Corvus*, or a different Guardian with the same equipment.

Or this is a remote image. They could have put him anywhere and spoken to him through the comm.

But the itch in the back of his brain told him the general was close by.

A mild scowl marred Cazin's brow while Sawyer stared at him, his body braced for a fight, and his mind searching for exits. He remembered how they'd gotten the doctor out, how it lifted like a cage without a door. Could he force the edge of the wall up if he had to?

His fingers twitched to try, but he remained as he was, not even standing at attention for the general since the box lacked height.

"We've lifted the ship's quarantine," General Cazin said, his voice loud in the confines of the box.

Of course they'd been quarantined. A Calypson on a Guardian? Defenders changed against their will, then released from that mental prison? It came as more of a surprise that another Guardian hadn't come and reduced the *Corvus* to space rubble just to be safe.

Sawyer forced himself to relax and wiped his hand along the thick hair on his jaw. "How long has it been?" His throat strained with disuse.

The general pursed his lips. "Twenty-nine days."

That explained the beard and his empty stomach.

Sawyer stared at Cazin, the questions in his head stacked a kilometer high. What could he get away with? What would see him sent out an airlock?

He settled for simple curiosities. "How many others were affected?"

He knew. He remembered everything, but wanted to see what the general would tell him.

Cazin tipped his chin. "Thirty-five people were attacked, changed, then reverted, including yourself."

The names of those defenders and scientists moved through his mind, their childhoods, their aspirations. It was too much and not enough at the same time. Sawyer forced his breaths to regulate.

"What do you remember of that time?" Cazin asked, his expression bland.

So much. It kept racing through his head. What he'd seen. What he'd heard in his mind. Thoughts skewed with visuals, making it a muddle. Memories that were not his tangled with his own.

"Not a lot." Sawyer cleared his scratchy throat. "It's a haze, really."

The general's eyes narrowed. "That's what most of you said."

"Most?"

"Some won't speak at all."

Sawyer had the sudden urge to see the ones who wouldn't talk, to find out if they were all right. Had their reversion been too much to handle? Or the pain?

His hatred for the Calypson increased tenfold.

The general stared at him, eyes assessing, and Sawyer rifled through the most appropriate responses to his last statement, but could only come up with, "Where are the other thirty-four now?"

He winced internally as Cazin continued to stare at him. "Twenty-four," he said finally.

"What happened to the ten?" *Stupid question.* It gave away too much.

The general didn't answer.

Experiments. Testing. Just shot out an airlock for fun. Sawyer wouldn't put any of that past the CORE government.

Cazin tipped his head, and a certain promise lived in his eyes while a threat hung in the silence: co-operate or end up like them.

"Let's move on to the second portion of your testing," the general said right before his image disappeared, and Sawyer was kneeling alone in a white box.

Hot rage bubbled up inside him, wanting to spew forth. He'd given his whole life to these fuckers, and when he needed them the most, they locked him up for *experiments*.

As quickly as the rage surfaced, it disappeared again, replaced by a cool resolve that felt like it infused his bones, as invasive as coalescing. Sawyer embraced that resolve, funneled everything he had into it, while he tried to access the general's mind.

There. If he pulled on the murmur, another thought followed, then another.

When he opened his eyes again, all four white walls rippled.

"Let's begin." The mechanical voice came from all around him. "State your name and ID number."

Thank you for reading!

If you liked STAR-BORN ANOMALY, I would absolutely love it if you would leave a review at your favorite retailer.

Not ready for this story to end? Join my reader community for your exclusive FREE copy of STAR-CURSED ODYSSEY, the story behind what really happened to the *Calypso* all those years ago.

GET IT HERE
https://bookhip.com/VZTJHTD

All of J.E.'s books can be found at:
https://books2read.com/jemcdonald

Glossary

administrator – This is a member of the ruling class who works under the Chancellor and has control over a smaller territory—usually a station or ship. Administrators can also be in the CORE military but it's not a pre-requisite.

agent – An operative of the CORE military, they work alone, often used for assassinations.

AL-22 – The standard weapon of a CORE defender.

autonomous shielding – Shielding that protects a person from laser fire. Does not protect against slower moving objects like blades. Standard in a defender's uniform but can also be a portable clip (often used by agents and enforcers).

bio-signature – A unique signature or marker based off a person's genetics, used as a security lock.

blast doors – The physical doors that protect docking bays, hangars, and viewers beyond the shielding.

bulkhead – The walls of a ship or station.

Calypson – The *Calypso* was the first inter-stellar vessel to carry humans to another solar system: Epsilon Eridani. Its intended mission was to research the first planet of the system and begin the terraforming process on its moon. The crew is presumed lost in space until they return over a hundred years later...

cardiovascular node – Same thing as the cortical node but used in the area of the heart.

cargo ship – A vessel used to haul cargo.

Chancellor – the most powerful person in the solar system. He/She has veto power over everything. Think of the Chancellor as the Prime Minister of the solar system.

comm(s) – Communications, communique. This is how people communicate with each other audibly. Sometimes there is a visual aspect.

common – The language universally spoken by all people no matter their origin.

CORE – Collective Organization of the Regulated Establishment. A civilized government body which has control over the terrestrial planets and Jupiter and all resources therein (Sectors One to Three). This government took control of the population through evacuating Earth and making the population dependent for its survival thousands of years ago, and was born from four major corporations known as the Corps before the evacuation. The only people who live on Earth now are conservationists trying to heal it.

CORE Military – The military force which, for the most part, protects CORE citizens from Tellusian raids. Ranks follow the current day American army but other terms are listed below.

cortical node – A device (the size of the tip of your thumb) placed on the head which can analyze brain activity, and send electrical impulses or nanos through the brain.

cred(s) – A monetary unit. Tellusians and CORE have separate identifiers for their currency but they both call them creds.

deck – The floor of a ship or station.

defender – Any rank of soldier in the CORE military. Their uniforms are white and silver and have autonomous shielding. This shielding works against laser fire but not blades, which is why Tellusian Warriors like knives so much.

dermal syringe – A futuristic version of a needle/syringe. It's placed against the skin to transfer narcotics or nanos into a person's system.

dispensary – The automated machine behind the walls of a ship or station that makes either food or drugs.

enforcer – A Tellusian warrior who works security, uses brute force a lot, not afraid to kill.

enviro-net – A force shield to protect crops from acid rain and other contaminants.

fighter – A small armed vessel used for precision fighting and attacks.

freighter – A large vessel used to transport large things such as a new batch of Marauders.

grid – The future equivalent of the Internet but it connects all things, encompasses the whole of CORE space by a network of relays, satellites etc.

hovercart – A surface vehicle. Made for two people with a back bed for gear, doesn't have a roof, so if on Earth, the persons would need to use UV suits to drive it.

investigator – Works under the Chancellor. They investigate anything from mundane crimes of station life to larger problems, but leave all the heavy lifting to the military.

jack – To override controls to gain access to a room, compartment, or airlock.

laser saw – A cutting tool made of lasers.

laser scalpel – A laser that is used for cutting. Quite small.

laser weapon/gun – A generic term for the weapons used by defenders and warriors. There are many types of laser weapons.

lifeline – A tracker which a person would purchase with their own money. Used especially by the ruling class.

lift – A multidirectional elevator used in ships and stations.

long-range shuttle – A small utilitarian vessel which can go longer distances on a single charge.

marker/markings – The documentation to declare ownership of a ship.

med bed or hover bed – A bed that can read a patient's stats and where a lot of the medical "action" takes place. Information is displayed on a control panel at the head or side of the bed, depending on the design. A hover bed is movable, a med bed is stationary.

med kit –A portable kit used to hold medical tools.

medic – Someone with the basic understanding of first aid.

medical aid vessel – A vessel with the sole purpose of saving lives. Often wounded would be transported to a medical station for specialized care.

medical assistant – Someone who is trained in medicine to aid doctors, a nurse.

nanos – Nanobot technology. They can be programmed to do a multitude of different tasks within the body.

ocular implant – This is a device implanted into the eye of CORE citizens at a very young age. It connects to the PALM and shows information in front of the right eye. It can be turned off but most CORE citizens are so used to it, that it stays on indefinitely.

overhead – The ceiling of a ship or station.

palette – This is a hand-held computer similar to our tablets but it's much more advanced. The Tellusian version of a PALM.

PALM – Personal Automated Link to Media. This is an extremely thin, transparent film and a collection of sensors which is worn over the palm of the hand and links the person to media, and any other information that is vital to their lives on the "grid." Information is displayed both in two and three dimensional form and is also connected remotely to an ocular implant. CORE citizens only use this, not Tellusians or Calypsons.

processing – This is the term used for when a CORE citizen is taken in a raid and then given rights as a captive. Their biometric information is recorded, they're given identifying bonds on each wrist before being placed in either a work pool for manual labor or a post specific to their occupation with the CORE.

pulse cannon – Similar to a rocket launcher but it delivers pulses of energy as its payload. Held over the shoulder and has limited charge, five shots max.

pulse rifle – Slender gun good for long-range situations.

reclaimer/reclamation unit – The compartment in the wall/bulkhead/ship where the item is received into the reclamation system.

reclamation – The recycling process of all ships and stations. Materials are disassembled in their base parts to be reused in different ways. Used for both inorganic and organic matter.

regeneration bath – A rejuvenating bath of thick medical fluid that repairs skin and is otherwise quite enjoyable when a person is immersed in it for ten minutes or more.

regeneration gauze – A fabric-like substance that helps skin heal and reduce scar tissue. Sort of like a super-advanced band-aid. (Some scars are not repairable. It depends on the extent of the damage.)

regeneration tool or regenerator – A tool which sterilizes, stimulates, and repairs damaged tissue. A **fine detail regenerator** would be used for small things like veins while a **broad spectrum regenerator** would be used for large areas like skin.

robocleaner – A robotic device used to clean up solids and liquids. An advanced vacuum that works by itself.

ruling class – This group of people stems from the original Corps and is responsible for all law-making and non-military control over the population. They have control in the military as well. Birth lines dictate who the next Chancellor will be.

scanner – A handheld device which scans a patient's vital statistics.

scribe – A recording device usually found on the overhead.

Sector Ten – Consisting of a man-made nebula, it is the area which is occupied by the Calypsons and avoided by everyone else.

sectors/hemispheres – The solar system is divided into sectors and hemispheres (based off of the Sun and Earth's positions) for navigation purposes. The CORE has complete power over sectors one through three.

shuttle – A small utilitarian vessel used for short distances: ship to ship, station to ship.

sluice – A laundry chute which cleans and folds laundry within minutes.

SNAP shielding – The automated shielding system that initiates when there is a loss of pressure/atmosphere on a ship or station. Very important for the CORE when Tellusians make forced airlock entries.

specialist – An operative of the CORE military who specializes in interrogation techniques and torture.

steam shower – Also referred to as a steam. An attempt to save water, steam and pressure clean the body with a burst of air to dry the body afterward.

sterilization – The process of sterilizing a surgeon's hands before surgery, inserted into a rectangular shaped device usually located on the end of a med bed.

sterilization film – A thin transparent film used in transporting sensitive medical equipment like prosthetics.

suspension chamber – A patient with severe injuries needing extensive surgery would be placed in this cylindrical pod so their condition doesn't worsen.

synthesizer – A tissue cloner (not a musical instrument). Where there is a void of tissue, a synthesizer can "replicate" new tissue to fill the void. There needs to be sufficient existing tissue for the bonding process.

tag – A digital marker Tellusians use to track enemy ships.

tech – This has two meanings, one is just a short form of the word technology. The other is the short word for technician. So either a person or a thing can be referred to as (a) tech.

techie – This is a slightly derogatory term usually used by warriors/defenders to someone with a technical mind.

Tell – This is a term used by the CORE toward Tellusians. Tellusians find it offensive.

Tellusian – The Tellusians resisted the evacuation of Earth arguing if the human population got rid of technology and advancement, Earth would not need to be evacuated and therefore would be able to sustain life. They were deemed terrorists and eventually run to the edges of the solar system. They developed into a fierce Warrior race. The have control of Saturn (their biggest asset), Uranus, and Neptune and mine each for their resources. They also steal what they can from the CORE, including people.

tracker – A chip used by the CORE to trace its officers, usually implanted in the flesh of the shoulder blade.

transfuser – A portable device with a store a fluids/blood product for emergency situations. Has a finite amount of material and can run out quickly.

transport – A large passenger vessel used for long distances. Would need creds to secure passage.

tyro – A novice training to be Tellusian warrior. A student.

UV-suit – A protective suit worn on Earth to combat radiation and other lethal conditions.

vambrace – Technology made of metal composite worn around the forearm of a Tellusian warrior. Used as a communication device, can detect life signs, and has a multitude of tactical uses but is not a weapon.

viewer – The monitor at the front of a ship that allows sight beyond the ship. Can either be a window or a screen depending on how it's used.

ward/warder – The relationship between the captive and the warrior who takes them.

warrior – A Tellusian soldier. They begin training very young and there is stiff competition to become one. Anyone who wants to be a Warrior goes through intensive training and "games." They have to be the best of the best. They have a penchant for knives.

CORE Ships:

Cruiser – A luxury, long-distance shuttle, usually meant for two people.

Condor – A single-person long-range CORE fighter.

Guardian – A CORE warship. The biggest, most heavily armed of the bunch. Used to fight Tellusians.

Marauder – A single-person short-range CORE fighter.

Raven – A multi-person CORE scout-vessel. Has weapons and is used mostly for reconnaissance.

Yacht – A larger luxury ship which the wealthy and ruling class use as pleasure vehicles. Meant for one or two families.

Tellusian Ships:

Destroyer – a Tellusian warship, similar in size to a Guardian, but with more exterior/visible armaments. Made of black composite metal so it blends in with space.

Cetan – A Tellusian stealth scout vessel. It's designed to house a Griffin that can separate and then work independently of each other.

Griffin – A one-person long-range Tellusian fighter.

Strix – A one-person short-range Tellusian fighter.

Tellusian Pod – These come from a Destroyer during raids to attach and force an airlock to ships and stations so Tellusians can people farm. They're round in shape and several captives can be taken and then stored in one until they are delivered to the Destroyer and processed as captives.

Star-Born Anomaly Playlist

These are the songs I listened to while writing this book...

1. DEAD ROSES.teis_ by NAMELESS TWIN, (DEAD ROSES.teis_)

2. Instructions for Time Travel – Recue Remix by Robot Koch, Savannah Jo Lack, Recue (Particle Fields Reimagined)

3. It's Personal by The Radio Dept. (Pet Grief))

4. Love Me – 4RR & Cutneck Remix by Damian Spider, Raddix, Giang Pham, 4RR, Cutneck (Love Me – 4RR & Cutneck Remix)

5. STATIC by ANTAGONIZER, AWAY, Crywolf (STATIC)

6. The Beast by Godford (I YOU SHE)

7. Us by WHIPPED CREAM (WHO IS WHIPPED CREAM?)

8. Maybe We Could by Kllo (Maybe We Could)

9. Let Yourself Go by Set Mo (Let Yourself Go)

10. Blinding Lights by The Naked And Famous (Blinding Lights)

11. Skynet by Vikentiy Sound (Skynet)

12. Black Magic by Ghostlo (Black Magic)

13. Half Way Home by PINES, Akacia (Dreamcycle)

14. My Heart by Sound Quelle, Gunnva (Trait)

15. Home – Covex Remix by Slow Magic, Covex (Home – Covex Remix)

16. Алая песня by Synecdiche Montauk (MMXVII)

17. I Follow Rivers by Marika Hackman (Deaf Heat EP)

18. UNDERGLOW by Tonebox, ALEX (UNDERGLOW)

19. Only by RY X (Dawn)

20. Talking in Your Sleep by Lia Rose (Talking in Your Sleep)

21. i could be your goddess by CASHFORGOLD (i could be your goddess)

22. Basic Instinct by The Acid (Liminal)

23. AZATHOTH by ALEX (AZATHOTH)

24. The Bird by SYML (SYML)

25. Restart by Carlile (Restart)

26. Move Slow by One True God (Move Slow)

27. Matter (Revel) by Arcane Roots (Matter – Revel)

28. What, Me Worry? – LP Giobbi Femme House Remix by Portugal The Man, LP Giobbi (What, Me Worry? – LP Giobbi Femme House Remix)

Acknowledgements

Phew! Another one done. I feel like I've run a marathon with this one, and it's ever so satisfying to cross the finish line. It might be a year later than I'd intended to release this bad boy, but a lot has happened since I first sat down to rewrite this book in the spring of 2024.

Like *Star-Crossed Captive*, the first iteration of this story came to me years ago. In fact, I had the storylines for *Star-Cursed Odyssey* and this book all tangled together in my first draft, jumping back and forth in time to tell two stories at once. But I soon discovered that it was a disservice to these characters, and the ones in *Star-Cursed Odyssey*, to deny them the time and space to grow.

Back then, I had a whole different set of readers for the bare-bones version of this novel. Thank you to Melodie and Caryn especially for all your guidance way back in the day.

A big THANK YOU goes out to my beta readers for this version of the story, Bevin, Amanda, and Mindi. Your insights and encouragement made this book stronger.

Thank you to all the readers who have reached out and asked when this series would continue. A good kick in the pants goes a long way, especially when given with such positive enthusiasm for Blueshift.

Another big thank you to Jess and Mary at Pages of Passion. You folks are so lovely. I adore that local support.

And thank you to my friends and family who continue to show up for me and my work. I get a bit teary eyed whenever I think about how amazing you are. Love you.

More Works by J.E. McDonald

https://books2read.com/jemcdonald

BLUESHIFT
Star-Crossed Captive
Star-Born Anomaly
Star-Cursed Odyssey

WICKWOOD CHRONICLES
Ghost of a Beginning
Ghost of a Gamble
Ghost of an Enchantment
Ghost of a Summoning

GOLDENLACH RIDGE SHIFTERS
Captive Wilderness
Caged Fury
Conquered Betrayal

About The Author

J.E. McDonald was born and raised in Saskatchewan, Canada, The Land of the Living Skies. As a child, she was either searching the clouds for identifiable shapes, or star-gazing way past her bedtime. She's an anti-morning person who wakes up at 5am to write. Needless to say, coffee is a morning requirement. She cut her teeth watching Star Trek, James Bond movies, and reading the Harlequin novels her mother left in the bathroom—which resulted in an extremely skewed sense of sex education by age eleven. All of these factors contribute to her love of writing paranormal romance with humor, mystery, and lots of spice. J.E. resides in Saskatchewan with her husband and three daughters.

www.jemcdonald.net
Facebook: /JEMcDonaldAuthor
Instagram: /jemcdonaldsk
TikTok: @jemcdonaldsk
Threads: @jemcdonaldsk